To Eileen
Happy 80
Best wishes

THE FACES OF THE FIEND OF BREYDON

CHARLES READER

Charles Reader

My thanks to:
MDA (early school years),
SMM (later school years)
and JMcND (university).

THE FACES OF THE FIEND OF BREYDON

CHARLES READER

PAUL DICKSON BOOKS

The Faces of the Fiend of Breydon
published by Paul Dickson Books, April 2023
Paul Dickson Books, 156 Southwell Road, Norwich NR1 3RP,
t. 01603 666011,
e. paul@pauldicksonbooks.co.uk,
www.pauldicksonbooks.co.uk

© Charles Reader, 2023

All rights reserved. No part of this publication may be reproduced or transmitted in any form or by any means, electronic or mechanical, including photocopying, recording, or any information retrieval or storage system, without permission in writing from the publisher.

Charles Reader has asserted the moral right to be identified as the author of this work.

ISBN 978-1-7397154-3-4

A CIP catalogue record for this booklet is available from the British Library

Designed by Brendan Rallison
Printed by CPI Group (UK) Ltd Croydon

ABOUT THE AUTHOR

Charles Reader was born in 1958. He read English Literature at University College London and went on to teach English in the UK, Kuwait and Germany. He now works as a foreign sales consultant and also conducts guided tours of historical sites in Britain and Ireland. Over the years he has written a large number of articles for very obscure trade magazines as well as a whole boxfile of outraged letters to the press, but *The Faces of the Fiend of Breydon* is his first novel. He lives in East Norfolk.

CONTENTS

Maps	1
List of Characters	2
Prologue	4

THE BOY JOHN — 7

Mr Cory's Bridge	8
The Phantom in the Chapel	35
The Pike-Queen	45
Figures at a Distance	69
The Wrath of Joyful Norris	83
A Brush with the Shuck	92
The Strange and Terrible End of Cork Norton	107
Once Bitten…	122
People, Too	139
The Riot	147
Two Broken Heads	162

HAVENS AND REEFS — 177

The Witching of Tealer Sayer	178
The Further Witching of Tealer Sayer	209
Paradise Postponed	220
Rio	227
The Mortuary	240

WHITE JENNY — 254

Jenny's Lair	255
The 'Green	268
The Demon at the Casement	275
Sandcroft's Ghost	293
Tealer's Last Shot	304
Back at the 'Green	315
Back on the Ice	329
Jenny's Last Victim	336
The Thaw	347
The Demon Drink	356
Day's End	370
About This Book	376
Acknowledgements	377

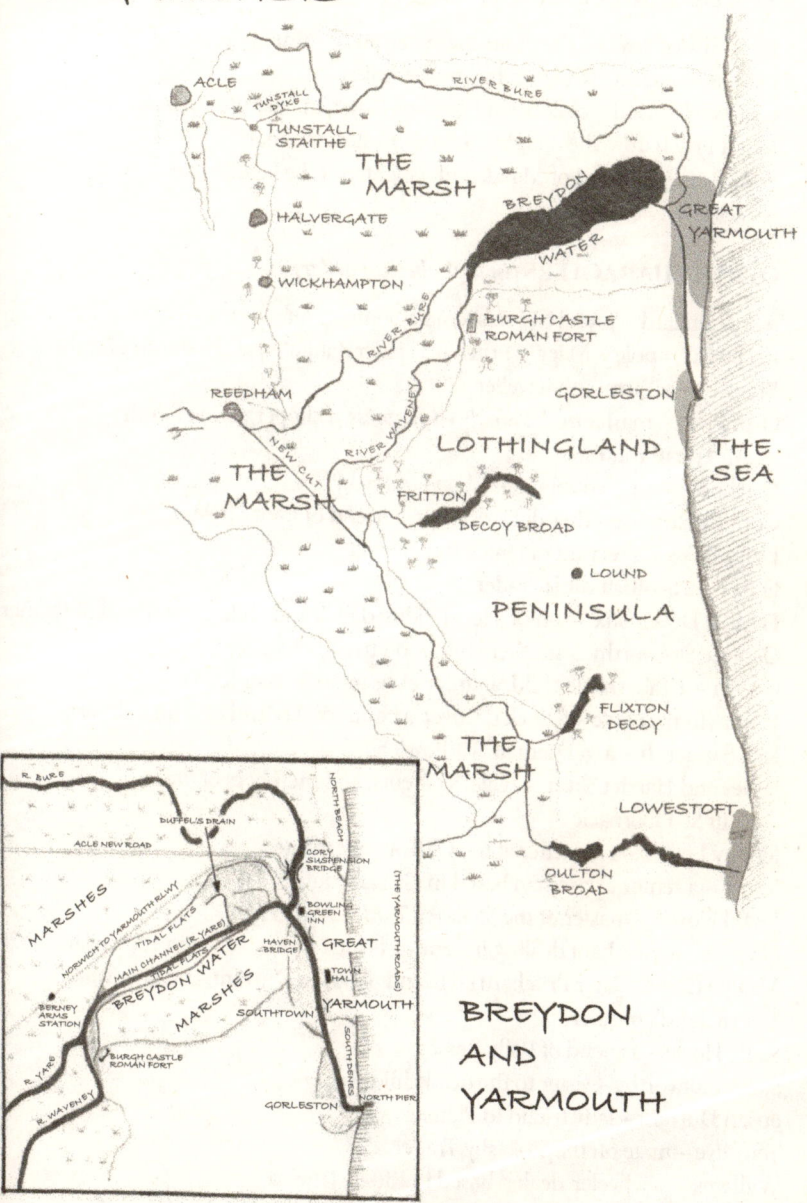

THE LEADING CHARACTERS IN THIS BOOK *(in order of appearance)*

John 'Tealer' Sayer – the main character, and victim of the Fiend
Palmer – uncle to Tealer on his mother's side
Charlie Harrison – childhood friend of Tealer, in later life a painter
Maud Pritchard – the daughter of a Gorleston milliner
Polly Bessey – friend of Maud, and daughter of the landlord of
 The Bowling Green.

OTHER CHARACTERS *(in alphabetical order)*

Annie Bullard – Joyful Norris's female 'companion'
Becky Catchpole – Maggie Pritchard's elder daughter, and sister to Maud
Bramley – a Yarmouth jeweller
Capt Press – master of the *Shadwell Empress*, a clipper plying South
 American routes
Catchpole – an accountant, husband to Becky
Cork Norton – another duck decoyer, a friend of Jointy Pole
Daisy Bales – a servant of James and Harriet
Fraser – a Scottish cattle-trader
Freddie Devereaux – son of a local industrialist, and childhood friend of Palmer
Georgie Stolworthy – another childhood friend of Tealer
Gooch – a Tabernacle child, a junior exciseman in later life
Harry (Jointy) Pole – a duck decoyer, a childhood friend of John Palmer
Jack Sandcroft – a 'gentleman' wildfowler
James and Harriet Sayer – Tealer's parents, and members of the
 Cliff St Tabernacle
Jeremy Lovett – a preacher at the Cliff St Tabernacle
Jermy – a senior exciseman based in Gt Yarmouth
Joyful Norris – master of the *Stokesby Trader*, a wherry
Levison – a merchant dealing in semi-precious stones, based in Rio de Janeiro
Maggie Collins (later Pritchard) – friend of Susan Durrant, and later Maud
 Pritchard's mother
Sadie Howe – a friend of Polly Bessey
Sarah Stolworthy – sister to the dead child Georgie
Susan Durrant – lady friend to Palmer
Tom Pye – mate on the Stokesby Trader
Williams – a 'wheeler-dealer' based in Rio de Janeiro

Various Town Hall officials, including:
Atwood (Town clerk)
Danford
Letts (commander of the local militia)
Simkins
The Mayor of Gt Yarmouth

Various wildfowlers and other regulars at the Bowling Green, including:
Cadger Brown
Deaf Watson
Fiddler Goodens
Generous Hunt
Poker Lamb
Saltfish Jex

PROLOGUE

*Oh, what can ail thee, knight-at-arms,
Alone and palely loitering?*

John Keats – *La Belle Dame Sans Merci*

January 1870

There have been some grim winters in recent years, but no-one remembers anything like this. The land is bound in iron, the waters of the dykes are thick, black glass, and the great, bountiful estuary of Breydon has become a barren place of ice-floes and whistling north winds. The main channel through the estuary is still open, but for weeks it has been carrying great plates of ice from the heart of East Anglia out towards Yarmouth harbour and the open sea. Duck and geese are sitting on the channel edge in silent masses, too cold even to look for what scraps are not locked in the frozen silt. The incoming tides bring no relief because the mud-flats they cover either stay solid or re-freeze immediately they retreat. Occasionally a small group of fowl might take to the air to scan the formless landscape for the smallest patch of open mud offering the chance of a feed. Most are too exhausted to bring head from wing. They are waiting listlessly for the thaw, or for death, whichever might come first.

The fieldfares and redwings, normally birds that race across the iron skies of January clacking happily at the bitterest cold, are dropping out of the air and fluttering uselessly in the snow. Sometimes a starving fox ends their sufferings, sometimes the sheer cold. A few that land near the town are caught by local boys who throw their hats at them, kill them and roast them over makeshift braziers.

Any horses on the grazing marshes surrounding the Breydon flats have long been taken upland or have perished. The estuary itself is entirely devoid of any activity connected with men. Its grinding bergs and fiendish winds have made it utterly inaccessible, and its desperate flocks of birds are sitting out this dreadful time unmolested at least by humanity. The wildfowlers, the hardy men whose living is to hunt the waterfowl of Breydon, can only sit huddled around the paltry warmth of the stoves in their shore-huts, dreaming of less bitter times. They know that out on the ice their quarry, usually so wary, is defenceless, but their spirits fail at the thought of taking their flimsy punts out into the deadly, grey-white nothing.

Only the scavengers are busy. With shining, merry black eyes alert to every detail, the local crows amble happily between the victims of the cold, tweaking a tail-feather here, pecking at the nape of a neck there, testing resistance. And in the bland skies above, a single great black-backed gull, the king of its tribe, is gliding up and down and across the void in a tireless hunt for weakness or carelessness.

As this tale begins, the great black-back is circling the corpse of a heron half-entombed in a frozen tributary of the main channel. What keeps the gull from landing is a small punt marooned nearby, also held fast in the ice, and containing the form of a man. The man is lying very still. He has greying skin and his lips are bloodless. There is no barrier between his exposed flesh and the vicious winds of Breydon, just as there's none between Breydon and the Arctic. The circling gull is patient. It knows that the man will soon die, leaving it to feed in peace.

Finally, it decides that all signs of life are absent, and it prepares to land.

Then the great bird banks sharply away. It has noticed that from deep within the folds of a white cape covering the head of the stricken form there's a glint of a moving eye.

The gull's right to be cautious; the occupant of the punt is indeed still alive – just. From time to time the cracked, colourless lips seem to attempt some utterance, and the eyes are never at rest. They look to be searching for something unseen, waiting in the limitless snowfield all around. Their gaze might be furious or it might be fearful.

It is hard to imagine those same eyes as they were five months ago: calm, optimistic and alive with the serene light of August. But then it's more than the simple passing of the seasons that has changed this man and left him alone in this boat, deranged, with the last of his vital warmth slipping fast into the infinite blank of a Norfolk winter.

THE BOY JOHN

And there I dream'd – Ah! Woe betide!

John Keats – *La Belle Dame Sans Merci*

Mr Cory's Bridge

As a small child, John 'Tealer' Sayer suffered badly from nightmares. The sequence of them was always the same. He had just been put to bed and would be drifting off to sleep when he imagined himself climbing up on to the chair by his washstand to look into the mirror. And as he looked he would see an indistinct, expressionless head like a marble bust staring back at him. And he would rush back to bed, only to find the same head watching him coldly through the garret window. He'd shut his eyes, but then he would hear the head bumping softly against the panes. The bumping would stop and he would dare to open his eyes. The head was perched on the end of his bed. He'd close his eyes and open them again – the head would have bounced a few inches toward him, and the more he closed his eyes the nearer the head would be when he opened them. He could keep the apparition at bay only by keeping his eyes on it. If he stared hard it would even drop back a little. But he would soon lose his nerve and hide, and then when he looked again the head would have advanced by a foot or so.

This would go on until he was woken by Daisy Bales, his mother's servant, who would then make him drink a tincture of nightshade in plum syrup and calm him with soothing Yarmouth songs about stormy seas turning placid and fathers coming safely home through tranquil sunsets with boatloads of fish for the family. Gradually the expressionless horror would recede and he'd relax, conscious only of a tight sensation at the back of his throat, the result of long bouts of shrieking that he himself could never remember. Then the tincture would work more of its magic and he would go into a curious state that hovered on the edge of sleep and was full of dreams that also he could never bring to mind afterwards – except an impression that he'd been floating or flying. Finally he would crash into a much deeper sleep from which he'd wake many hours later with a raging thirst.

Tealer was only eight when he witnessed first-hand the strange and terrible Cory Bridge incident, and the few people who ever got to hear of his nightly traumas naturally assumed that this experience was the cause of them. But Daisy Bales knew otherwise. She remembered that Tealer was not yet four when the nightmares had started, and from the first she reckoned she knew the real root of the problem.

"That int no wonder he get the dreamin', " she would mutter to other women on wash-days as they gathered to hang out linen in the back yards of the Cliff Street terrace. "Not with them two for parents, that int. They're a pair o' rum'ns. Neither on 'em understand littl'uns. They only ever read him biblical. All that there Rellyvations an' that. There int never no 'peace, be still' or 'suffer little children'. Not with them two, there int."

Daisy was certainly right about the bible readings, and perhaps about their effects. The solemn little gatherings were the only time Tealer's parents ever had any contact with him. Tealer would stand next to Daisy Bales in the front room (that his parents insisted on calling the "parlour"). His father James would always sit to the left of the hearth with an enormous family bible on his lap. Harriet Sayer sat at the other side, her gaunt features taut with attention. It was always dark and quiet in that room. In winter the windows were closed and shuttered however mild the weather, and in summer the curtains were drawn like shrouds against the offensive rays of the sun as it set over the marshes beyond the town. In the gaps between the monotone of James's prayers and the dutiful 'amens' of his tiny congregation the only sound would be the ticking of a clock that had been bought in a Hamburg flea-market by some Sayer forbear and now sat alone on the mantelpiece. Its dial was decorated with forget-me-nots, whose German name, *Vergissmeinnicht*, was written in crude Gothic letters beneath. (James often liked to remind his family that it was Time itself, not the Sayer forbear, they were enjoined not to forget.) The only other decorations in the room were etchings on the walls depicting Jonah being swallowed by the whale, Daniel in the lions' den and St Michael subduing the Devil. These were yellowed with age, stained with damp and covered with the corpses of generations of corn flies that had insinuated themselves under the glass and died of suffocation.

Tealer would exploit to the full any tiny diversion to offset the tedium of those dire meetings. The kind of the distraction depended on the season. During the winter months a meagre fire spluttered in the grate, throwing out more smoke than heat. Tealer would watch this fire intently, trying to guess when the next gust of the east wind would send a cloud of smoke far enough into the room to disrupt his father's incantations and send him into a paroxysm of coughing. Or in autumn there was always the chance of a moth blundering into the room - Tealer could follow its frantic spiral progress toward the lamp until it fried itself in the flame.

If he became too engrossed in such diversions Daisy would give him a gentle nudge. He always marvelled at how she managed this without ever seeming to change from her habitual pose, hands clasped virginally at her groin, head tilted to one side and eyes gazing without expression into the hearth. When the proceedings finally reached their yearned-for end Tealer might be asked a perfunctory question or two about what he had learnt at school that day. Then he would be expected to disappear to his garret. It was his mother's firm belief that, summer or winter, light or dark: "at the end of the day the only proper place for young people is bed". (Years later Tealer mentioned this one evening to Maud as they were lying together on the grass of the ruined Roman fort at Burgh Castle, gazing up at the stars. Maud giggled her wicked, liquid giggle and said "Then let us loiter here no longer!")

Ironically, it was during one of these family prayer-meetings that Tealer got to hear about the planned spectacle on the Bure. The meeting had started off as unremarkably as any other. There were lengthy prayers followed by a recital of some strictures for better living from Leviticus. As usual, Tealer sought diversions. For a brief period a flock of starlings set up a noisy squabble among the chimney pots so that muffled squawks echoed down the flue and tiny parcels of dislodged soot tinkled into the grate. When that finished he watched his mother grimacing at the intermittent yells of children playing outside in the street. When the children moved off to play somewhere else he turned to trying to find shapes of animals in the grimy marks on the ceiling above his father's head.

Then at the end of the reading James shut the huge bible with an uncharacteristic slam that made even the normally impassive Daisy start, and through his miasma of tedium Tealer began to register that his father was in a more than usually fervent mood.

Like many of the Cliff Street Tabernacle, James fancied himself as something of an orator. He wasn't gifted with the primitive powers of declamation of some of the Tabernacle elders, but the privacy of family prayers gave him a chance to indulge himself a bit.

Especially that night:

"...and we only have to look across the river to that there benighted town on the other side to find an example of just what St Paul meant, don't we?

We don't have to go to Sodom, or Gomorrah or Nineveh or any of them there hot places overseas. That we don't. That seem to me we have an example here! And what they ha' got planned for the night after tomorrow is a *perfect* example. People'll say that there's no harm in such things, and that thas just innocent pleasure. But I tell you what: that isn't! Thas the greasy pole, thas the slippery slope to perdition. Thas what that is!"

As usual Tealer hadn't been listening and didn't have the faintest notion what his father was talking about. But then James took up his newpaper and began to read aloud a description of the plan by Coke's Travelling Circus to stage a free entertainment for the 'enjoyment of the good people of Great Yarmouth'. The article explained that the spectacle was by way of a promotion for the circus itself a few days later – and was to feature one Arthur Nelson Esq., clown, and a set of performing geese.

When James had read the main part of the article he pulled off his glasses and looked at his three disciples. "How," he asked, glaring at them all in turn, "can people, as they do, laugh when they know that most of humanity is destined for a fiery end? How, I don't know. Look here! We're now approaching the Whitsun, there's typhus and the pox in the Yarmouth Rows, and yet there are those who see no cause for emergency, no need to settle their accounts with the Almighty. Instead they're prepared to go down to the Bure and watch…" (he put his spectacles back on to read) "… and watch… where is it now? Ah, yes… and watch: 'a unique and fabulous spectacle in which the clown, Nelson, shall be pulled up the river in a bath-tub by four trained geese.' He stopped, took off his glasses and looked at them all again to see if they were all as indignant as he was. "Geese! Lord have pity." He put his glasses on again. "That say: 'Master Nelson will start on the west side of the Haven bridge and finish on the north side of Mr Cory's Suspension bridge.' Once again he looked up at his tiny congregation, this time tearing his glasses from his face in his emotion. "Master Nelson'll finish in a worse place than that, let me tell you. They all will."

To anyone watching him, Tealer would not have seemed to be affected by this news at all. His eyes did not so much as flicker, yet behind the mask he'd suddenly gone from stupefied boredom to huge excitement.

Geese! He hadn't known there were going to be *geese*! And on the Bure!

He'd long known about the circus itself. Most of his school-friends had talked of little else for weeks, but Tealer had resigned himself to making do with second-hand accounts of the juggling, the sword-swallowing, the clowning and other outrageous delights. His parents were unbending in their interpretation of Holy Scripture, and, as Holy Scripture is not full of things to laugh at, neither James nor Harriet Sayer were much given to laughing – and certainly not at circus clowns. "We may live in jest, but we die in earnest" was one of James's favourite aphorisms (and the terrible events that indeed followed the goose show on that showery May evening two days after this prayer-meeting did little to budge him from that view).

Tealer therefore did not hold much hope of getting to the circus. But this show with geese was different. He hadn't heard about *this* from his friends. The circus itself was on the other side of Yarmouth, miles out of reach – but this was just up the road! And this involved geese! *Geese.* That was what made it special for Tealer, because his passion was bird-life. To him, a creature which could spread its arms and soar like a thought above the greyness of Gorleston was unutterably wonderful, and he'd spend hours watching the gulls wheeling and swooping in the skies above the herring-fleets as they came through the harbour mouth to unload. And geese were so much larger a symbol of this liberty even than gulls. Geese were from the marsh - the green sea that stretched away into a magical blur on the southwest horizon, and which Tealer had heard such tales about.

He continued to stare passively into the hearth, but his mind was racing.

Perhaps it's worth a small digression here to note firstly that Tealer's parents were well aware of this fascination of their son for birds, and secondly that they saw no good reason to encourage it. They did not forbid it, as they recognised there were worse things he could get up to: consorting with the offspring of Catholics, or playing ball-sports in the street. But James and Harriet were uneasy about their son's interest in nature, because nature had no central place in their world picture. It was at best a by-product in the creation of Heaven and Earth, a mere prop or backdrop. The struggle to ensure that piety and industry prevailed over sin was their overriding obsession, and it was a struggle they saw as one that took place in human society, not out in the empty wilderness. So they were dismayed to notice that this interest in the natural world showed no signs of diminishing as their son grew older. That they blamed entirely on Harriet's brother John.

John Palmer was a committed lover of the wild places and he kindled the flames of this interest in Tealer faster than James or Harriet could douse them. Palmer was a countryman and marshman to his boots. He'd often visit the Sayer household, deliberately (they suspected) to irritate his sister and her husband by telling Tealer stories of the *Gariensis*, the ancient estuary that contained the glittering expanse of Breydon Water and the great prairie of empty green marsh beyond it, separating Yarmouth and Gorleston from the East Anglian mainland. He would fill the boy's head with worthless tales of the howling winds, the strange black dogs, the jack o' lanterns, the pike as big as men, the pike as big as donkeys, the pike as big as tree trunks, the old boys who used to vault the dykes with poles and walk the mudflats with boards lashed to their boots, the eel spearing, the eel babbing, the dyke-fyking, the sluice-letting, the eel-netting, the mullet-fishing, the smuggling, and, above all, the wild-fowling. To a boy whose life was a mirthless round of prayer-meetings and arithmetic, these descriptions were truly wonderful. On the rare occasions his parents were not at home when Palmer paid a call he would ply his uncle with a breathless list of questions. But usually James and Harriet *were* present, like two dark clouds in a bright sky. Tealer then had to hope that Palmer had come primed with some marshland anecdote; Palmer seldom failed to oblige. With Harriet sitting ramrod straight in her chair, her hands clasped together tightly at her lap and her mouth locked into a grim smile, and James opposite her nodding politely but staring fixedly at the laces of his boots, Palmer would regale them with some outlandish tale of the fabled world, half-land, half-sea, just over the Cobholm wall on the edge of Yarmouth town. It was a world that called to Tealer more urgently than a choir of sirens, and he'd sit at his uncle's feet with eyes like saucers.

And just before we go back to the scene in the parlour of Sayer's house in Cliff Street that memorable Thursday evening, it might be asked why Tealer's parents put up with these visits from the wayward uncle John. Why did they have to let this merry, grey-haired, dark-bearded, twinkly-eyed prodigal brother of Harriet's into their front room at all?

Because he owned it. Their home was one of several old fishermen's cottages once belonging to the Palmers. John let his sister's family occupy it for nothing. This meant that they were able to spend the modest income from their small ship's chandlery on maintaining a façade of gentility. They were both remnants of families that had once commanded power and prestige in the area. But just as the proud little town of Gorleston had seen its herring fleets sold off and its influence lost to its brasher sister over the water, so several of its leading families, people like the Palmers and the Sayers, had seen their own fortunes melt away in a generation. Some had emigrated, others had turned to drink, others had quietly accepted the decline into proletarian obscurity; but James, and then Harriet, had found solace in the iron rule of the Cliff Street Tabernacle. Here they had found an immunity from society's humiliations not afforded by the tepid doctrines of their families' nominal Anglicanism. And also here, at forty-four and thirty-nine respectively, they found one another and married: evidence, you could say, that misery seeks company. After that the only upheaval in their sober lives was caused by some malefactor who substituted a strong cider for an apple cordial at a Tabernacle Easter feast, resulting in the appearance of their son John three quarters of a year later.

The Sayer fortune was almost completely gone, with the chandler's shop all that was left. The last few properties on the Palmer side had been left to John, who seemed intent on frittering the inheritance away on all kinds of half-baked enterprises. The project that that was occupying him at the time Tealer was growing up was a business selling wildfowl for the London table. As a sideline he provided gentlemen collectors with the skins of exotics like the Temminc's stint, the Asian plover or the Pallid harrier, whenever such rarities had the misfortune to stray off their migration routes and over the waiting barrels of the Breydon Water wildfowlers.

So always after a visit from Uncle John Palmer, James Sayer would ensure that Tealer was firmly reminded of *other* ways of looking at the wilderness. He would always wait a while, not wishing to undermine his benefactor too blatantly. But give it an evening or two and the next bible reading was sure to be something like the Genesis account of the expulsion of the First Couple from Paradise. The following night would perhaps feature the temptation of Christ in the Sinai desert. And by way of a sermon James would tell his small following to keep in mind the dangerous allure of the wilderness, the false peace of the wilderness, the cloying attractions of the wilderness. And what did he mean by 'wilderness'? Why… just as an example… Breydon. A useless expanse of mud, if ever there was one. A magnet for sinners and dreadworks of every sort. "Yes," James would urge, "and instead of a-ploughin' the land and sowin' it with wholesome grain, as does our Lord in the parable, or trawling the Yarmouth Roads for fish, like Christ's own apostles on the Galilee lake, it is well known that the men you find down on Breydon spend much of their time chattering inanely – and in the foulest language – about mud, tides and birds."

So passionate was Tealer's uncle about the wonders of Breydon, and so equally resolute was his father's loathing of it, that it took Tealer several years to be sure that there weren't two different places both called Breydon.

James and Harriet at least had the grace to acknowledge that Palmer's motives were not completely malign, even if his views were very warped.

"After all," remarked Harriet to her husband after one especially trying visit in which Palmer had regaled them all with an account of a mullet-fisherman's wife smuggling brandy off the South Quay in her corsets, "my brother John may have many failings – many failings – but he ent completely without his good points either. He do help us. He ha'nt run off to Jamaica like your brother Edmund. Nor is he known to visit the bordellos of Yarmouth, like your brother Timothy. And he still remain in contact with us, unlike your sister Mary, who you tell me now earn her living on the London stage."

"Yes you are right, my dear," said James. "And though he waste half his life in public inns, at least he ha'nt stooped to buying a share in one, as have your brother Albert."

Yes, they agreed, if their brother John was to be their only obstacle, then with prayer and fortitude they could ensure at least that their son John did not fall into the same loose ways.

All this was why subterfuge was Tealer's only hope of getting to see Arthur Nelson and his talented birds. Long before James had finished fulminating on the special risks to the human soul posed by performing geese, Tealer had resolved that this was one circus spectacle that he was going to see for himself. It couldn't be so difficult to find out enough about the event to plan a secret outing to watch it, he thought. In fact, by reading through the whole article out loud (to show how absurd it all was), his father helped him by providing him there and then with the details he needed to lay his plans.

Tealer was lucky that his garret was only reached by a steep staircase that neither of his parents had the joints for. They had no idea that their son's own greasy pole to perdition was the drain pipe outside his window, nor that the mossy roof of the lean-to privy was his slippery slope. These gave him access to the shadowy lanes of Gorleston, and to freedom. He'd been using this escape route for about a year, but till now only to steal across the town with his friend Georgie to play in the soft, night-chilled sand of the beach and watch the lights of the trawlers twinkling far out to sea. Tealer prided himself on these skills of escape, and he prided himself that he had never been seen in the act.

He had in fact been seen many times, because the streets of Gorleston, like those of Yarmouth on the other side of the Yare, were full of watchful eyes whose owners knew far more about creeping around at night than the boy Sayer. Thieves and poachers often made their silent way from their dwellings to their evening's business on the creeks of Breydon, or the pheasant coverts of the Somerleyton estate. They often saw Tealer and his friends skulking about the backs of houses in Gorleston, but they had no interest in a bunch of eight-year-olds up a little late. The last thing they wanted to do was to draw attention to their own use of this quiet route, laden with their various bulging sacks, bags and bundles.

In Tealer's home itself the only adult who knew about his forays was Daisy Bales, whose duty it was to clean Tealer's room. She often found sand and moss trodden into the floorboards, but she was not the sort to give the game away. Even so, Tealer knew that this plan to watch the geese was of a new order of daring, because this time it was to be carried out in the clear light of the early evening.

He needn't have worried. After prayers on that Saturday evening his parents sealed themselves away in their small parlour to read to each other from a batch of biblical commentaries. With the heavy door pulled to, and the windows firmly shut, the only sound they could hear was their German clock with the *Vergissmeinnicht* motif as it ticked its way away across the span of time that separated them from the Last Day.

The way was open! Yet come the moment of his flight Tealer was sitting in his garret having second thoughts. He was still in an agony of indecision when George Stolworthy`s owl-call, the pre-arranged signal, came up from the lane at the back of his house. He shinned down the drainpipe and off the roof ready to tell his friend Georgie that his parents had rumbled the scheme, and it had to be scuppered. But Georgie didn't give Tealer the chance to lie. He was waving a pamphlet showing Nelson driving his four geese on the water. Each of the birds was fitted with a plumed harness and looked as gay as any of the horses that drew barouches up and down the Yarmouth front for richer tourists. Tealer's sinews stiffened.

In a short time a small rout of lads had gathered, and once in force they moved off down the riverbank out of Gorleston, and through Southtown. It was a walk of some three miles, and all along the way Tealer felt the growing thrill of illicit pleasure. The boys quickly found themselves part of an excited, chattering throng that now included youths and adults. Soon they swung right to cross the Haven Bridge, where they were met by other, larger groups of people. The route along the riverbank was bathed in a watery sunset. The inevitable chill east wind was blowing in off the North Sea, rocking the brave buds and blossoms of the elder, ash and hawthorn against a largely featureless grey; but buds and blossoms there were, and the evenings for all their chilliness were getting longer, and people were thinking that carefree summer must be a week or two away, and a clown in a tub pulled by geese was just the kind of tomfoolery that seemed a welcome confirmation of it.

The crowd made its steady way round the curve of the river. It flowed on past the spur of land where the Bowling Green Inn stood at the meeting of the waters of the Bure and the Yare. It continued up the east bank of the Bure until the the towers of the suspension bridge came into view. For Tealer these were familiar, if bizarre, landmarks, though till now he'd only ever seen them from a distance. He was vaguely aware that this strange bridge had recently been the subject of discussion between his parents. This was because the builder of the bridge, a certain Cory, had fallen into an acrimonious dispute with the railway authorities over an issue of shared access, and the litigants on both sides had canvassed support from businesses across Yarmouth and Gorleston. This quickly widened into a more general argument that pitted supporters of the Acle New Road against those of the Norwich-Yarmouth railway, and a version of the controversy even permeated the closed world of the Tabernaclers. Many of the Tabernaclers had never been too sure about the rightness of Mr Cory's bridge from the moment it was built. It was 'new', and they were viscerally suspicious of 'new'. They worried that there was no mention of suspension bridges in Holy Scripture. But, countered those among them who favoured the bridge, no more was there mention of the steam trains that many of them now relied upon for their trade. And – had not both the bridge and the New Road provided work for idle Irish itinerants at a time when their own heathen land was being punished with famine? The doubters were unconvinced. There still seemed to them something unnatural, hubristic, even sinister, about supporting the weight of a bridge on flimsy bits of wire rather than good, solid masonry. So the pro-bridgers urged them to consider the role of the bridge as a means of carrying the Acle New Road into Yarmouth and on into Gorleston. Could not such a facility but bring trade and civilisation with it? And surely a bridge that offered a secure route into the town from the unwholesome slough of the *Gariensis* could only be from the Lord? It was this last argument that was eventually to win over the sceptics. There was further solemn, prayerful discussion. But the end was that the wise men of the Tabernacle decided they were in favour of suspension bridges.

Tealer himself had often wondered at the outlandish form of the Cory bridge. This evening it looked stranger still. People were swarming all over it. They were jammed up against the barriers on both sides, they were clinging precariously to the towers, they covered the foot-plates, some standing on the railings, others with their legs dangling through the wrought-iron latticework. All were waiting to catch sight of the clown and his geese.

Tealer's eyes were everywhere. Everything was strange and sinful. The people, adults and children alike, were dressed in greasy, grubby clothes of the kind that spoke of the squalor that Tealer was taught would be his lot if he didn't read his Bible and do his sums. In the air were the casual blasphemies and obscenities that marked the speech of the artizanry of the Yarmouth Rows. There was the thick, sour smell of bodies that had not known soap and water for weeks or months. There was raucous laughter, and the forbidding, forbidden smell of gin. This was the world from across the river, the exemplar so handy to the Tabernacle preacher in need of a Gomorrah. This was the ungenteel Yarmouth from which the good citizens of Gorleston sought to distinguish themselves. This, for Tealer, was wonderful!

Finally his part of the crowd reached the point on the bank which his friends had heard would offer the best view of the spectacle. It was here that he and Georgie found Georgie's cousin Charlie Harrison, a mercurial, sharp-eyed sign-writer's son with a passion for sketching things with charcoal on pieces of paper he always carried in his britches. He was already perched in a willow tree above Tealer's head, determined to make a picture of Nelson and the geese as they came up the river. Some of the other boys in their group immediately climbed up to join Charlie. At first Tealer was very reluctant to follow them, as he felt that this would make him conspicuous. His dread was being spotted by one of the Tabernacle faithful. However, there were several shouts from up the bank that the geese were on their way, and this put him in a frenzy of jumping up and down, and he realised that when the geese did arrive he wouldn't see a thing. He scrambled up the tree and swung from one bough to another until Charlie and the others could reach him to drag him to safety. He settled on a perch that gave a view right up the river to the Bowling Green in one direction and across Yarmouth to St Nicholas Church on the other.

Tealer's pal, Georgie, didn't join them. "I reckon I'll see more from the bridge," he said, and disappeared up the bank into the crowd.

And out of their lives forever.

"Thas only 'cause he dussn't climb up here," said Charlie to Tealer with a sneer, and Tealer nodded evilly. He was pleased at being able to show Georgie up. Georgie was always laughing at Tealer's early bed-times and the quaint ways forced on him by his parents. And who needed Georgie up here? It was exhilirating to watch the milling about below them and to feel the great tree they were sitting in sway with each cold gust of wind from off the evening sea. Tealer loved high places, for in a flat landscape like the *Gariensis* any high building, tree or mast invariably provides a view. Looking about him, he caught sight of the marsh stretching away to the south and the west, and for a while he stared quietly into the void while his friends chattered about the excitements in store.

Tealer eventually turned back to the river. The sheer size of the crowd gathering on the banks was itself something new for him. He was fascinated by the varieties of humanity on display. Now that he was down by the Bure itself, he was surrounded by folk from some of the poorest rows in Yarmouth. Many of them were very short. Many of them limped. Their clothes were uniformly tawdry. Some squinted through diseased or deformed eyes. A few were clearly imbeciles. Many others shambled along in a vague, clumsy way, and if they caught his eye would look through him with the bleary gaze of intoxication. Everyone, whatever their age or condition, spoke in voices that were hoarse, partly from rough tobacco or gin, but mainly from the effort of making themselves heard above the ceaseless racket of Yarmouth: busy workshops, the rumble of barrels and the rattle of clogs, hooves, and iron-rimmed wheels on cobble-stones, the clamour of street brawls, quarrelling parents and screaming infants.s

But tonight the crowd babbled, gabbled, gossiped and guffawed good-naturedly. The riverbank was filled with glottalized rhythm of the Yarmouth quayside, peppered with the tight-lipped vowels of cockney traders up for the May holiday and the lilt of Scottish fishwives. These folk were the famed Yarmouth bloaters – Barkis and Peggotty in the flesh – and one or two of them might well have lived in an upturned boat on the Breydon flats, but with rather more grit and less romance than would be suggested by Mr Dickens a few years later. Yet Mr Dickens would have been the first to recognise the determination among the poor of Yarmouth to have fun that evening, come what may. Arthur Nelson and his troupe of geese were later dubbed an 'absurd and worthless spectacle' by the sober, well-fed burghers who sat on the inquest into its awful consequences. But to the hard, simple folk who gathered that night by the Bure it had promised some jollity for once not brought by cheap gin. It meant a break in the drudgery of fish guts, night-soil buckets, blocked drains, leaking roofs, damp slimy walls, influenza, pox, rheumatism, scrofula, scurvy, impetigo, toothache, malnutrition, rickets, consumption, venereal disease, bitter draughts, rats, and squalor. It was fun, it was harmless, and on a chill evening in the grudging grey spring of the east coast it carried that vague promise of summer before the reality of summer with its own foetid, fly-blown horrors made folk yearn for the winds and rain of winter to return. Stunts like that of Nelson and his geese might have indeed have been 'absurd', but to these people they were not entirely 'worthless'.

As is always the case at such events, there was a delay and an anti-climax. The crowd began to get restless. Cat-calls, whistles, chants, and outbreaks of laughter surged up and down the banks in waves. People craned over one another to scan the unremarkable brown stream of the Bure for anything interesting, and seeing nothing disappeared behind the press of heads in front to continue gossiping.

Tealer began to forget his fear of being spotted. He listened with delight to the

Mr Cory's Bridge

coarse banter of the three fellows directly below him as one of them tried to watch events upstream with an ancient telescope.

"Can't y'see nothin'?"

"Just the back o' your blooda head."

"Are yer look'n down the right end o' that thing?"

"Hold you hard! I reckon I can see him comin'."

"Ho, yes? I reckon them on the market saw *you* comin' when they sold you that ole' glass."

"No! He's now comin'! Here he come. I reckon… ."

"Why, can you see him?"

"Well, no. That I can't, not yet."

"Well, don't talk s'much squit then. If he was a-comin' you'd hear them buggers acrorst th' other side a-hollerin'. They can see downriver better'n what we can!"

"They *are* a-hollerin'! Listen!"

"That they int, they're just standin' around blooda yarnin'. Just like my frigg'n missis on frigg'n wash day."

"He want to git a blooda move on with his geese, do the tide'll change and he'll end up out to sea and high an' dry on Scroby Sands. And I aren't blooda messin' about here all night. My woman's a-waitin' t'home for me wi' my tea."

"Oh, is that right? 'Cos that int what I heard she's doin'…"

A rumour made its way up the river that having left the Haven bridge the clown had been swept passed the river junction by the incoming tide and was heading uncontrollably, geese and all, toward Breydon. (As Tealer's father, with much shaking of his head, read in the newspapers days later, this was found to be true, and a major contributor to what was to happen.) The word passed up the crowd that the clown was now being dragged back and towed to the right point in the Bure so that the same tide would push him up the river under the Cory bridge. But people knew that this would take time, and they took the opportunity to come up the bank looking for vantage points on and around the bridge itself. The crowd was now packed tight as far as Tealer could see. For another twenty minutes it surged and jostled and swayed. It amused itself by waving to friends spotted on the other bank and shouting bawdy messages.

Then a regular pulse of sound was heard further down river toward the Bowling Green, and people cocked their ears trying to identify it. Finally it became clearer as a chant: *AIR-UH-eh-EE, AIR-UH-eh-EE*, and as soon as people recognised it they took up the refrain: *Here come the geese*! they shouted, *HERE COME the GEESE! HERE – COME – the – GEESE* ! And in their excitement they clapped and stamped in time.

Tealer and the other lads in the willow tree on the Yarmouth bank still couldn't see anything on the water, though they could see the folk further down the east bank as well as those on the eastern half of the bridge beginning to point.

It seemed like another false alarm – the chanting went on aimlessly for some time and then died down, and Tealer became tired with the effort of straining his eyes while trying not to fall out of the tree. He shifted his gaze again to the now huge crowds lining the Bure as far as the bridge. There were more people clambering on to the bridge, and others approaching it from the tollhouse. And beyond the tollhouse he could see yet more hurrying down Northgate Street so as not to miss the fun.

Suddenly there was a loud bang and a startled gasp went through the crowd, followed by a widespread outburst of laughter.

The fellow below Tealer turned to his friend and said: "Some ole bugger up there ha' got a gun - I reckon he want to see if he can get them blooda geese to fly off with that pissin' bath tub in tow!"

Tealer and Charlie thought this was very funny and hung precariously from their branches to see if they could see the culprit, but all they could make out was a pocket of people standing on the bridge pointing to something and arguing. Tealer was now feeling elated, as was everyone else, because the wind had dropped and the sun had come out from behind the watery clouds and was filling the concourse with bright evening light. Once again his eyes were tempted away from the main object and towards the sunset, and once again he forgot that he was part of the biggest crowd of people that there had ever been on earth, and he was carried away instead by the sight of the marshes with their flights of fowl and their limitless pools and creeks and dykes.

Finally he turned back to the crowd below him. The sunlight was now lighting up the faces on the east bank, including his own, and he looked up the river to marvel at the lines of humanity stretching along the bank into the distance.

That was when the elation drained out of him like the mercury from a broken glass.

He had spotted Titus Gooch standing on the east end of the bridge. By the age of eight Tealer had not yet met many people he loathed utterly, but here was one. Gooch was the son of Joseph and Charity, two Tabernacle stalwarts who ran its Sunday school, where they served their Creator by stifling any unwanted spirit of enquiry under a blanket of arid Tabernacle doctrine. During the week Titus was a nonentity who would skulk around in the shadows of the Gorleston school playground avoiding attention, and children not from the Tabernacle congregation paid him little regard. But the children of Tabernacle congregation didn't have the luxury of being able to ignore him. Squashed into the tiny annexe of the main chapel, they had to endure the weekly purgatory of Tabernacle Sunday school, where the Gooches used their pallid, bony, ginger-haired son as a monitor. He would sit at the back recording or fabricating misdemeanours amongst the other children. He revelled in the knowledge that any attempt by his victims to deny his accusations would imply that he was a liar and would cause his doting mother to apply the tawse with greater savagery.

With the sighting of this weasel all the joy of the goose show was suddenly a faint memory for Tealer. He sat cowering on the willow branch. Like many of the crowd Gooch had a telescope. Unlike them he wasn't searching the water for the goose show but scanning the faces on the opposite bank. And Tealer knew very well what Gooch was doing: he was looking for Tabernacle children he could report back to the hierarchy as having joined this godless crowd. Soon he would be turning his glass to the east bank.

"I go' get down from here" says Tealer to Charlie.

Charlie tore his gaze away from the river and looked at Tealer in bewilderment. "What, are you mad, boy? The geese are now comin'!"

"Thas Titus Gooch over there by the bridge. He'll see us."

"So what if he do? Cousin Georgie ha' told me about him. He say he's a girl's apron. I aren't scared o' him!"

"You don't have to be. He ha' come here to see who's here. He'll tell on me to his mother, who'll tell on me to my gaffer! There'll be hell-an'-all to pay."

Charlie thought about this for a moment "Well, you want to get to 'em first and tell 'em that you come down here for the same reason. To snitch on people. And when you did you saw him looking at the geese. Then he'll be the one that get wrong, not you."

But Tealer knew that it didn't work like that. Charlie wouldn't understand. Charlie's father's notion of firm parenting was the kind that came out of one of Mr Lacon's beer bottles. Bill Harrison couldn't have cared less if Charlie was out here watching geese pull some idiot up the river in a bath tub if that meant he wasn't under Bill's feet at home. Besides, the geese were coming, and that's what Charlie had come to see. He turned back to the geese and took no more notice of Tealer's woes. Tealer was left watching in fascinated misery as the telescope of Gooch swung over the river to where he was sitting in the tree. He couldn't have climbed down if he'd wanted to now, for such was the mass of watchers that he would have landed on their heads, and that wouldn't have gone well for him at this juncture. He tried hiding his face in his jacket, but it was too tight, and in any case to adopt such an unusual position when everyone else was craning to the left would have made him stick out like a sore thumb.

Gooch hadn't moved from his position on the east end of the bridge, whose elevation gave him a perfect view of Tealer's willow tree. Tealer fervently wished and then prayed that the callow bully would be jostled, or pushed, or that his telescope would be knocked out of his bony hands, or that something even worse would happen.

As the whole of Yarmouth, the whole of Norfolk, and indeed the whole of Britain was very soon to learn, something even worse did happen.

Though many afterwards said otherwise, it is not true to say that there was no warning. To a few sober-minded observers it'd been clear that some kind of calamity was imminent, and these few saved their own lives, and some others' lives, by taking action. They had realised that the loud report which had shocked and then amused the spectators was not a gun but the sound of a link in one of the bridge's chains snapping open under the sheer weight of humanity which had now rushed to its south side to see the geese. And even those who had missed this first sign reported noticing that the span, which normally hung over the river in a gentle arch, was now ominously horizontal.

But very few others were looking at the bridge itself. They were staring down the river watching as the four geese decked out with ostrich feathers appeared in the distance. Even Tealer – who wasn't staring downriver but bracing himself into a rictus against the moment that Gooch's panning telescope would form a perfect circle in front of his ugly face and bring a sadistic grin to his sallow features – even Tealer hadn't noticed anything untoward. He was as surprised as anyone when the southern side of the bridge simply gave way along its whole length and dropped into the vertical, so plunging the hated form of Gooch, together with four hundred other souls – men and women, adults and children, healthy and sick, guilty and innocent, fair and plain, brave and faint-hearted, rich and poor, church and chapel, drunk and sober, swimmers and non-swimmers – into the bland brown waters of the Bure, turning the river's surface white with spray.

Two experiences in Tealer's later life brought back most vividly the memory of the collapse of the Cory Suspension Bridge. One was of bullocks being pole-axed at a slaughterhouse near Acle. The other was a sheet of snow suddenly slipping off the steep roof of a Rotterdam church during a thaw. In the first there was the same sense of something very strong losing all its strength in an instant; in the second there was the same complete lack of warning. And along with every other witness Tealer did not remember there being a single scream between that final lethal shiver of the overwrought bridge and the point when the last torrential cloud of displaced water had slapped back down on to the surface of the Bure and the thrashing, gurgling forms of its drowning victims. Everyone later agreed that the pandemonium didn't really break out until after the huge splash created by the collapse had subsided and the river had returned to its normal state. The reason for this delay, of course, was that everyone was staring hard in precisely the wrong direction. And even when the shrieking began it took some time for those further down the bank, with their eyes still fixed down-river, to realise that the hubbub behind them was not being caused by the appearance of four decorated geese but by the sudden end of many human lives. Some didn't even look round until the great wave created by the simultaneous immersion of four streetfuls of people surged down the river against the incoming tide and into their field of vision, forcing them to turn round to see the cause. By the time the cries of "B'Christ, look at the bridge!" had begun to ring out above the happy clamour, most of those marked to die that evening were already dead. It was only then that Arthur Nelson and his geese were truly forgotten.

From their vantage above the main action, Tealer and his friends were able to see it all. They could watch precisely the stages in which the spectators realized the main spectacle of the day was not to be a jolly prank. First a few, then many, started running up and down the banks in a frenzy. Tealer saw how they were grabbing both at one another and at strangers with the same desperation, pointing at the bridge and yelling for anyone to go in to bring out a son, a daughter, brother, sister, father, mother, neighbour or friend from the wreckage. He saw others who were just staring nonplussed into the dull brown water into which so many people had simply disappeared. He saw how the more river-minded of the crowd were already in boats and rowing and poling their way frantically to get to the scene – so fast indeed were some of them that they had craft alongside the stricken metal-work within ninety seconds of its failure. He saw miraculous escapes; he watched as one man clung to the superstructure of the bridge with a girl clutching at his ankles until both were picked up. He saw one woman with an infant put the child's coat in her teeth and swim to the bank like a dog with a duck, where she clambered out and up the stairs black with silt. He saw that some folk were scrambling over each other frantic to get to safety, while others scrambled over each other equally frantic to get into the deeper water to save the drowning. And he saw that through it all the tide continued to race in, and he realised that a particular screaming could be heard above the general din and that this was from those who were still caught up in fractured metalwork as the water rose all around them. Several boatmen were reaching for knives, choppers and machetes to cut through shoes, clothing, fingers and limbs as was necessary to free them. Some casualties who had simply waded to safety were sitting on the muddy bank watching the mayhem with an amused detachment appalling to anyone unfamiliar with deep shock. Others were still floundering in the water, drowning. At least one rescuer was drowned with the victim he was attempting to save. A few of the victims seemed to be standing up in the middle of the river – this amazed many witnesses who rightly imagined that the Bure here must be very deep, since it was narrow, tidal, and the only outflow for all the northern broads of Norfolk. They didn't realise until they'd discussed it in hushed voices afterwards that the people they'd seen on the surface were simply the last to hit the water, and were standing on the bodies of the dead and living piled up below them.

Within five minutes, twenty or so boats were crammed into the area close to the bridge. There was a feverish brandishing of boat-hooks and grappling-irons. Heavy objects feet below the surface were being tugged at. Fresh waves of hysterical people were arriving by the water side; many were spectators from nearer the Haven bridge where the stunt had started and who had only just heard of the Cory bridge collapse. They only added to the mayhem of yelling, shrieking, pointing and aimless running up and down.

Now many bodies were lying in the water. Some were almost immediately taken by the tide and swept upriver toward Acle. Others were caught up in the wreckage of the bridge or in the unyielding clutch of their fellow dead and were slowly disappearing as the waters rose. Bodies and casualties also started to appear laid out on the bank. Living and dead were being put side-by-side because the rescuers had neither the time nor the skill to tell which were which. The eyes of most were wide open, and staring fixedly at some invisible thing. A few stared like this until they were convulsed by the deliverance of a wracking cough. Most stared on, their faces in death still showing their surprise at the sudden, brown darkness, the outrageous cold and the roaring and bubbling in their ears.

Order, authority and a semblance of coordination gradually emerged. Constables and soldiers began to appear, herding away from the scene those who were prepared to be herded. They also tried to stop some of the newly-arriving spectators from hurling themselves into the water in futile searches for missing family members who would now have been on the muddy river bed for more than twenty minutes. Other bystanders were being sold the timeless and preposterous untruth that there was 'nothing to see' – doubly absurd with the twisted ruin of the bridge so evident from all directions. For half-an-hour or more, with the light beginning to fade, more bodies were hooked, hauled out and laid on the bank, with the hook-wielders and netters combining their efforts to ensure that no area of riverbed was left unscoured.

The injured and the half-drowned were now being taken away on stretchers and hand-carts to the Norwich Inn a few yards up the bank. At one stage the net-handlers brought up a strangely colourful tin tub without even realising its connection to the tragedy around them.

A large waggon pulled by four big horses came to a noisy halt right below Tealer's tree. Some fast thinker had raced down to the Lacon´s brewery and had had four great barrels of boiling water winched on to the cart which he'd then driven back up at speed, causing the vehicle's heavy wheels to rumble like thunder on the cobbles of North Quay. The carter was heading for the Norwich Inn, but he whistled up help to manhandle one barrel down the ramp and on to the bank to save time. Yarmouth folk have never needed lessons in the treatment of those plucked from freezing waters. There was no time for modesty or ceremony – men, women and children alike were stripped, thrown into the huge steaming tub and subjected to a blur of rubbing hands. Other victims were simply prodded by helpers who shook their heads curtly and moved on without a word.

Tealer saw children his own age being carried home for the last time, the long wet hair of the girls swinging to the dazed steps of their fathers. He watched other people as they continued to walk up and down the bank staring intently at the opaque water as though it might defy the laws of nature and yield up a gasping relative or friend. The constables were now making no attempt to control or restrain such hopeless cases. With time the mixture of distraught shrieking and relieved shouts changed to a steady groaning.

Then from all along on the river bank, from survivors, helpers, police, soldiers, boatmen and onlookers there was a new alarm. People were pointing up-river past the ruined bridge and were shouting no! no! A late-comer to the festivities was galloping up the Northgate Street in a dog-cart. As it was the south side of the bridge that had collapsed, coming from the north he'd have seen nothing. He rounded the corner and started to straighten up to cross the bridge, and saw the carnage just as his horse was about to commit to the crossing. He lay back almost horizontally on the reins so that the horse slid for several feet and teetered on the edge of the newly-created precipice. To avoid falling the beast shied to one side so the cart itself slewed round and very nearly tipped its occupants into the river. It righted itself with a heavy jolt, and there was a great gasp of relief from those watching. The driver, the two women and the two dogs that were with him all stood up in the vehicle and surveyed the scene blankly. It was the horse that took control. It pulled them back on to firm ground where it waited calmly until the driver was able to gather his wits.

For Tealer in his willow tree the world below had become dreamlike from the moment the bridge had collapsed. What brought him back to reality was this near-fatality with the dog-cart. Suddenly there was something familiar before him. It was the white flash on the face of the horse and its white stockings that made him realise that it was Vulcan, a gelding that belonged to his uncle John Palmer. Then he recognised the retriever, Buck, and the terrier, Turpin, both with ears hitched back in manner of dogs who know there is trouble afoot that they are not involved in. In his dazed state it took him a while to think: if the horse in the shafts of the dog-cart and the dogs riding in it were all his uncle John Palmer's, then the man staring at the scene must be Palmer himself – as Tealer now saw it was. The women with Palmer Tealer didn't know.

The enormity of events had rendered Tealer immobile and incapable of speech, and in any case his thin treble would never have carried against the wind over the chaos below him. He could only watch helplessly as Palmer climbed down and surveyed the wreckage, hand on hips, too stunned even to shake his head. Having led Vulcan away from the bridge he handed the women down and disappeared with them into the throng. Then someone muttered in Tealer's ear:

"Didn't we ought be goin'?" Tealer had entirely forgotten that Charlie was there. "Yes" he said, and saying nothing more they climbed out of their perches and let themselves slowly down to the ground. They were stiff and slow from having sat motionless in the tree for so long. They were both shaking from a mixture of shock and the evening chill. The two friends who had been with them were nowhere to be seen. They began to pick their way through the corpses and the sodden piles of cheap umbrellas, coats, hats, shoes, pinafores and undergarments that marked the spot where the poor of Yarmouth had come to watch some fun with some geese.

The two lads walked slowly along the quay, very close to one another, utterly ignored by those intent on saving life or ascertaining death. At one point they had to pass a knot of men who were all standing in a circle around the prostrate form of a young woman in a white dress soiled almost jet-black with mud. They were cursing and pulling at some object obscured from view. Tealer and Charlie stopped and stared at the struggle. Finally something gave way causing one of the men to lose his balance with a muttered oath. They now saw that it was a small girl of about four that the men had been trying to release. The mother had been holding her hand when the green-brown darkness of the Bure closed around them. The child was clearly dead, and as it was released from its mother's grasp the woman herself shivered and died.

This was what Tealer was watching when a familiar voice behind him said: "I reckon I ought to be a-takin' you home, my man."

It was his uncle, now alone but for his dogs. Tealer was lost for words, but Charlie reacted immediately.

"We can't go yet," he said, "Georgie int back yet,"; and, as he said it, he and Tealer looked at each other, because both were thinking where Georgie had said he was going to make for.

"What's his second name, boy?" Palmer asked Charlie.

"Stolworthy, sir."

"And what was he wearing?"

"His weskit, sir. He was on the bridge with…"

"Yes. Stolworthy. A blond, curly-headed lad. A playmate of John's? I know who you mean," said Tealer's uncle. "Do you two wait here with the dogs till I come back."

He made his way over to the Norwich Inn, and joined the large group of people in and around the front entrance. Tealer and Charlie stood close together with the two subdued dogs, and all four watched the melancholy scenes on the river and its bank. A single goose was swimming amongst the watermen as they sounded the depths with their hooked poles and grappling irons. The goose still had a flamboyant plume stuck in a leather collar at the base of its neck. It was honking for its missing partners.

Tealer's uncle came back about five minutes later and said:

"George'll be late. Go you on home now."

They set off down the quay, and when they rounded the corner they glanced back to see him still standing on the quayside with his dogs, watching them as they went. As they came down North Quay towards the Haven Bridge they encountered a large group of older boys from the Rows standing in a tight huddle and talking in whispers. Normally this would have been a fatal lapse, but this time the older lads hardly looked at them. This was not a night for picking fights.

At the Yarmouth side of the Haven bridge they found the two other boys from the tree standing around waiting for them. With a quiet "See yer," Charlie left the others and made his way home through the stunned Rows. Tealer and his other playmates looked at one another, and without saying a word between them they crossed the river back into Southtown and made their way down the road to Gorleston. There they split up. Tealer pulled himself on to the privy roof, climbed up the drainpipe and crept into his bedroom without a sound.

It was by this time quite dark, and James and Harriet Sayer were preparing for bed. For the last three hours they'd been sitting quietly, drinking tea and reading, oblivious to the events outside. Their pious reflections had been disturbed at one point by a set of youths who had run up Cliff Street, clogs echoing loud on the cobbles, shouting their heads off about something that had happened in Yarmouth. Harriet had frowned in annoyance and James had got up and pulled the heavy curtains completely across to block out any further noise. They lived barely three miles from the scene of the catastrophe yet had no inkling of it until they were given a garbled, tearful version by Daisy Bales the following morning.

"Well, there we are," said James, when Daisy had gone to dry her eyes in the scullery, "there we are." It was much the same thing as he said whenever the *Norfolk News* reported another murderer hanged or another drunkard found rocking amongst the flotsam of the harbour mouth. A shame indeed, when so many had died in ignorance of the Lord and would not know Salvation. A Yarmouth shame, though, and no direct concern of James or Harriet.

But outside the Sayer household news of the disaster had spread rapidly. Within minutes it had coursed like a great sea-wave through the Rows and round the taverns and boarding houses on the quay. It had raced over the Haven bridge so that all the corners of Southtown and then Gorleston were awash with it. It had sped along the tracks of the new railway over the lonely marshes to Reedham, and to Brundall, and by road to the smaller villages along the fringes of the *Gariensis*. And by the new wonder of telegraph it was known about in Norwich within an hour of the collapse. There it soon created the same panic as it had in Yarmouth. Crowds of anxious relatives had swarmed around the telegraph office waiting for the latest postings of victims. From Norwich the news was wired to other towns throughout Britain; the wizardry of one new technology appraising the country of the failure of another. By the Monday morning, in towns far removed from Yarmouth or even East Anglia, and in accents utterly different from those of the dwellers of the Rows, people were talking of the Cory Suspension Bridge Disaster as though the bridge had been a crossing they'd used all their lives.

Yet a stranger visiting Yarmouth a few days afterwards might have been surprised at how unmoved its people seemed by the recent demise of their suspension bridge. The town had shrugged and returned to the hard business of living. This may have been because Yarmouth, like any port battered by the stern North Sea, was no stranger to the shock of multiple drownings. Or perhaps it was simply that displays of emotion were never the Norfolk way.

The truth was that very few had been completely unaffected, and the signs of this were clear enough to those who knew the place well. Boys weren't shouting and whistling in the streets, nor women gossiping in the market, nor men arguing in the taverns. Unsmiling nods were being exchanged instead of the usual 'how yer gittin on?' wherever friends passed in the road. Ponies pulling troll carts were being walked rather than trotted through the Rows. Even the dogs were barking less, it seemed, and were being kicked the moment they did.

Any drunkenness there was was not the loud, shanty-singing kind, but a maudlin, solitary business.

And there were other, less direct effects. For a few weeks the churches, chapels and the lunatic asylum all welcomed new faces. And it's said that there was a marked rise in the number of babies born about nine months after that evening. Did the young of the town feel the urge to create life to replace that snuffed out? Or merely seek the reassurance of physical contact in the face of such annihilation?

A few folk with the money and the inclination strove for other forms of solace. They didn't have to look hard for help in this, for before long there popped up in the town a small army of psychics, palmists, tea-leaf readers, tarot experts, necromancers, soothsayers, seventh sons of seventh sons and other charlatans hoping to capitalise on this rich seam of misery. But these soon realised what for all their gazing into crystal balls they hadn't foreseen: that the victims of the tragedy were mostly from the truly poorest Rows and hadn't even got the money for the simplest coffins for their dead relatives, never mind the dubious services of clairvoyants. It wasn't long before the booths were dismantled and the crystal balls, talking heads, smoke boxes and mirrors were packed up again as the magicians slipped back out of town. If nothing else, they were practised at seeing into men's minds, and there they'd seen that the mood in parts of Yarmouth was about to turn ugly.

And yes, after the period of shock and mourning, some of the hostelries turned rowdy again. A casting-about for scapegoats began. Word got round that the bridge had fallen because it had been tampered with. Insurance, religious hatred, jealousy, nationalism and subversion were all put up as the obvious motive. At different times – and sometimes at the same time – suspects included unpaid creditors, rival bridge-builders, Lowestoft fishermen, the Jews, Cornish fishermen, the Quakers, the French, the Masons, the Young Irelanders, the Germans, the Catholics, the railway interests and even the bridge-owners themselves. Some of the theories were ingenious, most were ludicrous, and none had any evidence whatever to support it. Seditious elements nonetheless saw their chance and did their best to raise Cain.

And yet they failed in this for much the same reason as the penny-mystics before them: the victims themselves were too taken up with the business of surviving from one day to the next to go looking for revenge. And they were simply of too little consequence to provoke much fury in the rest of the town. Anger there was, but no yelling mob laid siege to the house of the nearest railway baron. No-one, culpable or otherwise, ended his life dangling by the neck from the ruined metalwork of the bridge.

The answer to the question in John Palmer's mind as he had stood on the quay by the mangled bridge watching Tealer and Charlie slip quietly home – the question as to the effect on children so young of witnessing such ghastliness – was that they were not as traumatized as might be expected. Neither boy was left speechless or gibbering. Palmer mentioned this to Mrs Durrant, one of the two ladies in his nearly-doomed gig, who as a governess had had some experience of such things. She told him that most children of Tealer's age had so little understanding of death that they wouldn't necessarily link what they had seen by the bridge with mortality. And surely, whenever in later years Tealer himself remembered the disaster the image of the grisly scene was almost theatrical in its unreality: the remains of the bridge as a backdrop, the flurry of boats in the water and the rows of staring corpses. The screams and shrieks that had carried down towards him on the bank seemed to have no connection with the figures scurrying about between the recumbent forms of the victims. Any more direct sensation he'd either later blocked out, or hadn't registered at all.

This isn't to say he wasn't very curious about it all. His parents allowed Daisy to take him to Georgie Stolworthy's funeral (though cold and remote, they were not vindictive people). Georgie's death was the first time Tealer had had to face the finiteness of the human condition. He was full of questions about the boxes that Georgie and his brother were placed in, and the flowers sitting on them. He wanted to know why the holes had to be so deep, and what Georgie looked like now he'd been seen to by the undertaker, and how long he would keep looking like it – all questions that Daisy Bales answered in hushed monosyllables as they made their way slowly back home. Of course it took a while for him to realise that Georgie really never would call him to the window above the privy with his bad owl impression, but by the time it had truly sunk in Tealer's own young life had moved on. In fact, for a child who was so prone to night terrors anyway, it seemed for a while that Tealer had escaped the witnessing of the Cory Bridge tragedy remarkably unscathed.

But then he was to suffer two reverses whose effects ensured that this wasn't to be the case.

The Phantom in the Chapel

The first was caused by a sermon in the Cliff Street Tabernacle.

This was in July, fully two months after the bridge collapse. It was a cruelly hot afternoon in the airless chapel, and wedged between his parents in his starched collar and prickly Sunday weeds Tealer was whiling the time way by watching the courses of various insects buzzing around the chapel and hurling themselves against the translucent panes in an attempt to escape.

The preacher that Sunday afternoon was Jeremy Lovett, an up-and-coming Tabernacle elder. Listen to Lovett preaching and you soon knew where James Sayer had picked up his more irritating mannerisms.

Lovett's style of oratory was fascinatingly bad. His sermons were unhindered by any kind of structure, and devoid of any intellectual rigour. He would wade into each performance without notes, confident in his ability to keep shouting, whatever. As a young man he'd learnt the value of this – the less sure you are of what you are saying the more emotion you should say it with; that way, everyone imagines some especially telling point is being made, even if they themselves happen to be missing it. Another of Lovett's devices was to fire a rhetorical question at the half of the congregation to his right, look shrewdly at them for a moment, and then fire the same question at the half to his left, a ploy whose real purpose was to give him time to work out how he could answer the question himself. With these tricks he'd actually persuaded some of the simpler minds of the Tabernacle that he was an infallible mouthpiece of the Almighty – and, as is so often the case with men like him, he'd come to believe it himself. Even those who saw through the cant had to admire the illusion. And at least no-one ever *slept* during a Lovett sermon – the sheer volume of it made sure of that.

But this occasion, one or two of the congregation were more attentive than usual, and not out of any regard for Jeremy Lovett.

Rather the opposite. Lovett had long been one of the strongest advocates of the Cory Road Bridge from the day he'd lost his job as ticket clerk on the railway. He had cited all manner of references to show that the building of road bridges was nothing less than the work of God. Then, as we know, the wretched thing collapsed. This had left some of his Tabernacle rivals quietly cock-a-hoop. They were itching to see how he was going to explain his theological way out of this one. But when his slot on the preaching roster finally came round, they found they'd underestimated the pachyderm-thickness of Lovett's skin. His change of tack was truly breath-taking. Of humility or contrition there was not a scintilla. In fact, for the couple of months he'd had to wait for his turn to preach he'd been in an agony of suspense, fervently hoping that none of the other brethren would pre-empt him.

Finally, the first Sunday of his preaching week dawned. In his morning sermon he made no mention of the bridge, and the more cynical of his brethren smiled slyly.

They smiled too soon.

He'd merely been saving himself for the afternoon.

From the moment he had climbed up to the lectern, fixed his followers with an awful stare and fired off his first string of repeated sentences it was clear that Lovett intended to milk the cataclysmic images of the Cory Bridge tragedy quite uninhibited by any sense of irony.

"Brothers and Sisters in Chroist!" he thundered triumphantly, "Consider the victims of the fall of the Tower of Shiloam described in Luke. That tower – of Shiloam – that fell, didn't it? And 'at killed many people, didn't it? And what had them people done that was so especially bad? So especially bad? Nothin'…., thas what! Nothin'! Nothin'! Them people what perished was no worse than the people around them what was spared. And yet they perished and them other people around them didn't. Now, what do that tell us? Why were they singled out like that? Singled out? Now then! Now then! Yes! Why were they singled out? That's the question we should ask ourselves. Int it? Or… er…at least… no! *No*! That *int* the question we should ask ourselves. Is it? No, d'yer see, that *int* the question. Oh, no. Oh no, no, no. Because d'yer see, they *weren't* singled out. D'yer see? They *weren't*. All them *others* what *didn't* die – what *didn't* die – *they* deserved to be killed by the fall of the Tower of Shiloam *an'all*! Just – just – *just* – as every one of *us* deserved to be crushed into atoms by the collapse of that there bridge over the Bure river. *Every - one - of - us*. Every one of us deserved to be suffocated in the Bure river. Don't matters we weren't all there! Don't matters we weren't all there! For we were all as guilty as the four hundred what fell in the river on that dark day, yea, even as guilty as them seventy-nine wretches what were never to breathe again. No, brothers and sisters in Chroist, we shouldn't be asking why them particular souls were doomed - we should only ask ourselves: why did 'at happen in the fust place? Why did 'at happen in the fust place? Now then! Now then!"

By this time Lovett was beginning to move into that state of ecstasy that made preaching such fun. He could feel a new line of attack coming on, one in which he could use his favourite technique of singling out individuals from among his congregation. "Have you thought," he roared, pointing at different individuals in turn, "Brothers and Sisters in Chroist, have you thought *you* might ha' been the reason for that collapse? Yes, you! Or you! Or you! You might be the reason. Perhaps *you* are one of them that had so provoked God's wrath that He decided to sever the sinews of that there bridge – just as he smote the foundations of that tower of Shiloam what I mentioned earlier. So – *you* might have been the reason for that bridge fall'n into the river. And *you* could so easily ha' perished with it when 'at did fall. When 'at did fall. Yes."

Of course the moral that this ex-ticket clerk, Sunday afternoon visionary and self-inflated ignoramus was trying to instil in the hearts of his following wasn't original. Anyone tenacious enough to wade through the thicket of rhetorical questions and homeless clauses would find little more than a confused version of "ask not for whom the bell tolls…". It was really drivel of the most predictable kind; yet there was one small member of Lovett's congregation whom it affected out of all proportion.

Tealer was normally as good at dreaming through a Lovett sermon as he was one of James Sayer's homilies at family prayers. But it so happened that he himself was whiling away the time by recalling episodes from the bridge disaster at the same time as Lovett was sermonising on it. And he was remembering the sight of Georgie Stolworthy disappearing into the crowd just as Lovett from on high caught his eye and directed an especially ferocious '*you might ha' been the reason*' straight at him.

At an instant the harsh summer light streaming in from the high window scorched Tealer's eyes, the oppressive heat of the chapel threatened to stifle him, and the blood pounded in his ears. And his own voice resounded in his head "Yes, *I* might have been the reason! I *was* the reason! It was me! I wanted rid of Titus Gooch, so I wished the bridge would collapse with Gooch on it, and it did. *I* was the reason that bridge collapsed."

Tealer looked helplessly up at Lovett, but the preacher had suddenly become a distant figure in a mime-show, waving and gesticulating but making no sound. The boy then stole a glance across the chapel fearful that some of the other worshippers might have read his guilty response. He firstly found himself gazing into the lizard eyes of Titus Gooch. No ghost, this, for Titus had managed to scramble to safety in the melée of the collapse. He had been a white-faced wreck ever since, but he still managed a scowl at Tealer. Tealer looked away quickly, but as he did so he had just time to glimpse another figure at the far side of the chapel. This was only for the merest instant, but enough to take in the waxy, dead face of an unknown child – more like a child-mannequin – not watching the arm-waving form of Lovett like all the adults around it, but staring hard at Tealer himself. It could almost have been placed there by the righteous just to remind him, John Sayer, of all those lives he'd so wilfully wished away. Tealer quickly turned back to Lovett. He looked at his own shoes. He looked as his own hands. He watched numbly as a warble-fly hurled itself against one of the unforgiving panes above Lovett's head. There was no escape. Titus Gooch was quickly forgotten, but that second watcher, that child, or child-mannequin… there was no escape from *that*. *That* knew. It was so clear that it knew. And the voice in Tealer's head was stronger now, accusing and insistent, and no longer his own. 'Yes, you were the reason that bridge collapsed, John Sayer. See, one of them even knows. *You* were the reason. You.'

With sweat soaking his clothes he looked again – but the child mannequin had vanished behind the forms of the seated adults.

Thus was the conviction duly cemented in the young mind of John 'Tealer' Sayer that by willing the disappearance of the lank-haired gnome Gooch he had destroyed the life of his friend Georgie.

That night, just as he was going to sleep in his garret, he heard a familiar bad attempt at an owl-hoot and then Georgie's voice calling up to him from the bottom of the drainpipe. He jumped out and raced to the window in a flood of relief, only to find Georgie melting into the cobbles of the yard below. And waking up the following morning he found Georgie staring down at him from the edge of the bed. He rubbed his eyes and Georgie was gone. Later that day when he was walking to school he thought he saw Georgie among the children going in through the gates ahead of him. But when he caught up there was no Georgie.

These apparitions alarmed Tealer and caused him to believe he was being haunted. This growing certainty led to a return of his night terrors, and these in turn led to a second major trauma.

Daisy Bales was on hand to cope with the first two or three of the bad dreams when they returned. She brought Tealer round and administered her tincture and sang the songs and coaxed him back to sleep.

But as the summer became hotter there was an outbreak of typhus in the Rows which spread out across the town and into the hinterlands. One victim was Daisy's aunt in Caister. Daisy was given leave by the Sayers to help tend to the dying woman. This meant that she was not in the house on the night of Tealer's worst nightmare. James and Harriet were disturbed during their evening devotions by an outbreak of hysterical wailing from the little garret, and it was Harriet who had to grasp the rope bannister and haul herself up the steep stairs to Tealer's bed. She eventually managed to wake him though she could do little to get him to calm down. Then she remembered Daisy's nightshade in plum syrup. But Harriet wasn't versed in folk remedies and in her haste to stop Tealer's yells she poured out three times the correct dose, which only had the effect of doubling the intensity of the visions.

Tealer later remembered very little of this descent into Hell. Perhaps whole legions of drowned, silt-covered victims were rising out of the Bure to point accusing fingers at him, and perhaps they even pulled him down into the muddy waves with them. Perhaps the stolid, humourless face that stared back from the mirror was now a baleful, black-eyed troll that fixed Tealer in its glare and licked its dry lips. Perhaps these, and perhaps much worse.

Not only his parents but the whole neighbourhood was roused by his dismal howling and screaming. The racket was so dreadful that James later confessed he thought his son might be possessed by demons. Finally the noise abated as Tealer fell into a coma that lasted until the following evening. And, when he finally came to, he didn't speak for another three days, and everyone thought he'd been struck dumb. It was Daisy who realised that at least part of the problem was that hours of sustained shrieking had damaged his vocal chords. She poured pints of lemon and honey cordial into him and finally managed to get him to utter a few cracked syllables. When he could produce a few words she urged him to tell her what had so terrified him. He told her that there had been many terrible things in his nightmare but that he couldn't remember any of them. This wasn't the whole truth: there was one image that did survive the amnesiac effects of the nightshade: he had dreamt he was running frantically through the lanes of Gorleston with the faceless form of George Stolworthy following at a relentless walk. But this he daren't tell even the trusted Daisy. She might guess what he'd done to bring such a vengeance on him.

Everyone said that little John Sayer was never quite the same after that night. Even when his speech had completely recovered he only ever spoke sparingly and quietly. People didn't know that an accusing voice was often ringing in his head. It was a wordless monologue that he now took to be the voice of the child or child-mannequin he'd seen in the chapel, and which was now beginning to haunt him by day…

It started to loiter at the end of each street at he entered it, while at the same time muttering into his ear as though it had climbed on to his back. But children are resilient, and accept horrors that might drive their elders insane. And so despite the unlovely presence of the child or child-mannequin loitering at the end of his street, or perched on his shoulder muttering into his ear, Tealer was soon back to climbing down the drainpipe to meet up with the other lads. They'd often go down to the quay as a gang to watch ships from the harbour mouth. Yet just as he was beginning to enjoy the sense of freedom Tealer might glance away from the sea and spot a small child of about their age watching them from across the river on the Yarmouth side. It was always too far away to see who it was. So, very casually, he'd ask his friends about it. He'd say something like "Look at him messin' about there," or "Who d'you reckon that is on the other side there?" And Charlie, or Sammy, or Davey, would look at where he was pointing and shrug, or say "Dunno," and get back to arguing about the rigs of the ships they could see.

And the figure wouldn't go away.

One such time Charlie was drawing a brigantine on the back of a laundry list and the others were carving model boats out of jetsam. And Tealer asked "Who's that boy a-standin' and starin' at us, Charlie? Who d'yer reckon that can be?"

"Jiggered if I know" said Charlie, not even bothering to look up, "but he might as well lose hisself, 'cause I aren't puttin' him in my picture. I just want the ship."

"But who do you reckon he look like?"

Charlie squinted briefly at the far-off form. "No-one," he said finally.

"Do you reckon he look like Georgie?" persisted Tealer.

"*Georgie*?"

"Yeah. What d'you reckon?"

"Georgie's dead, Johnny." said Charlie. "You don't go walking down South Denes Road when you're dead. He's a-laying up in in the churchyard at St Nicholas. He ha' been ate by worms b'now, I sh'think."

But still the figure on the far bank lingered. Tealer looked at it and then at his friends and then back at it again. Eventually, without a word, he left the quayside and ran home. One of the other boys looked casually up from carving a wooden boat and said "I reckon Sayer's mad."

"Thas what I reckon, an'all." said another, and they returned to their boats, not giving him a second thought. The figure looked on for a while and quietly drifted away. If the other boys noticed it at all they said nothing to one another. They were busy with their sketching and their carving.

For weren't there were always figures on the far bank, or out on the marsh, or at the other end of the market, not quite recognisable?

By the time high summer had become late summer Yarmouth seemed to have moved on from the tragedy. A town that wrestles a livelihood from the sea has no choice. Tealer himself remained the plaything of many phantoms, and they were mostly Georgie Stolworthy.

Then the dreams that gave rise to the phantoms – or the phantoms that gave rise to the dreams – were for a while brushed aside as another chapter in the life of John Sayer was written.

Towards the end of that same summer the typhus that had killed Daisy Bales's aunt also claimed the lives of both James and Harriet Sayer.

A panel of enquiry was set up by Yarmouth Borough Council to investigate the effects of the bridge collapse on the families of its victims. It was this panel which discovered that in the growing heat of the summer typhus had become rife in the most foetid of the Rows. By the time the authorities had been able to do anything sensible the disease had swept out along the water-sides and had infected most areas of the town, sickening and killing as it went.

How it got across the river and into South Town, and then Gorleston, no-one could rightly say – but, pew by tight-packed pew, it worked through the faithful of the Cliff Street Tabernacle, and many succumbed, leaving their brethren wondering at how this could have happened to them of all people… and scratching their heads all the while. One of those struck down stricken was Tealer's father. His mother followed, and after some ten days of illness they died within several hours of one another.

And, perhaps because Tealer was never treated with any warmth by either of them, he never afterwards remembered feeling anything like grief or mourning. He only felt a natural fear that the security of his home had been removed at a stroke.

In fact he couldn't have been in better hands. Daisy served the office of the laying out of his parents and so ensured that Tealer's last sight of them at least didn't resemble the traumatic jumble of pallid skin, crushed chests and splayed limbs which till then had been his only acquaintance with human mortality. He was taken in to see them where they lay side-by-side in the shuttered front room. He found their expressions much as they had been in life: distant, intense, and suggesting that death, rather like performing geese or noisy children, was nothing much to laugh at.

John Palmer saw to the funerals. A few days later he sat down with Daisy one evening after Tealer had been put to bed. They discussed what was to be done. The following morning before school Tealer found that Daisy had been joined by a slim, smiling young woman of about thirty with a mountain of hair plaited and piled beneath a jaunty bonnet. She was called Mrs Durrant, and Daisy told Tealer she had come to help Daisy to clear belongings and tie loose ends. Tealer later realised she was one of the two women in Palmer's dog-cart on the night of the bridge disaster. She was a sometime governess and piano teacher to one of the richer families of Norwich, and she had a placid, slightly careworn beauty that made her compare very favourably with the grim-faced harridans who were the only female teachers Tealer had ever known. She also had a gentle way with her that Tealer in his confused state readily responded to. She had a scar from her ear to the corner of her mouth that Tealer was never to ask about. He was also never to ask about Mr Durrant.

After a few more days, some time around mid-September, Daisy called Tealer down from his garret to tell him his uncle wished to speak to him. He walked in to the little front room to find it unusually full of an autumn evening sunshine that was illuminating the thick dust of the musty furniture. Someone had pulled the curtains right back, something never done in James and Harriet's day, and Tealer literally saw the room as he'd never seen it before. Even the windows were open. Daisy was standing behind the chair where his mother used to sit, and his uncle was sitting at the dining table with Mrs Durrant. They were all looking at Tealer.

"Did you want to come live with me, Johnny?" asked his uncle without ceremony.

"What about Daisy?" asked Tealer.

"She says she'll come to look after you," said the smiling Mrs Durrant, stroking his hair.

Tealer was naturally hesitant, like a long-captive animal whose cage door had been left open. He was, after all, only eight. He nodded slowly.

Yet that uncertain nod was Tealer Sayer's break with a life of closed windows, starched collars and contemplation. His lot seemed set to become immeasurably happier. The prospect of what lay ahead – a life of birds and boats and guns and the great, bad, wild, green marsh – all at once seemed wonderfully bright. His expression was as impassive as ever, but he was quietly ecstatic. His heart leapt even at the sight of unfamiliar rays of light dancing on the familiar walls as the curtains caught the evening breeze.

Then for an instant the sunlight fell on a grubby print of Harriet's that showed Satan importuning Christ in the wilderness, together with the caption 'Get thee hence!' It was only for an instant, but it was long enough for Tealer to see that the Satan-figure had turned its bug-eyed leer from Christ to Tealer himself. Tealer looked up into Mrs Durrant's face and then back at the picture, sure that she too must have witnessed this manifestation. She glanced briefly in the direction of the print but saw nothing and turned her kindly face back to Tealer. Tealer looked back at the picture. But a cloud had crossed the sun. The sombre print was once more part of the dusty drabness of the rest of the room. Satan had returned to his business with Christ.

As before, only Tealer had seen the evil. As before, he must keep it to himself.

But make no mistake, there most certainly was something or someone malign and destructive hidden in that room that evening. And wonderful though his new life with his uncle would turn out to be, Tealer was set to confront this same demon in still stranger forms.

The Pike-Queen

The Jesuits say that if they have the child at seven he is theirs for life. Jesuits were not numerous in Gorleston, but if the principle is correct for all shades of religion one would expect John Sayer eventually to have acquired a Tabernacler's sturdy indifference to the wonders of nature.

But it was an indifference he never did acquire.

Or perhaps Jesuitical theory makes no allowance for a man like John Palmer.

Palmer had seen the burgeoning naturalist in his nephew even when the child had been confined to the airless Sayer household. Having once taken him in, John senior was able to spend the next five years turning his nephew into a fowler, sailor and countryman. He quickly managed to make sure that the boy's guilty fascination with nature became an outright love for it. Palmer wouldn't have set much store by the predictions of Jesuits in any case. He made no distinction between the various persuasions of priests and preachers, but dismissed them all equally as a 'damned lot of tricksters'.

John Palmer's own wife had died in childbirth. The couple had already lost their first child to smallpox, and the second died of measles shortly after the death of its mother. At a little above thirty, a childless widower, Palmer felt no urge to found any more dynasties. He resolved instead to lose himself in travel. In this he was lucky. He was a youngish Englishman in the hey-day of youngish Englishmen. The British Empire – the world by any other name – lay at his feet. He knew that among the Queen's overseas dominions there were opportunities for yeoman adventurers like him – men whose marked regional speech and ways weren't the bar to advancement that they were in the mother country. He decided he would go off 'to seek his fortune' in these far-flung places. He therefore used much of his remaining inheritance in sailing from continent to continent, telling everyone, starting with himself, that he was exploring the potential for tea-planting or ship-building or tin-mining or cattle-ranching. The real purpose of these quests was to see as much of the world as he could before the arthritis and cynicism of middle-age began to curb his energies. His adventures had left him very wealthy, but only in experience. He still retained part-ownership of three Yarmouth brigs, all that remained of the once-large family shipping concern. With this income he was able to live simply but comfortably, indulging his twin passions of sport and nature. His house was full of mementoes of his wandering life, and these gave him much pleasure.

But increasingly of late John Palmer had taken to ambling around his small dwelling in Row 111 in a pensive mood. He would find himself running his finger absentmindedly over the broken teeth of the man-eater he'd shot in the Sunderbans, or leafing through his beloved first edition of Col. Peter Hawker's *Instructions to Young Sportsmen,* or gazing at his own sketch of the mynah bird he'd been given by the padre's wife in Kerala (shortly after she'd found out what its favourite Hindustani expression actually meant).

Much as Palmer had enjoyed this travelling, sailing, shooting and exploring, he was beginning to find that something was missing. It was his visits to his sister's house in Gorleston which made him realize what it was. It was the thought that he might go to his grave without ever having passed on these accumulated skills and experiences to a successor.

Because one of the greatest joys of association with the outdoors – and ask any hunter, sailor or fisherman and he will tell you the same – is the opportunity to pass on its changeless lore to the next generation. For a man of Palmer's generation this need was especially pressing. Palmer was intrigued by science and innovation, but at the same time he realised that many of the old ways he'd grown up with were fast disappearing in the burgeoning tide of steam and steel. He was no man of books (except of course his bible, which was Hawker's *Instructions to Young Sportsmen*) and the idea of sitting and writing everything down had no appeal. He wanted to hand down the fruits of his experience by word of mouth and by practical demonstration.

His newly-orphaned nephew appeared the perfect oblate.

So Tealer's re-education started immediately. Palmer decided to introduce him without delay to the several different wildernesses that lay just beyond Yarmouth's crumbling walls, and the first and most formidable of these was the one from which Tealer would eventually earn his living.

The North Sea is not a lovely sea. It usually presents a grey face that reflects the cold sky above it. It doesn't create majestic ocean rollers but vicious, choppy waves that bounce a boat around like a cork. Not many of its beaches are sandy but instead are swathes of sterile pebbles that clash and grind with each surge. Its waters are usually bitterly cold from being separated from the warming

Gulf Stream by the island of Britain itself. It fills the east wind with a drizzle that even in midsummer has the capacity to freeze and numb and to leave one wondering if the sun will ever shine again. When the wind's in the west, those in small boats off shore need to look to their seamanship or find themselves pushed far out into the sharp peaks and steep troughs of the 'Yarmouth Roads' in a matter of minutes.

The North Sea is a young sea, and the marshlands and forests which it swamped in prehistory have produced deposits that shift and shove with every strong storm. These sands make its waters turbid and unfathomable. Powerful longshore currents sweep along the beaches, so that the waterlogged corpse of a bait-digger who steps into one of the treacherous holes in the shallows on Blakeney Point can be attracting a silent ring of onlookers thirty miles down the coast in a matter of hours.

But there's been enough drowning in this story already, and the North Sea also has its charms. If you look hard at the unchanging grey you can see flocks of tiny waders whisking effortless between the breakers, or the dark heads of seals that watch you sorrowfully from the safety of the open water before they disappear back into its gritty opaqueness. And the restless sands and shingles are ever revealing ancient and mysterious relics – elephant bones, antlers, spear points, tree stumps. The seabed here was once the floor of a thick green forest, echoing with birdsong. Shimmering swarms of herring now pass over the bland plains which once witnessed struggles between ancient people and huge beasts, whose dramas, with their heroes, triumphs and tragedies, are utterly unrecorded save for the shards and fragments brought up in trawlermen's nets.

Young Sayer was introduced to the sea in stages. On the very first day of his life in Row 111 he was taken by his uncle on to North Yarmouth beach to look at the grey seals basking on the dunes. This simple journey, no more than a walk along the strand, was transcendently new. The sharp tang of the seals might have wrinkled the nostrils of another child. To Tealer it was the smell of adventure. He laughed at their bovine slowness – and he looked at his uncle sceptically when Palmer told him how they chased and caught fish through the murky water.

The next week they went on to the pier to watch the fishermen preparing fish for the market. Tealer was thrilled by the thump of the breakers as they pounded the supports.

"There y'are, boy! Look at your clumsy old seal now!" Palmer was pointing to a bull of some three hundred pounds as it twisted and glided through the breakers, never taking its eyes off the cod fisherman as they gutted their catches all along the jetty.

Another week on, Palmer hired the services of a smack, and they went out on to the open water. Tealer was enthralled by the rolling and the pitching of the craft and the creaking of the sheets. He gazed down into the grey spikey waters of the Roads trying to make out what lay beneath them. The peaks and troughs of water mesmerized him; they all seemed sure to swamp the modest vessel, and the boy who rarely spoke much above a whisper yelled with excitement when one actually slopped over the gunwales.

Then his uncle tapped him on the shoulder and pointed back to Yarmouth, which was now just a line on the horizon, so distant that the beach itself was hidden beneath the tops of the waves that were rolling away from them towards the Gorleston cliffs. This was the first time Tealer realised that that the sea was a much bigger place than the town he used to view it from. And for an instant he imagined a particularly huge wave sweeping over Gorleston, brushing all before it – all the schools, churches, tabernacles, school teachers, Sunday school teachers, school monitors, Sunday school monitors, school bullies, preachers, inspectors, shuttered parlours and prayer meetings. All washed away in a frothing wall of water, cascading into every dusty nook in the town and leaving this vast uncontrolled, sun-spangled, heaving, noisy world in which boats sailed and seals, gulls and terns swam, all untroubled by rules or limitations.

Palmer noticed the ease with which the boy accepted the water without showing any real fear, and he later quietly remarked on it to Mrs Durrant as they strolled arm-in-arm along South Quay one sunny evening. She maintained the reason for this was Tealer's implicit trust in Palmer. "He can't imagine you placing him in real peril. You'd find that an older child would never have such complete confidence."

"But he saw more people drown in five minutes than many of the oldest herring-men I know ha' seen in a life time. Yet there he was, a-laughing at the waves as though he were born in 'em."

"I still think he saw that tragedy as an adult might view a massacre in a stage play: unsettling, dreadful, but not affecting him any more than as a spectator. Now had he been dragged barely alive from the water under that bridge, why then I warrant you'd now be having a harder task getting him used to the sea."

Having been introduced to the elemental sea, Tealer was then taken by his uncle to learn about the subtler ways of the rivers that poured into it.

One hot afternoon, so hot that Vulcan the horse was soaking in his harness within minutes, they clopped up the lanes from Yarmouth, passing between sweltering fields of ripened wheat whose only sign of life was the wheezing of the yellowhammers in the bordering hedgerows. They drove through the hamlets of Ormesby, Rollesby, and Ludham, all drowsy and Sunday-silent. Vulcan's hooves echoed like gun-shots off the baking walls of the cottages where the only other sounds were half-hearted chirrups of sparrows amongst the pantiles. They entered cooler stretches of woodland that were filled with the strident calls of chiff-chaffs. Finally they could hear the sounds of coot and duck promising open water, though long before any water was to be seen. Only when they made their way down a long loke that ended in a staithe did Tealer catch his first sight of the river – and even then it seemed no more than a large pond. It was in fact one of the bends of the Thurne. Tied to one of the jetty posts was his uncle's yacht, the *Hermione*. Her sleek carvel lines were planed to a fault, and her brass fittings gleamed in the August sun. From within the womb of this elegant half-decker Tealer was to learn his river lore.

At first the *Hermione* seemed a confusion of ropes and pulleys that creaked and squeaked and rattled as she left her secluded mooring. And the yacht moved glacially slowly, so that Tealer began to think this rather dull next to the thrilling junketing they had had in the Yarmouth Roads. It was when they came out on to one of the broader, straighter reaches of the river that the magic of Broadland sailing was revealed. Once free of the tall willows that surrounded the staithe, the sails billowed out in the now-stiffening north-westerly and a gurgling came up from the bow as the craft picked up speed and slipped down the Thurne. Tealer Sayer's life as a sailor was underway.

He was put on the tiller, and was taught to hold his course as the boat sped towards the reedy margins that marked the bank until the bowsprit actually began to disappear into the undergrowth. Then he would shove the rudder hard to port or starboard so that the boat would do almost an about, and there would be a rush of water under the hull and the wind would send the boom creaking and ringing over from one side of the craft to the other. He was to shout "lee-oh!" when he did this.

On their next outing on the river Palmer took the tiller and told Tealer to act as look out on the prow. They were tacking against the westerly, gathering speed across a wide reach towards the opposite bank. Tealer now knew that at the last instant the tiller would be thrown from one direction to the other, causing the boat to slew round back into the open river. But this didn't happen. Palmer didn't react to the fast approaching bank, and the boat careered into the reeds. Tealer shouted in alarm and with eyes shut he braced himself against the bow as he waited for the jarring crunch of a collision with the bank. But none came, and Tealer heard his uncle laughing merrily in the stern.

"What, did I give you a turn, boy?"

The echoing rhythms of the river were suddenly muted, the powerful summer light was dimmed and there was a great rustling and whispering all around. Tealer slowly opened his eyes and found that he was in a reed world. Reed blotted out the view, even the light. It scraped along the sides of the *Hermione* and filled her hull with seeds. Palmer brought the sail down and poled the boat along a barely discernible course of water through the wall of green-brown stems. The dominant, universal sound was now the chafing of reed-stalks, permeated only by the chattering of reed-warblers deep in the undergrowth. Tealer's clothes and hair crawled with the beetles and spiders that had been dislodged as the *Hermione* had crashed through the reed bed.

Then as abruptly as they had entered this suffocating world, they left it. From the choked dyke the boat burst out again into open water. But this wasn't the river. They were on a huge pond, whose surface was utterly still. The fence of thick reed that surrounded it made it insular, and the intermittent duck-calls and *w'pink*-ing of the coots were greatly amplified. Tealer looked over the side and could see straight to the bottom nine feet below them. He even caught the occasional movement of large fish amongst the fronds of waterweed.

It was Tealer's first experience of a broad, though it could have been a lake in the Garden of Eden.

It was a fierce Eden. Dragonflies crackled everywhere. Some settled on hull of the boat or on Tealer's clothes or hands, and surveyed him with a compound stare of cold ferocity. Equally colourful were the horseflies, though Tealer soon found their beauty belied their intent, for any wet skin they found exposed they punctured with their stiletto mouthparts. Swallows and swifts darted about with the dragonflies and the horseflies, feasting on both. A hobby was flying sorties from a vantage in the treetops round the broad, killing dragonflies and feeding as it flew, and on one occasion taking a swallow and feeding on that. There was an area on the fringe of the broad where the reeds had been cut back to reveal a muddy pool like a miniature of the broad itself. The water was only an inch deep, but even in this tranquil spot a huge raft spider scuttled back and forth through the idyllic haze, searching for fry.

They sailed around the broad for a while, and at one point Palmer reached out to grab a small piece of willow that was floating near the far bank. He pulled it in board and it brought with it a length of rope with a sack on the end. He stored both rope and sack in the fore deck well out of sight.

"You didn't see that, boy," he said.

They returned to the broad one evening the following week, this time in a rowing boat. And it was on that return that Tealer was introduced to another fearsome broadlander. As always his uncle gave no warning of the coming lesson. They had reached the middle of the broad when of a sudden Palmer dropped anchor and then poked around in the foredeck to produce a short thick rod of split cane and a reel of polished applewood around which was bound a strong silk line. He opened a jar and took out a freshly pickled mackerel and a straw. Tealer was intrigued. Palmer passed the straw through the vent of the fish and blew down it, making the fish puff up. Then he sealed the vent with a clip and passed a metal trace through the gills. He attached two hooks, one fore of the fish and one aft, and held it up to the light to admire his handiwork. Tealer continued to watch him wordlessly. He now knew without asking that they were to fish for the terror of the still waters.

"We'll try to find a jack for you to look at, Johnny,"

Tealer watched as Palmer took the simple arrangement of rod, reel and mackerel bait and steadied them for a moment over his shoulder. Then he swung the tackle back and forth to get the measure of it and then flicked it over the side of the boat so that the mackerel's metallic blue scales caught the early autumn sun and flashed for an instant before landing in the water some thirty yards off. The splash set ripples journeying away across the broad's mirror surface.

Palmer reeled in, at varying speeds, jerking the rod and flicking it from one side to the other so that the tiny bow wave created by the floating bait appeared and subsided and reappeared as it approached them. Tealer watched carefully, but nothing much happened.

Once having reeled in, Palmer cast again, this time a little to the right of his previous cast. Again he reeled. Again he cast, now at two o'clock to the original. On the third cast the bow wave of the lure seemed to be joined by another at an angle, but then the tiny ripples of this second, tangential line subsided into nothing – but not before a small grunt of satisfaction came from Palmer.

"Did you see that? Jacko like the look of our little sick roach-mackerel. We'll give him a better view." Palmer cast out into the same patch of water as before, and then said "Your turn, boy." Tealer hadn't seen very much, but he was willing to have a go. He started turning the reel as he thought his uncle had turned it.

"Don't make it so rhythmic, boy. And not so fast. That's how healthy fish swim, and Jack Pike haven't the energy to be a-chasing healthy fish around the broad after a hot day like we've had today. You want to make him think your fish is peggin' out." He took the rod back and reeled at different speeds, sometimes supplementing the chicanery with slight jerks on the rod that caused the deadbait thirty yards off to splash slightly. "Get the idea, boy? Try again."

Tealer did. He pulled the deadbait into the boat and his uncle cast it out for him again, always dropping the lure six feet or so to the right of where it had last landed. On the fifth or sixth cast there was a sound between a snap and a clap almost as soon as the bait had landed, and the split-cane came alive. A small pike, perhaps two or three pounds, became the first in a long line to nurture in Tealer an undying fascination for all fierce toothed things from dark waters. The reel squalled and the rod nodded furiously as the pike swarmed across the water to the nearest reed to shake out the hooks. Tealer was very excited and started pulling furiously at the fish.

"No, no boy! Let him swim himself out before you try that or we could lose him. It won't be long. Pike are all fire at the outset but they soon wind themselves."

Sure enough the line soon went limp, though when Tealer began to reel in he could feel a new and unaccustomed weight on the end. Yet from the uniform blue-green there was still nothing to see. Then two smouldering eyes glared up from the gloom, and the long, sinister shape and the tiger-striped back broke the surface. Palmer netted the jack and hauled it in. Tealer was chilled by the cold fury in those eyes, and more so when he saw that they actually swivelled in their sockets to watch him as his uncle pulled the fish out of the net. His uncle showed him how to hold the pike over its shoulder, and he felt the spasms of power course through the little predator as it sought with its last energy to free itself from his grip. It was too small for eating so his uncle decided it should be disgorged and put back. He told Tealer that there were those who killed every pike they caught whether they planned to eat it or not, because they believed it a murderer of other fish and no good. "…but the waters would be foul with dead fish if Mr Pike weren't there to clear them up". So he showed his nephew one of the many ways to disgorge hooks from a pike, and told him that however he did it the rule was never to allow fingers past the teeth "or one day you will surely pay".

He then took out a u-shaped spring with which he forced the jaws open, and a pair of flat-edged forceps to unhook it. The pike's mouth opened impossibly wide and it revealed a set of needles large and small that all sloped toward its huge gullet. Then as if to make his point for him, Palmer's gag slipped on its mark and the pike's jaws snapped shut on the forceps so that its teeth grated audibly on the metal.

Palmer handed Tealer the now subdued pike for him to put back in the cool green broad. He threw the fish in so that it hit the water with a splash, and was immediately upbraided by his uncle.

"He gave us sport today, boy. Now look! You ha' thrown him in and stunned him! Is that a way to treat him?" His uncle leant over and grabbed the stupefied fish again and swung it back and forth through the water. "We may knock him on the head to take him home and fry him, or we may let him go, but whatever we do, we don't do mischief to him and leave him to starve, for then we're no better than hooligans." He gently let the pike slip out of his hands, and with a slow undulation it responded and swam slowly down to about two feet below the surface. Then with a flick of a tail it vanished into the green. Tealer watched the point in the water whence it disappeared, and then looked round, scanning the broad carefully. As his uncle prepared the tackle for another cast, Tealer picked up the forceps his uncle had used to disgorge the hooks. He studied the deadbait carefully. Then he looked at Palmer's bag, which held two sets of hooks about twice the size of those they had just used, and made safe with corks. He reached for them and felt their points and barbs, all surgically sharp. Again he scanned the placid waters of the broad.

"I know what you are thinking, boy," said his uncle, who had been watching him with sidelong glances. "All good piking men have the same thought after they caught a pike or two. They get to thinking: just how big can a pike be? Well, I can tell you that myself. One of the biggest in England came out from there – out of this here very broad. Nigh on forty pound, and its head was wider than yours, boy."

Tealer searched the water for any sign of such a creature, but the placid surface of the broad gave no sign as to the whereabouts of the demons beneath. He half-feared catching the stare of such a killer transfixing him from the twilight depths. He remembered the pleasure of feeling the split-cane bend and bounce to a force other than his own as the small fish he had caught had fought for its freedom. He tried to imagine that feeling magnified twenty times. He was hooked as surely as the jack!

And that night he had a pike nightmare, but he rather enjoyed it. He was being chased through the water by the kind of pike he'd imagined when he'd been looking at the massive hooks he'd found in Palmer's creel. Its head was a huge version of the little monster he'd caught with Palmer. Then its face became more human as it rose up from the depths to grab him in its maw. But for once he woke up before he had started screaming. And the image it left him with in his waking hours simply added to the thrill of staring into the blue-green waters of the Broads.

Together they visited other broads, including one even more secluded that the first, and this new broad became special for Tealer. It had a name, but his uncle always termed it the 'hidden' broad as if to emphasise the importance of keeping quiet about it. Tealer would learn to fish in it, but also to swim in it and to row, sail and shoot on it.

The fishing came first. By the time summer had drawn to a close Tealer had been introduced by Palmer to several kinds of fish. They'd ledgered for carp and bream, and laid out floats for perch, roach and rudd. He'd learnt to read the signs in the movement of his porcupine quill float, telling of the tiniest nibblings of roach at his bread paste lure. And no fish ever gave a greater fight than a carp that he'd taken with his uncle. For forty minutes they fought together to bring one gulping leviathan out of the depths of an old stew pond stocked centuries before by Benedictine monks.

But nothing supplanted Tealer's fascination for the Tiger of the Broads. Nothing compared with that maniacal rush out of the tranquillity of a reedy corner on a sunny afternoon, or the frantic dash for cover once hooked, or the uncompromising glare of those huge eyes, or the shocking, unfishlike array of daggers and needles revealed when the great mouth was opened. As his uncle let the boy use larger baits to entice the females from the deeper waters, and as the pike they caught got bigger and bigger, the drive to catch something semi-mythical became a small torment. When he wasn't fishing Tealer would gaze into the depths, half-yearning, half-dreading to see some fish of impossible dimensions staring back at him from the jungle of weed below.

"What sport do you like best, boy?" his uncle would ask, as if he didn't know. "Is it the sailing? Or the rowing? Carp angling? Is it the perch or the tench? Do you like bending your rod to a big old bream. Yes, thas the bream you like best, I reckon."

"The pike," Tealer would answer in his characteristic mumble.

"Oh-ah, the pike" answered Palmer on one of these occasions. "But you've never tried shooting yet. And… you've never had a turn with White Jenny". He chuckled at his own small innuendo.

Tealer idly wondered who White Jenny might be. He didn't think she was Mrs Durrant, and he was right. For the time being, though, he was thinking only of pike.

It was late summer of that same year, or perhaps the following, when the afternoons were still hot and lazy and the surface of the water still glassy. Uncle and nephew were again alone on the broad, this time scouring its bed for bream to take home for Daisy Bales to boil in brine and bake for the following Friday. They'd caught no bream, but an eel came up writhing and twisting in Gordian knots in its efforts to escape. Tealer watched as his uncle untangled the eel and knock it on the head ready for Daisy's smoking tray. It was a tedious business, and Tealer scanned the water idly as he waited.

"Look!" he said and pointed to a shape just below the surface right in the middle of the broad. "Someone ha' thrown a big old gatepost into the water." And in a softer voice "That isn't something left with bottles on, is it?"

"No, boy: no bottles to collect to-day. Where are you looking?"

"There. About twenty yards. But not quite on the surface."

His uncle shaded his eyes, but peering through the haze of dancing gnats and darting dragonflies at first he could still see nothing. Then he spied what Tealer had seen:

"Ah, yes" he said "Yes, I can see where you're lookin', boy. Perhaps thas an old branch half-waterlogged. Strange we didn't see it last time. Sometimes you get… you get…" And Palmer laughed with disbelief. "Good Lord! Thas…!…. Ah, but God help us all if it…"

It dawned on Tealer what his uncle was saying, and they gazed together, still disbelieving. The long, nameless shape remained unmoving, but also indistinct. Then as they continued to stare, slowly and surely it sank from view. And it was only as it was disappearing that Tealer made out the huge head and the crown-sized eye that he realised had been watching them closely all the time.

"I don't suppose we'll ever know how big they can be," said his uncle that evening as they fried sausages and drank tea on the bank by the jetty. "Perhaps thas better we don't, do we should never venture out on to the water again! Thas so rarely fished here – that's why they can grow like that. Cha! Such a calm, peaceful sort of place, almost like the lake Adam and Eve might have bathed in during their innocent days. And yet haunted by… by a great ole' beast like that." He burst out coughing, for they were sitting on the smokey side of the fire to avoid the massed ranks of gnats. "Ah, yes," he said when he'd recovered, "Nature is full of all manner of contradictions like that."

For several minutes they sat in silence looking into the embers and listening to the wood owls hooting in the carr around the broad.

"So," said Palmer, after a yawn, "Are we go' try and catch her?"

"Yes" said Tealer in the darkness. "Yes, I reckon we should."

It seemed like hubris.

They told no-one of their plans. There are few ears more attuned to rumours than those of anglers listening for talk of big fish. But Tealer was already used to keeping his uncle Palmer's secrets, some of which concerned things weightier even than great pike.

They decided to fish with an inflated mackerel some seven inches long, and decided to use the largest hooks they could find in Palmer's creel. The day they chose for their quest was sunny, but cooler and windier than that of the original sighting, as autumn was approaching. The wind was southerly, so Palmer decided that they would sail the Hermione up the Yare and moor on the bank, and then row a reed-flat up the dyke and on to the hidden broad. This they did, and when they arrived they found the water in a very different state. Now the breeze was whipping up the surface so that rows of glittering wavelets slapped against the hull of the reed flat and daggers of light were penetrating for the briefest instant the dark blue depths of the broad.

Tealer knew that he wouldn't be allowed to cast this time – this fish would be nearly as heavy as him. Palmer cast out, well into the breeze so that the lure described an arc and landed just shy of the reed beds at the edge of the broad. He reeled in. Both watched the lure quietly. An hour passed, though it seemed no more than fifteen minutes. Palmer casting and reeling in; Tealer clutching the gaff; both of them watching the mackerel and every ripple and eddy around it.

They had both seen the pike with their own eyes, and they knew such a huge fish would not leave so good a feeding ground as this broad, and that it was therefore *here*. Somewhere in this twelve acres of uniform, choppy water it was watching, and it was waiting.

The sun sank lower in the sky. The lights on the water became magnified so that the whole broad on their west side was a sheet of flame. The wake of the dragged mackerel broke the regular wavelets of this light into diagonal patterns.

As Palmer later logged in his diary, it was about five in the afternoon, just as the surface water was beginning to cool, that there was tiny irregularity in the sparkling parallel lines left by the bait.

"Uncle John…,"

"Yes, boy, I saw it too."

But the bait continued unmolested on its journey back toward their reed-flat.

Palmer cast out again. The bait disappeared into the sun, but reappeared far down the broad, sending an explosion of light in circles away from it as it landed. Jewels of illuminated water dripped off the following line until it settled on to the surface. Palmer began reeling in again, and they stopped breathing as the bait reached the point at which they'd seen the changed pattern.

The strike, when it came, was no more than a click on the surface of the water. Palmer and Tealer looked at one another.

"Is it her?"

For a moment Palmer didn't answer. Then he sighed.

"No. It is some cheeky jack with eyes bigger than its guts. And Jack Pike is not what John Palmer wants tonight, is he, boy? That he ent. But we`ll put him to good use, shall we? Set a thief to catch a thief, what?"

In its rush to escape the little pike had come out of the sunlit water and had made for a shady area in the lee of some willow trees. It soon tired and Palmer began reeling it in. His plan, he explained to his shaking nephew, was to kill the fish and use it as dead-bait for the evening feed.

"There isn't a supper your big pike like better than a smaller pike," he told the boy. "I've often found…"

What Palmer had 'often found' is lost to tradition. It was as though an invisible boat had suddenly moved across the main body of the broad toward the little bay, for a bow wave appeared from nowhere and made straight for the hooked pike as Palmer's reeling brought it in towards their reed-flat. With a surge of water that was almost a roar the pike and the lure disappeared and the reel screamed at a pitch that Tealer had never heard. He and his uncle gasped in a treble and baritone harmony.

But then there was silence. Only the wind in the alders and the steady slap of the wavelets against the boat.

"We 'a lost her, uncle."

"Yes, boy, I reckon we have. Don't forget she could only have been caught up on the tip of the hooks. The rest were buried in the jack. She must have a funny strong bite to have been caught by them at all!"

They stood looking at where the bubbles left by her rush were dissipating. Then from way across the other side of the broad came a large splash.

"Another pike," said Palmer, catching his breath. "That must be another large fish, an' all. The big'uns must be feeding tonight." He began reeling in. Then he cried out: "No, blast, that was her! She's still on! She's coming towards us. Get that gaff ready! No! get an oar. She's coming under the boat! If she does that we really will lose her. Bring us about!"

Tealer dropped the gaff and scrabbled to unship the oar. With all the energy

The Pike-Queen

In his small frame he rowed frantically to get the boat parallel with the line, which was still limp. Palmer's reeling hand had become a blur, and yet the line remained limp. He peered over the gunwale. "Yes, here she come! Here she come!"

Tealer looked over the side and just glimpsed a vast ugly head as big as a calf's pass six feet below them just parallel to the dinghy. The rod bent further than Tealer had thought possible without breaking. The pike made for the shallow water and then started another run along the edge of the broad. The reeds in the shallows marked its progress as in each in turn swayed in its wake. Gradually the fish slowed and Palmer started another frantic bout of reeling in. The pike didn't oppose the pull directly but at a tangent that took it into the middle of the broad. Then it relaxed and allowed itself to be drawn in toward the boat. Tealer with his gaff waited for the great form to come into view. But another splash created a fountain of spray, and a curse from Palmer told Tealer that the fish had run again. Tealer could feel the reed-flat being pulled to the extent of its anchor rope.

For thirty minutes or more this cycle of reeling and running continued. The fish would appear to give in, then as its tormentors came into view it would gather itself in another mighty effort and Palmer would have no choice but to let it run. But gradually the pike's escaping runs diminished in vigour, and finally Palmer was able to set about bringing it alongside. Even he was mesmerized for a moment by its awesome size and had to bring himself around sharply to concentrate on the job in hand.

'Right, boy. Be ready to hand me the gaff and take the rod off me. If she run while you're a-holding the rod don't try to stop her – either we'll lose her or she'll have you in the water."

Palmer reeled until the pike's head came out of the water. The mackerel, which had once swum over the Dogger Bank with millions of its brethren far away from this still-water mayhem, was reduced to a fish paste. Its pulped flesh was just visible in the mouth of the still-gasping jack, which itself was dangling hopelessly from the side of the matriarch. Palmer took the gaff and slipped its hook under the pike's jaw-bone, and then handed the rod itself to Tealer. Palmer then prepared to lift the fish in, but his position was awkward and he found he could not lever the great weight over the gunwale. He unhooked the gaff and, incredibly to Tealer, reached down to put both hands over the murderous jaws.

He slipped a thumb into each eye socket. The ferocious brows above the deep-set eyes gave Palmer enough purchase to haul the fish up, over, and into the boat's flat bottom. They she lay immobile save the occasional spasmic pump of her gills.

Palmer had determined to kill her and to have her head preserved for a plaque in his study and her flesh divided up between the many deserving marshmen and farmworkers living along the banks of the Yare. He still had hold of her with his left hand as his right fumbled for the varnished wooden priest in his pocket, only to find it had fallen out and was lying in the bow beyond arms length.

"Damnation," he said as he manoeuvred to pick it up.

In later years it would take Tealer whole minutes to describe what happened next, yet the motion as it happened was so fast that it was all but invisible. His uncle had relaxed his grip on the pike and had half-stood to pick up the priest. He had taken his eye off the fish for an instant. And it was in that instant that the cavernous mouth opened, revealing a Molochian gape. Tealer wasn't yet experienced enough a piker to know that this gape presaged a violent flicking in order to be rid of the irritating hooks. When it came, the left-right shake of the head was not even a blur. The hooks were thrown off and the might jaws (no 'were') clamped on to Palmer's balancing hand. Palmer roared with pain and shock, and before he could stop himself he dragged what was left of his hand out from the terrible vice. The momentum of his effort caused him to career across the reedflat and over the side into the water, leaving an empty space spattered with crimson drops. The fish lay with her mouth open and strips of flesh from Palmer's hand were clearly visible on her largest teeth. For a moment her great orange eyes swivelled slightly to capture Tealer's image. Then in a final victorious pulse she heaved her forty-five pounds upwards so that her head was resting over the gunwale. Now she could see the water that was her world. With another great ripple of movement she tipped herself right over the edge and into the water with a heavy splash where she sank like a stone out of view.

Tealer's head was full of many things, but a part of him calmly noted how completely such a big fish can become invisible in clear water. Then he looked over the other side for Palmer and immediately saw that the water was reddened from the wounds in his uncle's hand. Palmer had already swum to the stern of the boat and was preparing to climb back aboard. He hitched one leg over the stern and reached for Tealer who pulled himself horizontal to help drag the man out of the water. Palmer flopped into the boat and slowly regarded his right hand. Two of his fingers were bitten to the bone, and the rest of the hand was a mass of deep lacerations from which the blood continued to flow profusely – but to his great relief the wrist, at least, was unscathed. Tealer was stunned, but was brought to his senses by his uncle's curt instruction to take off his shirt and rip it into strips with a clasp knife which his uncle had given him for a present. Then Palmer instructed Tealer to row the reed-flat back to the little jetty on the far side of the broad. The boat wasn't light and Tealer not much more than four feet tall, but he was effervescing with excitement.

At the jetty his uncle didn't try to climb out but instead without a word reached down into the water where a willow stick was floating. With his good hand he pulled it up. Tied to it was length of hemp, and on the end of that a cluster of unlabelled bottles. He took the smallest of these and uncorked it with his teeth. Then he took off the shirt-bandage and soaked it with the bottle's contents. This he then applied to the injured hand with the good.

"I don't know if this'll work," he hissed through his teeth, "but I've heard enough seamen say that washing a wound in spirit's even better'n seawater." He then took a swig from the bottle and his white face forced itself into a grin: "Deep breath, boy. You've got some more rowing to do!"

And Tealer took the heavy oars and stretched every sinew to get the boat out of the broad and into the river where with the help of the tide they made the haven of Rockland. Once ashore at Rockland, the still-dripping Palmer went along the bank to where the *Hermione* was moored and took a canvas bag from a locker under the half-deck that contained a change of clothes. Then he led Tealer up to the village inn where he had decided they would have to spend the night. A group of old men was sat outside taking in the weak autumn sun before it disappeared below the alders. They looked on in undisguised curiosity but said nothing, and those that caught Palmer's eye acknowledged him with deferential touches of their peaks. Tealer saw that they knew his uncle. Inside was a clamour of marshmen, reedcutters and farmworkers, and a huge pall of smoke wafted out of the open door at intervals.

Palmer pushed his nephew through the throng to negotiate a room and a meal. Tealer had never yet been inside a tavern and was fascinated by its rich adult aromas and the muttering of many male voices. Yet he was uneasy. He remembered that such a place was the 'parlour of Lucifer' or the 'ante-room of

Perdition', where men drank 'the vomit of Beelzebub'. And several miles across the marshes, deep down in the clay of the Gorleston graveyard where they lay, perhaps the mouldering corpses of his parents turned in their twin cells and despairing groans emanated from their shrivelled lips as their son followed his uncle across the threshold of the New Inn. Then perhaps these groans were followed by subterranean grunts of satisfaction – because Tealer never relaxed for a second he was there.

The following morning Palmer and Tealer reappeared in the now-empty lounge to take breakfast. As the landlord, a heavily whiskered man by the name of Pearson, came out to attend to them, Palmer said:

"Before we take breakfast, Pearson, I want to show you something. Shut the door." He walked over to where his jacket had hung all night on a brass hanger to dry over the ingle. He pulled out the flat, half-empty bottle with his good hand and showed it to the landlord. Pearson looked at the bottle and then at Palmer without expression.

"Do you know whose this is?"

"Yours, I should imagine, Mas' Palmer."

Palmer smiled and shook his head. "No – or, not yet, anyway. That come out of the hidden broad."

From under his shaggy brows Pearson darted a look at Tealer before resuming his expressionless mien.

"Don't worry about Johnny here," said Palmer. "I reckon he already have enough on me to secure me a berth on the next transport to Tasmania. He's no mardler. Are you, boy?" Tealer shook his head without a smile.

"Well now, if 'at come out of the hidden broad, and you took it out last night, 'at could only be Norris's, I believe sir."

"Norris's? Are you sure?"

"Night follow day, sir."

"Damnation," said Palmer. There are twenty other wherrymen I would prefer t'have to deal with than that old devil. Where's he to be found?"

"His man Pye told me last week that they were due back at Tunstall Staithe. As you'll know, sir, he skipper the *Stokesby Trader* for Mr Powley, who have his yard there."

Later that morning Palmer was sitting in the stern of the *Hermione* steering the craft with his good hand and Tealer manning the sheets as they drifted back down the Yare, across Breydon and up the Bure. They were seeking the wherry *Stokesby Trader* for the unwanted meeting with Daniel Norris.

Or 'Joyful' to his friends.

Of whom, Palmer told Tealer, there weren't so many.

But Tealer wasn't listening; all that he cared about was that they might be going aboard a wherry!

Tealer was as familiar with the sight of wherries as was any other Yarmouth child born with eyes. They were common enough on the town's waterways as they sailed out to unload cargo ships and bring goods back to port, though they somehow never seemed at home amongst the coasters and clippers tied up on the quay. Here in the broads Tealer had already begun to see the great black-sailed barges in their true setting. In narrow stretches the *Hermione* had several times passed one close enough for the boy to reach out furtively and let his hand brush the thick, rough woodwork of its massive clinker hull. Yet even here both the wherry and the wherrymen seemed aloof, apart. Whenever the *Hermione* had met a wherry on the water Tealer had noticed the brisk nods of the crew to Palmer as they passed, coupled with an unsmiling glance at the boy himself, before they returned their gaze upriver. Doubtless the responsibility of steering many tons of fast, wilful oak in strong winds through confined waters was a serious affair. But Tealer came to realize that there was more to your wherry than even its great size suggested: those cavernous holds might be loaded 'to the binns' with mountainous piles of reed or coal – so much so that river could sometimes wash clean across the midships – yet such spectacular loads were only the cargo you could see. The business of the wherry was largely unspoken, and was conducted in the very inaccessible corners of the Broads. The days when wherrymen would sail out under cover to meet Dutch and Spanish merchantmen far out in the Roads were long gone, along with the import tariffs that had made it worthwhile, but the smuggling of cigars, brandy and other desirable goods that had grown legs was not quite dead, and the authorities were always mistrustful of the black-sailed barges and the men who sailed them.

Yet for the humble folk who lived their solitary lives amongst the reeds, the surly ways of the skippers were of small issue. They only cared that it was the wherry that brought their supplies of coal, corn, ale and gossip from beyond the fastness of the swamps. It was the wherry that brought the bricks and timbers with which they repaired their homes. It was the wherry that carried off the monumental piles of reed from which they earned their paltry living. The cribs they lay in as infants had been brought up river by wherries, as had the rough-hewn beds in which they conceived their own children. It was a wherry that would one day take their coffins on the last journey along the river for burial in the sandy Broadland churchyards on the bluffs above. Your wherryman was as trusted as your parson and your blacksmith.

Except for Norris. From Hickling to Oulton the skipper of the *Stokesby Trader* was known and loathed. "and seeing how broadspeople worship their wherrymen, that must ha' taken some doing," Palmer later growled to Tealer.

Progress was slow on the last leg of their journey to the staithe. It was situated at the end of Tunstall dyke, a small watercourse that led from the Bure, under the New Road and away towards a thick stand of willows. Palmer had to moor the *Hermione* at the mouth of the dyke, and they set off down the tow-path. Further and further they went until they could see the tall willows, but there was no sign of any great black canvas or even the bare mast of a wherry. Only when they arrived could they see that Pearson had been right, for there, tied up, was the *Stokesby Trader* with its rig and mast down. Tom Pye, Norris's mate, was swabbing the deck. Pye helped them aboard, and Tealer took his first steps on the hallowed timbers, hard as rock beneath his feet.

The staithe was a place of quiet industry. In one of the waterside buildings someone was planing wood. The air was full of the smell of bitumen. Chickens scraped about in the yard, and white duck and coot dabbled in the water around the wherry.

Pye, a placid giant of a fellow, greeted them warmly. He told them that Norris had had 'business ashore' the previous night and was having 'a rest'. He grinned shyly down at Tealer and whispered to Palmer. "Ha' the littl'un ever been round a wherry before, sir?"

"No, I don't believe he have. Ha' you got the time?"

Tom looked at the cabin, and said even more quietly "I think Joyful could be a while yet. Come you wi' me, young sir."

He led the child round, and Tealer's eyes were everywhere, taking in the sheer scale of rigging laid out ready for deployment, and the tree trunk mast that stretched practically the length of the vessel.

"Is she the biggest wherry there is?" he asked.

"No, my man. She int that big at all. No more'n eight-and-twenty ton when she's a -carryin' a full load. There's wherries twice as big."

They walked down to the stern. The main hatch was open and Tealer could hear his clogs echoing in the deep empty hold as he followed Pye. He gaped at the tiller, which alone was as long as a rowing boat. His eye followed it down to where where the huge rudder lay submerged in the deep, gin-clear waters of the staithe. He started to ask Pye how many men would be needed to bring the boat about, but Pye put his fingers to his lips and pointed to the cabin where Norris was still asleep. The brightly-painted door was ajar, and Tealer stole a glance into the interior. Of Norris there was no sign, but Tealer realized they were being watched by a young woman of about twenty-three. She was taller than average with tanned skin and with a sullen look about her. She seemed to be wearing a patch over one eye, but Tealer had just time to realize that it was black and swollen before Pye gently hustled him away. The woman didn't introduce herself and wasn't introduced by Pye. She stood staring at them from the shadow of the galley, a large, rusty bread knife hanging down from one hand.

To get Tealer's attention back, Pye unhooked the forestay and in a blur of thick forearms pulled the single great mast into the vertical, so that its long red burgee was level with the tops of the willows. Then having secured the mast he picked up a crank handle and slotted it into a barrel winch and began to wind it round. Slowly but surely the spar began climb up the mast causing the sail to unfurl like a huge black wing. Then Pye took the handle out, let the sail down on a brake, and slotted the handle in a second time. He turned to Tealer with another shy grin.

"Did *you* want to put it back up, master John?"

Tealer looked at him and at Palmer and at the sail, which with its spar must have weighed more than a ton.

"Go on, boy," said Palmer, "wind it back up. That won't bite."

Tealer gripped the crank-handle in his small hands and began to turn. To his surprise it moved easily. The top of the revolution was so high that he had to stand on tip-toes to keep hold, which caused the two men to laugh. But as he turned the huge black sail began to unfurl again. He stopped suddenly to check he was not being tricked, but sure enough the spar stopped with him. He started again and the spar continued on its way. The men laughed some more, but quickly stopped at the sound of some banging and crashing at the other end of the wherry.

"Ah, well." muttered Palmer. "All good things come to an end."

A large unkempt figure shambled unsteadily out of the hatch and made his way to the side to relieve himself into the staithe. Mid-purgation he caught sight of Palmer and Tealer, and scowled. Scowling came easily to Norris – he had light eyes that glittered rather than sparkled, set deep in a face etched with forty years of sarcasm and ill-humour. He pushed himself back in.

"What do you two blooda want?" he asked, by way of a greeting.

"Mr Palmer want a word, Dan," said Pye.

"Do he now?" said Norris. " That int often we get such fine gentlemen come to see us on the *Trader*."

Palmer didn't waste time with courtesies. "I think this here bottle belong to you."

Norris looked at the bottle and his narrow eyes narrowed further so they almost shut.

"What make you think that, then?"

"That came out of the hidden broad."

Norris said nothing at first but simply glared at Tealer, whom he'd never seen before. Then he looked at the bottle:

"But thas nigh on empty."

"I needed it to wash a wound. I was bitten by a large pike and there weren't anything else to hand."

No wherryman would have extended much sympathy to anyone being bitten by a pike, though a good few might have guffawed at the idea. Norris merely surveyed Palmer, trying to work out what the trick was.

"Can this here boy be trusted?"

"Yes, that he can. More than a few men I know."

"I blooda hope so," said Norris, not taking his cold, bitter gaze off Tealer. "Them what can't end up getting' wrong off me."

Palmer glanced at the silent girl watching them from the shadow of the galley. "Yes," he said, "I reckon." He fumbled in his pocket and counted out some coins, which he slapped down on the hatch with the bottle. "There you go. Settled. Come on, boy, we're now goin'."

Norris grabbed the money with a speed not unlike that of a lunging pike and counted it.

"Hold you hard! That was a bottle of ginnever, not a mug of ale."

"*Half* a bottle," called back Palmer as he and Tealer jumped ashore. "You can still have the other half yourself…" and added quietly as he turned his back "only don't bend over afterwards, do that'll all spill out again." Honest Tom Pye chuckled to himself, and there was even a smirk from the silent girl in the hatch.

Palmer and Tealer set off down the down path back to the river with Pye following on behind. When the *Stokesby Trader* was out of immediate earshot, Tealer whispered to his uncle.

"Did you see that lady watching us?"

Palmer stifled a snort and whispered back. "The *lady*? Yes, boy, I saw the… er… lady."

"Is 'at Norris's daughter?" whispered Tealer.

"No," whispered Palmer.

"Tom's missus, then?" whispered Tealer.

"Not her either," whispered Palmer.

"Who then?" whispered Tealer.

"Norris's wherry-woman," whispered Palmer.

"But what do she *do*?" whispered Tealer.

"Well, she help about the boat. And she… look after Norris," whispered Palmer.

"But he's too old to be looked after," whispered Tealer.

"Yes, boy. That's what most o' Norfolk say," whispered Palmer, with a grin at Pye.

Finally they reached a bend in the boat dyke and Tealer turned for a last look at the receding wherry. He found both the sour face of Norris and the dark, damaged face of the girl still watching them. Then the great black barge was hidden from view. At the entrance to the Bure, Pye helped them into the *Hermione*, threw the rope to Palmer and watched the river wind fill the *Hermione*'s sail, which now seemed handkerchief-sized after the great spread of the *Stokesby Trader*. Once back on the open river, Tealer told his uncle that that he should like to be a wherryman. Pye could be his mate, he said. He little knew then that he was destined for adventures on even larger vessels. A good thing he was, too, for the railway trains were already reaching across the marshes, each pulling the load of ten wherries. And as for Tom Pye – not five years hence poor Tom Pye was lying buried in Tunstall churchyard, his young skull shattered by the very winch handle that Tealer had turned to such effect.

Figures at a Distance

These, then, were the events and sensations now filling Tealer's life. With such new experiences and adventures on the sea, the rivers and the Broads, it might be asked if Tealer was still prone to what Daisy Bales termed 'the dreamin''. He was, but very much less. Daisy learnt never again to give him tincture of nightshade, for since his near-poisoning it had the effect intensifying his sufferings. Now she used the gentler fumes of valerian to keep the mannequins at bay.

And this lessening in his nightly torments was all part of a change that had been taking place in the boy from the day he had been taken in by his uncle. His sallow complexion had become ruddy, and where there had been a weary, resigned look in his eyes there was now a sparkle. He was eating more. He was growing apace, and the untried bones and weedy muscles of his limbs were responding to the walking through thick mud, the hauling on sheets and the lugging of heavy bundles aboard boats. And though he occasionally had flashbacks and nightmares ('screamers' as his uncle termed them) they seemed to be a phase he was fast growing out of.

But the figure which haunted Tealer's horizon in his waking hours was different. This had never gone away. Regularly he would spot it disappearing round the corner of one end of a Row just as he entered at the other end. On several occasions when he was standing on the South Quay waiting for the herring fleet to come in when he saw a child across the river on the Gorleston Quay sitting on a pile of swills looking straight back at him, knocking its heels against the baskets, just as Georgie had done. However, this 'Georgie', or whatever it was, was more often to be found lingering in lonely places beyond the town. If Tealer was on the river with his uncle it would be almost always appear at some point during voyage, watching motionless from up on the bank. If they were at sea, the figure would be standing alone on the deserted shore, following the course of their boat.

Tealer was in no doubt that the apparition was Georgie. Who else had he wronged so shamefully? He feared and disliked it, but over the first few months, as he settled down to his new life with his uncle, he reached an accommodation with it. It hadn't harmed him, and it was no longer accompanied by the demonic visions that had wracked him in his Gorleston life.

Yet it was *there*, and he rather wished it weren't.

One thing was clear to him: he must never mention it to his uncle, who had more that once said that those who spoke of the 'haunted' marshes were weak-minded coxcombs. Tealer's greatest dread was therefore not the ghost itself but the fear that he might inadvertently let on about it to his uncle. He worried that Palmer might the think him 'touched', or 'an egg shy of a clutch'. He might even have his nephew 'put away'. (The very week Tealer's parents had died one Tabernacle brat had relished telling Tealer he was due for the orphanage.)

No, he told himself, 'Georgie' must remain his private Fury.

And Tealer might have continued for years to believe that it was the reproachful wraith of young Stolworthy that was glaring at him from the fringes were it not for an experience late that autumn, when Palmer decided it was time for his nephew to become acquainted with the sublime world of the Breydon estuary and its surrounding marshes.

"Did you want to learn to shoot, boy?" asked Palmer, one day in November.

"Yes," said Tealer.

"Are you sure, boy?"

"Yes," said Tealer.

"Well, before ever you handle a gun, you have to know what you can shoot, and when you can shoot it, and where. Let's go down to marsh. We aren't go' shoot anything, mind. We're just go' look. In any case, the big flocks of duck won't start a-swinging in from the north till next month at the earliest."

Firstly, Palmer took him to the Roman fort to survey their hunting ground. They climbed up on the flint walls to take in the huge scene before them. The joining waters of the Waveney and the Yare, the Breydon estuary and the marshes stretched away from them in the autumn sun. These were the very badlands that had been forbidden to Tealer for so long. We are talking only of a tiny remnant of the ancient estuary and a few thousand acres of grass, but Tealer gazed at the expanse as Cortez must have gazed at the Pacific.

"How long do you think thas all been there, Johnny?"

"For ever, I should think."

But Palmer told him he was looking at the newest land in Britain. All 'borrowed from the sea'. Palmer pointed out the various windpumps that were working to move the water of the November rains back to the estuary wall to be dumped in the river. "And if them pumps stopped doing their work, the sea would come and take it all back again. And Yarmouth and Gorleston would go back to being islands." Then they walked off the bluff of the fort, and took a long detour back through Yarmouth to Cobholm, where they left Vulcan tied up. There they made their way back down on to the marsh and climbed the Wall, an earthen rampart between the two faces of the *Gariensis*: stretching away to their south was the glistening, glittering mud of Breydon at low tide, alive with the pipings and whistlings of countless waders, while to their north and west lay the quieter and more secretive marshes – not quivering bogs but a series of grazing meadows crisscrossed by ditches. Tealer was torn between gazing at the two worlds, but Palmer told him to ignore the estuary for now and look at the marshes "They are where you'll be learning to shoot, boy. We'll only go out on the estuary when you know how to handle a gun in a boat without blowing your mate's brains out. *And* when you've spent a few hours on the Wall learning about the tides and the currents."

"What wall?"

"This here wall we're now on."

Tealer was also beginning to learn of the wayward nomenclature of the Norfolk marshlands, where 'walls' are really dykes, and 'dykes' are what other Englishmen call ditches. He would soon learn to tell the difference between his mill dykes, his spring dykes, his soke dykes, borrow dykes, drains, gutters and dry dykes. Some good for pike, others perfect for eels. Some offering the blue lighting of the kingfisher in summer, others the green flash of the cock teal in winter. Even the same dyke might change its nature utterly in one week, from gin-clear to the colour of milky tea. He was also introduced to the marshmen who understood the flow of water over tiny gradients as though they were raging torrents, and could juggle sluices and windpump gears to flood or drain marshes in hours.

On this his first day on the marsh Tealer found his eyes drawn like magnets to its horizons. He let his gaze trace a course from one pole through the zenith to the other pole. Then he turned three hundred and sixty degrees and marvelled at how the landscape now seemed so small. He began to see that it was not the marshes themselves that presented such sense of space but the infinity of sky beyond them.

He would never tire of this. On starlit December nights he would stand in the middle of a field of curious horses as his uncle picked out the constellations in all four quadrants, and Tealer came to know the power in the word 'firmament'.

He also learnt his clouds. On those special sunsets after a rainy day he could spend a quarter hour staring all around him at the critical minutes of arc just above the skyline, only visible in truly flat country, where patches of glowing cumulus stretched away to impossible, visionary distances. There were the cold February days when the sky was locked in grey and featureless stratus, and was uncanny in its impenetrable nothing. But the most spectacular and humbling were the days when the glowering cumulonimbus would swell up to apocalyptic heights as forks of lightning raked the heavens, and colossal cracks of thunder shook the land to its core.

There was one time, a particularly clear, frosty November day, when Tealer said on an impulse:

"Uncle John, we are the last two people alive in the whole world!"

Palmer looked at the boy in surprise, for Tealer rarely spoke unless spoken to. "Well, yes, coming down here can make a man think that, Johnny. But I tell you what, boy: never believe it. There's more eyes down here a-watching your every move than you would think possible. Thas because thas all so flat, and you think everything is nearer than 'at really is, and that anything higher than a walking stick would stick up on the skyline. But look around. Go on, take you this here glass and look around."

And Tealer took the glass and swept the marsh in a complete circle. Sure enough, a mile to the north of them a marshman was standing still as the gatepost he was leaning on, watching as his two dogs brought a herd of bullocks off the marsh for the winter. To the east a gang of men was clearing dead scrub from the bank of the railway line. On the other horizon a figure was just visible winding the handle on a sluice. The deserted landscape was in fact full of activity. Yet the effect was singular, for all noises – the shouts of the men and the lowing of the beasts from the bullock field; the rhythmic clink of the railwaymens' mattocks; the grating of the rusty bearings on the sluice winch – were utterly swallowed by the distance. This soundlessness rendered them all characters in a dream.

Then Tealer caught sight of another figure, and this one made him catch his breath. About three furlongs from where they were standing someone else was visible. Unlike the others, this individual was not tending animals or working on some manual task, but merely sitting very still and watching Tealer and his uncle. At the distance he was at it was impossible for Tealer to determine his age, not just because he was sitting, but also because the flatness of the marshes, devoid of any perspective, can make a child of a man or a colossus of a child. The face was simply a white patch in the telescope lens, yet to Tealer it was clear what the figure was doing. It was sitting on the bank of a dyke looking steadily in their direction. It was watching Tealer.

Tealer had a dreadful notion as to why that was.

He put the glass down and looked with the naked eye. He realized the figure was actually perfectly visible, but very, very still, and this was the reason he'd missed it in the first place. Tealer looked at his uncle, but Palmer was gazing into the opposite direction, and he put his glass up again. The figure had not moved and was continuing to stare straight at them. It was the inimitable Stolworthy look: indistinct, bland, but undeniably – undeniably – *there*.

"Well? How many people can you see?" asked Palmer

Tealer tried to answer but his throat was dry. He mustn't let on. He must not let on. No-one must know of this haunting. If he did not want to be thought unhinged, and put away, he must not even hint at the watching figure not half a mile distant.

The watching figure carried on watching, but Tealer turned away as though it weren't there.

He tried to speak a second time. "Well," he cleared his throat, "well, th-there are some men working away on the railway line."

"Yes, that there are. Anyone else?"

"There are some people moving bullocks about up by Breydon Wall over there."

"Yes, I saw them too. What about looking west?"

"An old fellow is workin' a winch."

"Marshman Gedney. Any more?"

"No," said Tealer.

"Sure?"

"Yes. I reckon so."

Palmer took the glass from him and swept it slowly round all points of the compass, stopping wherever something caught his sight.

"Hmm," he said. "You did well, but you didn't see everyone, y'know."

Tealer said nothing.

"Look beyond where Gedney is. There's an old woman a-shuffling about on the Halvergate Poor Marsh. I wager she's after mushrooms." But where Palmer was indicating was nowhere near the figure Tealer had spotted. Then he said "And what's more, there is someone loitering about on Gallants marshes." This time he pointed straight at the unmoving figure.

This observation by Palmer left Tealer speechless, for it caused him to be assailed by many conflicting ideas. Palmer looked at him.

"Blast, boy, you a' gone white as a sheet! Bless you, thas no hanging offence, missing people with your spyglass. Not unless you shoot…"

"Who is it?" Tealer practically shouted, when he found his voice.

"Eh?"

"Who is it there?"

"Which one?" asked his uncle. "The woman or the one on Gallants?"

"On Gallants," said Tealer. "Who is it?"

Palmer looked down at the child strangely for a moment, then held the telescope up to spot the figure again.

"Well, now, too far to say. I can't even rightly see if it be man or boy."

"What is he about?" And he tried to adopt a calmer tone. "I… I should like to know."

"He seem… he seem to be watching us. Which come as no surprise to me."

"Why?"

"I should imagine he is up to no good. Setting springes for the snipe. Or poaching fish with a fyking net."

"So… why don't he run?"

"He know there are too many wide dykes 'twixt him and us."

"So who *is* he?"

Palmer turned round again in surprise at the vehemence of his normally quietly-spoken young relation. "I just now said, boy: I don't know. I can't see from here, as he know very well himself. Could be anyone. Could be anyone's ghost for that matter."

Palmer might have meant this last comment to be whimsical, but he got no apologetic grin from his nephew. They walked off the marsh and back up the track to their trap, with Tealer silent all the way. Only when they were actually trotting back up to the Acle New Road did Tealer speak.

"I didn't reckon you believed in such things, Uncle John," he said.

"Such things as what?"

"Ghosts."

"Oh, who am I to say there are no such things, Johnny? All I can say is that I ha' never seen the proof of them myself, and as I have told you before, there's a few old boys down here would have the rest of us believe that the ghosts on the marsh are ten-a-penny, because then we might stop coming down here, and they could get up to their mischief undisturbed. And that would make life very much easier for them! But if you were to put a pistol to my head I'd have to admit that any of them there figures we ha' now seen *might* be ghosts. But we can hardly go a-chasing across the marshes to ask them, now can we? Look now, there's a marsh harrier. See how he glide about with his wings in a 'v.'"

Tealer pretended to look at the marsh harrier, but was really scanning the marsh for the lone figure again. It had vanished into the green.

Thus was Tealer introduced to the marsh, a place which would always have the ability to delight, chill and humble him all at once. The boundary between what was natural and what defied natural explanation seemed lost in the haze that existed along the blue grey of the horizon. And on top of this uncertainty he had now to consider the possibility that he was not alone in being haunted. It seemed other people might be followed across the plains by figures at a distance. If they were, he wondered why they were. To him it seemed the answer, whatever it was, must be simple, yet he was greatly puzzled.

The Faces of the Fiend of Breydon

All this he decided to put to the placid Mrs Durrant, whom he had come to trust over the months since he had come to live with his uncle and to whom he had come to refer on the kind of questions that are perplexing to a nine-year-old boy – but which that his uncle would laugh at or shrug off as unknowable. He'd ask Mrs Durrant what she thought of the business of haunting and being haunted…

The two of them were sitting in Palmer's living room the night after this first trip to the marshes. Palmer himself was out on 'shore leave'. Tealer was promoted to 'acting first-mate' and was therefore allowed to sit in Palmer's chair on the condition that he protect Mrs Durrant from 'pirates, brigands and hostile boarders' while Palmer was away. Mrs Durrant was on the other side of the hearth, working at some embroidery.

Tealer was trying to copy an illustration from a book of hunting prints. The room was lit by two ship's lamps on either side of the hearth that spread a light rich in double shadows. He was watching his uncle's mistress from the corner of his eye, waiting for an opportunity. When he reckoned the moment to be right he closed the book and asked Mrs Durrant if she believed in ghosts, such as 'you might see down at marsh'.

The governess put her needlework down, raised her eyebrows and blew elegantly through part-closed lips.

"Ghosts. No, Johnny, I don't believe I give such things much credit. I can never remember having seen such. Perhaps I have and have not realized that that is what they were!"

"That's what Uncle John said. Have you ever known anyone who has died?"

Mrs Durrant was used to the directness of such questions from children. "Oh, some," she said.

"And ha' you seen their ghosts?"

"No, I can say with some certainty that I have not. When I think of all such dear people – friends, members of my family, both my parents who passed on from this life long since – I imagine them to be in Paradise – as I am sure, Johnny, yours are also, God rest them – and as I hope myself to be one day, for all that I…that I… am… Well, anyway, I don't imagine them still to be wandering around here on earth. What would it avail them?"

But Tealer wasn't yet satisfied. He pressed her on places such as those where people had died in the most unhappy circumstances.

It was then that he saw Georgie's face spring out of the pattern of the curtains in the darkness behind Mrs Durrant's chair. He froze, and then forced his eyes away towards Mrs Durrant who was gazing into the fire.

"What about the Suspension Bridge?" he asked, clearing his throat to conceal, as he thought, the tremble in his voice.

Mrs Durrant looked up sharply; till now the child had not talked of the bridge collapse at all. She could see the question was significant to him, though she wasn't to know he'd been prompted by the wraith of little Stolworthy developing over her right shoulder. She studied him for a moment and then turned back toward the fire. She became sad and serious.

"Well," she said, "I suppose if there are such things, they should be found around where that bridge used to be. Many poor people perished there in a most dreadful manner. As we both have reason to know."

Tealer said nothing, but watched the face in the curtain folds quickly become more Stolworthy-like.

Mrs Durrant noted his silence and asked him:

"And you remember clearly those events, do you, Johnny?"

The face behind her was silent, unmoving, ashen-faced, glassy-eyed, watching Tealer as closely as she was.

"Oh yes," said Tealer, "I remember everything."

"Do you know, you are quite right to wish to discuss it? To raise it with me. Your uncle has only ever referred to it in the most passing manner – but I am a firm believer that these things are best… off ones chest." She put her embroidery to one side. "And since you have asked me about the bridge I will tell you about my experiences of it, and then you may tell me yours. It will do us both good. The ancient Greeks called such exercise of deep feeling *catharsis*."

Tealer gritted his teeth; he rightly suspected that his Aunt Durrant was about to go off at a tangent. He hadn't wanted to talk about the bridge collapse itself. He'd only wanted to know if she'd heard of anyone else who had been at the bridge and who'd been followed about by a ghost as he had been. But she clearly thought it was time Tealer was allowed to express the pent-up feelings she imagined he had about the collapse.

What Susan Durrant did not know was that Tealer had actually talked about the incident a great deal, though only to the two friends who'd been there with him, and always in his barely audible mutter. In fact, the three lads had discussed the collapse with one another so many times that it had lost its immediacy and had begun to take on a pantomime quality in which the falling spectators were no longer tragic but ridiculous, or even comical, like so many skittles, or like the competitors in a tug-o-war when the rope breaks. *Splosh-splash-kersplosh!* And nothing funnier than the reptile Gooch, thrown in so abruptly that his telescope was still glued to his leering face as he disappeared into the water. By sharing this mixture of memory and imagination the lads had learnt how to make themselves hysterical with laughter. It was only when the other two mentioned Georgie that Tealer's part in the hilarity tailed off to a skull-like grin and a mechanical nodding of the head.

However, like it or not, Tealer's question had set the poor governess off on her own exercise in *catharsis*. Whether or not he wanted to listen, she wanted to describe it to him.

As it turned out, he was very lucky she did.

"My own memories of that awful day are so… vivid," she started, and went on to describe to Tealer how his uncle Palmer had collected her and her friend Margaret Collins from Miss Collins's parents' dwelling in Caister, and had sped with them into Yarmouth, making haste in order to be in time to watch 'some nonsense they might find highly diverting'. As they had driven toward the bridge they'd heard people shouting, she said, but had merely supposed that the entertainment had started, and had not realised that they were being implored to stop. Then they rounded the corner and were very nearly dragged on to the stricken bridge. The scene that then presented itself to them, as well as the near-accident with the dog-cart, left them stunned. Mrs Durrant related how she had seen wild-eyed, shrieking women tearing at their own hair. The bodies both of the living and the dead covered with the blue-black silt of the river-bed. Corpses floating face-up or face-down in the river. And in the background the wrecked structure of the bridge itself, its back broken "as if by some thunderbolt or other apocalyptic agency". And the naked forms which at first sight looked as though they were being boiled in a cauldron and tormented by devils (though she had since come to realise that that hot water tub had in fact been the saviour of many lives). "But for that first shocking instant it looked like nothing so much as one of those frightful tableaux by Bosch," she said, forgetting in her growing passion that Tealer might not know who Bosch was.

Her friend Miss Collins had found it all too much, and Palmer had had to carry her bodily away from the scene so that he and Mrs Durrant could apply salts to her. Then they had come back to see what assistance they might be of, which is when Palmer had seen Tealer in the willow tree. He'd decided that the child was in the safest place under the circumstances, and besides, it was already too late to prevent him from witnessing the horrors on show, so they resolved firstly provide what help they could offer. They thought that perhaps they could use Palmer's dog-cart to carry casualties, but it turned out that there was little to be done that was not already in hand. This is when they came back to look for Tealer.

By this time Mrs Durrant's eyes were wet with tears, and she was choking back the occasional sob. Without taking her gaze off the fire, she said:

"You will remember, Johnny, that you were concerned for one of your little companions."

"George Stolworthy," said Tealer immediately.

"Yes, I seem to think that that was when we went into the Norwich Inn."

She told him what then happened in the Norwich Inn. The tavern had been converted into a makeshift ward and a meeting place for the several surgeons who had been hastily assembled to attend the injured. Being respectably dressed, Palmer and Susan Durrant had been able to walk into the inn unchallenged – Palmer had perhaps been taken for a surgeon, she could not say. She recalled how others, frantic to know the fate of relatives, were being pushed back with a mixture of soothing words, threats, and truncheons.

As she told more of her story Mrs Durrant seemed all the more to forget that she was supposed to be reminiscing for the sake of Tealer sitting across the room from her. In fact she seemed to forget he was there at all, because she began to recount details that, regardless of any need for 'catharsis', she might at other times have thought unwise to repeat to a child as young as Tealer. But Susan Durrant was by this time talking into the depths of the fire.

And Tealer had had much training in not interrupting adults during monologues.

She described how she'd found the scene in that public house to be, if anything, worse than the sorry spectacle outside. The rooms in the inn were so thick with steam from the barrels of Lacon's hot water that it was very nearly impossible to see whether shapes six feet away were of the victims or those administering to them. Just as on the quay outside, people were being stripped and jammed into barrels regardless of size, age or sex. Shouted orders mingled with the screams and croaks of the injured. Some victims still imagined themselves in the Bure and were fighting wildly with their helpers. Others, having been saved from the river, now had to be stopped from sinking quietly and drowning themselves in the very water meant to restore them. Assistants rushed here and there with towels, smelling salts and jugs of brandy. There was a feverish rubbing of pallid limbs that were hanging down the sides of the crowded tubs. There was coughing and retching, and the harsh sound of air being drawn into damaged lungs, and the expectoration of heavy Broadland water mixed with blood and phlegm, and there was a cacophony of shouts as helpers yelled warnings to one another, or sought to encourage those teetering between recovery and eternity. As Palmer and Mrs Durrant walked through the lounge some victims were being declared dead and were being hauled out of the barrels and replaced with others still showing vital signs. "In fact, if the scene from the collapsed bridge was Bosch, then inside that Norwich Inn was Dante," murmured Mrs Durrant.

However, they could see no boy-children, alive or dead, who fitted the description of little Stolworthy. Palmer had shouted the child's name to an orderly from the militia who was trying to pour brandy down the throat of a two-year-old girl. Without even taking his eyes off the girl the orderly (who also must have assumed Palmer was a surgeon) had said 'dead littl'uns are in there, sir' and had gestured with his head to a door at the back of the bar which led through to a small store-room. They followed his advice and went into the store-room which together with the yard beyond it had become a makeshift children's morgue. Everywhere helpers were laying out the dead as the small, limp forms were carried in from off the hand carts brought up from the ruined bridge.

Palmer had stopped a woman who was carrying a book and a quill to tell her that he was looking for Georgie Stolworthy. The woman had asked him gently if he was a Stolworthy himself. No, he'd said, but he knew the child by sight as it was a playmate of his small nephew. The woman replied that they thought they had both Stolworthys in there. *Both* of them, Palmer had answered, Lord have mercy. But, she'd continued, they didn't know which was which as the lads were much of an age, and she would like to be sure before the poor mother arrived. Perhaps the kind sir could help? He'd agreed, and they had been taken over to two small corpses, both wearing cheap cotton weskits. He'd looked at what he took to be the older child but saw no face he recognised from the streets of Gorleston. It must be the other one, he'd said, and asked the woman to remove a cloth from the upper half of the smaller child's body. Alas, she'd answered, that would be no help: it seemed the child must have stuck his head through the metalwork of the bridge the better to see the clown with the birds as they passed below…

It was at this point in the narrative that Tealer sat up.

"Aunt Durrant, do you mean that…?"

Mrs Durrant came out of her recall with a gasp at her own insensitivity. She put her hand to her mouth and began to gabble apologies to Tealer, firstly as though she were talking to his uncle, and then remembering she was addressing a child. But Tealer said that it was all the same to him, because poor Georgie was dead either way. After several such reassurances, Mrs Durrant carried on, though she was much less graphic in her descriptions.

But Tealer was no longer listening. He was thinking. He was applying the pure logic of the child to a metaphysical conundrum. Surely ghosts of the dead haunted you in the form in which they'd died? He knew this because Mrs Durrant had recently read to him from a book of historical fancies that said that the corridors of Hampton Court Palace near London were haunted by a headless spirit, and that it was believed to be the ghost of Queen Catherine Howard whose head had been chopped off. Yet the Georgie Stolworthy he'd kept seeing was always a wraith with head intact. A cold, miserable, blank, pale, staring kind of head – but unarguably a head. Yet now he learns that Georgie's head was crushed in the collapse! Therefore: whatever it was that had tormented him so that summer, and was still coming back to put in the odd appearance from the banks of rivers or from distant marshes, *could not be Georgie Stolworthy*!

Ms Durrant still had tears in her eyes as she came to the end of her descriptions, and Tealer tried to look as solemn and sympathetic as he could, but in fact he was feeling a glorious sense of release.

And the shape in the curtains seemed now just a shape in the curtains.

This elation lasted for several days. The poker face that had hidden a weary torment now hid a sense of triumph. Those who knew Tealer noted a small opening up in his demeanour. Susan Durrant was one of these, and che congratulated herself on her wisdom in getting Tealer to talk about the bridge collapse.

Yet as soon as others began to note this change, Tealer himself found that clouds of doubt were beginning to form on the horizon. Something, he felt, was unresolved. Something was still… there. Certainly this nameless presence, this child, man or mannequin, was no longer George Stolworthy, the small son of a Gorleston draper. But Tealer slowly realised that this hadn't spelt its demise. It became his Tormentor. It took various forms. It could enter, vampire-like, the body of a living creature or an object. It could be a face-shaped cloud on a thundery day. It could be an unexplained far-away groaning in the small hours. It could be the gleam in the evil yellow eye of a herring gull sitting on a chimney pot, following Tealer as he walked along the Row below. Sometimes it was a single creak of a floorboard, or a rustle of dead leaves in a hedgerow, or a feeling of not being alone on a lonely road. But mostly it was the familiar, unknown watching figure across the river or at the far end of the quay. Now less of a child, and more of the man, or the mannequin. And whatever guise it adopted, it never allowed Tealer to imagine he was quite free of it.

In fact a month or so later, a series of incidents took place that left him feeling more persecuted than ever by this private, newly-anonymous, demon. It was an unplanned and unwanted reunion with some of the other Tabernacle children that caused the succubus to manifest itself in a strange and horrible manner.

The Wrath of 'Joyful' Norris

With going to live over the river with his uncle in Yarmouth, Tealer lost all contact with the community of the Cliff Street Tabernacle. Over the next few months he might see the odd familiar face in Yarmouth market when he went with Daisy to buy provisions, but if he did there was never a hint of recognition – on either side. There were also certain times a party of the Tabernacle church would make a pilgrimage over to the Yarmouth side to hand out improving pamphlets in the market-place. Daisy never allowed him anywhere near them.

But on one afternoon of his second Yarmouth winter Tealer had been sent to buy bread, and had Charlie Harrison for company together with Harrison's dog, a bull terrier that on a good day responded to the name Grinder. As they came up the King's Road and into the square they chanced on a group of the youngsters, demurely caped and bonneted. There was a moment of mutual surprise, and then the Tabernacle children turned their backs, whispering. Tealer looked at Charlie, and they both shrugged. Although he didn't know it, Tealer had been warned against by the parents of this pious huddle from the moment they knew he was to live with his uncle, the notorious Palmer.

The two parties might simply have ignored one another had not one of the young evangelists, a podgy shrewlet by the name of Modesty Pratt, decided to foment some trouble. When she caught sight of young Harrison in the dim light of the market she turned with a smirk to Faith Mullin, the girl next to her "Who's that with John Sayer?" she whispered loudly "He look like a charity boy."

"His name's Charles Harrison," answered Faith in the same whisper. "He's a cousin of them Stolworthy boys what were drowned on that new bridge. He live in one of the worst Rows. My mother say his father is a drunkard and a wastrel."

General giggling.

Tealer and Charlie overheard as they was supposed to. Charlie's eyes blazed and he told the girl to mind her 'humbugging tongue'. Her brother heard this and told Charlie to mind his. Tealer told the brother to mind his. Mullin said that Tealer was a bad sort whose uncle was a cove who spent his time with bottle-smugglers.

Tealer himself flared up at this mention of bottle-smuggling. "That weren't his bottle, if you want to know, that was Joyful Norris's. He only borrowed it to clean a pike bite – and then he only took…" Tealer realised he had committed a serious lapse, and he froze as Mullin's pimply face puckered into a frown. But then Mullin went on to say that Palmer was known to 'keep a fancy woman'. Tealer had no idea what he meant but reckoned he was being damned rude – which therefore gave Tealer convenient cover for his earlier slip. So he punched the older boy in the mouth. This caused a fight in which size left Tealer at a disadvantage. The Mullin boy grabbed at his jacket and slung him into the icy slush in the gutter. From the ground Tealer kicked up at the older boy, catching the back of his knee joint, causing it to buckle. Mullin crashed down on to the cobbles next to Tealer. Tealer was able to wriggle away and get to his feet. Then his hair was pulled so violently that his eyes watered and his teeth rattled in his head. A bony arm slipped round his neck and a foul-smelling breath filled his nostrils. He didn't need eyes in the top of his head to know that it was Gooch that had crept up on him. This grotesque youth, whom the last six months of adolescent development had done nothing to beautify, had heard the fracas and had hurried over to join in as soon as he had seen who was on the receiving end. He held Tealer in his knobbly grip while Mullin got up, wiped the mud and slush from his jacket and proceeded to slap the hated Sayer in the face and box his ears.

After what the two bullies reckoned was a sound hiding, Gooch croaked into his ear "Well, Sayer, 'at'll teach you not to get saucy with your betters. Aeeegh! Agh!"

These last two exclamations were the result of the addition to the fray of Charlie's dog. This brute had disappeared up into one of the Rows searching for any cat crazy enough not to be sitting up on the wall-top. As soon as he'd heard the scuffles and shouts of a brawl he had scampered back down the road as fast as his stumpy legs would carry him. His young master, standing just beyond the pool of light where Tealer was being thrashed, might just have given the old terrier some small urging – it mattered little, for Grinder would have joined in anyway. Gooch's screams marked the point at which Grinder's teeth buried themselves in his scrawny buttock.

Mullin aimed a half-hearted kick at the animal's ribs; but people who kick them soon find out that bull terriers wear coats of steel. Mullin's boot bounced off, and showing all the courage of his type he disappeared smartly into the night. After a few shakes Grinder let go of Gooch who fled in the opposite direction bawling loudly and attempting to cover the massive tear in the seat of his britches with his hand. Grinder turned with one foreleg raised debating whether or not to give chase. He decided against it and instead waddled over to decorate Gooch's knapsack which was still lying in the road where Gooch had thrown it down.

The other Tabernacle children had disappeared.

Meanwhile Charlie helped his young friend, winded and bleeding, off the numbing cobbles. Tealer had many bruises, a spit lip, a torn jacket and a dousing in freezing slush. He'd get a few clucks and tuts from Daisy when he got home. But none of that worried him at all – so long as all the onlookers had only forgotten what in his fury he'd said about 'bottles'. He fervently hoped they had, for by blurting out what he'd blurted out he had betrayed the comity of moon-lighters whose secrets Palmer had so confidently allowed him to share.

He lived in a state of unease for several days.

This unease subsided as time passed.

It reasserted itself when he heard his uncle remark to Mrs Durrant one Sunday lunch that Joyful Norris had been caught by the Excise, and "after what they'd found on his wherry the old devil'd be lucky not to swing for it."

Mrs Durrant asked in a casual manner where Norris now was.

"Norwich Castle prison. Where he belong," said Palmer. "But I know that old fox. He'll spirit himself out somehow. And I fear for the poor soul who squealed. Norris has a way of catching up with his enemies."

Tealer suddenly had no appetite for his junket and prunes.

And soon after this he was all alone on the hidden broad, standing on the alder-wood jetty with a fishing spear. The broad was winter-clear, so that he could see every plant, leaf and waterlogged twig eight feet below him, and even the submerged contours of the far extent of the broad. The scene was still – yet somehow not tranquil. The sky was black with storm, and there was a strange green haze on the water. A sense of expectation hung in the air as though a dark secret, already half-guessed at, was about to be confirmed.

He suddenly noticed two orange lights in the water that seemed to be approaching from the middle of the broad. He was held in a fascinated horror as they revealed themselves to be the eyes of a monstrous and outlandish pike. It was perhaps the giantess they had hooked in the autumn, but now grown to mythic dimensions. It held him in its stare until it was right beneath him, and it then underwent a hideous metamorphosis. The smouldering orange glare turned to a bitter blue, and the great duck head was contorted into a human face. Now the great form rose, and Tealer knew that the lunge and snap – faster than thought – was imminent. Some unsuspected reserve gave him strength and he hurled the spear at the fish, and there was an enormous swirl of water and it was gone. Tealer turned to walk shakily off the jetty, but found his way barred by the gross form of Joyful Norris covered in silt so that only his burning blue eyes showed through. The blades of Tealer's fishing spear were sticking into the front of his chest. He moved wordlessly towards Tealer and seized the boy's throat in his two muddy hands.

Tealer woke to find both Palmer and Mrs Durrant shaking him out of one of his 'screamers'.

Two days later a harsh voice woke him up and brought him to his window, and there was Norris in the Row beyond his yard, glaring up at him when he pulled the curtains across.

Then the day after this he saw the sour-faced wherryman staring angrily at him the opposite bank of the Yare in much the same way as Georgie once had.

And yet this man was languishing in the damp bowels of Norwich Castle. How could he be walking the streets and quays of Yarmouth unless he had indeed, through some black miracle, 'spirited' himself out to catch up with the unhappy orphan Sayer and wreak a terrible vengeance?

That must be it! Even his uncle had said that Norris had this ability.

And finally there came the evening Tealer had been sent to buy some candles, and by the time he was ready to come home night had fallen. He was now very twitchy, and he had no wish to be walking the Rows in the darkness a moment longer than was necessary. He decided to take a short cut down the Kittywitch.

In those days the Kittywitch was the smallest and vilest of all the Rows. At its narrowest point two men couldn't pass. Even in daylight scowling shapes appeared and disappeared in its grimy doorways. Dogs slunk in the shadows. Malign-looking cats spat at the drunks and were spat back at in turn. The Kittywitch smelled of ordure, sweat and all manner of corruption. Yarmouth children were always warned to keep out of its narrow confines. They were told that it was named after a witch who once lived there who could change herself into a cat. Any child she saw she would remember – and that night she would jump over the roof tops in her cat-form and slip into their rooms where she'd resume her witch state and eat them. And children sneaking fearful glances up the dingy little alley had no difficulty in believing this. Even the silhouette of created by the buildings – which leant so far into the street from either side that they nearly touched – could be the hooked nose and bony chin of a sleeping witch.

Tealer knew stories of this alley from other children, but his uncle's scorn for make-believe meant that Tealer's own head was never filled with *this* kind of nonsense – the evil spirits of his universe were at once more real and more vague than cackling crones with pointy hats. (And Palmer would one day tell him the truth about the Kittywitch: that in fact its name came from the many 'kittywitches' who worked their crude spells in its darkest recesses, and that it was not the small children of the rows they sought to entice but their fathers and older brothers – whose furtive visits to this unwholesome place were the true source of its reputation.)

So when on his shortcut down the Row Tealer heard a terrible shrieking from up ahead of him he was nonplussed rather than terrified. A harpy came out of one of the doorways screaming at someone inside. She had unnaturally red cheeks, black-ringed eyes and straggly, greasy hair and she was wearing a cloak that hung off her as a series of rags. The hag continued her tirade until a large dark form came out from the gloom of the stair well, grabbed her and flung her against the opposite wall so hard that it vibrated with the force. The string of obscenities became a formless shrieking.

"Hold your row, yer filthy crow! You ent go' git no more off me," growled this attacker and he aimed a kick at the prostrate form. The boot seemed knock her unconscious and there was the snap of breaking teeth. Then he darted a look up and down the Row to see if his brutality had been witnessed. At first he didn't see Tealer and looked back down at the woman, but then he brought his head slowly up again as he realized that the small shape in the darkness was a watching child. The poor light prevented any real recognition on either side, but Tealer reckoned he knew that voice.

The thug roared out and started to give chase. Tealer's legs came to life and he fled down the narrow passage, crashing into rails, low walls and hard objects, and he broke his nails and barked his shins as he scrambled to get away from the heavy tread coming up behind him. He disappeared into the pitch-black warren of alleys, slippery with winter slime, and eventually dived over a low wall into a heap of coal where he shoved himself into the far corner and tried to stifle his panting. The clump of boots came up the alley and stopped.

And carried on.

He waited in the coal for an hour, unaware of its lumps and sharp edges digging into his back, buttocks and thighs. He spent the whole time in a transport of fear, turning rigid at the scrape of the clogs of every drunken sailor, the cries of every hungry infant, the screams of every domestic quarrel and the yowl of every arguing cat as the poorer Rows settled down for another night. He expected Norris's murderous face to leer in at him from over the low wall before pulling him out to throttle him; whether for blabbing about the bottles or seeing the assault on the prostitute. Finally he summoned the courage to creep back over the wall and make an uneventful way home, more terrified than ever.

And yet Norris was supposed to be in the stern custody of Norwich Castle Prison!

It was another casual mealtime conversation another day or so later that neutralized this Norris version of the Tomentor. Palmer came home from a night at the Bowling Green Inn, whose various customers knew exactly where Norris was. It transpired that the old brute had not been arrested for possession of contraband at all, or even a suspicion of it. It was true the Excise had subjected the *Stokesby Trader* to an inspection, but in recent times such searches had become little more than a ritual, a hangover from the far-off days when smuggling was a real business on the Broads. But what the inspectors had found was Annie Bullard the wherry-woman lying motionless on the galley floor, her head blue from having had it pounded against the varnished timbers of the wall. Matthew Jermy, the chief exciseman, was a fair-minded fellow with no great desire to persecute the hard-working poor of the Broads for the sake of a box or so of untaxed cigars. But he had a daughter of the same age as this wretched girl, and he wished to see Norris pay for his viciousness.

The girl survived – and then wouldn't testify. Heaven only knew why, said Palmer (and it was to be many years before anyone found out). Norris had been able to walk away a free man. "That won't be long before we see the old devil in his usual state, a-staggering about in the Rows and a-shoutin' at all and sundry," said Palmer.

Tealer with mightily relieved. "I think I ha' seen him already, uncle," he said.

The irony was that he hadn't. The scowling wherryman across the water might well have been Norris, and the face below Tealer's bedroom window might just have been, but the unsatisfied patron of the Kittywitch Row certainly wasn't. Norris would never part with money for such a service when he had it for free on board his own wherry.

No matter. Tealer had not been 'to blame' for Norris's arrest. More importantly, if it *had* been Norris blundering after him in the Kittywitch, then at least he now knew the vicious old brute was no Springheel Jack of the Yarmouth Rows, able to appear at will whenever Tealer was alone and vulnerable.

No, that Norris wasn't.

But someone, or something, was.

Over the next two years of his life Tealer would find that the dead of night continued to produce its far-off screams; the eyes of the gulls in the chimney pots continued to gleam; the floorboards continued to creak; the leaves in the hedgerows on the outskirts of the town to rustle inexplicably on winter nights. And every now and again he would have a night time visitation. He'd shoot upright from a deep sleep, and the Tormentor, the cause of all these twists of the knife, would be watching him from the foot of the bed. And on one or two of these occasions he had the overwhelming feeling that at last he knew who it really was.

"What do you want?" He would demand. "What do you want with me?"

But it's not in the nature of such apparitions to answer questions like that. In any case, by morning Tealer would only remember that *something* had happened. What, and at whose hands, he invariably had no idea.

Yet this was also the time of Tealer's life when Palmer started to make him think about what he was seeing whenever they went out on their forays into the countryside. Man and boy would gaze avidly at mundane things like feathers, tracks, droppings, sloughed skins, frayed twigs and flattened grass, and they would argue excitedly about what might have happened the previous night to leave such signs. Tealer was taught not to let the imagination override the facts, but merely to use it to fill the gaps in the evidence and arrive at a sensible conclusion. And if he could arrive at no satisfactory deduction, why then, Palmer taught him, this could only be because he didn't have enough of the facts – meaning that the solution was unknowable – and he shouldn't trouble himself unduly about it.

Inevitably Tealer also started to use this same system of thinking to dismiss all the creaks, rustles and far-off screams that he had never dared tell anyone about.

So: when he was stealing through the darkest Rows late on a winter's afternoon he might be as convinced as ever that there were footsteps other than his own echoing off the dreary walls. He might shoot looks, just as before, into the void behind him. But, if he did, he was now just as likely to stop and stamp one boot on the cobbles, and to grin into the darkness as he decided that his pursuer was no more than the echo of his echo.

So: the figure in the distance that was also the face in the curtain, the glaring stare of a herring gulls or the merest rustle in the undergrowth – resolved into a nothing. A dose of sober Reason and even the half-remembered, uncommunicative visitor of the small hours could be passed off – just – as a vivid dream.

So: Tealer Sayer's tribulations at an end.

If it had only been that simple.

Perhaps with a dose of sober Reason a few of Tealer's night terrors and other flights of fancy were exposed as foolish notions – but to imagine the Tormentor Itself, that had stalked John Sayer almost from his cradle, could be annulled so simply, would be to forget that this Tormentor was real in a way that its disguises were not – and that when one of these masks was lifted, then, virus-like, this same Tormentor would surely take on some new, more convincing form. This is what It now did, and this time Its tactic was devious and truly malign… Hitherto It had teased and taunted the mind of young Sayer with sensations that were perplexing because the rest of the world seemed not to acknowledge them.

Now, It would play the opposite trick.

And so the Fiend appeared in the marshes. A monster that stalked the ronds and reedbeds around the old port of Yarmouth. It had been lurking there for years, centuries even, but to a young mind it must have seemed suddenly to arrive. Firstly, strange and ghastly cries, as though a large creature were being strangled, were heard from the depths of the Somerleyton woods. Young people remarked on it, older ones kept their silence. Then animals, and then a boy, died, horribly. At frst a draught horse, a Suffolk gelding known on its estate for its gentle ways, was possessed. It smashed its stall into kindling and crushed its teamsman of many years to a pulp against a barn wall. Then the same doleful shrieks were heard at night in the lanes around Burgh Castle by a party of boys returning from rook-scaring. Not long after this some two miles downstream in Cobholm, a boy no older than Tealer himself, died; again, it was said, in dreadful circumstances. It emerged that this boy been one of the bird scarers. One rumour even had it that in his last seconds of life he was trying to bite himself in the small of the back.

Lurid details aside, the two deaths were fact. In the case of the boy, even the local paper reported on the fuss there was when the Bishop refused leave for an exorcism in the room where the death had occurred. The older folk, those with long memories, looked ever grimmer. They recognized this demon and remembered all that their ancestors had said about it, including that it might be destroyed never so many times, it would always return. All contact with it, even the smallest glimpse in the moonlight must be avoided. Certainly it must never be discussed. Only then would it disappear. Some fools still contrived to laugh at it – they gave it pantomime names: 'Galleytrot', or 'Shugmonkey' – because, of course, they feared it.

Tealer was soon aware of this dire creature, and was almost immediately convinced that the Tormentor had called it up and in some way merged with it expressly to track him down. He came to know it by its ancient name, which was 'Shuck', and meant 'dog of the devil'.

A Brush with the Shuck

Dogs featured much in Tealer's life from the time he joined his uncle in Row 111. Before then he'd had very little to do with them. There were always a few strays to be seen in the streets and along the docks of Gorleston, scavenging amongst the drying nets for discarded fish or dessicated crabs. Across the river the Yarmouth Rows were full of them: busy-looking curs, ever trotting purposefully to some meeting point or other, ever just out of range of boots or stones. Tealer's parents were terrified of them and would send Daisy with a stick to drive away any that came near the house. James Sayer even once gave his son instructions as to how to defend himself in case of attack. He was to stand with his back to a wall or tree and use one arm to cover his throat while keeping the other firmly by his side as he kicked out (it was left to his brother-in-law to tell the boy that the other hand was actually better employed covering the privates.) As a result, Tealer came to live with his uncle with an inbuilt distrust of dogs.

It was a phobia he had quickly to lose in order to settle in John Palmer's house. Palmer had two dogs, one of which, Buck, was about three years old when Tealer came to live with him. Buck looked suspiciously at the boy as the boy did at him. "Don't worry about that fellow, old partner," said Palmer, "He just in't sure about you. No dog with a brain trust a young'un from the off. He'll come round." And after three months, when Buck found that Tealer was not the kind of urchin to poke him with sticks or pull his tail he began to accept the small figure around the house without watching him out of the corner of his eye. He even allowed Tealer to scratch his ear.

The other dog, Turpin, had disappeared before Tealer went to live with Palmer. He had been a jolly little foxhound, but when Tealer asked Daisy what had happened to him, she told him that a devil had got into the little dog, and Palmer had had to shoot him.

And a third dog that Tealer had to come to terms with was the formidable Grinder, Charlie Harrison's bull terrier. This bow-legged, slant-eyed, canine thug was dangerously fond of its young master, but was only ever regarded Tealer with cold indifference. He was scared stiff of it at first, and his friend Charlie had to work hard to persuade him not to back off whenever Grinder came to sniff him. He learnt to ignore the dog as it ignored him.

A Brush with the Shuck

Yet it was this Grinder that gave Tealer his first real lesson in the simple, brutal rules of nature. We don't talk here of that (by Grinder's standards) trifling nip on the back-side administered to the ghastly youth Gooch, but a more elemental, terrible display.

Tealer arrived one afternoon after school to find Charlie picking up pigeon carcases from the tiny yard at the back of his parents' house. A large tom-cat had been disturbed raiding the pigeon coop that Charlie's family had at the back of their dwelling. Charlie said it would be back, and that it would be fun to wait up for it with Grinder. Tealer had imagined the dog would be used to rush out and scare the cat away. Instead, as night fell and the unsuspecting cat jumped into the yard, Charlie leapt up from behind the rain butt and cut it off from its escape route, a pile of unused washing-line poles leaning against the outer wall of the yard. The cat spat at Charlie and quickly scanned the yard for an alternative exit. Then it saw Grinder trotting towards it. This caused the animal to arch its back, double in size and give vent to a deep and terrible growling of a kind Tealer had never known a cat could make. It presented a spectacle that might have caused a hungry bear to pause, but Grinder did not even slow. There was a flurry of fur as the cornered tom unleashed its twenty stilettos into the dog's face, but bull terriers have their eyes set deep in their skulls against such tactics. He grabbed the cat and began the classic figure-of-eight worry that silenced the screams of the unfortunate beast in seconds. Then he tossed the carcase into the air and caught it again, breaking the spine in his bald, scarred jaws. He tore at the mangled corpse, crushing the head into a pulp, ripping off limbs and tail and splitting open the stomach full of half-digested pigeon. The boys watched without speaking as he ate every scrap. He then licked the pool of blood remaining, and sniffed the ground all around just in case a morsel of cat-flesh had been overlooked. Finally he looked briefly at the two small boys, wagged his tail, and sat down to scratch himself.

"That'll learn the ol' bugger to kill my pigeons!" yelled Charlie with excitement. He had seen several cats destroyed by his squat, ugly companion, and was inured to it. Tealer smiled too, but wanly. He'd already seen for himself the natural world was a good, intriguing, wholesome, innocent, splendid world; but until that night he'd only read, or been told, that it was also merciless and violent. Now he had seen this at close quarters. In particular he'd witnessed the uncompromising, unnegotiable savagery that can lie simmering in any dog. It was this that sowed the seeds of a wonderful and terrible new trauma in his life.

By the time he had been living with his uncle for a couple of years Tealer was ranging free with Charlie across the hinterlands of Yarmouth and its marshes. Far from disapproving, Palmer positively encouraged this, provided Tealer was with another boy. He was particularly anxious that Johnny should go out and 'learn his birds'.

"After all, you don't want to be a *Cockney* Johnny, do you, boy? Your cockney Johnny come down off the London train, pockets a-bulgin' with all his new-made money, and a-kitted out with all the latest in shooting wear. He blunder about in the reeds, scare all the quarry away before he've even primed his gun, blaze away at his own shadow, wing some poor old cormorant… and then back he go, back to London to tell his friends how he 'nearly 'ad a goose up in Naw-folk'. So go you down the marsh and learn your birds, boy!"

Tealer needed no encouragement. One of the favourite haunts of the two lads was the ruined Roman fort and the marshes of Cobholm just below it. Like any real boys of their age they would spend the spring and early summer looking for birds' nests.

As always, Charlie would be followed by the dog Grinder, a perfect surety against other, larger boys who felt that the fort was *their* terrain. Grinder seemed happy with this arrangement, as he could dig for rabbits in the sandy bank above the marshes. The scrub around the old fort was a wonderful area for bird-nesting and the two boys would go to painful and dangerous lengths to seek out crows' nests in the hawthorns – driving up through the tight, brittle branches, almost oblivious to the scratching and stabbing thorns in their excitement to find the big, blue-green eggs for their collections.

There was one May evening when they were out so late that the light was going. They decided to split up and meet back at the Burgh Castle church. Charlie would search the fort perimeter for songbirds' nests in the crumbling flintwork, while Tealer would go down to the marsh and use the last of the light to search for waterhen eggs. (He loved presenting Daisy with a few of the sweet-tasting, sandy-brown prizes wrapped up in a packet of plaited reed.)

From where he was hunting close to the river he could hear Charlie and Grinder making their way through the trees to the massive centre of the fort. Tealer began searching for the waterhen rafts in the dykes. At one point he looked up and realized that it was too dark to make out where his friend was up on the bluff, though he could hear the occasional bark as Grinder surprised a rabbit.

Then the darkness intensified, and Tealer's senses sharpened. The gristle in his ears twitched to every sound, and his eyes ached as they sifted the darkness. He stopped searching and began simply to enjoy the night noises around him.

And this was when he heard the breathing.

It was close, and was coming closer. It was not human breathing, but something else. It was the rhythmic panting of a running dog. There was only one dog anywhere near, and the thought of this made Tealer's heart race a little. "Charlie, where are you, man?" His voice seemed only to carry a few yards, and there was no answer. The panting continued and was closing in. In the darkness Tealer saw an image of the wretched tomcat being dismembered. Such a small prey was a mere game for such a killer. Tealer froze and he listened. The panting hadn't stopped. Tealer could only wait for Grinder's barrel shape to emerge from the darkness. He knew that Charlie was out of earshot. He knew he was alone.

And there are times when you can feel very alone on the marsh. No trees to climb or hedges to hide behind. Just you and your nemesis. And Tealer's nemesis that night was a large brindled assassin of uncertain temper that might just wag its tail, or that might just kill him and then wag its tail. Men far away in Yarmouth might shoot the dog afterwards and shake their heads in pity at the tragedy, but that would be little help to Tealer out here on the Cobholm marshes.

Then the panting stopped. Tealer dared not breathe. The panting started again and seemed closer, and Tealer's nerve failed him. His instinct was to find Charlie before Grinder found him. He ran back across the marsh and up the church path, past the church and through the woods to the fort.

"Charlie, where are you?" he shouted through his own panting.

There was no running sound behind him so he carried on toward the fort. The flint wall of the castle appeared as a white line in front of him, and he raced up the bluff through a gap in the wall and out on to the meadow in the centre of the ruin. He saw Charlie at the far end, and next to him in the dusk stood Grinder. Tealer froze rigid as Grinder came forward and sniffed him. Recognising his scent, the dog merely turned his back on the boy and went off to investigate some more interesting smell in the undergrowth.

"Have he been with you all the while?" Tealer asked when he had the breath.

Charlie looked round him, genuinely puzzled. "Have *who* been with me all the while?"

"Grinder."

" 'course he have. Where else?"

"I thought he followed me down to marsh. I heard a dog runnin' around and pantin'."

"Well, that weren't Grinder. What'd he want follow you for? You don't smell *that* good."

"Whose dog was it then?"

"I don't know. Perhaps that was the Black Shuck."

"The what?"

"The Shuck! Hell, man, you must a' heard on it. That were only last month that boy up Cobholm died from it. You know, Woodyard's boy. They say he went down a-twistin' and shriekin'. They reckon he seen the Shuck. Which was why, they reckon."

"Why what?"

"Why he croaked. 'Cos... Oh never mind that. We didn't want t'be talking 'bout things like that up here. Not when thas gettin' dark, we didn't. Let's get home, do our people'll be a-worritin'."

Tealer was only half-listening. He was still watching the squat shape of Grinder through the twilight, and shaking.

Then in the June of that same summer Tealer was on the river with his uncle. It was a still evening, and there was quiet on the water. Murmured conversations between wherry crews wafted out from various galleys on the heavy air. They passed the toll gate and a wherry moored beyond it. As they came upwind of it a huge dog jumped out of the cabin and gave throat to a volley of deep barks that rang across the water, shattering the evening peace of the quay.

Palmer laughed. "Well, now, would you want to make free with the bottles and chattels of that wherryman, young John? No? Neither would I. Not with a Black

Shuck like him on guard!"

This casual statement rang a small, sharp bell. And they sailed on for a bit, and with a lull in the wind Tealer asked:

"Uncle John?"

"My man?"

"What is a 'blackshuck'? You now said that's what that there big old dog was like."

"Yes, so I did, boy. Black Shuck, they say, is one dog you should not want to meet. He's very big, and you only see him at night, and when you do your seal is up, for you won't last the year. He's black with great red eyes. Sometimes you see him in the lanes upland, sometimes as a shape moving fast acrost the marshes at dusk. Sometimes you hear him a-snuffling in your yard as you're a-dropping off to sleep. There are those who reckon he's attacked people. They reckon he ha' jumped on men and torn their throats out. But mostly the fear he cause people is the curse that go just with having laid eyes on him. You're doomed. That's what they say. Ha!"

"And is it all true? Ha' you seen it?"

"No, boy, that I haven't."

"Do you believe it?"

"No, boy, that I don't."

Tealer thought long and hard about this demon dog. He thought back to the strange pantings and breathings in the dusk below the fort the month before. He thought of Grinder's ungentle figure-of-eight worry. He fretted less these days about the unknown human figures at a distance, but his unwished-for relationship with the Tormentor was very much undiminished. His mind kept coming back to the panting and the breathing. *Something* was there! Against his wishes, his powers of observation and imagination began to conspire.

He began to ask people questions. His young friends, his uncle's friends, other marshmen and fowlers. He would ask them with a broad grin, as though the question was part in jest. What he found gave him little comfort. Most people laughed, but did not actually dismiss the Shuck stories as nonsense. Some folk shrugged. But one or two told him very sharply to hold his tongue, and it was these, he told his uncle in an off-hand manner, that he found the most 'interesting'. His uncle looked at him and laughed.

"You mean you ha' got it into your head that the Black Shuck is a real dog?"

"No, that I haven't. But why did some of these men tell me to keep quiet? Do *they* think thas real?"

"And who is it who told you to be quiet?" his uncle asked.

And Tealer told him: Simon Gedney the marshman was one.

His uncle laughed aloud. "Well, there you are! I might ha' known. Simon is one of the sharpest relievers of other men's game in the business. Do you suppose he want you or anyone else down there at dark when he is a-plying his trade. No, that he does *not*. And if he said to you, 'Boy! Do you keep away from that marsh do you'll surely be eaten by the demon dog,' you might think 'thas only old Gedney trying to scare me off'! So he just say nothing – because he know saying nothing will make you *far* more nervous. And blast us all to hell if we don't find he's right! I reckon you ha' got yourself in a twiddle about this demon dog. Ho, ho! Thas what I reckon!"

Tealer was alarmed that his uncle should think such a thing "No, no, that I haven't! I'm only interested, that's all."

"Thas good, then. Because there is no Shuck, boy, just stories told by mischief-makers and believed by bird-brains."

Ah, but the problem for Tealer was that it turned out that one of these 'bird-brains' was Harry 'Jointy' Pole, a man whose views Palmer valued almost above all others, a man he had always told his nephew to listen carefully to. And it was the gruesome, believable account of Shuck the Hell Dog related by Jointy Pole that was to do Tealer Sayer no good at all.

In Lothingland, in the north east corner of Suffolk, there lies a long, quiet finger of fresh water marked on the map as Fritton Lake, but known to many as Decoy Lake. It is a broad, but not at all like the shallow broads of Norfolk. There are no thick banks of reeds waving and hissing under an open sky. Here the water is deep and it is fringed with quiet woodlands of pine. The area is infested with rabbits which thump the sandy floor when there are stoats, foxes or men about. At night, the only sound is of the wind washing through pine-needles.

The decoy is part of an ancient estate whose original owners had held it since medieval times. In 1780 the estate had passed into the hands of William Devereaux, a man made rich from the production of dye, and whose family made it their business to fill the void left by the ancient, penniless lineage they had replaced. By the time of Tealer's boyhood, three generations of the Devereaux already lay in the huge vault in the tiny churchyard overlooking the decoy lake.

Both the Devereaux and their predecessors had long received peppercorn dues from local decoy-men who had lived solitary lives working the duck-decoy from which the lake first took its unofficial name.

The last of these decoyers was Harry 'Jointy' Pole.

Few people knew Jointy very well. In all his life he'd never been more than five miles from the place of his birth, which was the same hut he still occupied alone on the banks of the decoy broad. He seldom left the confines of the decoy wood except on Sundays and other high days when he would make his way down the sandy path to the little church on the edge of the estate. He was a devout Christian in the low Anglican mold – hating pomp but loving ceremony. Although unable to read a word he could recite whole chapters of the New Testament; although a mumbler and mutterer in speech he could make the gentlefolk in the front pews start and smile with the clarity of his responses during divine service. Men at work in the fields around Decoy Wood often heard the sound of psalms being sung in a powerful bass echoing from its centre; they imagined that it must be Lord Devereaux himself, strolling along the banks of his lake, because he was known to have a fine bass voice. No-one would never believe the singer could be 'ole Jointy'.

But for all his quiet piety there were those who looked askance at Jointy Pole. Only the oldest locals knew exactly where he had come from and how long he had been working the decoy, and they had the good sense not to discuss the matter. To younger villagers and newcomers it was as if Pole had emerged fully-formed from the silt of the lake itself. People mistrusted his solitary ways. They were unnerved by his ability (which gave him his name) to turn his head almost one hundred and eighty degrees like an owl to watch who might be coming up a woodland path behind him. Even his curly mop of gypsy-dark hair, only ever combed by the wind and the rain, was viewed with suspicion, for colouring like that was rare in an area where the Vikings and Flemings had left so many descendants with straight fair locks. (Such suspicions were only voiced quietly, mind – the Devereaux people themselves were also dark-haired.) In earlier times, when the plague struck or the wheat failed, men of Pole's appearance and reclusive habits did well to make themselves scarce. Even now there were locals who reckoned that deep down in Decoy Wood old Jointy Pole might well be engaging in some black art or other.

And if they had ever seen him about his business they might have felt vindicated. He *was* a wizard and an enchanter. But it was not people Pole bewitched, it was duck; and not a few at a time, but whole flocks. Through some uncanny jiggory-pokery with a dog, a few screens and a net, he could beguile huge numbers of fowl into his traps. Within hours of a flock arriving on the water he could have it trussed and dressed, ready for the cart to take it to market. The whole operation would be conducted in near silence; he had never fired a weapon in his life. The privileged few who had seen him in action could only conclude that he entered the very souls of the birds that landed on the waters of Decoy Lake.

One such witness was the middle son from the 'big house', the Hon. Frederick Devereaux, who as a boy had spent most of his idle hours down by the lake, and had become a disciple of his father's strange tenant. By the age of ten, the lad could drive the rest of the folk up at the 'big house' to distraction with his 'Pole says this…' and his 'Pole says that…' Most of his family were quietly appalled at the idea of Freddie spending so much of his leisure time with a duck decoyer – and this dismay seemed to go beyond the fact that the man was an illiterate rustic. But Lord Devereaux himself, from whom Freddie seemed to have derived so much of his love of nature, had no objection, so the boy had free rein to learn from Pole as much as he could.

Because he was a sickly lad the young Freddie had not been sent to Harrow with his brothers, but was educated at home. Thus he came to know the boy John Palmer, whose family were known to his father through business, and who had been invited to join Freddie as a study companion. Freddie found in Palmer a kindred spirit, and they went out together on shooting and bird-nesting expeditions. It was therefore inevitable that Palmer would come to be introduced to the strange inhabitant of the hut down at Decoy Lake. At first Palmer was not impressed with the idea of consorting with a decoyman. The shooting members of his family all had the gunner's natural distrust of those who killed duck by means other than a gun, and John was no exception. But Freddie repeatedly urged his young friend just to come down and meet 'the capital fellow who works on our decoy.'

"I think he knows more of wild beasts than anyone on earth, Palmer. He sees and thinks about nature as you and I do. You really must come with me to meet him. I shall think you have something to fear if you do not..."

So John Palmer was persuaded to make the first of many visits to the shores of Decoy Lake, where he was introduced to a rough, fearless black-bearded fellow of about thirty who spoke sparingly and to the point, whether to a farmworker's child or to His Lordship. And Palmer was soon as intrigued by the decoyer as his friend had promised he'd be. And what country lad could fail to be? A man who would place live worms in his mouth and coax wild thrushes and robins to fly down and take them from between his lips. A man who could pluck adders from the sunny patches of sand between the lakeside oaks and handle them with impunity. Who could curb the young Master Freddie's endless cough by blowing the smoke of henbane leaves straight into his face, and who could staunch the bleeding of a cut with cobwebs. Whose hut was decorated with gin-traps, eel-traps, mole-traps, rat-traps and at least one man-trap. Who could glance into the summer sky for less than a minute and then tell where all the local bees in the area were swarming. And, of course, a man who had the sublime talent to persuade duck to fly down into the Decoy Lake, swim towards him and give up their lives.

Palmer thus became the next acolyte of this illiterate, all-knowing hermit. But he was the first to admit that even the deep friendship he struck up with Pole never came close to the unspoken understanding there was between the rough decoyer and the middle son of Lord Devereaux. Palmer was often fascinated how in their thinking and speaking they were like peasant and patrician versions of the same character.

"Do you know, Devereaux," he'd once said to his friend a few years into their friendship, when they were both about eighteen, "I reckon if you'd been left in Decoy Wood as an infant for the gypsies to find, you'd ha' ended up looking exactly like old Jointy, what with your dark hair an'all. If you ever grow a beard when you get older I shall be pushed to know who's who 'twixt the pair of you. That must come from all the time you spend round that hut a-yarning with him."

Devereaux had laughed loudly at that. "Don't be an ass, Palmer," he'd said. "I seem to remember you are also seen down at his hut very much." Then he had changed the subject.

Freddie Devereaux's slight, tubercular corpse had been turning to dust in the family vault for fully ten years when Palmer decided it was his turn to present a new initiate at Jointy Pole's simple dwelling down at Decoy.

As they drove through the low hills and modest woodlands of the Lothingland peninsular, Palmer readied Tealer for the meeting with Pole rather as a priest might school a novice for an audience with a cardinal. Tealer was not to ask questions; he was simply to watch and learn. So the boy gazed in wordless mystification both at the strange figure of Pole and at the bizarre arrangement of parallel screens of alder and reed down the path from his hovel. They were set at a diagonal on either side of a channel leading off from the open water, and a huge conical net, whose mouth lay just beyond the innermost of the screens, snaked away as a diminishing tunnel, rather like the web of some gigantic house spider, to some sinister place well away from the open water.

Pole had glanced briefly at Tealer and then ignored him, addressing what little he had to say – which was little indeed – to Palmer. He led uncle and nephew round the back of the decoy to where the screens were erected in ranks. The three of them hid in the wood and watched. A flock of sixty mallard had collected out on the open water of the broad, so they crept forward and took up their positions behind the screen.

"Now watch this, boy. Just you watch this," whispered Palmer as they both squinted through tiny peepholes in the screen. Pole whistled a low whistle and a mangy-looking cur-dog appeared from nowhere. "That's Mart," whispered Palmer. "Don't look much, do he?" Mart did not; he was the kind of dog most people in Yarmouth threw things at. He didn't approach the duck directly but slipped behind them into the wood, so that Tealer imagined he was going to swim up behind the duck and drive them toward the net.

Mart did no such thing. He suddenly appeared on the bank in full view of the birds. Their heads shot up, suspicious, but not unduly alarmed, as they had thirty yards of clear water between them and the shore.

Then started the sorcery.

A Brush with the Shuck

From behind his screen Jointy whistled a series of low whistles and the dog Mart began to weave his way in and out between the furthermost screens, slowly making his way to the mouth of the net. At first the birds simply watched. Then, as if pulled by sixty individual threads, they began to drift slowly towards him. Mart didn't look at the duck, but merely carried on his erratic way. Various whistles from somewhere in the undergrowth told him when to slow, when to stop, and when to start again.

"Can you see? You'd think they'd been hypnotized…" whispered Palmer, deep into Tealer's ear.

The duck came in closer to the mouth of the net.

"… but they aren't. The real reason is that they're curious, and nervous. All they can see is that there dog keep appearing and disappearing, and they want t'know why."

Then as the duck approached the mouth of the net, Mart disappeared altogether. But he reappeared on the bank behind the duck, which by this time were some way up the channel, and he jumped into the water. There was a roar of wings as the duck shot into the air, but it was too late. They had passed the mouth of the net and were therefore stopped short. With the dog now cutting off their escape route to open water they panicked and headed up the channel into the 'pipe' where the net got progressively smaller. Tealer and Palmer left their hideouts to find Pole had already cut off the ducks' escape route back to the net's mouth.

There followed the grim final act of this strange spectacle. Pole pulled his victims one by one from under the net, broke their necks and slung them in a pile so smoothly that he had the next flapping bird in his hand before the previous one had hit the twitching pile of its dead brethren. Tealer might have found this hard to watch, but there was a rough poetry in the instantness of the execution of so many birds in such deft hands. There was no triumph, nor was there anything casual in this killing. There was only the earnestness and concentration of a man performing the task that was his means to a living. Even at ten years old Tealer now knew enough of the wild world to realize that for a man like Jointy Pole such gathering of fowl from the water was as natural a task as gathering apples from a tree or honey from a hive.

"Well, did you enjoy your visit to the Decoy, Johnny," asked his uncle as they made their way home from that first day by the pine-fringed Suffolk broad.

Tealer said he had, and his uncle saw that he meant it.

"And what d'you think of friend Jointy?"

"He don't say much, but I don't think he's angry with anyone."

"Yes, you're right, old man. Thas just his way. Do you know, he's never even set foot in Yarmouth? Yet he seem to understand the world better than many men I know who ha' sailed right round it."

So they went back, many times. Slowly Tealer began to get the measure of this reclusive, mumbling, black-bearded man. He realized that Pole never smiled, but was full of the simple humour often called 'dry' (a term that later in life Tealer found was often misapplied to people simply because they managed not to laugh at their own jokes).

Pole was meticulously clean in his habits, though he never washed more than his hands, face and neck in water he pailed from the broad. ("A bath would kill old Jointy." said Palmer when Tealer mentioned this to him.) Yet so pure was the life he led that he never smelled of anything more than the green water of Decoy Lake. He wore a smock that seemed to keep him dry in wet weather, warm in the winter and cool in the summer heat. Under this he wore rough linen trousers. These were tied round with an eel-skin thong to 'ward off the rheumatics'. In the summer he wore no footwear at all, while in the winter months he wore a pair of high boots, first given to him by Lord Devereaux, repaired many, many times, and which were probably first cobbled for a redcoat under Wellington. His main source of food was the potato patch he tended on a small piece of ground in the woodland that surrounded the decoy. He would boil his 'spuds' in a big black cauldron that simmered permanently outside his hut. He would also dine on whatever he had to hand – duck, of course, a-plenty, but also eels, pike, waterhen, crawfish, woodpigeon and rabbit – and accompanied by water-cress, hazel nuts, blackberries, crabapples, carrots, ground elder, shaggy parasol and whatever else was in season, pickled in earthen jars, or clamped in the soil along with the 'spuds'. He kept large sacks of barley, most of which he would spread in the shallows to keep the duck coming in, and some of which he would use to brew strong ale to whose effects he seemed quite immune; and to Tealer's utter delight he used the empty sacks as blankets.

When not about his main business of tricking duck up his decoy pipe Pole made hurdles out of hazel, screens out of reed, and chairs out of ash. He mended nets, laid snares, 'hulked' rabbits and plucked duck. He speared eels under the September moon, standing in a reed flat like a giant heron with his glaive at the ready. All year round he worked the warrens with his long net, using Mart and two sullen ferrets he kept in a hutch just by his pillow.

To Tealer, Pole lived in a rough, hessian-covered heaven. "I can't think of anything that could be more fun than to be a duck decoyer," he admitted to Palmer after another of their afternoons with Pole.

His uncle laughed at that one. "Steady there, boy! You haven't yet tried the shooting method with duck. And – *and* – you haven't met White Jenny."

"But who is she, uncle? You've talked of her before." said Tealer, who was still at an age when girls and young women seemed a largely superfluous act of Creation.

"You'll meet her soon enough, and then you might find that decoying's not the only pleasure in this life," said his uncle with a grin. "But howsomeever – I ha' spoken to old Jointy: now he ha' seen you he's happy that you should go down when you want. But don't keep pestering him with mardle. He won't like that. Blast! not that you're much more talkative than he is! But *don't* go asking him about guns. He hate 'em. He ha' never even fired one. Thas why he ha' got no time for them boys down on Breydon. He reckon their way of taking duck is underhand. Mind you, that's just what the gunners say about decoyers like him."

Palmer smiled at the irony of this as he urged the horse Vulcan to greater things.

And thus begun Tealer's friendship with Jointy; a friendship which in later years – when the decoy men were all dead and the decoy nets had rotted away and the decoy channels were vague inlets, clogged with bulrush and reedmace – a friendship which in later years Tealer would think back to with a sad pleasure.

He began visiting Jointy Pole as regularly as Palmer and Devereaux had before him. He would always find him busy – skinning, bodging, weaving or plucking – and always staring furiously at the task in hand with a clay pipe clenched between his teeth, smoking an acrid blend of tobacco tricked out with mugwort leaves. He would only greet Tealer with a nod, but there would always some surprise prepared. Perhaps no more than a glimpse of a blackcap's nest in the shrubs, or perhaps something more substantial. He might have set his old mantrap ready to spring with a branch. He might show Tealer how to catch a pike from the stony bottom of the broad with nothing more than a loop of wire on an ash-pole. Sometimes Jointy would have a gift for his student – a piece of alder carved into an owl, a pike skull boiled clean and white, the blue pinion of a jay, or a rare egg for his collection. "Here y'are, boy" is all he would say as he handed it to him unsmiling, and Tealer knew that he should thank him only in the briefest terms.

During those mystical afternoons amongst the sun-dappled woods of Decoy Broad, Tealer kept his promise to his uncle that he would keep quiet and watch. Sometimes, though, curiosity would get the better of him; but he learnt very soon that if he asked a question which Pole did not wish to answer – either because he was too busy with some other task, or because it was a time for even more quiet than usual – the duck decoyer would simply ignore him. At other times, Jointy might be in a more forthcoming mood, and sensing it, Tealer would try him out with a few choice questions he'd saved for the occasion.

And this is how he was forced to draw nearer still to the Tormentor.

It was through learning of the manner in which a man called 'Cork' Norton lost his life.

The Strange and Terrible End of Cork Norton

They were sitting in Pole's hut, cooler than the bank of the broad, and – when the eyes became accustomed to the darkness – full of delights. There were rabbit snares, glaives and fishing rods. There were strange medieval-looking tools with long handles for cutting channels and clearing weed from the surface of the water. There was a fiendish instrument called a 'devil'; a beer barrel impregnated with six-inch nails and weighted with ballast so that it sat in the cool depths of the Decoy Lake, ready to snag and tear the drag-nets of the poachers who might seek to clear the water of its fish while Pole was at his devotions in church.

Pole was making a sheep hurdle for a shepherd, one of many jobs with which he would fill the hours between decoying. Tealer was quietly watching as the decoyer's strong brown fingers threaded withies between the hazel uprights. Mart the dog lay in the gloom, panting in the heat and snapping at the odd horse-fly.

Pole darted Tealer a quick look, and Tealer now knew that this indicated a willingness to engage in some rudimentary conversation. So he started on the usual unsequential list of things he had stored up to be asked of Pole next time he saw him.

"What did you catch last week, Jointy?"

Without looking up, Pole answered: "Two score mallud."

"That's good, isn't it?"

"Int so bad." Still without looking up

"What's the most you ha' ever caught?"

"Much more'n 'at."

A silence. From outside the hut came the *quack-wack-ack-ack-ack* of mallard, the *quark* of waterhen, and the *plink* of coot from the decoy broad. Inside the hut the buzzing of flies and the occasional snapping of Mart's thin jaws mixed with the creak and swish of the withies, and the intermittent whack of Pole's mallet on the hurdle to make the weave tight, and a sucking noise as he drew the last fumes from his pipe.

"Ha' you caught any pike since I last come?"

"Yuh."

"Big'n?"

"Nigh on twe'eh poun'."

"Where'd you catch it?"

"Langham's pit."

"What d'you catch it with?"

"Rudd."

"Live or dead?"

"Dead." No look up, no halt in the rhythm of the fingers on the hurdle. Pole didn't even glance at the boy as he reached to take the next strand to weave into the frame.

"Were you ever married, Jointy?"

"No."

"Were you ever a-courtin?"

"Long while ago."

There was another period without communication, with only the buzzing, the snaps, the creaking and swishing, the mallet thumps and sucking on empty clay.

"Where's Langham's pit?"

"Acrorst th'other side o' th' decoy."

"Is 'at deep?"

"Two fathom or thereabout."

More hurdle-making.

"Jointy, who'd win between a rook and a crow?"

"Crow, I reckon. But then a rook usually have friends about…."

Buzz, snap. Creak, swish. Thump. Thump.

"…so Mr Crow, he keep out the way."

Buzz, snap. Creak, swish.

Tealer then took a deep breath.

"Jointy, do you reckon there's such thing as Black Shuck?"

The buzzing of the flies and Mart's tormented snappings went on unabated, but – just for a second or two – there was a break in the rhythmic sounds of Jointy Pole's hurdle-making. He did not look up, but his hands had frozen mid-weave.

Then he carried on with his hurdle. He said nothing, and Tealer was resigning himself to the fact that this all-important question, the one that had made him swallow hard before asking it, was one of those that Pole was going to ignore.

But then Pole said, almost as if to himself, "The Shuck dog. What do *you* know about him then, boy?"

Tealer was caught slightly off-guard by this reversal in roles. "Well, thas a big old ghost dog that go about frightening people in the lokes and the marshes."

"Oh-ar." said Pole, reaching for another withy, still without looking up.

"He howl very much."

"Oh-ar."

"And he a' got red eyes."

"Oh-ar. What else?"

"Well…He don't stay in one place, but wander about."

"What else you heard about'm?"

"Sometimes he come after you and kill you," said Tealer, remembering all that he had been told by the various others he'd questioned. "But sometimes he don't, but even if he don't bite you – even if you just see him – you're still done for."

"Oh-ar."

"But…"

"But what?"

Tealer didn't want as valued a guru as Pole to think him foolish, so he said "But I know some people reckon thas all squit, and there int such thing as a devil dog."

Pole finished his row and banged it down with his mallet, which he then put back under his seat.

"Well then they're wrong," he said. He said it so matter-of factly, so without emotion that Tealer wondered if he'd heard right.

"What did you say?"

"I said, they're wrong. " Pole was now holding his hurdle up, checking that his withy strands were lying parallel between the hazel uprights.

"D'you mean you think thas real?"

No immediate answer. Pole was concentrating hard on the hurdle, following the line of each withy from start to finish. Then: "Oh yes, thas real, alright."

Tealer would have dismissed such nonchalance from anyone else as artificial. But Pole was a man devoid of artifice, and Tealer knew it, which was why he was awestruck. This was a simple affirmation of the existence of the demon dog by the man, the very man, whose opinion on marsh lore Tealer's sceptical uncle Palmer prized above all others! It caught Tealer short, because he was expecting to be told the opposite.

This was unnerving, and was about to become more so.

There was a long silence now, broken only by Mart's attempts to rid the hut of warble flies. Tealer hardly dared breathe.

At length:

"The Shuck." said Pole. "You want t'know about him, do you? Oh."

He took another withy and carried on his work. And he began to talk at more length. His tone throughout never wavered from his habitual, undramatic mumble. "The eyes int just red. They glow like gret ol' crimson balls in the dark." He began to weave another line. "And that don't just howl. That make a noise like nothing I hint navver heard n'my life. Thas just like thas stranglin' isself." He finished the line and walloped it with his mallet. "Thas just as though 'at loathe every man and beast on earth." For a moment Pole's fierce brown face gazed at some point half-way between him and the wide-eyed child perched on the wicker stool on the other side of the doorway. Then he carried on weaving. "And 'at wander around for days and days before 'at come to claim its own." He finished his line and banged with his mallet, which he put down again. "And thas certainly right that 'at don't have to bite a man's throat out to kill'm..." He shook the hurdle and pounded it a few times with his fist, and, satisfied with its resilience, he leant it against the wall of the hut. "...as I know only too well." Then he reached for his wallet of tobacco and started filling his clay.

After a while he said "A good deal o' people say old Shuck is always a dog." Then he got up and went out, followed automatically by Mart. This was only to light his pipe from a taper he took from the eternal flame at the back of the hut. He came back in and sat down "...but thas wrong," he said.

The story Pole then went on to tell was a long one, and his mode of narrative made it longer. Snippets of information were inserted into the natural breaks that occurred in whichever task he was about, whether the building of a hurdle, the sharpening of a tool or the filling of a pipe. The result was a series of simple sentences or phrases, each one an island of speech in a sea of busy silence. As he spoke he didn't look at Tealer at all but stared the while at his handiwork, only glancing occasionally through the doorway of the dark hut at the sunny waterscape that seethed with insects outside. If it was a ruse to keep Tealer's attention, straining for the next morsel, it worked – yet this was incidental. When Jointy said anything to anyone at all he only spoke as he thought: slowly, methodically and only at those intervals that were convenient to him.

"Yer Shuck can be whatever he want," he said. "He can be a cat or a crow or a lizard. But really old Shuck is a demon. Like them demons what the Lord Jesus driv into them Gadderin swine. As we learn about in church. But he *prefer* to live in dogs. Thas why everyone say he *is* a dog. An they say he's always evil. Thas wrong an'all. He come to *punish* evil. To my way o'thinkin'. But sometimes the good pay with the bad. Like when King Herod killed all them littl'uns. As we know from St Matthew. You only hear the Shuck's about after someone ha'done suffin' bad. Suffin' right bad. Or after suffin' right bad ha' been brought into the area. Suffin' what navver oughtera bin allowed."

Tealer then heard himself asking Pole if that meant the Shuck could appear as a person as well as an animal.

"That he can. As you'll hear."

"Oh," said Tealer, "thank you."

Pole puffed meditatively on his pipe, purposefully blowing jets of blue smoke round the hut to drive out the flies. Then he inserted new uprights in the 'mould', the baulk of timber with regular holes that served as his hurdle frame, and he started on a second hurdle, grunting and frowning with concentration. A casual listener might have thought he'd lost interest in the subject, but Tealer knew that nothing ever hurried Pole any more than it ever delayed him.

"Cork Norton was the last man I knew fell foul o' the Shuck," the decoyman said finally. And still with the pauses, and still without any fluctuation in tone or emphasis, he proceeded to tell the strange tale of a man, another Suffolk decoyer by the name of Stanley 'Cork' Norton. And even though he was now cutting to the chilling heart of his account, the inexorable, matter-of-fact tone and single sentence delivery was unchanged.

"We used to call him 'Cork'. Thas 'cause as a boy he was always a-fall'n in, yet navver did drown. Perhaps that was his bad fortune. What *did* happen to him was a sight worse than drownin'. *I* reckon, anyway. I heard that Cork had come back from the sea. He come back to find a woman. Settle down. Poor ole fool.

"His father had been the decoyman down at Flixton. Next broad down from here, other side o' Somerleyton, t'ward Low'stoft. After ol' man Norton died there wunt no-one else on the estate knew the decoyin'. 'Cept his boy Cork. So Cork get offered the job, an' he took it."

Pole's fast hands had already built up one quarter of another hurdle in the time he had taken to vouchsafe these stages in the sad biography of Norton. He went on "Yer see, we'd been boys together. Learnin' decoyin' from our gaffers. So now he was back I thought to go down the road to see him. Have a mardle."

He shook his head in private despair at some unstated recollection, and then carried on:

"Thas when 'at all started." The next pause was also a long one because Pole had found a withy that had split during the weaving. He pulled it out, cast it aside, and picked another from his pile. And then, once more with short pauses between each instalment, he picked up the thread of his narrative.

"There's a big ole wood right round Flixton village and the Flixton decoy. Road from Lound go right through the middle on it, so I had to go through it to get to Flixton. That was where I began t'feel suffin' wunt right. Felt I was bein' a-followed. Felt I was bein' a-watched. From the trees acrorst 'way. So I stop and look. But I couldn't see nothin'. So I look back ahead. Then I suddenly stop an' look acrorst the way again. And thas when I seen what I seen."

At this point Pole broke off from telling his story and for once looked Tealer straight in the eye.

"Perhaps I didn't oughta be a-tellin' you this. I don't want to get wrong off your uncle Palmer."

"He won't mind," said Tealer, possibly truthfully. "But what did you see? Was that the Shuck dog you saw in the trees?"

"No, young sir, 'at wunt the Shuck dog.' 'Least, that might ha' been the Shuck… but that wunt no dog." Pole stopped and took a deep breath. He was still unsure whether he should carry on. "That was an ole man."

"An old man?"

"Yes."

"Well…, what was strange about that, then?"

"Nothin'. 'Cept his head worn't no bigger'n an apple."

Tealer looked at Pole to see if he was still being serious, just as Pole glanced at Tealer to see if he was being taken seriously. Neither need have worried.

On Pole went.

"…and his face was… red. No, not red, scarlet. That was jus' like one o' them there devil faces. One of them devil faces what you get a-paintn'd in old bibles. And then 'at disappeared."

Jointy stared at the roof of the hut as though he had just had an idea for its renovation.

" 'course, you get no end o' rum tricks on the eyes in these here woods at night," he said and returned to his weaving. "Thas what I reckoned that was. A trick o' the light. I didn't think nothing more of it for the while. I was just happy to see my old mate Cork. We got to talkin'. We talked about what he'd done in foreign parts. We talked about what we used to get up to as young'uns. Then I mentioned what I seen in the woods. For a moment Cork din't say nothing.

He dint smile. He dint frown. But he looked right queer. Then he laughed and told me to stop talkin' squit. He said I'd lived in Decoy wood long enough. Long enough to know better than to be fooled. Sunlight comin' low through the trees, he said. So I dint think no more on it.

"Next few times we met up was when he come up here to help me at Decoy Lake. So 'at was a good few weeks 'fore I had any reason to go down to Flixton. But when I did, more strange things happened."

Pole took a swig at a mug of ale, and as he did so his eyes swept the whole hut, taking in everything except the motionless face of his listener.

"I'm a-walking down the Flixton road. Hadn't even reached the wood. I see this here fox a-comin up the road t'ward me. And I thought at first that couldn't ha' saw me. But 'at had. 'At was coming stret toward me. And 'at was a-givin me the evil eye. 'Goo on!' I holler at it. 'Goo on!' And 'at just disappeared back into the wood. Then there was this squirrel. 'At dint run up the tree and hide, as they do. 'At ran up and down the tree, up an'down, up an' down, for no reason. Then I saw a stoat that was just layin' in the grass. Just a-starin' at something in the middle o' nowhere.

" Well, I said suffin' 'bout it to Cork. But he just shrug his shoulders. Well, I'd heard o' evil spirits taken over a wood or a piece of land. I was beginnin' to get worrited. But I dint want to upset Cork with such talkin'. After all, he'd only just lost his old chap. So I still dint say nothin'." Pole shook his head again.

"Then I went down there about twelve week afterward. I was go' stay o'ernight in Cork's hut in Flixton woods. I was go' help him with the early decoy. And 'at was gettin' dark when I got to Flixton. And I got to the spot where I had seen that goblin thing. That thing wi' the red face what I just now told you about. I dint see it again. But I wunt happy. 'Cause I reckoned suffin' was up. I couldn't see nothin' this time. There weren't no strange creatures about. Then I thought t'myself: yes, and thas it! There ent *any* creatures about. Not e'en the sounds or noises of creatures. Well, you know yourself, boy, there's always noises of a summer evening. You get voles scrabbin' about in the sedge. Or rabbits runnin' around in the ferns. Or thumpin' on the sand. Owls kek-kekkin'. And when you hear none o' that…. When you hear none o' that, you know suffin' int right. Made me shug, that did. Then, blust, I *did* hear suffin'. And what I heard then… well 'at made me more'n just shug. That was a pantin'.

"Panting?" asked Tealer before he could stop himself, "What – you mean – panting like a dog?"

"Yes."

"Ah," said Tealer, quietly.

"Yes, a-pantin'..." continued Pole, "That was gettin' closer and closer. So I turn round to see what 'at was behind me. But at that seal o' evenin' in summer there's all kind of shadow and what-have-you in a loke. So I couldn't see nothin'. And then... I seen a shape like a dog. Like a dog. And a-zigzaggin' about as though 'at was arter suffin'. Then 'at stopped. Then 'at look up. And thas when 'at seen me. An 'at let out a noise. Not a bark, nor nothin' like a bark. 'At wunt even a howl. An 'at started a-comin arter me. I thought that was time to git myself somewhere else. So I run down the road. And along the path to Cork's hut. Thas when I knew for sure that dog was arter me. 'Cause I heard it a pad-paddin' behind me. I had a good start on it, mind. But when I got to the door... When I got to the door, that was locked. 'Course, I banged, and banged, and hollered. And by-and-by that opened. There was Cork lookin' even more scared'n what I was. 'Come you in quick!' he shout. And he drag me in. And he shut the door behind me. An' he bolted it. He told me the dog ha' chased him into the hut, and 'at ha' been about all day since. So we sat in that hut. A listenin' an a-listenin' till our ears nigh fell off. But we dint hear nothin'. Arter an hour or more we thought we'd have a look. We slid the bolt. We unlatched, and we began to pull the door open. And that was when there was this almighty gret thump against it. And a right terrible growlin'. 'Course we both on us pushed. But that could ha' been a hoss on the other side. At first that forced the door back inch by inch. An' thas then I seen the eyes. Through the crack. They were like two gret ole balls o' red glass. A-glintin' an' a-glitterin'. Angry, wick'd eyes. That wunt like no dog I ever seen. Nor heard, neither. That was like...,

Pole looked out at the water briefly and screwed his eyes up, trying to find the right adjective. He gave up.

"And 'at was bitin' gret ole chunks out the door. If ever you go down to that hut on Flixton Lake you want to have a look. You can still see the dints."

But Tealer did not see himself going down to the Flixton Lake in the near future. He was seriously alarmed, perhaps more than Pole realized.

By this time Pole had put his next completed hurdle down and was simply puffing on his pipe between phrases. Suddenly he seemed to realize this, and he started on a new hurdle. But the story went on:

"We did get the door shut in th'end. I can't imagine what'd ha' happened if we hint. But we were lucky. Well, Cork *did* get bit. But just a nick on his arm. I soon had that stopped wi' cobwebs. Out the corner of the hut. And for the rest o' the night… for the rest of the night we could hear that hound a-prowlin' and a-paddin. Back and forth, back and forth. Outside Cork's hut. Then toward dawn I remember that began to rain. And 'at seem to drive the creature away. 'At set up a worse din than ever. But acrorst th'other side o' the wood. Then that went quiet. We dint hear it n'more.

"But we dussn't come out that hut for two days. Cork had already been inside for hours afore I got there. He reckoned the beast had chased him there all the way from the decoy. So we sat in there an drank ale and ate cheese and listened. Neither on us said the word 'Shuck'. Neither on us wanted to think thas who 'at was. But we both knew. Both on us.

"When we come out I went straight t'church. To thank the Lord for my escape. I dint hear nothin' about the dog n' more. I reckoned that was the end on it. Perhaps that'd died. Perhaps someone'd shot it. I thought that was the end on it. Arter all, what'd happened was bad enough…. But…" Pole shifted his position slightly on his wicker chair which creaked, causing Mart to jump up and watch his master with ears cocked "…but what come next was wust of all."

He ordered the dog back down and then settled himself more comfortably to tell the last chapter in the tragedy.

"Cork had said he'd come up to Decoy Lake. T'see how I was getting' on once the winter flightin' had started. But he never did come. I never heard nothin' from him. Not until the fellow who bought my ducks in them days… Not until he told me he'd visited Cork earlier that week. T'see if he had ducks for sale. But he said Cork had been laid up wi' the sickness. And he hint done no decoyin'. So come the fust week in March down I go to Flixton lake again. Nothin' to upset me on the road, not this time. And what wi' the snow-drops and primroses in the banks… with the flowers, and 'at, I was feelin' quite happy. That dint last long.

"I got to Cork's hut an' found the door locked again. I shouted out to Cork.

'Are yer there, ole partner?', I shout. Well, fust of all I dint hear nothin'. Then I hear someone a-movin' about. 'Cork?' I go, 'are y'alright?' Then I reckon I hear a noise like gaspin'. That was as if someone couldn't breathe right. So I reckon Cork ha' got a problem. So I took a run at the door and fetched it down."

Pole stopped. This stop wasn't for effect but because he had decided to start on a new hurdle, and he was concentrating on driving the uprights into the mould. His tone of voice seemed more humdrum than ever as he resumed.

"Well, what I found a starin' at me was a fiend. An evil spirit. 'Cept that weren't. That were poor old Cork. I hint navver seen a man in that way. He was a-stand'n up on his bunk. With his back 'gainst the wall. His hair was standin' on end. There was a terrible smell, an'all. Well, 'course he'd been a-layin' in his own mess for days. And he was a-starin' at me. As if *I* was Satan come to take *him* down to Hell.

" 'Get you away from me!' he go. 'Cork,' I say, 'thas me, Jointy.' But that wunt no good. 'Get you away from me!' he go. 'I know what you want,' he go. 'You want drown me in the decoy,' he go. 'That I don't,' I say, 'whatever make you want t'think a thing like that?'

"So I tried to get him a drink from the butt. But 'at wunt no good. He start a-loutin' an' a-hollerin' and a-bendin' his back. Bendin' his back just like what an adder do when you fetch it a crack wi' a stick. Well… well… Well, there's a deal more I could tell you. But I aren't goin' to. Bein' as you're a young'un. But that wunt much fun to see."

Tealer asked. "Did he die?"

Pole didn't answer, nor did he even acknowledge the child's question. He simply took up where he'd left off.

"He began to calm down. He began to breathe easier. He let me come up and put a damp dwile on his head. Then he began to talk some sense. Not much sense, mind. On account he was right sick. But.. but.. at least he had stopped sayin' I wanted t'drown him. I could just make out what he was on about. Though that was hard. You see he was still pantin', gaspin' and sweatin'. E'en though he'd stopped his loutin'.

" 'I'm done for, bor,' he go. 'I'm done for… Thas 'cause I stole that… wakri… from the market in Salv'dor,' he go. 'An' I brought it here.' 'I'm a-payin',' he say,

'I'm payin'. 'At was a wicked thing what I done' he say. 'Thas why the Shuck come for me', he say."

"*What* did he say he stole?" asked Tealer.

"Thas what I couldn't understand m'self, Mas' John. So I ask him. 'What do you mean, a "wakri", Cork?' I ask him. 'You seen it,' he say. 'Red-faced devil.' An' thas when I remembered that thing what I seen a-watchin' me in the Flixton wood. But then poor Cork started a-mutterin' to the fairies again. I could see he was a-goin' back to how he was before.

"I reckoned I ought t'get help. But I dint know what to do. You see, all Cork's folks were dead – his father'd been a six-month's corpse up the church-yard when Cork got back from the ships. So up I go to the big house. So up I go to the big house to get someone to tell Mas' Frederick. He was a good man, Mas' Frederick. Allus was to me, any rate. He come to the door an' I told him what'd happened… He nod and look right serious. I thought he might send his keeper down, but he wanted t'come hisself.

"Course 'at took us a fair while to get back to Flixton. When we got back to the hut we go in together… There's old Cork a-layin' on his bunk. Right still. Not how he was when I left him. Mas' Frederick, he go up to Cork an' say… He say 'Stanley,' he say, 'my good old fellow, can you hear me?' Cork lay there right still. He didn't say nothin'. Mas' Frederick say to me, he say… he say, 'I have seen this before, Harry. It doesn't look well,' he say. Then he put his head right close to Cork's. And suddenly Cork wake up and tried to bite Mas' Frederick in the face. But Mas' Frederick was ready. He jump back and left Cork a-twistin' an' writhin' on the bunk. And Mas' Frederick look at me very serious. He didn't say nothin' for a moment. Then he pull this pistol out o'his pocket. He go back to Cork and say… He say 'Stanley,' he say, 'can you hear me?' he say. 'You must get ready to meet your Creator,' he say. I remember them were the exact words what he used. And he was then go' shoot Cork in the head. But blust me if Cork dint shug an' die afore Mas' Frederick had the chance to fire his gun."

Pole by this time had finished his last hurdle. He piled it up with the rest. Then he filled his pipe again and re-lit.

"So there y'are, young Mas' John… There int nothin' pretend about the Shuck. Nor about what he can do. I wonder *I* aren't dead…. Seein' as I laid eyes on him. But then I trust our Lord Jesus. He keep me from such evil spirits as there might

The Strange and Terrible End of Cork Norton

be in the carrs and the marshes. Every Sunday I go to morning service at the Decoy church. Sometimes evensong at Somerleyton. I am a wretched sinner. I know that. But I don't believe I ever done anything *right* wicked. But anyway, the Lord Jesus Christ is my avvercate in Heaven. An thas only the guilty what have to fear from such things as ol' Shuck. Only the guilty."

There was silence again as Pole regarded his last hurdle, and then he started taking the completed hurdles outside one by one.

When he'd finished and was sitting down again it was Tealer that broke the next period of silence, fully three minutes, by clearing his throat carefully and asking what Pole supposed Norton might have done to bring the Shuck down on him. Pole, ever busy, continued in his interrupted style of narration:

"Why, any man can see what he done. He brought that there red-faced hobgoblin over from foreign parts. What he call a 'wakri'. An' 'at was that what brought the evil into the marshes. Thas clear: there never was a place for such a creature in a Christian land. As I said, thas always suffin' from outside… Always suffin' from outside what cause the Shuck to… "

But Tealer interrupted him this time. "But did you ever see this goblin with the red face again? Are you sure 'at was real?"

"Why, yes, young sir. I still got it."

"*What?*"

"I found it where Cork had killed it. Round the back of his hut. I keep it in a basket at the edge of the Decoy. 'Cause they say you can use the remains of one such evil creature… To keep the others away. An' thas right. I hint never seen the Shuck back here. Not since that night 'at come arter us. So I reckon 'at must work."

He was cleaning the mallet-head in a pail of water, possibly not even aware that Tealer was staring open-mouthed. Before Tealer could speak, Pole added:

"Did you want to see it?"

Tealer nodded slowly. It had occurred to him that he was having one of his bad dreams, and that the worst part was just coming.

"That int pretty! Are you sure?"

Tealer nodded again.

"Stay you here, an I'll get it. Stay there, dog! – don't want *you* nowhere near it."

He went out leaving Tealer alone in the hut with Mart. Mart looked intently at the doorway and then at Tealer to see if the boy held any clue as to why Pole had disappeared outside without taking Mart with him.

Eventually the decoyer came back with a wicker basket which he set down on the floor. He pulled the lid off and said: "There y'go, boy. But don't look for too long, 'cause I reckon 'at still have the evil eye."

Tealer looked in.

No more than a foot long, and dressed in grubby miniature clothes, lay the shrivelled, mummified, grinning corpse of a red-faced goblin.

An hour later Tealer was sitting beside his uncle as Vulcan took them back to Yarmouth.

"He's a good old boy, Johnny," his uncle was saying "and you want to listen to everything he have to say. Especially as he seem to have taken to you. He's very choosy about who he talk to, especially young'uns. I reckon thas because you're a quiet one, like him."

Tealer was quiet on this occasion, too. He did not feel like broaching the tale of the dead Cork Norton immediately. He watched the swallows gathering on the gateposts ready for their journey south and listened to his uncle's tales of adventures with Pole.

Then his uncle asked: "What did you talk to Jointy about this time?"

"Flixton Decoy."

"Flixton, eh?"

"And a fellow called Cork Norton who was the decoyer there," said Tealer.

"Oh yes," said Palmer, "Poor old Stanley Norton. Served on my ship a few times. And… er… what did Jointy tell you about him then?"

"Nothin' very much, 'cept they used to help each other sometimes. But what was up with him? Why was he 'poor' Stanley?"

"Oh, only that he died young."

"How?"

"How? Oh, never mind that now. Long old story. Tell me what Jointy had to give you. He always give you somethin' when you go round there."

And at the same time as Tealer and Palmer were having this discussion on the way back to Gorleston, Jointy Pole was poking the embers of the fire outside his hut. To an observer he would look no different from how he ever looked: deliberate, serious, thoughtful. There was no way to tell that the object of his pondering was Tealer Sayer.

He was thinking that the handful of other people to whom he'd shown the contents of the wicker basket had all recoiled with exclamations of revulsion. Yet that was not how the boy Sayer had acted at all. He had looked sad and resigned more than anything else, as though some familiar, unwelcome guest had arrived unexpectedly.

That puzzled Pole mightily.

Pole didn't know that an old succubus in new form, invisible to him, invisible to everyone except John 'Tealer' Sayer, had crept up so close behind the boy that as he had left Pole's camp he could feel the thing's hot, foetid breath on his neck.

We must understand that before that meeting with Pole, Tealer had actually become a little attracted to the stories of Black Shuck, notwithstanding his own experience on the marsh.

Once Bitten...

Oh, yes, the Shuck!

The Shuck was not merely an evil presence that had chosen to haunt the marshes; it *was* the marshes. It was the unfettered beast, dark, wonderful, malign and free. It was the shiver in the reeds by day that might only be the wind. Shuck was the shape in your yard by night that might or might not be a cloud crossing the moon. Shuck was a steady rhythm of four feet following you from the other side of the hedge that you heard, or thought that you heard, as you made your lonely way home through the pitch black of the back lane from the inn.

But now? Now Tealer's head was full of a sad and sickening tale, and told by none other than the uncompromisingly honest Jointy Pole. And the central fact, the existence of the Shuck-dog, was corroborated by almost everybody else worth listening to (with the important exception of Palmer). And then in the back of Tealer's mind was that frenzied figure of eight and the yowls of the dying cat in Charlie's yard. And then also that urgent, remorseless panting of a pursuing dog he'd heard down by the fort. And the strange sight of that shrivelled gnome-thing, glaring as it was glaring when it had been killed. And the image of the decoyer Norton, perhaps a man very like Jointy himself, writhing around in his own excrement, and so lost to reason that he feared drowning in his own water jug. No romance now; only the dread of a hateful and loathsome thing, sent to condemn the wicked to a terrible end. And who could be more wicked than the fallen young Gorleston Tabernacler?

This was now the Shuck that padded in the twilit lanes of Tealer's mind.

The next scene in this final episode in the childhood of Tealer Sayer is a cloudless summer evening about a week on from that vivid meeting with Jointy Pole. Tealer was sitting alone in a field on the Wickhampton road, across the marshes from Yarmouth. Nothing could be further from his mind than the sombre tale of Cork Norton and the red-faced goblin. He was now eleven, and this was the first time he had been allowed to tote a firearm without close supervision, and he felt great pride at the weight of the 28-bore on his arm. It was late August, only a day or two after harvest, and he was hiding in amongst the barley shocks. He was scanning the sky for the wild mallard which had been seen over the last few nights coming in to feed on the gleanings.

He also had his fishing rod with him, because he and his uncle had spent most of the afternoon alternately fishing and swimming in the Fleet Dyke. His straight blond hair had dried and curled in the sun, and his clothes had the unmistakable earthen odour of fresh dyke water. All-in-all he was very excited to be there. His uncle was in a wheat field half a mile down the road towards Reedham. What ever could dislodge him from such a perfect position on such a perfect night, ready to bag his first plump mallard unaided?

He was about to find out.

The air turned cooler as evening advanced. For whatever reason, the duck weren't flighting early. After an hour of intense scanning of the pink sky, Tealer's concentration began to wane. He started noticing features of the landscape. He was intrigued to watch a sea-mist roll in from Breydon and across the marshes below him, leaving the grazing cattle and horses floating on a placid sea of vapour. He knew it could be another hour before the whicker of mallard wings would set his heart racing. He opened his knapsack and took out the cheese and bottle of ginger wine it contained. He sat chewing on the cheese and taking meditative gulps from the wine bottle. He stared into the blank of the mist, and found himself thinking about his younger life, and in particular about his parents. What would they have thought of him now? Would they really have disapproved? Nowadays he only occasionally felt twinges of guilt that he now lived a life so alien to their strict code. They were not bad folk, he thought. Daisy was always telling him that they'd done their best for him, even if they were a little stern in their manner. The best bird book on his book-shelf was not in fact given him by his uncle, but by his father. He had given it quietly, furtively, unsmilingly, and with something muttered about the glory of God's creation. Couldn't have been long before they both died. And for all that people were convinced otherwise, Tealer never remembered either his parents laying a finger on him, however flagrantly he'd transgressed the unbending rule of the House of Sayer. Yet look at Charlie Harrison, whose freedom in those far off Gorleston days Tealer had been so jealous of. Charlie was often black and blue with the hidings dished out to him.

This wasn't the only time Tealer found himself thinking like this.

He was no doubt much happier now. Every holiday his uncle would have some new adventure in the shooting, sailing or fishing line planned for them. Every evening there would be some anecdote of boar hunting in the Punjab, or mahseer fishing in the Indus or a brush with dacoits in Burma, and Tealer cared not a jot if half of it was make-believe. And then there was the endless stream of new curios that they would dig out from his uncle's wooden chests. The skull of a maneater, complete with broken teeth ("which is what caused it to start eating men, boy"); a series of ivory balls of grotesque oriental shapes that revolved one inside another, all carved with ineffable patience in a nameless alley in Macao; the awesome cartridge of a Sharps breech-loading rifle, almost like an artillery round.

No, the grim fare of bible readings that were the evening entertainment in his parents' house were hardly much to compare. But had James and Harriet actually been so hard…?

Still, this was his first night out alone with the gun, and he had to concentrate on scanning the orange-pink-blue of the horizon for duck. Yet twinges of guilt poked through his excitement. He wondered…

But his wondering was halted by the sight of something moving fast across the marsh below him, right at the edge of his field of vision. He watched it blankly. It seemed as big as a deer, but moved with the motion of a dog. He watched through the mist, but there was no reappearance. Then, almost immediately the rhythmic whicker of duck wings forced his eyes back to the sky. But he had been indiscreet: the turn of his head had been spotted by his quarry. The birds veered off to some less suspect quarter of the upland stubble. Tealer's ears strained the field for any other sounds of duck.

The next sound was neither the muttering of mallard duck nor the whicker of their wings. It was a noise that turned Tealer's vitals liquid. It was a familiar panting. He spun round trying to place it, but couldn't. It stopped for a moment and started again. He stood up, knocking over one of the sheaves. Three duck that had not seen him braked and changed direction with a desperate whooshing of wings, but he didn't even look up at them. He was turning round and round, trying to place where the creature that was hunting him was coming from.

Still there seemed no direction. Yet the insistent, relentless noise bore down on him.

All the images crowded in: Grinder's figure of eight, Cork's anguished death, Pole's hideous mannequin. Tealer was breathing hard in bursts and then holding his breath. The panting in the dusk was urgent and unremitting. He looked around in the evening light for anyone to call out to, but Norfolk fields are big, and he was alone.

Finally, his nerve broke. He jumped out from behind the barley shock with his gun, not bothering to pick up his fishing rod and the rest of his gear. He raced up the hill, slipping on the dry, shiny stubble, and finally arrived gasping at the Reedham road. He stopped to listen. The creature in the gloom behind him came on. He was still being chased! He was exhausted now, but the image of the dread dog forced his legs to drive on. He stopped again. The panting came on after him. On he went until way down the road he could see the top-hatted form of his uncle sitting in the shelter of a straw-rick.

Even with his muscles awash with the spirits of fear, Tealer was now beginning to buckle and stumble. He had been running flat out for five minutes, with a (for him) heavy gun in one hand. Under his stout tweed waistcoat and breeks his body was swimming in perspiration. He tried to shout to his uncle, but before he could make a sound his Palmer bawled out:

"Stop! Is that gun cocked?"

It was. Normally Tealer would have been mortified at having broken one of the most basic rules of shooting in such a clumsy way on his very first day alone with the gun. Now he was too shocked to care – with shaking fingers he took out the percussion caps and eased the hammers off cock.

Palmer was preparing to give the boy a major dressing down for the breach of so much safety and etiquette, but the words died in his throat when he saw that was that Tealer was not even listening to him but was staring all around in a state of distraction. Clearly something had left the child petrified.

" 'Deuce is the matter, Johnny?"

Exhaustion and fright had rendered Tealer speechless. "D-dog. D-d-d-dog Cha-chasing me."

"I see no dog."

"Thas there. B-b-behind me. I heard it."

Palmer looked around in the misty sunset.

"There's no dog behind you. Sit you down here and get your breath back. Good

God, you're wringin', boy."

Gradually Tealer relaxed, as his uncle took out some water from a flask to give to him. Then he stiffened again and jumped up from the straw as he heard something. It was very faint, but to his sensitised ears, very definite.

"There it is!" he yelled. " There! There! You *must* hear it. There!"

And his uncle cocked his head, listening for any sound other than the lowing of cattle coming up from the marsh, and the summer evening songs of blackbirds in the hawthorn hedge at the top end of the field.

"I can't hear a thing, boy, but then too many guns ha' gone off right by my poor old lugs for me to hear very much… " Then he stiffened too, and listened harder. He put his own gun down and cupped his ears in the direction that Tealer had come from. He listened for about half a minute. But instead of picking up his gun again and drawing back the hammers in preparation for the coming horror, he merely smiled faintly. He looked at his nephew:

"Where's your rod? And your knapsack?"

Tealer pointed to the field he had just left in such a hurry.

"Well then, you'd better go and get them, hadn't you?"

Tealer looked at his uncle in disbelief. Palmer's eyes were screwed up against the last fierce rays of the sunset, making it impossible to read his expression. He went on: "And if you see old Shuck…"

"But I… I never said anything about the Shuck!"

"No. Well, *any* old dog, then. Anyway, take your gun, and if you see *any* wild dog a-comin' for you, whether thas a ghost dog, or a real dog, or some in-between sort o' dog – well, do you give him a dose! And watch out for them old Frenchmen too. There are a fair few of *them* about in the wheat tonight, an' all. A right fair few."

Tealer looked down the deserted path, which the mist was beginning to obscure. He did not much care for the idea of going back along that road on his own. He looked at his uncle again, whose expression in the setting sun was still not to be read, though Tealer reckoned from his tone that he was mightily amused, which the boy could not understand.

But there was nothing for it.

Tealer set off out of the field, and back down the road toward his own hide. He was a little less apprehensive now that he had seen his uncle so relaxed; but as the watching form of Palmer disappeared from view Tealer felt alone again.

As if on cue, the panting noise resumed. There *was* something there. A dog following him, waiting for him. He *hadn't* been wrong.

Should he go back?

No, he decided, he would not. He was armed – and he would persevere.

Then there was an explosion of sound in the gloom ahead, and his heart nearly came out through his mouth. He brought the twenty-eight bore wildly to his shoulder, but didn't fire. It took only half a second for him to realise that he had put up a covey of red-legged partridges that had been feeding on ants in the dust by the road-side. He watched the birds speed away upland, some calling their *chuk churr-churr* as they became lost in the gathering dusk.

Partly to give himself time to recover, Tealer stood for a minute or two listening to their calling as they landed and settled out of sight. He noticed that at a distance their calls were reduced to a faint *churr-churr, churr-churr,* with the distinctive first syllable lost in the thick evening air.

This made them sound like nothing so much as a large panting dog, always approaching, but never arriving out of the darkness.

So, then - both here on the Wickhampton road and below the Burgh Castle weeks ago, Tealer had been fooled by the calling of red-legs. 'Frenchmen', as his uncle liked to call them.

Tealer shot no duck on that first solo expedition. By the time he got back to his own hide the light had gone. The critical fifteen minutes – which are what the preparation of any duck flight is all for – had passed. On their way back to Yarmouth that evening his uncle said quietly and not unsympathetically, "There's *always* an explanation for everything you see and hear in the field, boy. You'll only be a sportsman and an Englishman if you make it your business to find out what that explanation is."

He never again mentioned that evening duck flight on the Reedham road.

A few days further into that formative late summer found the *Hermione* at a regatta on Oulton Broad. Tealer and Palmer were sailing with Mrs Durrant and Mrs Durrant's cousin Miss Collins, as well as Tealer's friend Charlie Harrison. Miss Collins was a pretty but vapid red-head of Anglo-Irish stock who was shortly to marry Pritchard the Gorleston hatmaker, and she was wearing one of his most flamboyant creations to keep the August sun off her freckly complexion.

It was one of those glorious late summer days, when everything around – the water, the sails of the yachts, the parasols, the swans, the men's linen jackets, the women's dresses, the picnic cloth – seemed not just to reflect the sun but to glow with light of its own.

The *Hermione* had joined a convoy of other vessels that had tacked down the Waveney from Yarmouth in the early afternoon either to watch the racing or to take part in it. Now most of the waterborne spectators were setting set off home up the river, their faces flushed from the sun on the water and their eyes full of the lights of the day.

They had the gentlest southern breeze to push them along the Oulton Dyke and then the Waveney where the ebb tide would speed their journey back into Norfolk. The river itself was supremely peaceful, with just the creak of the sheets, the call of the coots and the faintest wash from the bow, mingling with the muttered conversations from other crews ahead of them echoing down the water. The reedbeds were filled with the incessant rhythms of the reed warblers, each one continuing where the last left off, creating a chain of chattering song as they journeyed along. Beyond them in the marshes were the fainter songs of the yellowhammers and skylarks. Tealer was lodged in the bow with a small telescope watching a rare grebe diving into the opaque brown waters of the river. Charlie was next to him sketching wherries and other large craft as they passed. Mrs Durrant and Miss Collins were sitting either side of the tiller, each with a dainty hand on its long, firm polished surface. Palmer was sitting amidships smoking a pipe and watching the sail.

Mrs Durrant said: "Do you know, John, I am sure I have been here before."

"That you have, my dear. Last winter we brought the *Hermione* up here. And you might remember I have a small boathouse hidden in the reeds on the next reach." And he turned to Ms Collins and added in a lowered voice that Tealer nevertheless caught: "Thas where I meet my white lady, don't you know?"

Miss Collins simpered, and Mrs Durrant added in a rueful tone, also very quietly,

"Ah, yes. My rival. Take my advice, Maggie dear, don't mix your affairs with those of these hunting men. They keep other loves hidden away in these marshland fastnesses. You're much better off with your hatter, however mad he may turn out to be."

There was more simpering and murmuring. Fingers were no doubt put to lips and then pointed to the backs of the two boys.

And in a louder voice Mrs Durrant said: "But it is so different in this season. Now it is friendly, but then it was all so stark and … sinister. There were no people or boats. I confess I found it quite disturbing."

"Thas the best time, the winter, for coming down here. Ain't I right, young sirs?"

Yes it was, the boys said.

"What do you think then, Charles Harrison?" asked Mrs Durrant.

"I reckon thas much better without people, miss" said Charlie, looking up from his sketch. "I don't like to draw people."

The adults laughed at this, and Miss Collins said: "Well I shouldn't like to come down here alone as you brave men do, even with a gun in my hand. I should be very nervous."

"Nervous? What of, though?" asked Palmer with a laugh.

"All manner of horrid things."

"Such as?"

"Oh, I don't know," said Miss Collins, vaguely.

Up in the prow, Tealer wasn't relaxed. He had an inkling where this conversation might now lead. He pretended to scan the far bank for birdlife through his lens, though he was listening to every word.

"What about that demon dog, for example, that is said to prowl the fens?" said Mrs Durrant.

Tealer squirmed.

"Marshes, my dear," said his uncle. "Fens are in the west of the county."

"Marshes, then. Though I don't suppose the dog is much exercised by the distinction."

"Yes, I have heard of it," said Miss Collins. "Black Jack, or somesuch."

"Black Shuck," Palmer said. Tealer found himself a coot to watch through his telescope and studied it intently.

"Yes, we have a story like that in Ireland. My grandfather used to tell of a similar creature that was said to roam the hills in Wicklow. The locals believed it was a ghost-dog that had been there since the time of the Viking hordes. I remember you telling us that this area was also in thrall to the Vikings, Mr Palmer. Perhaps Black Jack is a ghostly cousin to the Irish dog!"

"My dear Susan, my dear Miss Collins", said Palmer "let me tell you fond ladies what I think about such notions. The man that shun the world's wonderful, quiet, lonely places is the man with a guilty conscience. Because if he *is* guilty, then, yes, if there is anywhere where all the devils from hell will seek him out, then thas in these here marshes. If he have nothing to fear, then this wilderness is a paradise he can enjoy to his heart's content. Thas my belief that both the good and the evil come from the people. The place is only the place. One man's heaven, another's hell. For me thas the first."

"But what if you came to grief down here, Mr Palmer," asked Miss Collins. "I think you would not look up upon it quite so benevolently."

"Pshaw!" he said. "If I come to grief down here – and I may well – then I promise that'll be no doing of Nature but only my own carelessness – or (he grabbed the tiller from the two ladies and jerked it round to keep the wind in the sail) – perhaps the carelessness of others."

"It'll be your liaisons with that other mistress of yours that do for you, John Palmer," said Susan Durrant. "Mark my words."

After some more adult laughter the conversation drifted on to other topics.

But for Tealer this had to come to a head. A mixture of hair-raising tales, terrifying encounters, flat denials and humiliating experiences had left him in no small pother. He decided he must confront his uncle with what he knew. He would lay bare what he had now learnt to be the facts concerning the dog Shuck.

He wouldn't rush in. He'd choose his moment.

But things had to come to a head.

The head was come to in Palmer's study a few days after that sunlit boat-trip to Oulton. It was just before supper, and Palmer called both Tealer and Mrs Durrant into his study. Amid his feathers, books, rocks, eggs, and weapons he was sitting in a pool of brilliant yellow light. As their eyes accustomed to the contrasts they saw that he was staring down the eyepiece of a large brass microscope set in a space he'd hastily cleared amongst the clutter on his bureau. Tealer had never known this microscope existed, but then one of the delights of Palmer's study was the manner in which such unsuspected wonders materialized from nowhere. The microscope had in fact been stored for years in a nondescript box in one corner of the room. The box itself had served humbly as a base for a stuffed mongoose and cobra locked in a battle that was slowly being won by moths and weevils. Now mongoose, cobra and weevils were relegated to the gloom along with all the other curios and bric-a-brac. Now it was the brilliant glow from the body of the newly-resurrected instrument, catching the gleam of the four candles set in brackets on the bureau, that dominated. Around it was scattered a series of slides, each with a minute stain of brown gum at its centre, and each identified in a tiny copperplate: 'foot of beetle', 'scale of worm', 'mouthpart of flea', and so on.

"Bought this from a pawn-brokers in Southwark years and years ago, and thas only now I've had a chance to use it. Look, dear. What do you think that might be?"

Mrs Durrant brushed back various straying locks and and squinted down the eye-piece.

"I have no idea," she said, "but it is something very revolting, I'm sure."

"Wing of a gnat," said Palmer. "Go on boy, have a look."

Tealer climbed up on to Palmer's chair and looked down at a scene like a map showing the rivers of a delta.

"What about this?" Palmer took a slide with a glass cell attached to it. Mrs Durrant sighed indulgently and peered again down the metal tube.

"I can see noth…Oh!" She backed off with a hand to her mouth. "Really, my dear John, and just before supper! I have no time to look any more. Daisy may need some assistance in the kitchen, and I shall leave you two gentlemen to your… researches."

Palmer winked at his nephew. "Go on, boy, your turn."

At first Tealer could see nothing but white light in the eyepiece, and was only conscious of the heavy fumes of Mrs Durrant's French scent that suffused the brass and glasswork of the instrument. He was a bit apprehensive because he knew what he saw would be alarming, but he did not want to be caught reacting like Mrs Durrant. At first he could only see the yellow light reflected by the mirror below the slide. Then a monstrous spider-form suddenly crossed and re-crossed his view. It stopped and stared up at him with malevolence in each of its six black eyes. Its fangs pulsed like daggers being sheathed and unsheathed. He drew a sharp breath, but kept looking.

"Good, eh?" said his uncle.

Tealer agreed, but looked around the microscope to see where the spider was.

Palmer took the slide out and held it up to a candle on his desk, showing that the glass cell contained a speck of dust that moved about inside. Tealer could just see it was a money spider scuttling about looking for an escape.

"See how small! Strange to think that there are demons such as these a-runnin' around in our very eating and sleeping rooms, spearin' and poisonin' and grindin' one another up, and we are none the wiser! Did you want to see some more?"

Tealer said he did, and they rushed around the house, scraping at the skirting boards and cornices of the study looking for bread crumbs, the shells of insects, and bits of dust. As the aromas of their steak and kidney supper wafted through from the kitchen they studied the intricacies of some dessicated scrap from a similar meal of a month before.

Before they went through to take supper, Palmer leant back and yawned happily.

"Amazing what an unseen world there is around us," he said. "So many things that men ha'n't understood till now are being made clear with such instruments as this." He stroked the body of the microscope admiringly. "Do you know, we're living in a rum age, boy. I've often told you, I fear for many of the old ways, especially marshland ways, what with all these machines and engines and gadgets that appear with every year that pass. But thas not *all* bad. Every now and again humankind come up with something like this here microscope, and suddenly things that we could only explain with fables and fairytales are clear to us. And those of us prepared to learn the lessons put ourselves at an advantage. Most people still live in ignorance, you know. They never bother to find out what's behind things. They don't want to, half the time. They hear something odd when they lay in bed, or they see a strange light in the sky, or their dogs bark at the thin air, and they'll prefer to believe all kinds of witless blather by way of explanation. But if we have a mind to, and we ha' got the courage to, we can rise above all that. Just think, Johnny, you and me, a-sittin' here in this little room, with equipment like this here set of tubes and lenses to help us, might one day find any number of answers to so many mysteries. We'll be able to put paid to so many trumpery notions that people fill one another's heads with."

Palmer meant this as no more than a piece of wholesome advice. He always tried to speak to Tealer as his own grandfather had spoken to him: as if to a man his own age, and avoiding condescension. He had no idea of the ferment of confused ideas in the head of the quiet, thoughtful boy studying the labels of the other slides on the table. In particular, he didn't realize how his advice to reject superstitious explanations only added to Tealer's quandary.

Palmer had started to pack up the microscope and the slides when Tealer spoke out.

He said: "Uncle John, Jointy say the Shuck came after Cork and he died six month later. And he said that was all 'cause he brought a goblin into Decoy wood. *Jointy* said."

Palmer stopped what he was doing and looked at Tealer, utterly nonplussed.

Tealer added "He shew me the goblin, so I know."

These occasional outbursts from his soft-spoken nephew often caught Palmer on the hop, and this one certainly did. His lips twitched wordlessly as he sought some marker by which to find his way through this cryptic jumble of references. Then a spark of understanding flashed in his eyes. He put the microscope down, leant back slowly in his chair, looked up at the dark ceiling of the study and drove his hands through his thick hair.

"Oh, dear," he said.

Tealer started to believe he might have revealed some great truth that had shattered his uncle's faith in rational explanations for things.

"Oh, dear," said his uncle again, still with his eyes shut and his hands on his head. Then he looked at Tealer and clapped him on the shoulder. "Old Jointy ha' been talking to you about poor Stanley Norton. *Cha*! Yes, I remember you said he' told you about Flixton. I should ha' realized. He must have taken to you to want to talk about *that*! He never told me – I only learnt about it from Freddie Devereaux, just before he went abroad that last time. *Cha*! No wonder you ha' been even more quiet than normal just lately."

"Jointy said 'at was the Shuck that did for Cork Norton," said Tealer again.

"Jointy said the Shuck did for Cork Norton, did he? Well, boy, I suppose you could say that's true – that is, if you saw things as Jointy would see 'em. Yes, you could say it *was* the Shuck that did for Norton. Others might put it differently, but... well... let's say the difference would be lost on Jointy." He sighed and said, "Go and tell your Aunt Durrant to tell Daisy to keep the pie warm. We shall be a good few minutes. I need to talk to you."

When Tealer came back, Palmer made him recount everything Jointy had said. Tealer obliged, complete with 'Shucks', 'wakris', goblins, foxes, squirrels and stoats. Palmer listened carefully to every detail, nodding, mostly looking serious, but sometimes with a rueful smile playing around the corners of his mouth. When Tealer had finished, Palmer poured himself a glass of sherry, took a sip and folded his arms.

"Very well. Now listen to me. Stanley Norton, God rest him, was a good old boy. He was a first-rate seaman, and he crewed with me on several voyages. I know how he died 'cause I got most of it first hand from Devereaux himself. And as Jointy told you, Freddie was there when Norton passed away. What I *didn't* know – not till you now told me – was what poor old Jointy had made of it all. Now you *have* told me, though, that all make sense." He clicked his tongue and shook his head.

Then he asked "Have you ever heard of hydrophobia, boy?"

Tealer hadn't.

"No, why should you at your age? Thas a disease, but a disease like no other – I believe 'at mean 'fear of water', from the Greek. I think 'at must be the worst disease known to science. That leave you crazin' for a drink, and yet you're terrified you'll drown in it when you get it. Some poor coves who go down with it even start to fear they'll drown in their own spit. I saw it once or twice in India. The British there called it 'rabies' – I believe, from the Hindustani."

Palmer looked at Tealer to see if he was making any headway.

"Let me try to tell you what happens to any poor dog that has such a disease, because I believe you'll then begin to understand what happened down there by the Decoy Lake all them years ago.

"Your dog with hydrophobia is a right sorry creature. Firstly he can't settle. He go round and round the country for miles. Thas like he's a-tryin' to find who or what's makin' him feel so bad. Then he start losin' control of his movements. He can't bark properly. All he can manage is a sort of strangled howl. And that's when he start lookin' right strange. Day or night, the pupils of his eyes open right up, and they start a-glowin'. He start a-frothin' at the mouth, and a-twistin' and a-turnin'. And that's when he start attacking anything around him: that might be a tree, or his own shadow. Or you, if you happen to be near. But strange to say, he very rarely kill outright anything he attack. That isn't because the disease don't make him funny strong – that certainly *do*! But he don't have the coordination. So he might come for you, and still you end up with just a slight wound. But if he do bite you, and he ha' broken your skin with his teeth, well then you're still done for. It's just that you won't die straightaway, because the venom in his bite take some time to poison your brain. I think you can see what I'm at now, can't you, boy?"

Tealer said nothing. He suddenly felt his hand being pushed from behind by something wet in the darkness. It was the nose of Buck. The retriever was looking to have the backs of his ears scratched.

Palmer looked at the dog. "What could turn a soft beast like that into a fury? I pray that when my time comes the Lord above will spare me an end like that. To be honest, boy, I think we would be better torn apart by the phantom dog than nipped by the mad one." He took another sip from his sherry.

"You remember little Turpin, don't you, boy?"

Tealer said he did.

"Best little terrier I ever knew. He'd had a fight with some sailor's cur on the quay, and I thought he started actin' queer a few weeks later. Could ha' been anything. But I weren't takin' chances. I seen what happen with people who did. Poor little devil." This was the nearest Tealer saw his uncle ever to having a tear in his eye.

"Anyway, thas what did for Cork. Somehow hydrophobia got into Decoy wood. Or so I reckon. That could ha' been a weasel brought it in that bit a stoat that bit a fox that bit a gypsy's dog, and there you had your animals acting strangely, and there you had your Shuck. And when old Cork got that bite on the arm, he was done for. Jointy was right lucky he weren't caught himself. Freddie as well. 'Fact, any of them round the Decoy Broad."

Tealer was setting all this against his memory of what Jointy had told him. It seemed to fit the facts, but the inconsistency that remained was the principle one, the one that had been jarring and grating throughout:

"But you always say to me to listen to Jointy because he always know what he's talking about. But he never said any of this."

"Yes, John-boy, I reckon I am to blame for that. What I should have said is: men like Jointy are never wrong in telling you *what* happen. *What* happen. Jointy will never miss a detail, whether that be the size of the duck flock, the positions of the stars at night or how many times a poacher in the next village sneezed. In that sense I ha' never met anyone else the like. But – and this is where I reckon I let you down, Johnny – I should have added the Jointys of this world know nothing of *why*. Jointy'll tell you how many colours of dragonfly you may see down on the Decoy, and you'll look in the finest handbook of British insects and find there's just that number to be found in the Broads. But ask him what their great long tails are for, and he will tell you they're for sewing up the mouths of liars. He will tell you the exact hour – never mind the day – when the first swallow appear in the spring. But he reckon they spend the winter with their heads in the mud at the bottom of the broad. No point in telling him they fly back from Africa."

Palmer was watching the candlelit face of his nephew with some concern. As so often, the poker-face of the boy betrayed very little. This time it was hiding his elation. He was beginning to feel the same relief of burden as when he first learnt that Norris had been arraigned for battering some woman rather than for smuggling. Or that poor Georgie Stolworthy had gone to his grave minus his head. It seemed as though he were about to be freed from the curse of the Shuck!

But before this long-remembered conversation in the candlelight was to finish another loose end came to his mind.

"But what about the goblin thing?" he said, "I saw that myself!"

"Not a goblin, boy, a 'uakari'. Thas a small monkey from the South American jungles. And nothing to do with the Black Shuck dog; just a coincidence that Norton was keeping one at the time he was bitten. Thas a monkey with a face just like a man's, but only about one tenth the size – and as Jointy said, thas bright red. Some of our crewmen used to buy them as pets. 'Wakris', they used to call them – 'course they couldn't get their tongues round the native word! I remember Norton had won one in a card game with some of the locals on one of our South American runs. He forced them to give it to him when they couldn't pay cash. The other crew were agin it, because the locals told them that that had an evil spirit, but I didn't see any harm, and so I let him bring it home. What I *don't* know is how Jointy come by its corpse, after Norton had died. But anyway, that wouldn't have anything to do with the mad d... ,"

Palmer had stopped, and was running his hand thoughtfully over the head of Buck the dog, and staring the while into the flame of one of the candles on his bureau. There was now no trace of a smile, and when he spoke again his voice had dropped to a murmur "Unless… 'at was the uakari that… Good God, thas never occurred to me before… and I let…"

Palmer poured another sherry from his decanter and downed the contents in one. And just as many other adults were apt to do with Tealer, he'd momentarily forgotten the boy was there. When he came-to again, he said "Go you and get your supper, and tell your aunt Durrant I shall follow presently."

He did not emerge to toy with the congealed remains of his pie until long after Tealer had disappeared to bed.

But the Black Beast of the marshes - no more than a mad dog!

And with the dog destroyed, another ghost laid! Another dragon slain!

Perhaps the demon itself, the troubling spirit behind all these monsters, was disappearing as Tealer changed from child to boy.

Sadly, not. Hauntings like that of Tealer Sayer are never quite so simple.

Even as Tealer stood exulting as the Hound from Hell was reduced to a sickly cur, unknown to him the real Demon of the Marshes, the true Fiend of Breydon was present with him in that dusty study on that evening in late summer.

Perhaps it was smiling a glittering smile, nodding its head in mocking agreement at the sober rationale, triumphant in the knowledge that it was not done with John Sayer yet, and that it could wait.

And wait.

And wait until we find ourselves back where we started, years later, with this same boy as a man, freezing to death out on the Breydon ice.

People, Too

For the time-being, though, other forces would crowd in on the life of Tealer Sayer. Other events would surprise, delight, appall or shock him – and these were not of the netherworld-kind, but very much part of this world.

Haunting or no haunting, Tealer was growing up.

Take, for example, the occasion when, now aged about twelve, he was sent home from his school to avoid an outbreak of the chicken pox. He arrived to find that Daisy wasn't in the house. The place was silent but for the odd muffled clopping of a horse on the cobbles of the Row outside. He decided to go up to his bedroom and label birds' eggs.

What stopped him on the stairs was a mournful groaning. He first thought somebody, either Daisy or his uncle John, might be ill, and he carried on up to see who it was.

Then he stopped dead again.

A voice, at once strange and strangely familiar, seemed to be whispering his name urgently.

The old, dread chill went through him.

But Tealer had come a long way:

"There's always an explanation for everything you see and hear in the field, boy. You'll only be a sportsman and an Englishman if you make it your business to find out what that explanation is."

He found himself shaking, but this time he was determined to ride out the fright and investigate – which is what he did. He crept down to get an ebony cudgel from the stick-rack and then crept back up. Having never had to creep around in his uncle's house he'd never made a precise note of which parts of the staircase creaked – and so one board made a noise which to Tealer seemed like a volley of musketry, and it caused him to freeze. Yet the groaning continued unabated. No longer did he hear his name being called, but the voice was still quite audible, and mixed with a hissing like an angry swan.

He hesitated.

"You'll only be a sportsman and an Englishman…"

He continued till he had traced the sound to the room in which Palmer slept amongst yet more floribunda from his seafaring years. Like any good hunter Tealer went down on all fours so that he didn't present a human silhouette. This also spread his weight more evenly across the treacherous floorboards. In this prehistoric position he was able to approach the door, which was ajar, and he looked through the gap.

The bizarre creature he spotted, the one responsible for this noise, had a series of effects on him in very quick succession.

It was a strange, white, multi-limbed thing that lay on his uncle's bed like a huge, beached starfish. Then he realised that it wasn't one animal but two. Then he realised that one of the creatures was not a creature at all but his uncle, with a face twisted in agony, while the part that wasn't his uncle was lying on his uncle, trying to suck the very life force from his mouth. Then he realised it was this other creature that was groaning, and simultaneously he realized it was not his, Tealer's, name, but his uncle's, that was being chanted. Then he realised that this other creature was Mrs Durrant with her luxuriant hair let down so that it covered most of her back and thighs. Then he realised that both Mrs Durrant and his uncle John were entirely without clothes, which for the most infintesimal instant reminded him of drowned bodies by the Bure. Then he realised what was happening.

The reason that Tealer wasn't shocked or stunned by what he saw – that he didn't put two and two together and make three, or five, or sixty-seven – was thanks to the instruction in the ways of the natural world in which he'd been immersed. From his earliest days with Palmer he had been told why the little terns on the North Beach climbed on one another, and why the tom-cats on the privy roof would yowl so much at night, and why great angry bulls were put out on the marshes with the docile cows in the months of May to October. It was explained to him in such a matter-of-fact way by his maverick relation that none of it seemed strange, despite the fact that Palmer had never actually said "And people, too, boy."

And as he watched the scene from the floor of the landing, even its astonishing effect on his own body was not too terrifying or too incomprehensible, though it was wonderfully new.

So Tealer crept down back downstairs in a whirl of emotions, but the first of these was a great satisfaction at having had his suspicions confirmed: men and women *were* like animals. Take away the tweed jackets, the shirts, the neckerchiefs, the bustles, skirts and the corsets, and people were no different from the cattle on the marsh, the dogs in the Rows or the fecund terns on the North Beach.

And he went out and re-staged his entry into the house, with a theatrical banging of the door, throwing down of satchel, clonking of hobnails on the kitchen floor, and squeaky pumping at the well in the back yard – and his uncle presently appeared on the stairs with Mrs Durrant behind, both properly dressed if a little dishevelled, both quite composed if a little flushed, exactly as they had appeared so on many other occasions – and there and then the remaining pieces in the jig-saw started to fit rapidly and unremarkably into place.

Take also the time, another year later, when Tealer was forced to confront the real possibility of his own end. We know that as a child he'd been chased by ghosts and spectral dogs, but not by Death itself. We also know that he'd witnessed the real demise of many other people on Cory's Bridge, but he himself had never been in any real danger.

But one quiet October night out on the marsh there were a few seconds when Tealer really was dead if he didn't look sharp, and he knew it.

It was one of the many evenings at that time of year when he and Palmer went on an ambush of the wigeon.

Flighting wigeon was the most exciting of all the marshland sports his uncle had yet revealed to him. The two of them would go down to the marsh and each would choose a field, separated from its neighbouring fields by drainage dykes.

They'd wait until dusk on adjacent marshes, sometimes just uncle and nephew, at other times with other sportsmen.

They'd wait until the silent, disciplined ranks of gulls had all flown eastward to their roosts at sea, and the noisy gangs of rooks and jackdaws had flown westward to their roosts inland.

They'd wait until after the mallard had landed noisily in the dykes.

They'd wait until after the dunlins had raced through the dusk above them, squeaking hoarsely.

They'd wait until the piteous complaints of the lapwings had begun to die down.

They'd wait until a more regular rhythmic whistling could be heard…

And then their chilled hands would tighten on the stocks of their guns. This was the sound of the squadrons of wigeon. Birds in fours and sixes would begin to appear out of the dusk to hover wasp-like over a chosen flash of water. For an instant they would present targets against the sunset before they disappeared below the skyline into the gloom of the earth. Great speed was needed to bag even one or two birds.

This was one such evening. Before dusk Palmer and Tealer had taken up their positions on adjacent marshes, both empty of stock. The evening air hung with the promise of burgeoning sport. It had rained earlier in the day, the first rain for several weeks. Now the clouds had cleared, and the webs which blanketed the grasstops and thistle heads glittered with millions of droplets of water where they caught the sunset. Across the boundary dyke and half-way across the next marsh stood Irstead Supreme, an English shorthorn bull with his harem, placid and content on this lush, sparkling evening. The bull and a few of the cows watched casually, chewing all the while on the last fresh grass of the year as the two hunters took up their positions. The other cattle didn't even bother look up. Beyond the cattle were sheep, and even these flighty souls seemed lulled by the sense of autumn calm around them. Across the marshes came the dibbling sound of swans feeding on duckweed. A barn owl began its restless search for scraps of life in the long grass.

The marsh that Tealer had chosen to stand in had several separate flashes that had collected with the recent rain. He and his uncle had had a happy debate as to which flash the wigeon would drop into for the night feed, for there's always a favourite. They'd scanned the ground for feathers and chippings to get a clue from the previous night but knew it was useless. The recent downpour had wiped the slate clean. They must guess. They must whistle just like a lonely cock widgeon wanting to be joined by others, and they must hope that the birds above would respond and visit the selected flash.

The night fell and its players arrived on cue, adding their voices to the concert of wader calls now ringing around the marsh. But as the widgeon appeared, Tealer realised with anguish that he wasn't under their flightline. He wasn't standing directly beneath that route to a charmed pool selected by the first one or two birds and then used by squadron after squadron coming in to feed. He watched his prey pass over him, way out of range, calling provocatively.

The very young hunter is so enthusiastic, so determined and so headstrong that no obstacle no matter how formidable will prevent him from closing with his quarry. As he gets older, he realises that wild attempts to rectify a mistake rarely come to fruition, because they are the wildfowler's equivalent of changing horses midstream. The patient philosophy of 'another time' is the only remedy when the hunter is outwitted by his quarry as Tealer had been on that October night. But Tealer still had that to learn. Instead of straining the sky for a stray flock that might not use the main approach, he made his way across the marsh in a foolish attempt to get under the imagined flight-line.

He decided they were coming down in the next marsh, so he unlatched the gate and let himself through. With his eyes peeled to smarting and his ears aching with the effort, he tried to place the line of the whistling birds in the night sky all around him. To his intense irritation he caught sight of one or two hovering shapes about to land in the marsh he'd just left, so he raced back through the gateway to his original position. The sound of two shots from his uncle's stand on the next marsh did nothing relax him. He wanted to be in amongst the birds too!

He splashed over to a new pool of water in the grass and set up shop, trying to still his own panting so that he could listen for the arriving duck.

Events speeded up at that point.

Of course, Palmer heard all this 'gallivantin' about', as he later called it, and from his own marsh he shouted out to Tealer through the darkness:

"Them birds better be deafer than me, boy!" Then he chuckled. Then he shouted in a voice that was utterly different – loud, urgent, with no trace of the usual irony: "Johnny, get off that marsh! *Get – off – that – marsh – now*! Into the dyke, Johnny! *Quick*!"

For an instant, perhaps half a second but no more, Tealer had stared uncomprehending into the quadrant of dusk whence his uncle's voice was coming and had realised that Palmer was moving towards him very quickly. Then he felt the ground shaking around him, and his legs began to work at a speed he had not thought them capable of; he found himself running very fast across the marsh to the big dyke that separated him from his uncle's stand. He didn't stop and turn to be transfixed by the pitiless giant Death bearing down on him. This was no mixture of fascination and dread for some shadowy fiend, but a desperate rush to avoid a peril that was in no way abstract. Instinct made him do just what his uncle had schooled him to do should this ever happen. No thought this time of uncocking his fowling piece or fumbling in the dark for other items of kit; in fact he threw away his gun and ran for his life. Three yards out of from the dyke he leapt and landed exactly in the middle of the water. He had no time to gasp at the cold as it saturated his tweeds. He swam furiously for the far bank and tried to scrabble up its steep side, but could only gouge holes in the soft blue mud.

Everything slowed, and then stopped. And only then did Tealer find himself looking up the bank into the more familiar, hated, mannequin face of old. With casual interest it looked firstly down at him and then at the monstrous shape bearing down on him, as though musing on how long it would take for him to die when he was caught. Then the world came crashing back to life, and where the apparition had been there was Palmer, whose long wiry arm reached down and dragged Tealer up the bank and into the next marsh, well away from the water's edge.

Once well clear, Palmer and Tealer turned and looked into the dark, ready to get back into the water if need be. But there was nothing to see, and the only sound was a retreating rumble and a rhythmic gasp. In all the episode had lasted no more than fifteen seconds.

And Palmer started a desperate laughing in which Tealer joined in. Palmer whipped out a hipflask of his favourite sloe gin, and handed some to Tealer. Tealer swigged at it not knowing its strength and dissolved into a fit of violent coughing made worse by his panting. He handed the flask back to his uncle and he noticed that Palmer's hand, for all the mirth, was shaking as much as his own.

"We'll come back tomorrow morning to get the gun," said his uncle, slapping the quivering, dripping boy on the shoulder.

They did, and the morning was as glorious as the night before. The swans were still in their dyke. The reed warblers were chattering ceaselessly in the reeds, and there was also a busy twitter as gangs of goldfinches flew in streaks of red, gold and white between the clumps of thistle along the dykes. Irstead Supreme was feeding in his marsh with his cows, a sea of tossing heads, flicking ears, twitching flanks and swinging tails. A hare on the other side of the marsh got up and loped away at no more than a canter before stopping at a prudent distance to fix her unblinking gaze on the dog Buck, hoping that she wouldn't be forced to sprint away on such a hot morning. There was no sign of the drama of the previous night other than the gun lying in the damp grass.

Palmer picked the weapon up, eased it off cock, brushed the worst of the mud and dew from it, and handed it to Tealer. They went over to the gate which Tealer had left unlatched in his haste to change position. Two of the cows had come through during the night, and Tealer drove these back and his uncle closed the gate behind them and re-latched it. They leant on the gate and regarded Irstead Supreme – docile, uninterested – as he continued to work his way through the dew-wet grass.

"Lesson to be learnt here, boy," said Palmer.

By a week later it was all a huge joke. Sitting with his nephew in his study among all the trophies and curios, Palmer said: "There's a few things any good countryman learn never to trust, boy, and one of 'em you learnt last week. We might be talking of the friendliest, docilest old mangol-chewer in all England, the kind as never move except to cover his heifers or brush the flies off his back – that make no odds. The moment you relax is the moment he'll have you. There are too many men I've heard about who ha' ended up all dossed about with horns through their backs, or their spleens trodden into the mud, for me ever to doubt what I was always told as a lad. *You never trust a bull.*"

He puffed on his pipe, and looked around his room, and back at Tealer. "I've had a few scares myself, but I don't think I've had as close a scrape as you had that other night down on Halvergate triangle."

Tealer asked "And what are the others, uncle John?

"What others?"

"The other things a countryman never should trust."

"Ah yes, the others. Well, one is a mended ladder. Another is an empty gun. Another is a shallow swamp. Another, as I once found, is a dead tiger. Another, for when you go to sea, is weather set fair. Another, for when you're a mite older, is a cast- iron investment. And another, also for when you're a mite older, is a woman fast asleep."

They both chuckled at the last, though Tealer had just the beginnings of an idea what he was laughing at.

What he did know was when the danger was real, and the fear justified, he was actually elated by it. When he next saw Charlie he proudly gave him a detailed account of his escape.

The Riot

And what of the greatest of these tests, another that this time could have claimed not just Tealer's life, and also that of his uncle, and actually did claim another life, and very nearly set the whole of Yarmouth to civil war?

Why, *that* all started on a wild day in mid-September when uncle and nephew had gone down to watch old Gedney the marshman pull up his fyke net for the first time since winter. Tealer was always absorbed to see the mysterious community of the deep dyke hauled up tossing and flapping in the depths of Gedney's net. But this time Gedney himself kept stopping and cocking his old ear toward Yarmouth. Then he would carry on and haul up a little more net and then cock his ear again. Being such a blustery day, the east wind was noisy in Tealer's own ears; he could hear nothing. He looked at his uncle, who shrugged.

Then Tealer himself noticed in the gusts of wind small but distinct snatches of sound like those you sometimes hear on the threshold of sleep.

Finally, Gedney had pulled up all his nets and bagged all the eels they were going to take home. He stood up from his task, and said:

"Yarmouth's a noisy ole bugger this arter noon."

They all listened intently into the wind.

Gedney went on: "Course, there's hell'n'all rum noises come outa that there town these days. What wi' all them engines an' all. All bangs and whistles and shrieks an' 'at. All that thumpin' and bumpin'. Thas a wonder you Yarmouth people can put up with it. That'd craze me."

He cupped his ears with his muddy brown hands and listened towards the smokey skyline of Yarmouth.

"But thas different today..." he said, frowning, "...from what I normally hear." He listened some more. "Yes, this time thas people! That int none o' them steam machines a-making *that* racket. That it ent. Thas a parade, thas what that is. Listen, there's drums and music and all sorts! What, you got the army in town, Mr Palmer?"

Palmer said: "I should hope not, Simon, not today of all days, because the seamen are parading, and that would be asking for trouble." Then he snapped his fingers: "Of course! Thas the seamen themselves. It's *their* drums and bugles we can hear."

"In September, sir? Whatever are they a-celebratin?"

"Well, I wouldn't call it a celebration, Simon. A parade, yes. But hardly a celebration. No, they're angry. There's been this new Mercantile Marine Law passed just recently that's set them about with all manner of regulations. I do feel for them. I have always found Yarmouth sailing men brave and sturdy fellows, and I reckon thas time we started treating them fairly. But the thing is, they also want the same pay in summer and winter. Fifty-five shilling year round. No shipowner is ever go' agree to that! We can't – we aren't getting the trade ourselves! The railways ha' taken a lot o' our coastal work, and what they haven't taken the Lowestoft ships have. Still, thas nothing for you to worry about, Simon. You're well out of such disputes here."

Gedney spat into the dyke. "Them seamen want to see if they can get fifty shillin' down here a-slubbin' dykes or fyking for eels. Blast! Or twe'eh shillin', for that matter!"

Palmer took the point and felt into his waistcoat pocket. Then he and Tealer climbed abroad the trap with their sack of eels. Off they set along the Acle New Road, straight against the wind all the way into Yarmouth.

And as they got closer they found the sharp ears of Simon Gedney had been right. They firstly heard the thump of the heavy drums from way down the New Road; then as they passed over the now re-built Bure Bridge they were beset all around by the rattle of snares and discordant blasts from bugles and trumpets. Pockets of men were going marching up the Conge and along the North Quay shouting and chanting. They could see that this was to be no ordinary September morning in Yarmouth.

What they couldn't see was that at that very moment a rattled conclave of shipowners, clerks and civic leaders was gathering in an upper room of the Town Hall:

Jermy, Superintendent of Revenue: (peering nervously through the window overlooking South Quay): "I like not the look of this business. Not one jot. We'll ha' be careful not to provoke unnecessary trouble."

The Riot

Simkins, a Ship Owner: "Take courage, sirs. We mustn't flinch. Our man Graystone must be brought to his ship. As an example. Then this hubbub will quickly peter out. They'll see there's no point to their disobedience."

Letts, Colonel of the local militia: "Quite right. But first the streets around the quay must be cleared."

Jermy of the Excise: "Why, though? These men are doing no harm – beyond that infernal din. Let them let off steam, I say. There's little point in goading them. They can't stand about on the quay all year."

Danford, a Magistrate: (with no time for rebellious sailors, but whose fine sash windows are but a stone's throw from this very spot): "Well now, there may be some sense in that appr…"

Letts, Colonel of the Militia: "No harm? They could very well do harm. At any instant. We must clear the streets."

Jermy of the Excise: "I tell you, they will only cause trouble if they are provoked. They seem content to march up and down and bang on their drums. If we make no performance about it we should easily get Graystone to his ship. It will be a fait accompli. There'll be no further point in them waiting around on the quay and their protest will come to nothing."

Simkins the Ship owner (who, as it happened, owned no property in Yarmouth): "No, that is wrong sir. Thas Graystone's right to ignore the strike of his fellows and our duty to support him by transporting him back to his ship. And to do it in the surreptitious manner you suggest would be tantamount to admitting these troublesome sailors are in the right, which they assuredly ain't."

Letts, Colonel of militia (who, incidentally, also owned no property in the vicinity): "Exactly."

Atwood, Town Clerk (another with no house on the quay – and, it must be admitted, with various ship-owning friends): "Exactly."

Jermy, Excise: "So then, we clear the streets. But how, pray? How, if we are to avoid doing a great mischief to our own town."

Letts, Militia: "Militia."

Various: "Militia?"

Letts: "Militia. Cold steel."

Palmer took Vulcan to his stabling on the Cobholm marsh, and having unhitched and watered him, he and Tealer made their way home for lunch through the groups of seamen to the house in Row 111. Tealer was going to try to add to the eel catch by 'babbing' for them that afternoon with Charlie Harrison. His uncle did not even stay to eat, saying 'some pressing business' had come up.

Having gobbled his midday meal Tealer grabbed his stick, spade and line and made his way back down to Cobholm to meet Charlie. All along the south Quay there were still little knots of sailors standing round: talking, smoking, spitting. Some had banners and bells, others had horns and whistles, and every now and again the general hubbub of the quay would be drowned out by a deafening concert of discordant sounds. Tealer hurried on. He was mildly interested in all this unusual activity, but large noisy crowds had an unhappy association for him.

When he was back at Vulcan's meadow, he started to dig for the worms he needed for eel-bait. At length Charlie arrived, without any eel-tackle, but with a worried-looking girl of about eighteen.

Tealer gave the girl a quick puzzled look and then turned to Charlie.

"Where's your bits and pieces, boy?"

"Hang the babbin', boy!" said Charlie. "We go' watch the march. Come you on. That'll be good!" He started back up the hill before Tealer could say a word. Tealer had to drop his eeling kit in the dog-cart at the corner of Vulcan's enclosure and run to catch his friend up.

"There's go' be some fun, boy!" promised Charlie, though he looked deadly serious as they hurried up the lane back toward the town. "My gaffer told me that the owners ha' got a strikebreaker called Graystone. They want to get him out to his ship to show they int afraid o' the sailors. Sailors reckon they are go' stop 'em. Everyone's meeting outside the town hall."

"And who's *she*?" muttered Tealer, nodding towards the girl.

"Sarah Stolworthy. You remember Georgie – what was killed up the Cory Bridge. Well, his sister. Don't you recognise her?"

Tealer sneaked another look at Miss Stolworthy.

"P'raps I do."

"Well, she's now married my cousin Jed what sail on the *Vindicator*."

"But why…?"

"Family way."

"No, I mean, why's she *here*?"

"Jed's up the front with the other strikers, and he told me to look after her 'case 'at get rough."

Tealer followed Charlie and his protégée back over the Haven Bridge to rejoin the stream of people making their way to the town hall. The noise of so many clogs all moving urgently in the same direction was still making Tealer very uneasy. Why didn't Charlie seem worried by it too? he wondered. After all, Charlie had been there with him by the Cory Bridge on that dark day. But Charlie lived in amongst a large crowd, and such clamour of moving feet was a commonplace for him. Plus – and already at fourteen this was noticeable in him – Charlie harboured passions more pressing to him than a dread of reliving ancient traumas. In particular he held an increasingly withering view of authority. Oppression and injustice made his sharp eyes blaze with fury, and today's issue was one such. It didn't seem to have occurred to the sign-writer's boy that his friend's guardian could be seen as one of the guilty owners – or if it had, it hadn't changed anything for him.

Once they had crossed the Haven Bridge and joined the main body of the marchers they had to slow right down to a shuffle. There were no convenient trees to climb as there had been down by the Bure five years before. Tealer had to stand on tip-toe to get any idea of what was happening. The front of the procession seemed to have stalled and bunched. Tealer looked round at some of the others who had gathered there.

"Most o' these buggers ha' never been on a ship in their lives," he murmured to Charlie. Charlie shrugged. He was having too much fun to be bothered by such detail. Meanwhile somewhere in the crowd a song was got up, a sea-shanty that both boys knew. Charlie nudged Tealer and joined in lustily. Tealer sang a little half-heartedly at first, but then was surprised to find himself singing along as merrily as the rest.

In the town hall – where enjoyment of the parade was rather less in evidence

– the lively debate had just been further enlivened by the arrival of a second ship-owner:

Simkins (to this second shipowner): "And a very good-day to you, sir. So glad you could attend. And how do you propose we manage this situation? I think you should tell us, you know. I seem to remember that 'at was you that condoned the rascals pressing that outrageous petition for fifty-five shilling that ha' been the cause of this… this ado."

Palmer (who was the second shipowner): "I never condoned any such thing, sir. I merely pointed out that their grievance is genuine and that we should pay heed to it. They ha' been a-suffering much more than any of us from the present difficulties. But – whatever the ins and outs – I hear you plan to use foot soldiers to clear the way. Is that right?

Letts, Colonel of Milita: "Indeed it is, sir.

Palmer: "May I ask how? Will you shoot the front line of the marchers down?"

Letts: "No, sir, not if there is no need, but we'll fix bayonets. My coast guards will form a ring – but an impenetrable *ring – that will surround the fellow Graystone and see him to his vessel. The sight of uniforms'll bring some sense."*

Palmer: "But – begging your pardon – the road around the town hall is flat. Your men will be no higher off the ground than the crowd. Only the front will see them, and those behind will have no idea what's a-happenin'. Either your men will be a laughing stock, or they will be forced to impale the frontmost of the procession. Then you'll surely have your riot."

Letts: "I think, sir, I should know my business better than you."

Palmer: "I'm sure you do, sir. But your business, I believe, is warfare. By God's grace that's not yet quite what we face."

Jermy: "And hope not to."

Danford: "Aye."

Simkins: "No! That's weak talk! That's surrender! And we must *prevail. And here is a way. What say you, Your Worship?"*

Mayor: (with several excellent properties along the South Quay, but also many powerful ship-owning acquaintances) "Um…"

Atwood the Clerk: "Well! There we are then. All in favour? [Here there was a show of hands, in which Jermy and Palmer showed 'no', Danford havered, and the remaining ten or so of the council showed 'aye'.] *There, decided! I'm sure His Worship agrees? Yes? Thought so! Colonel! Form your ring, sir. Form your ring."*

Five minutes later, Tealer and Charlie noticed the singing suddenly stop as a murmur went through the crowd. Then everyone went quiet.

The next sound was an angry sigh that quickly transformed into a roar, and for several minutes this prevailed until cheering and clapping spread back through the procession from the front – it reminded Tealer of the delighted jeers you hear in a playground when a bully is getting a hiding from a more popular boy. This went on for some time until another spell of relative quiet came over the parade. The two boys were beside themselves with curiosity. Finally a garbled version of what had happened got back to where they were. An attempt had been made to use the militia to shoehorn Graystone through the throng; the soldiers had even fixed bayonets, but the crowd had stood firm.

"There, look." said the girl Sarah, who till then hadn't uttered a syllable. "Thas that. They can't do it 'cause Jed and the others ha' stopped 'em. Didn't we ought be goin' back home now?"

"Now whatever would Jed say if we did that?" said Charlie.

"But that man in front of you now said they'd got guns, an' 'at," said Sarah, getting more to the point.

"But they didn't do nothin' with 'em, did they" said Charlie. "They dussn't. There are too many of us. But I do want t'know what they are go' try next."

Yet the 'they' he referred to weren't too sure themselves:

Jermy: "Well now, we have *achieved a lot!"*

Colonel of Militia: "Pshaw! We only need to show a little more force. Identify the ringleaders, then a few shots in the air and the rest'll scatter like chaff."

Jermy: "I can think of no better recipe for mayhem. Most of the assembly would have no idea where the shots were from. There'd be widespread panic, with who know what result. And as for reasoning with the saner elements – well, there'd be no trust 'twixt the ship owners and their men for years to come. I say again, let them have their head. They'll think they've won and they'll go away. Forget this half-cooked business with Graystone."

Palmer: "Alas, Mr Jermy, I fear it's now too late. We must take some action – if these men remain till nightfall, they will start drinking, and then we could see real damage. For their own sakes we should make them disperse."

Colonel Letts: "Aha! You see sense at last, Mr Palmer."

Palmer: "Well, an idea at least. We need a troop of Hussars".

Letts: "WHAAAT?"

Palmer: "Cavalry. Men on horses."

Letts: "Damn you sir, I know what Hussars are! Are you suggesting my coastguard men are not up to…"

Palmer: "Men on horses can be seen from further away. And if they're deployed carefully they can break up the gathering without causing a headlong panic. If we are fortunate there will be no serious risk to either side. And certainly no need for shots."

Letts: (when he can speak without spluttering): "In Yarmouth? Are you mad, sir? This is a town. A maze of streets! Alleys, sir! Alleys! Into which these wretches may escape!"

Palmer: "Forgive me, but I thought their dispersal was our intention. And I once saw this technique used to right good effect in Hyderabad. Not one injury to any party. That was a religious disturbance, mind, not like this, but…"

Letts: "Hyderabad? Hyderab… Sir, this is Yarmouth, and these sailors are unlawfully assembled, and their ring-leaders must be arrested, not allowed to escape! And, lest you forget, the nearest cavalry squadron is stabled in Norwich."

Palmer: "And 'at could be in Yarmouth in a very short time, if we wished it."

Simkins the shipowner: "By which you mean half a day. The devil take your 'if we wished it', Palmer! We look to have complete disorder in the streets within the hour!"

Palmer (with sigh): "You telegraph the commandant of Hussars in Norwich, and tell him to send a detachment of horse by special steam train down to Yarmouth immediately. They wait up on the Conge. You address the trouble-makers. If they refuse to be about their business, you send a runner with a message for the detachment to appear at the top end of the quay. If they still refuse, you give the signal, and the detachment can advance along the quay. Once the Hussars are visible to the main body of troublemakers you will find your assembly will disperse in moments. And, er… for what it's worth… the commandant in Norwich has already been alerted, so there would be no time lost at that end."

Letts: "The commandant has been alerted? By whom, pray?"

Palmer: "By me."

Letts: "Damn your impudence, sir! Damn your impudence! Who gave you leave?"

Palmer: "Why, the fellow in His Worship's telegraph office."

Letts: "Damn you sir! But no matter – you have wasted the commandant's time and yours. Hussars? Arrant nonsense! I will prepare my men again. They are well able to handle this shambles themselves. Confound it all, what does it say of us if we have to call on Norwich to deal with every disorderly parcel of scroundrels that shows itself on the quay…"

Jermy (very quickly): *"Now, there's a point. Now there is a point. Yes – I confess that, on reflection, you are right, Colonel. 'At'd be a damned poor show. I think we are persuaded. No need for horse warfare, what? But…I do suggest we let things be for half an hour. This'll give most of the rabble time to lose interest, which will isolate the hard core, whom we can then apprehend with your militia."*

Simkins: "Hmm. Well, I grant that seem sensible."

Danford and others: "Aye."

Letts: "Hmph."

Jermy: "And also, before we sally forth again, I move that His Worship should appear at the door with Mr Atwood, who should read the Riot Act. To further legitimise our position…"

Mayor: "Er…"

A show of most hands ratifies the decision. Exit Palmer, in some disgust, quickly followed by Jermy, who stops him on the landing. And, *sotto voce*:

Jermy: "Palmer, send for your Hussars."

Palmer: "But you now said in there…"

Jermy: "I'm well aware what I now said. Now send for your Hussars."

Meanwhile things had got rather slow down on the quay. Most people were back to standing in small groups, and several games of dice had started. After about forty minutes Tealer was heartily bored and all for going home, and he only changed his mind when he smelled hot pastry. Some enterprising baker had sent his lad out into the crowd with a basket full of muffins and pies and was doing a brisk trade amongst the protestors. Tealer found some coins in his pocket. He nudged Charlie.

"Fancy a pie, man?"

"That I would."

Tealer bought a bag of small pies. He, Charlie and Sarah all had one each planning to save the rest for later. But then Tealer noticed Sarah turn her back and quietly stuff the remaining pies in her mouth. Charlie caught this too and winked at Tealer – he was from a big family and already knew about women in Sarah's condition. Tealer, not so well-informed, was about to whisper indignantly to Charlie when the crowd in front suddenly got to its feet.

Again, it was difficult to know what had happened.

Tealer thought he could hear a tiny voice up ahead intoning in some official way. Whoever it was must have been important because the crowd around him started to shush one another. Everyone strained in vain to make out what the speaker was saying, and, for a moment or two, silence fell on the gathering and the only sounds were gusts of wind and the incessant slapping and creaking of halyards from vessels moored along the river.

A buzz of gossip filtered back, the gist of which Tealer missed. Then he saw something fly through the air from somewhere close behind him. There was some angry shouting from the front of the procession and a few seconds later everyone was pushed sharply backwards as a ripple of energy passed through the press. There was another roar from the crowd, this time at a higher pitch, and in an instant the grey wind-blown sky above the lads was filled with stones, bricks, bottles and other missiles that sailed towards the doors of the town hall

It took Tealer and Charlie more than a moment to realize that this good-humoured protest of hard-up seamen, with its shanties, its drumming and its muffins, had just turned ugly.

Sarah tugged at Charlie in desperation, but it was too late to escape. All three were pushed violently one way and the other by men behind them fighting to get to the action. People were now shouting and yelling wildly, but above the general hubbub there arose a chant of "Let-them-go!" What had happened to bring this violent turn of events Tealer had no idea. From his position behind five hundred other marchers, most as tall as or taller than he was, he had no inkling that a body of militia men and constables had made another attempt to get the man Graystone to a steamboat in order to take him to his vessel. This attempt had been foiled by the seamen simply blocking their path, which had led to the mayor appearing on the town hall steps accompanied by Atwood the clerk who'd read the Riot Act – this was the thin-voiced recital Tealer had heard. When news of this spread through the assembly there were general expressions of contempt – and by way of expressing his own disgust, young Charlie Harrison had been moved to throw a half-eaten pork pie as hard as he could in over the heads of the protestors in front. Unbeknownst to him, the pie had caught the wind and knocked the Mayor's hat off just as the clerk was finishing, and the special constables with them had waded in to seize the man they wrongly thought responsible. The result was the mayhem which Tealer and Charlie now found themselves part of.

What Tealer felt – indeed was caught up in – was one irresistible wave of movement followed by another; back and forth they went as the tightly-packed mob charged the arresting constables, were counter-charged, and charged themselves again to release the men who had been seized.

The chant "Let them go!" now resounded across the quay, and Charlie took it up. Tealer was surprised to find himself enervated with a mixture of sympathy and confidence. Here were a thousand men shouting in the street, men his uncle had called 'honest, sturdy fellows', and they were all shouting the same thing. They *must* be *right*, he thought, they *must* have right on their side! He joined in. They charged forward with the crowd, but then were sent running back by another determined counter from the constables, specials and militiamen. This was a rare game! As they raced backwards and forwards Tealer became convulsed with a fits of laughter.

He turned to yell something encouraging to Charlie but found that where Charlie should have been there was only a youth Tealer didn't know. For a moment, he had the curious impression that this unknown boy wasn't interested in the main action, but was regarding him with scared, wondering eyes. He stopped laughing, as for the tiniest instant this impression sparked an old dread. But what was new was the speed with which this old fear, hitherto so unconquerable, was then swept aside by a new, unfamiliar, euphoria. Tealer felt waves of energy course through his powerful young frame, and he became invincible. The strange youth was swallowed in the bubbling cauldron of the riot and utterly forgotten. Tealer then located Charlie, and they joyfully redoubled their efforts to push forward with the rest of the throng.

The din of shouting, yelling and cursing now intensified, as did the scuffling of clogs, the thumps and thwacks of fists, sticks, boots, stones and truncheons hitting or missing their mark, the breaking of glass, the splintering of wood, the crash of falling metal objects, the screams of women, the crying of children and the barking of dogs.

At one point a huge knot of struggling, fighting men staggered straight toward the quay's edge where they would have pitched headlong between the moored vessels into the seething brown tide but for the stout railing that buckled under the strain yet did not give way. This knot of fighters grew bigger as men of both sides raced to the edge of the quay to help their fellows. It teetered again on the quay edge, and then as if by mutual consent surged away from the river and back to the town hall.

What was goading folk on all sides, and was spurring Tealer himself to action? What evil genie had surged out of one of the many broken bottles littering the quay and was swirling around amongst the men and women gathered there, turning the steady old herring port into this maelstrom? Who remembered? Who cared? Away from the sharp end, this was sport!

The crowd swayed back and forth. The rushes of the police were ferociously repulsed by the sailors, and the attempts of the sailors to storm the town hall were equally vigorously resisted by the authorities. Tealer caught sight of a body of constables dragging two sailors up the stairs of the station house next to the Town Hall. The great oak doors swung open to let them in. The foremost demonstrators raced up the stairs behind them, but were too late to stop the doors from being shut and barred. This provoked a special paroxysm of rage in the crowd, and Tealer himself yelled angrily with the rest. Up ahead some of the burliest of the seamen tried to shoulder-charge the huge timbers. They bounced off, and one or two were knocked down by missiles thrown by their own side. Then the crowd drew back – a second group had armed itself with a spar from one of the nearest ships and was now preparing to ram the doors. Desperate not to miss this Tealer actually slipped under the legs of the rioters in front and fought his way closer to the town hall steps.

He was not able to get as close as he wanted, but as he forced himself back on to his feet amongst the sweating mob he could see that the ramming party had come to a halt on the stairs and seemed to be in deliberation. Cries of "Hold hard!" and "Wait!" began to be heard amongst others calling for the doors to be dashed into splinters. It was as though a negotiation had begun. Tealer still couldn't see properly as the sailors with the spar were in his line of sight, but he could see that one or more of the defenders appeared to have risked taking up a position between the business-end of the spar and the massive doors. There was clearly spirited remonstration on both sides, but the actual violence was suspended, and the attackers had put their spar down the better to argue. The crowd behind them was still dangerous: coiling, heaving and twisting, but not actually striking. People in front of Tealer were shouting angry opinions and telling each other to be quiet in equal measure. People behind Tealer knew nothing of events at the front and were impatient to hear the crunch and the cracking of wood as the doors were breached. For a moment the outcome seemed uncertain. Then the crisis seemed to have passed. The party with the spar walked down the steps leaving a single figure at the top exposed.

There was still a fair racket coming from the back of the crowd, and it could only have been the front few who heard what was being said. Heads in front of Tealer bobbed about, trying, as he was, to see, and he still couldn't get a clear view of the man facing the crowd, though at last he could hear snatches of what was being said – and this roused in him a desire to put a face to a voice that for all the noise seemed familiar to him. This meant that he was not concentrating on what was going on around him, and that was very nearly his undoing.

The doors of the hall burst open and a body of constables charged out to seize the spar-wielders. The lone negotiator was apparently trying to stop them but was brushed aside, and the chaos resumed. The infuriated crowd surged forward again shouting about "liars" and "tricksters", and the man from the town hall party was apparently being dragged to safety into the Hall by the defenders who beat back the crowd and slammed the doors shut again, though not before a flint had been hurled at the retreating party and had hit a human skull with a jarring thud.

A moment later an upper floor window opened and a town hall official leant out and waved a large cloth as though taunting the mob below him. He was actually signalling to some entity at the far end of the South Quay, but he had no time for more than a couple of flourishes. Volleys of stones flew up towards him, smashing the glass of the window as he slammed it shut.

The cloth, though, had had the desired effect and the entity took its cue to move forward, revealing itself as a troop of armed horsemen, all waiting for a second signal: this being the downward swing of the troop commander's sabre.

About four hundred years before this unhappy scene, a certain flint fragment had been dislodged from the walls of a nearby Greyfriars monastery during the fires of the Dissolution. For the intervening period this unremarkable cobble had lain undisturbed before being plucked with feverish anger from its matrix of sandy clay and hurled wildly at the cloth-waving figure in the window. The flint failed to connect with the window – in fact it missed the building altogether. It arched high into the grey sky before hitting the branch of one of the South Quay limes. It bounced down through the other branches before ricocheting off at an angle back into the mob below, and it caught young Tealer Sayer square in the side of the head, just as the troop commander brought his sabre down.

Tealer saw a bright red-yellow light and heard a noise like a piano hitting the ground from a great height. The flint had lost most of its momentum in hitting the branch, and much of its remaining force was absorbed by Tealer's blond thatch. He was out cold for only a few seconds, but long enough to miss the fact that the crowd had thinned with astonishing speed and had left him entirely alone in the concourse, and that a rigid line of brass and scarlet complete with waving plumes was clattering straight towards him like a legion of avenging angels. Tealer was still too dazed to be fearful, and he might actually been left alone to face this new threat had not some unknown rescuer run up, reached out an arm thick from a lifetime of hauling heavy canvas, and half-dragged, half-lifted him off the quay to dump him against the river wall.

He was dimly aware that above the general hubbub a woman was yelling his name. He was too concussed to realise this was Sarah, who'd seen his predicament and was screaming for help… and so didn't see that she herself was pulled off the quay by Charlie, but not quickly enough – and that there was a loud *thwunk* as she was struck by the broad chest of the outside horse of the formation, wrenched from Charlie's grip and spun like a wheel under the beast's hooves before being dragged away by a group of seamen, leaving behind her a trail of blood and vomited pie.

Seconds – or minutes – or hours – might have passed.

Tealer's sense of who he was, and then of where he was, gradually returned, together with a growing awareness of a shocking soreness at the point on his head where the stone had struck him. He gathered that he was sitting propped against the river wall, though he still had no clear understanding as to how he got there. He watched dumbly as the last vestiges of the riot were cleared off the quay by the cavalry, whose unexpected appearance had had such a galvanizing effect on the crowd.

After about half an hour the clamour had died away completely. From having been like the arena in a Roman circus the South Quay was now eerily quiet. Even the wind had dropped. Tealer climbed unsteadily to his feet, and winced as the throbbing in his head intensified. He wobbled across the road, not heeding the shards of broken glass that crunched under his boots.

As he walked off he registered vaguely that he was being watched intently by the same strange youth he'd seen earlier. But Tealer was too dazed to pay the lad much attention.

Two Broken Heads

Something akin to a survival instinct led Tealer to pick up his eel-babbing gear so that his movements that afternoon wouldn't attract awkward questions at home. He walked down to Cobholm past sullen groups of sailors – most were standing around muttering, and some, like Tealer, were nursing cuts and bruises.

When Tealer returned home he was still feeling distinctly otherworldly, but through his pain he had the dull feeling that he should try to go in unobserved. But it became clear this wasn't going to happen. As he crept into the parlour he could hear a low urgent conversation going on in the kitchen between Susan Durrant and Daisy, and then Daisy saw Tealer and hurried over to him.

"Here y'are! We were then wonderin' what had happened to you." Tealer was about to start his eel story when he noticed she was carrying a bowl of bloodied bandages.

"There's bin a to-do up the quay. Your poor uncle ha' been knocked about suffin' dreadful. Doctor say he ha' broke his head. But he's still breathin, so 'ass better'n 'at could be. Your poor aunt Durrant ha' bin howlin' her eyes out. She's with him now. You'll ha' wait till mornin' if you want 'see him."

In his dazed condition Tealer could dimly recognise that the kitchen and scullery were spattered with blood. He groped around for something to say, but by the time any words came Daisy had bustled away upstairs with a fresh dressing. She hadn't seen his own injury under his blond thatch and she was far too concerned for her employer to have noticed Tealer's complete lack of reaction to her news.

Tealer staggered up to his own sleeping quarters and lay down on his bed. He had no appetite for supper, and didn't reappear downstairs, though no-one noticed. After a strange night of half-dreams he woke early in the morning to find himself lying fully dressed and in the position he'd lain down in. His head still ached appallingly, and it would still be a while before he could begin to reflect on an afternoon that had begun with his preparing for an eel-babbing expedition on Breydon and had ended with him nearly being trampled by a detachment of Hussars.

Two Broken Heads

A hazy, formless period followed in which days and nights merged into one. Tealer was quite badly hurt, but his famously quiet demeanour disguised the weak state he was in, and Daisy and Mrs Durrant must have assumed that his pallid look and his lack of questions about Palmer's condition were the result of shock at what had happened to Palmer. They had no idea that Tealer himself was in a not dissimilar condition.

Then Tealer began slowly to emerge from the half-light of concussion. Images that had been lost in a fog began to resolve themselves. Memories of recent events became clearer.

But as they did he began to see the strangeness of them.

He remembered with a growing astonishment what he himself had done. He was now quite unable to imagine how he could have joined in the riot so easily. Away from the hypnotic chanting of the mob it all seemed so inexplicable.

The scene that lay beyond the walls of Palmer's house was unchanged – the town hall of warm brick, the stately rows of planes and limes, the arching Dutch gables – and filled with all the familiar and accents. The South Quay, with the glass swept up, the railings put back, and all the rough, genial characters of the town busy about their work, gave no hint of aught amiss. How could he reconcile all that with the bedlam of that Saturday afternoon, when the bedrock of timeless old Yarmouth had suddenly seemed no more than a brittle crust covering a seething lava of anarchy?

Only one fact prevented Tealer from regarding the whole experience as a strange dream, and that was that his uncle, John Palmer, was very ill, and likely to succumb.

Then came the first time Tealer was allowed to tip-toe into his uncle's darkened room. His uncle still couldn't speak, and Tealer had been told not try to talk to him. He found it difficult to associate the shrunken, bandaged form in the silent gloom with the powerful presence of John Palmer. Then as he tiptoed out again he happened to ask Daisy how the injury had come about.

"He was tryin' to talk to 'em in front o' the town hall and some dirty devil threw a stone at'm."

Which was when the last of the buried images from that day came back, and Tealer realised that the unseen figure trying to calm the rioters had been Palmer himself.

And, in Tealer's mind, the question – that of whether Palmer had seen Tealer in the crowd – followed swiftly on. And Tealer's not knowing the answer was destined to make the next few days for him a miserable affair.

Then one evening Susan Durrant, whom Tealer had seen very little of, gently took his hand and said very quietly.

"John, your uncle is able to speak."

Tealer nodded slowly, using all the training of his early childhood to betray no emotion.

"And he wishes me to tell you something…"

Tealer didn't allow an eyelid to flicker.

"It is… that he feels he is on the mend. There, now, is that not good news?"

It is, thought Tealer. Or it should be.

Mrs Durrant went on to tell him that he could visit Palmer again, and could stay for a short while. Tealer duly went upstairs, took a chair, sat down by his uncle's bed, swallowed hard, and asked him how he was. But other than a grunted 'not so bad' and a few monosyllables the bandaged face in the gloom of the shuttered room gave little away.

Then other visitors arrived. Most were acquaintances from the shipping trade, but one was Jermy from the Excise. He stayed for about half an hour, during which Tealer heard quiet voices coming from Palmer's bedroom.

Eventually Jermy reappeared downstairs. Tealer was at supper in the kitchen, which was where Jermy spotted him as he made his way out. The exciseman fixed him with a long, hard exciseman's look.

"So you're the boy Sayer."

"Yes, sir" said Tealer, standing up with the blood crashing about his ears.

Jermy nodded, never taking his eyes off him.

"I ha' seen you before. I've just been talking to your uncle about you."

"In-indeed, sir."

"Yes, indeed, sir." He nodded again, and grinned a wolfish exciseman's grin.

"But last time I saw you, you were in a cot. I knew yer father. James Sayer – he was a... dependable sort. We were both young men in the Priory Lane Tabernacle. Bless him, I once played a terrible trick on him with some cider. I don't think he ever forgave me. Ha! D'you remember him?"

"Yes, sir, a little."

"But talking of good sorts, you should be proud of your uncle, an' all. It's the belief of more than a few of us that he saved a lot of lives out there on the quay th'other day. Don't suppose you were anywhere near the place to see, though...".

"No, that I wasn't, sir, I'd gone eel…"

"... so you wouldn't know. But it was his idea to get the horses on the street. Saved a lot of lives. You won't hear that from anyone else who was there, mind, 'cause they were all agin the idea. Damned shower, the lot on 'em! But your uncle shouldn't ha' tried to reason with the strikers once the trouble started. That *was* a mistake. Things were too far gone by then. He wouldn't be layin' up there in bed with his head split open. But… that's John Palmer for you. And, as I said, he saved a few lives. 'Fact there were very few injuries at all, bar his – just some stupid girl that got herself right under the feet o' the horses. How, I can't imagine, seein' as they never rode at anything above a slow canter. Apart from her, 'at was just a lot of sore heads, I reckon!" He laughed, and Tealer smiled nervously, mindful for a moment of his own throbbing skull. "But I tell you what, boy – and just 'twixt you an' me, now – 'at was a job persuadin' the others, specially that coxcomb Letts. Blast, if *he'd* had *his* way – well, there'd ha' been shootin' and all sorts! But do you keep that to yerself, do they'll brand us all liars."

He turned to go out, and then added with another laugh: "And d'ye know, boy, the stupidest part of it all is that there wouldnt ha' been any real trouble at all but for some clown in the mob hullin' a pie at the mayor during the Riot Act. Can you believe that?"

"Er, no, sir. Thas a rum thing. As you said."

"And, 'course, Lett's men weren't lettin' *that* past! So what happened, happened. Chuh, chuh, chuh!"

Tealer hoped the sharp-eyed inspector had finished at last, but just as he turned to go, he turned back again. "Still," he said "I reckon we all seen a bit of history down the quay last week. I say 'we', but 'course, I don't mean you. You were well out of it, I'd say."

"Yes, sir, I was eel babb…"

"What a business, though! Chuh." He put on his hat, smiled another lupine smile at Tealer, and walked out.

Tealer had lost his appetite again. His head was aching furiously, partly from the still-tender lump, but more from the questions that were now beginning to race through it.

He sat alone in the kitchen for an hour or so, as Susan Durrant was upstairs sitting with his uncle, and Daisy was out. He was now an apprentice in his uncle's office, and without Palmer to direct him, he had not much to do, except think.

He decided to get some fresh air, and walked out into the Row, which was warm and bright in the early autumn sun. The ageing Buck, who had hardly moved from his basket in the kitchen since Palmer's injury, decided to hobble out with Tealer. Tealer stood with the dog, breathing the salty air, still thinking hard. This stopped when Buck set up a deep growling. Tealer looked where the dog was looking, and saw a shape at the river end of the Row, dark against the strong September sunlight. Tealer could only make out a broad brimmed hat. Then the shape disappeared. Buck relaxed, and walked back into the house. Tealer stood watching the end of the Row with a host of feverish questions still raging in his tired head.

Then he turned to look up the other end of the Row and found the same shape not three feet from him, watching him from under the broad-brimmed hat with a fierce blue stare.

"Are you alright, man? I heard you an' your uncle both got hurt in the fight." A familiar voice, but with an unfamiliar, teeth-clenched quality to it.

"Hell, thas you," said Tealer. "Yeah, I'm alright."

"You sure? You're as white as a sheet."

"Yes, well… you made me start, creepin' around the streets like a thief. What were you doing up the Row just then? And whyever are you hidin' behind that great ol' hat?"

"I heard the authorities are still looking for faces they recognise. An' I heard that fellow Jermy was round here 'bout half an hour ago. He's one o' them buggers – you want to watch him."

"Oh, I don't know. My uncle ha' always said Jermy int so bad."

This got no response from Charlie, and Tealer noticed his friend was trembling slightly.

"Anyhow, come to tell you Cousin Jed's Sarah died last night."

Tealer tried to find room for this in his crowded, damaged head.

"Sarah? You mean Georgie's sister. How?"

"Well, you know she fell under the horses on the quay. Women wi' a cargo can't be dossed about like that. The little'un wasn't due for another three months, but that come out, an' they say the blood wouldn't stop coming out after it."

"Do you mean... that was *her* got trampled? Whyever was she in the way?"

"Hell, didn't you know? 'At was *you*. She saw you go down and was hollerin' at me to help you away."

Tealer's colour must have drained again, because Charlie quickly added "Blust, boy, 'at weren't *your* fault. An, Jed ha' told me 'at weren't mine, neither. We both reckon 'at was the bastard that called out them cavalry. Evil bloody thing to do, against men who just wanted enough to live. And wi' women and kids about. But no-one seem to know who it was."

It was then Tealer realised that Charlie wasn't shaking from fear, but rage.

"Any way, just thought you'd want to know." said Charlie, and he turned to go. Then he hesitated: "Oh, I never asked – how's your uncle Palmer?"

"Fairly," said Tealer.

Charlie took this in for a moment, and went.

The sea is a great clearer of heads, and a little while after this meeting with Charlie Harrison Tealer decided he needed a walk along the quay.

The breeze was stiffening, and carried autumn flavours. The river banks and the streets that opened out on to them were alive with commerce. Whistling, singing, banter and blasphemy drifted along the quayside as seamen and stevedores swung craneloads of goods in and out of the holds of the ships. The strike seemed to have been forgotten as men got on with the business of the port.

Then the wind dropped and there was silence. The whole of South Quay, right up to the harbour mouth, stopped moving. No screaming gulls, no slapping wavelets against the hulls of the vessels. No more shouts or whistles. Tealer might have thought his injury had suddenly rendered him deaf but for the crunch of his boots on the cobbles. He realised there was no other sound because nothing on the quay was moving.

This silence lasted for a few seconds, and was broken when every worker on the quay dropped whatever he was holding, and crans, sheets, brushes, lathes, planks, pails, shovels, ladders and saws – all the innocent tools of industry – fell with a series of thumps and ringing sounds that worked their way along the river. Everyone, as one, turned to look at Tealer. And in a second single movement they all picked up, or took down, or pulled out, the more ambivalent items of trade: claw-hammers, crow-bars, flensing-knives, marlin-spikes, pitchforks, hatchets, axes and grappling-hooks.

Tealer knew the reason, and he ran, and with a shout the whole of Yarmouth chased him. His route back home was blocked, so he was forced up to the Haven Bridge and along a Row into the market place. Here the fishwives screamed oaths, picked up their filleting-knives and joined the pursuit. This wasn't like the night-time escape from the drunken whoremonger – this time there could be no doubt how far behind his pursuers were, or why they were after him.

He somehow got to the top of Row 111 and tore down it to his uncle's house. He had no thought what he might do there – perhaps barricade himself in until help arrived. As he slid to a halt outside the house he found his uncle, still heavily-bandaged, standing in the doorway. He shouted out some warning, but his uncle turned his back and slammed the door in his face.

Tealer pounded uselessly at the door and then turned to face the mob which was now appearing at the top end, with a few more cutting off his exit out on to the quay. A long, pointed shard of cast-iron lay nearby where in the recent wind some guttering had fallen from the roof and shattered. Tealer picked it up, backed into a recess in the wall opposite and prepared to fight off his assailants. When they realised their prey was cornered the leading group of pursuers slowed and prepared to attack. Tealer hurled his guttering with a desperate strength. It flew spear-like through the air and impaled the closest of the mob through the neck. This was one of the shrieking harpies from the market. She clutched at the shard and crumpled. Then Tealer went down under a shower of blows from assorted weapons, but not before he'd recognised the woman he'd struck as Sarah, with her faced puffed and bruised from the hooves of the charger and her hair matted with the sweat and blood of miscarriage.

"John! John! John Sayer! *John!*"

Tealer was being shaken about, but could feel no hooks or blades tearing at his flesh. This was because his uncle was standing over him shaking him as he lay slumped and moaning over the table in the kitchen.

"Blast, boy, I thought you'd had with all them dreams years ago!"

This was true – Tealer still had a few, with adolescence providing a few exotic variations on the theme – but it had been a while since he'd had a corker like this. He looked at his uncle, now with much-reduced dressing, smiling down at him.

"Damn it all, I thought *I* was the one that had had the crack on the head. You look as though you don't remember me! Thas better! Now, listen: I han't had a good swig of ginnever in weeks. So I might need you to carry a message. Don't go telling your aunt Durrant. Then in a few days we can go after the mullet on the estuary mouth. The quack say I shouldn't have any loud bangs around me still I'm completely healed, so no popping at duck for a while. So I been layin' upstairs and thinking. I reckon that mullet-fishing is the next best thing. It's about that time of year."

Normality then quickly returned to the house in Row 111. The various forces that seemed to close in on Tealer simply dissipated. The cataclysm of recrimination and blame remained a feature only of vivid dreams. If Palmer had ever suspected that eel-babbing was not the sum of Tealer's activities on the day of the riot, he never let on. When, over supper one evening, Susan Durrant happened to mention she'd heard some of the ringleaders had been hauled up before the magistrate, Palmer only made a remark about some 'dashed hotheads amongst the lads' who'd let things 'get out of hand'.

"Reckon we all learnt a lesson," he said, and started talking about something else.

Of course Tealer never let on about his role in the strike, nor the injury he'd sustained.

And he didn't tell Palmer that Charlie Harrison's pork pie had most likely sparked the riot.

Nor, for that matter, did he tell Charlie.

And he didn't tell Charlie about Palmer's role – as far as he knew Charlie still believed Palmer's main contribution to have been a brave attempt to mediate.

And Charlie never told Tealer that he'd since found out the cavalry was Palmer's idea.

And Palmer never told anyone that the only reason he'd gone out to talk to the rioters was to give the Hussars time to form up.

And so Tealer never told Palmer when later he realized that must have been the case.

And Palmer never told Tealer that he'd paid for Sarah Stolworthy's funeral as soon as he'd heard she had died.

In fact, once the shock of the riot had subsided, no-one on any side really showed much enthusiasm for talking about it at all. And this unwillingness to prolong the issue was not confined to people Tealer knew. Within days of the riot the strikers had returned to their vessels, and within weeks the shipowners had agreed to their demands. Each side decided it had made its point and the dispute that had engendered the fury of the riot was laid to rest.

The reason for this swift new harmony came from the sea. The squally weather that accompanied the riot got worse. A vessel at anchor off Gorleston was cast adrift, and the huge waters smashed it against the wooden lattice of the harbour mouth, causing much damage. Then during one especially fierce night several smacks were lost with all hands. Down on the beach there was soon the familiar, doleful spectacle of splintered timbers, life-boats, debris, detached rigging, and, not long after, the line of water-logged corpses laid out on the shingle. Little huddles of people, mostly women, spent hours and hours standing on the strand gazing out into the angry grey, ever seeing the tip of a mast where there was none.

And as always these losses reverberated around the town in the special manner reserved for deaths at sea. The dispute over pay, with all its ugly consequences, was to all intents forgotten. It was as though all the people of Yarmouth had been reminded that their rickety old herring-town, perched a few feet above the pitiless North Sea, couldn't afford to allow itself to be torn apart from within when it had so much to threaten it from without.

But Palmer still wanted his ginnever! A month after these events he was still recuperating, and Tealer, still aged only fifteen, was sent by his uncle on the 'mission' to Joseph Powley on the Tunstall Staithe.

Palmer had said "Besides, that look less conspicuous if you go, boy. I'm a bit better known than I'd like at the moment."

The message for Powley was simple: 'Rockland'. Tealer didn't ask what it meant, because he knew. Every few months a certain Dutch vessel would be met off Yarmouth by a fleet of three wherries and relieved of its cargo, which usually was several hundredweight of Delft packed in crates of straw together with a few boxes and bottles. Palmer had no interest in the Delft, but like several gentlemen in the area, he could often find houseroom for some of the boxes and bottles. After a decent interval he would pick these up from strategic positions in the reedbeds and creeks. This had been going on for years, and Tealer suspected he did it as much for the spice as for the gain. "Let's give old Jermy the runaround, boy!" he'd say with a grin, knowing that Jermy probably cared not two hoots. Tealer firstly had to pass on word of the hiding place Palmer wanted the wherrymen to use. 'Rockland' therefore meant the bole of a convenient willow on the edge of Rockland Broad.

So as was planned Tealer sailed the *Hermione* up the dyke, and then walked along to the staithe where the three wherries of Powley's fleet were moored. There was no sign of anyone on either the *Sister* or the *Alexandra*, and so for the first time in seven years Tealer climbed aboard the *Stokesby Trader*. Powley wasn't there either, but Tealer found Joyful Norris glowering at him from the hatches.

"Rockland," said Tealer, and turned to go back to the *Hermione*.

"You can tell your uncle I aren't dropping no cigars up Rockland on his say-so."

"I believe they're bottles."

"Don't make no odds. I aren't doin' it."

Tealer stopped. Though still wary of Norris, he found the sour wherryman less intimidating than before. As some boys grow, some men shrink. He was determined not to look at a loss. He said in a neutral voice "You aren't. Right. I'll tell him."

"Tell him I dussn't. Them reedbeds round Rockland is full of Excise. Hell'an' all Excise. He know that."

"If he did know, he'd a' chose somewhere else," said Tealer. He shrugged as lazily as he could, and added "but I'll tell him anyway."

"I know where Excise is and where they int!" shouted Norris. "I was a-dodgin' them buggers when John Palmer was on the tit. I aren't goin' up Rockland wi' his fancy smokes – or his bottles – an' that's that!" And he went back down through the hatch into the galley.

When Norris had disappeared out of sight Tealer suddenly felt a smooth arm snake tightly round his middle and and a hand press itself against the bare flesh under his open shirt where it was tucked into his britches. Another went across the top of his chest and pulled him slowly backwards. He jumped at the touch, for he'd thought that he and Norris were the only two on the wherry.

Then a deep female voice said in his ear:

"Excisemen int why the ole bastard dussn't go up Rockland." Annie Bullard the wherry girl was by then a buxom thirty-one, and had recently taken to giving the lad Tealer a sly smile whenever the wherry had passed the *Hermione* on the river. "Do you ask your uncle!" she added with a grin.

"I… er… will then," said Tealer, going a bit hoarse.

"An' 'ass all you have to say to a lady? I'd 'a thought…" but she was interrupted by some cursing from below. She shrank away into the galley; but not before she had given Tealer's hand a hard squeeze.

Tealer tottered back along the tow-path to the *Hermione* and sailed down the Bure to Yarmouth. When he walked the last few yards up South Quay it was deserted but for one youth of Tealer's age. Tealer looked briefly at the boy, and then looked again. He was trying to place the face, and he found himself taken back to the riot.

But then he forgot him. Tealer now had other concerns, and they were all linked to the feeling of Annie Bullard's arm around his waist.

When he got back home he told Palmer what Annie Bullard had told him, if not the manner of delivery.

"No, the Bullard woman is right," said Palmer, "Norris would never be caught on Rockland after dark. He's scared of meeting Tom Pye. Rockland was where he did for him."

Palmer explained that he was referring to an accident, but one that was Norris's fault. It had been a rough winter's day on Rockland. The wherry was due to pick up reed, and while Pye and the cutters had been loading up, Norris had been in the galley with a bottle of the contraband.

"Necked a glass or two more than he could take," said Palmer. Later that day, they were just setting off from Rockland when a gale of wind blew up and Norris decided to drop the sail. He was still shakey from the brandy. His hand wasn't steady on the pawl, which failed to engage on the windlass gear. "Often happens," said Palmer. But more seriously Norris had broken the golden rule: he'd left the winch handle in the winch, so that when the spar and sail crashed to the deck, the windlass spun round "screaming like a scalded witch" and the handle came adrift and went whistling through the air in an evil, flailing arc, and brained poor Tom as he was clearing the hatches to receive the sail's gaff end. His corpse was knocked over the side. Norris could only sit and watch the waters of the broad turn red with the failing of another of its sons. It took them most of the day, Palmer added, to hook poor Pye out from the mud at the bottom.

"And what don't help is that other people reckon they still see Tom Pye a-standing on the water on misty nights, waiting to point his finger at Norris. And as I ha' said more than once: there are too many misty nights on these rivers of ours for men with a guilty conscience."

That last bit about Tom Pye is the part that we know would have riveted Tealer in earlier years – more proof that your accusers *do* stand watching you on marshes, by broads and at other lonely places! But Tealer was growing, and the notion of Tom Pye haunting the miserable wherryman Norris had less resonance with the boy than it might have done with the child.

All that was in his head was Annie Bullard's constrictor-smooth grip.

Tealer had to set up an alternative drop for his uncle's illicit gin, and this took him out on to the Broads several more times. And when he finally came home with the requisite bottles in the folds of his coat he looked warily around for any of the more officious excisemen as he crossed South Quay.

Again the strange youth was standing just where he had before. But this time, if Tealer noticed him, it was only from the brief notion that he could be an exciseman's lookout. Any deeper suspicion was subordinated utterly to the recurrent sound of Annie Bullard's husky voice in Tealer's ear.

These, then, were some of the formative experiences in the youth of John 'Tealer' Sayer. Over the next two years he would find himself subject to all the usual influences. Ale continued to taste bitter, yet he came to like the bitterness. Tobacco made him choke, yet through the choking he felt its calming effect. Females were ever perverse, yet he began to be charmed by the perversity. These were all the standard distractions, but none would cause his downfall.

And a yet more powerful siren was calling, drowning these others out.

The sea, the first real wilderness he had ever been shown, had come back to steal Tealer's soul. He found himself ever more interested in Palmer's shipping business; perhaps more than Palmer himself. Even on days when he could have been shooting or fishing he had taken to wandering down to the quay to compare the rigs of the brigs, the brigantines, barks, the barkentines, the sloops, the ketches and the schooners.

His uncle responded to this welcome interest by securing him a position as a junior, and his life as a man of the oceans was underway. He was already travelling abroad before his sixteenth birthday. However wide the skies over the marshes and the broads, there was a now bigger world beyond.

It was when Tealer was eighteen and sailing on brigs out of East London that he received a communication from Susan Durrant telling him that Palmer had died in a shooting mishap.

"Poor John, hoist by his own petard", she added, smiling her sad, patient smile as they drank tea in the house after the interment. "But how else would he have wanted to end his days?"

Susan Durrant decided then that she was middle-aged, and she went to live with her sister in Swindon, where a newly-rich railway-owner had children he wished to be put on the right track.

Thereafter Tealer only visited Yarmouth between voyages. The man who had saved him from a childhood of mumbling introversion and shepherded him through the tribulations of youth was dead. Yarmouth had become as grey as the sea that churned on its shingly beaches. Tealer kept the house on Row 111 as an occasional dwelling and as a store for his uncle's effects. He rented out the Gorleston property he'd grown up in. He also maintained one or two houseboats down at the riverside. On occasions he visited old friends like Charlie, Jointy or Simon.

Other than these, he thought, the threads that tied him to 'the old place' were all broken.

That's what Tealer Sayer thought.

When he looked around the other mourners who had gathered for his uncle's burial in the unkempt Palmer plot, he could not know how closely acquainted he would one day be with a then eight-year-old pair of freckly hands that had helped in the preparation of the smart, sombre Pritchard headgear that many of them were sporting for the occasion.

But before we leave Tealer Sayer to sail away into adulthood there is one last scene from his early life that we should record, because it introduced to him a character who later very nearly destroyed him, or saved him from destruction, depending on your view.

It was mid-October and Palmer's first foray out on the marsh after his injury. He and Tealer were standing on the shores of the estuary fishing for mullet in the silky swirling mud of the incoming tide. Tealer had caught a fine specimen which his uncle helped him unhook. Tealer mentioned to Palmer that he thought mullet an ugly sort of fish, even though its great pouting lips were like those of a 'beautiful woman'.

"Well, yes," said Palmer, "Yes, I reckon you could say they are, boy. Though I should like to know what beautiful women *you've* met to know a thing like that."

And as they re-baited and re-cast into the shallows Palmer laughed again, shaking his head. Then he looked at Tealer as though something had occurred to him.

"Boy," he said, "can you keep a confidence? Yes… I reckon you're old enough;

I reckon you can. That's time. Come on, we ha' caught enough mullet, and that seem you've got an eye for a fair maid. Well let me take you to meet the fairest maid in Norfolk. Let's go and call on my White Lady."

They gathered up their fish and dismantled their lines and set off by boat to a most secret place.

They were watched by the inevitable youth in the distance. Tealer had marked him earlier and not thought anything more. Perhaps he should have, because it was this figure that ten years on would leave him a wild-eyed, hypothermic wreck in that stranded punt circled by several hungry crows and the single huge gull out on the ice of this same Breydon estuary.

But that was still a long way hence. Right now Tealer was being led away to be initiated into the life-changing rites of White Jenny.

HAVENS AND REEFS

La Belle Dame sans Merci
Hath thee in thrall

John Keats – *La Belle Dame Sans Merci*

The Witching of Tealer Sayer

In late August on the estuary of Breydon, the shortening of the evenings only serves to enhance the feeling that summer might be everlasting. Men and women can stand along the Yarmouth shore of the estuary and stare across it into the mighty sunset with the residual warmth of the day still in the pebbles and dust under their feet. The gathering gloom makes them wistful. No-one talks. People gaze into the dusk. A few who know about such things might dream about the time when Roman commanders first stood in this same place and gave the estuary, then far bigger, the name *Gariensis*. Others simply dream.

There's the smallest breath of wind and it is in the kindly west. From its birthplace above the wild Atlantic it has blown across the moors of Ireland and the hills of Wales before passing over the farmland of central England. It has soughed and sighed through nameless groves and quiet valleys, and has ruffled the leaves of fifty million oaks and beeches. It has eddied around churches, barns and spinneys, it has set up tiny dust clouds in kitchen gardens and sent slow waves across the ripening corn. By the time it has reached Norfolk it is merely a breeze, heavy with the scents of harvest. As evening comes it doesn't even cause a ripple on Breydon's grey waters. Higher in the sky it has still a little of its strength, enough to be caught by the single mighty black sail of a wherry. That great craft, laden with thirty tons of bricks, is slipping silently down the estuary towards Yarmouth.

These are the evenings when the world seems made for leisure, and even those with a job go about it slowly, as though they were working on the Sabbath. Someone with some unpressing business upriver rows with an oar-stroke so slow that his boat scarcely moves, even with the water at slack. As he slops his way along, he stops after each pull to watch the wherry ply its way in the opposite direction.

From the Bowling Green Inn comes the mutter and laughter of competitors and the click and clatter of the sport which gives the place its name. The Bowling Green is an ideal tavern for Breydonsiders. It lies on a spur of land at the point where the combined waters of the Yare and the Waveney, flowing out of Breydon, meet those of the Bure coming down from the north to form the great muddy current which then swings south through Yarmouth town and out from the harbour to the open sea. This spur gives a clear view of the meeting waterways and their banks, and even the lane leading up to the tavern from Yarmouth.

In the air above the river black-headed gulls are wheezing half-heartedly to one another. They have the skies to themselves, for the legendary flocks of wildfowl will not be honking and whistling their way from the arctic wastes for several months yet.

There is even something subdued in the relentless thump from the other end of town where the new-fangled steam hammer is driving piles into the clay of the harbour mouth. Only the dancing, singing swarms of gnats show any urgency as they prepare to fan out across the evening sky.

Down below the wall at the end of the lawn, in the mud at the water's edge, and looking as though they've just sprung from it, five or six boys are sailing a variety of boat-shaped scraps from the timberyard downstream in Yarmouth. Even as they watch their precious craft negotiate the jetsam of broken pots, waterlogged beams and dead seabirds, the ways of the wind and the water are being etched on their minds. Generations of the town's seamen have played at this spot in their childhood, and many a passenger brought safely to land through the angry swell of the Yarmouth Roads has had reason to be grateful.

The sharp ears of one lad catch a change in the pattern of chat coming from the 'Green, and he puts his head over the wall to find a newcomer has walked out to join the bowlers. His friends haven't caught on – each one is watching the wherry as it slides silently past, dreaming of a day when he might be the one sitting nonchalantly in the stern smoking his clay, with one foot rested on that tree-trunk of a tiller. But this particular child is listening hard. He hears snatches of talk – only snatches – but enough to glean that the newcomer is a sailor, and that he has just come into port. The boy knows what this means. He doesn't even glance back at his friends, but quietly slips up the steps and scampers away down the path to the town – the other boys are still watching the slow progress of the wherry.

The lad knows exactly where he is going. He tears down the North Quay road, over the Haven Bridge and on into Southtown. By this time he's panting hard, but he catches the sight of an unfamiliar set of masts towering up from behind the quayside church of St Mary's and vying for dominance of the skyline with the legendary High Mill of Southtown, the tallest in England. It makes him run even faster. A clipper has berthed! And such is the speed with which dock gossip gets across Yarmouth that it can only be a matter of time before the other boys come running over the bridge into Southtown to have a look. By these few minutes' advantage he will have sole rights to any oranges or other treats thrown over the rail by its chuckling crew.

There's everything to play for!

He races the last hundred yards down St Mary's Lane and out on to the quayside. There the *Shadwell Empress* sits at her mooring, and for all his running the child has to stop breathing for a moment as he takes in the enormity of the vessel. Though not yet nine years old he knows his sails. He can see that with three masts square-rigged, and the stern-most rigged fore-and-aft, the *Empress* is a bark. He doesn't know that she has spent her thirty years shifting coal to South America and coming back with coffee, nor that her owner is a Yarmouth man who has brought her home from Brazil via London to sell her to some Dutchman wishing to sail the Antwerp route. If the deal fails the owner will simply take her back out into the Atlantic and leave her to her own devices.

She's therefore all but empty. There's no spare fruit to be had. There's only the bizarre whiff of a hold that very recently has held coffee. Although he's disappointed, the boy knows the value of loitering in the area. There's usually something of interest to see when a clipper docks. Last time it was a giant scarlet and gold macaw which flew out of the galley, across the river and on to the roof of the town hall where it sat and screamed insults at the crowd below. On another occasion a hairy spider as big as a rat darted out of a crate of pineapples and ran across the quay, causing hardened stevedores to scatter. The lad has also seen men with black skin on every part of their bodies except the palms of their hands; he has seen brown men with eyes like coal and yellow men with their hair in plaits.

Alas, no parrots, spiders or coloured men appear. Only one fellow comes down the gangplank, and he is of the local tint, if a little sunburnt. He's tall, with blond hair and a close-cropped beard. He has large canvas bag on his shoulder and a leather pouch attached to his belt. At the bottom of the gangplank he lets the bag fall with a thump, feels the pouch and looks around him. He sees the boy, and to the latter's astonishment makes straight for him. He has a surprisingly quiet voice for a sailor.

"Well now, my man, what ha' been going on in Yarmouth since I been away?"

The child is dumbstruck at being spoken to by a man straight off a clipper, so the sailor asks again. "I said, what ha' been going on here?"

The child hesitates, still incredulous that it is him the seaman is talking to. Finally, he says:

"My front tooth ha' fell out."

"Fairies come?"

"No."

"What else ha' happened?"

More thinking: "Mrs Barker upstairs died of the cough'n."

"Sorry to hear that."

"Sally's had a l-litter of ten b-but two died and Joe bashed all the others with a lead pipe 'cept Smudger."

"Sorry to hear that, an'all. Still, think on it this way, old partner: Smudger's brothers and sisters'll never know the marsh damp a-seizing up their back legs. But poor old Smudger will one day. Keep you a-goin'. What else come to mind?"

With his most immediate stock of gems exhausted, the boy moves on to second-hand material. "Mr Preston's the new mayor but he int a labourin' man's man…"

"Mr Preston, eh?" says the sailor, looking up and down the quay and nodding almost absent-mindedly. "Mr Preston. Is that so?" Then he looks at the boy again. "What else?"

"Um. Charlie H. ha' joined the militia."

"And Charlie H. in the militia? Did you mean Charlie Harrison?"

The boy's squirming shows that he does not have a clue if he means Charlie Harrison, so the man smiles and says "Cause thas a laugh if you do! Thought thas the last thing *he'd* join. Blast! There *is* a laugh. Anything else come to mind?"

The boy thinks again, mouth open, desperate to oblige. He is wringing his memory for drops of recent gossip; mutterings that have wafted over the wall from the Bowling Green; comments his mother has whispered to other women in the Rows; murmurings he has picked up through the curtain on the nights his father has been sober.

"Oo-ar," he says, 'Arty Ruddock's Joyce ha' had a boy, but 'at'll look more like their lodger than 'at do Arty. Holland the timber merchant is on bad times, but his foreman look better off every day. Cadger Brown's punt ha' grew legs and walked."

The sailor's grin broadens. This is what he has been questioning the boy for: not the news, but to hear the familiar tones of Yarmouth for the first time in months.

And seeing the man smile, the boy relaxes a little and goes on: "Tealer Sayer's girl ha' run off with a Scotchman. An'…, oo-ar! An' you want t'be careful by Breydon 'cause every day there's an exciseman a-layin' about in the reeds there. Oo-ar! An' Deaf Watson reckon he 'a seen a ghost up the top o' Berney mill."

And being not yet nine, the boy still has something to learn of the world, so when he looks up at the sailor and sees the smile has frozen on the man's lips he doesn't know if it is mention of excisemen or mention of ghosts which has caused the bigger shock.

"Got go home now," says the lad, and vanishes.

And this is how John 'Tealer' Sayer learns that his long-awaited haven has turned out to be a reef.

August is also the month when Mr Jeremy Lovett, now a senior elder at Gorleston's Cliff Street Tabernacle, makes sure to warn the younger elements of the Tabernacle congregation of the special end-of-summer traps that Satan lays for them. Lovett threatens them with the terrible consequences of being drawn into 'devil worship' and 'heathen rites'. He refers, of course, to the dancing and the merriment that mark another successful conclusion to the year, with crops brought safely to barn and fruit saved from birds, wasps and blights. Being several generations Gorleston folk, Lovett and the other Tabernaclers don't have much to do with the land. They know little about its cycles and rituals, and what they do know only makes them suspicious. They certainly find nothing godly in August's dubious celebrations of fertility; they see them instead as excuses for licentiousness and idolatry. They deplore even the sober harvest festivals of the Anglicans in St Nicholas church. A flummery of apples, flowers and loaves baked in fancy shapes, if you ask the Tabernaclers. A half-step from corn dollies and Green Men.

But Jeremy Lovett himself reserves his most terrible denunciations for the Burgh Castle 'horkey', a harvest dance that takes place in the vast interior of the ruined Roman shore fort of *Gariannonum*.

No-one knows when the tradition of this frolic started; only that it has always been permitted by the owner of the land, is linked to a regatta down on the water earlier in the day, and is paid for by the local church. It's always held once the crops are just in, and the space at the centre of the huge fort is still a sea of stubble. It's known to the locals simply as 'the horkey up the fort'. Although nominally a church event, it brings together villagers, workers from the upland farms, marshmen, wherrymen, dockers, wildfowlers, fishermen, clerks, tinkers, musicians and sundry other sinners. And once the sun is safely down, the church-goers have made their excuses and the cider has really begun to flow, people from the Gorleston side of the river – quite respectable people by day – begin to sidle through the gap between the fort's massive flint walls; then they are soon indistinguishable from the rougher offspring of Yarmouth as they drink, jig, and giggle.

And the ruined fort of *Gariannonum* is a perfect site for such outrages. It sits on a bluff of land sheltered from the stern sea breezes by the sand dunes of Yarmouth behind it. On clear days it offers heady vistas of the Breydon estuary, the courses of the Yare and Waveney rivers as they flow into Breydon, and the marshes beyond. When the fogs of autumn swirl around on the swamps below, the fort takes on a mysterious and romantic character, and standing on its walls you can feel as though you are on a great ship at sea. When the thunder clouds are piling in the marshland skies, or the east wind is whipping in from the coast, the fort offers a sheltered vantage from which to view the flatlands at their wildest. Being a good way away from the nearest habitation, it is rarely visited except by the occasional antiquarian. And the whole site is surrounded with whispering shrubs of willow and elder that form thick, secluded groves.

Little wonder that young revellers have always met here to dance, drink and forget that the gentle green marshes will soon be in the icy grip of winter.

Little wonder that a good few people in the area have birthdays in May.

Little wonder that Lovett and his flock regard the Roman ruin as the playground of Beelzebub.

Little wonder that it was here John 'Tealer' Sayer was seduced by Maud Pritchard the witch-maiden.

So… the Roman fort is the object of Lovett's special fury.

He summons all his energies for an attack on the 'horkey' on the Sunday before it is due to be held. Till then he is ominously silent. But on that dread day he gives vent to such fits of lectern-pounding that his magnificent beard is soon flecked with the spittle of righteous passion and his metacarpals are bruised for days afterwards. (This violence to the lectern is a relatively new feature in a Lovett sermon. It appeared a few years ago – at about the time a falsetto squeak had started to compromise his devastating crescendos – and now the relentless pounding is a mainstay of the performance.)

"People try to tell us that that there fort is 'old', don't they?" he thunders, thumping the oaken frame of the lectern with both hands. "They tell us thas 'old', don't they? And then they tell us there's suff'n special 'cause thas 'old'. Well (*thump*), brothers and sisters in Chroist, I can't see it m'self. Can't see it m'self. In fact, I'm go' tell you something different (*thump*), brothers and sisters in Chroist. Somethin' different (*thump*). I've bin a-readin my bible (*slap*). My bible (*slap*). And that don't say nothin' (*thump*) about 'old' things being sacred or special. There int nothing (*thump*) sacred about 'old'. No, that there int. And do yer know, brothers and sisters, just recently I ha' been a-readin' another book, an'all. Not the Bible, now. No, another book. Now, normally, all the reading I ever do is from the Good Book (*slap*) what lay here in front of me. The Good Book (*slap*) what lay here in front of me. That's all we need to read, int it? That that is. Normally, any rate. But I *did* come by a book gi'en to me by a fellow brother in Chroist several year ago what I want to tell you about. What I want to tell you about. Thas a book about the people what lived here in ancient times. And 'at brought suffin' to my mind what I want to share with you today in our Tabernacle. This is what I want to share with you: all these here 'wonderful old places' what we ha' got hereabouts – I mean all these here 'forts' and 'mounds' and ancient stones and suchlike – weren't (*thump*) put up by Christian people at all. Not (*thump*) by Christian people at all. I don't just mean these was people as were born in the light but then went astray or joined the papists or the Anglicans (what we know are papists by any other name). I don't just mean *that*. No! I mean they weren't Christian (*thump*) at all! Not (*thump*) at all! Not (*thump*) at all! I mean them there old ruins and monuments were put up by people what sacrificed in human blood! And worshipped idols such as were worshipped by the Canaanites! The Canaanites (*thump*)! Right here, not twenty minutes' ride from our Tabernacle. The very bricks, the very mortar what you can break off and crumble in your hands was put there by people what practised idolatry (*thump*), and fornication (*thump*), and all manner of other (*thump*) er…er…. immoralities! Yes! Other immoralities! And yet (*thump*) – AND YET! …and yet… er…and yet – each year young people from this here town – this (*thump*) here (*thump*) town (*thump*) – go and join all and sundry for drinkin' and dancin' and… and… I know not what… within (*thump*) them (*thump*) there (*thump*) very (*thump*) same (*thump*) walls (*thump*)! Well now, need I say more? Need I say more? Brothers and sisters in Chroist (*thump*)…" and, exhausted, he takes hold of the sides of the pulpit to catch his breath. He can barely whisper the concluding, triumphant, repetition, "Brothers and sisters, need I say more?"

He needn't, but when he gets his breath back he usually does. He usually goes on to cite the case of Godfrey Atkins, an earnest curate at the Church of St Nicholas in Yarmouth with an interest in history. A few years ago this Atkins wrote an article for the local paper in which he suggested, if you please, that there was no *better* site for a church harvest dance than the Roman fort as "this was the place where Christianity was first brought to the East Coast by Fursey the Missionary".

"And who, pray, was Fursey the Missionary?" roars Lovett as he has every year since the offending tract first appeared. "Who was Fursey the Missionary? I'll tell you who Fursey the missionary was. An Irish monk, that's who! An Irish (*thump*) monk! A monk! (*thump*) Now then! Now then! A Roman (*thump*) Catholic! I rest my case. I rest my case."

But Jeremy Lovett can rest his case as many times as he likes – the drinking and dancing and sweating of the horkey at Burgh Castle go on, as immutable as the harvest it celebrates. Indeed, as if to prove Lovett's point, it was at the same frolic two years ago – indeed, two years ago to this very evening of Sayer's homecoming – that Tealer Sayer was first ensnared. Yes, an ensnarement of just the kind – *just the kind* – that the folk of the Tabernacle are always warning against!

And the particular temptress selected by Satan for the ensnaring was a dreamy redhead by the name of Maud Deirdrie Pritchard.

Was Maud Pritchard really a witch? A daughter of Satan?

Maud certainly wasn't a typical daughter of Gorleston. She certainly wasn't the sort to shuffle along the pavement under a mousey shawl like one of the flat-chested, bony, browbeaten young women of the Tabernacle. But then neither was she like any of those town girls who could often be seen wobbling up the High Street of a Sunday afternoon, decked out in their catchpenny finery, stealing glances at themselves in every shop window and brass plate. Instead Maud would stride around the town, bonnetless, unchaperoned and purposeful, her stunning head held high and her thicket of auburn ringlets streaming over her shoulders and down her back like some kind of gypsy princess. And if this alone weren't proof enough for any Tabernacle witchfinder, there were the eyes. Maud's eyes were green. Not the greeny-brown that is often called 'green', nor the 'green' that is just a nice term for a certain insipid shade of blue. Maud's eyes were *green* – a scorching, emerald green. A green with a vividness that not only lit up her own face but seemed to light up everyone and everything she looked at. Yes, to the holy men of Gorleston it was her eyes that showed Maud to be unusually dangerous. For surely any God-fearing young woman graced with such stunning eyes would be all the more careful to keep them lowered to the floor. And even if she were some run-of-the-mill slut she would drop her eyes... if only in that lewd, mock-modest fashion of sluts. Yet Miss Pritchard did not lower her gaze modestly, nor did she drop it coquettishly, nor did she conceal it in any way at all. Instead she directed it straight at anything that interested her, and straight through anything that didn't.

None of the stern Tabernacle fathers ever knew Maud well enough to speak to – she was of Anglo-Catholic stock, and Tabernaclers have never had much to speak to Anglo-Catholics about. But they could hardly miss her, especially on those high days and holidays when they left the sanctuary of their Tabernacle and sallied forth into the very wilderness of Gorleston to do battle with the Powers of Darkness. They would erect a little booth on the corner of High Street and Baker's Road. They would cover it with placards bearing pithy texts from the Scriptures, and from this portable citadel they would berate, harangue and plead with the sinful of the town. As they shouted their message across the street they would scan the faces of passers-by for signs of 'guilt'. If they spotted any such 'guilt' they would step up the passion in their voices, glaring pitilessly at their target as she (and it usually was a she) tried to lose herself in the throng.

And they were more subtle than you might think. They never pointed or named names, but they never left you in any doubt as to the intended victim. And if, as happened from time to time, some shameless little strumpet chose not to be cowed but to stare straight back at them, their righteous passion could change effortlessly into reasonableness and unctuous, head-shaking pity. And best of all was when the gin-soaked invalid of the Crimean, whose begging pitch they habitually blocked with their stand, would stagger right up to their podium and shout some choice vulgarity straight into their faces, making the onlookers howl with laughter. This the Tabernaclers positively loved, for it was only important to them that they were the centre of attention; they cared not one jot what kind of attention it was. And in any case, there's nothing your religious zealot loves more than being laughed at; it appeals to the martyr in him.

What your religious zealot finds harder to cope with is being utterly unnoticed. It is those who are neither furtive nor scornful but genuinely indifferent that he finds truly vexing. The Tabernaclers were skilled enough at promoting their cause for this not to happen very often, but one who managed such indifference, and managed it repeatedly, was Miss Pritchard. The Tabernacle elders secretly came to dread the sight of her pre-Raphaelite silhouette appearing at the top of the street, for the result was generally the same each time. If she happened to pass the Tabernacle stand she might look casually up, she might not, but she never so much as broke her stride. Of course everyone else in the street, covertly or openly, would turn to watch *her*, for she was uncommonly lovely, and the unfortunate preacher of the day would suddenly be preaching to himself. He would probably begin to stutter and bluster as he lost his thread. His fiery sermon would fizzle in his throat. What was worse, he would find himself doing what everyone else was doing, which was watching spell-bound as Maud floated on down the road.

And what infuriated the preachers most was not the suspicion that Maud created these distractions on purpose, but the realisation that she didn't.

So, when subsequent, disgraceful, events took Maud far away from Gorleston, the Cliff Street faithful were not sorry to see the back of her. Thereafter they only had to contend with the unchallenging husseys who spent the weekends loafing and preening in the High Street. If any of the elders did ever think back to that torrid summer of 1867 they'd assure themselves that there'd been 'something different' about the girl Pritchard...

There'd been something unnatural about her.

Unquestionably.

A handmaid of Beelzebub.

A daughter of Satan.

Maud was actually the daughter of Maggie Pritchard, widow to the late G Pritchard of F Pritchard & Sons, Milliners and Haberdashers to the Gentry. And the gaze that left Lovett and his followers feeling so marginal was not a product of unspeakable pride but of uninterrupted dreaming, usually prompted by whatever romantic novel Maud was reading at the time.

If Maud did seem a little 'different' it was only because 'different' was exactly what, from the age of three, she'd been told she was. Maggie Pritchard never let her daughter forget that she was descended from a family of Anglo-Irish landowners, lords of the verdant, magical hills around the sacred site of Glendalough. And if, Maggie would add, Maud's poor late father did not stem from such distinguished stock – if making hats in Gorleston was not quite the same as owning swathes of County Wicklow – well, it was at least a trade 'a little apart' from the common run.

It therefore never occurred to Maud to doubt she was chosen for better things. Yet simple vanity was no failing of Maud's. The thought of Gorleston, with its three straggling roads of shops and squat cottages, did not cause her broad, sensuous mouth to curl; she was so confident that the fishing town would never figure much in her destiny that she bore no resentment to it at all. She was never unkind to the dowdy coterie of female friends, daughters of other small businessmen in the town, with whom she was wont to associate. She never bolstered her own sense of superiority by putting them down. But she knew in her heart that they were never going to be setting out on the same great adventure as the daughter of the late G Pritchard.

It was in fact two years and three months ago – a Sunday afternoon in May – that Tealer Sayer first sailed into the view of this young visionary. She was taking a walk under the lime trees along Yarmouth's South Quay. She was with her friends Sadie Howe, whose family ran a small fish-curing business, and Polly Bessey, eldest daughter of the Bowling Green landlord. Maud loved nothing more than to come along the quayside with her friends to gaze at the ranks of schooners and Indiamen. The tangle of masts, sails and ratlines would mesmerise her as they creaked and rocked in waves from the Haven Bridge all the way down to the harbour mouth. She would take in the wonderful odours of salt water, fish, pitch and spice, and would imagine the places the ships had seen, the hurricanes they had weathered and the baking doldrums they had languished in. For Maud the quay was gateway to a world beyond the hat-making and gossip of Gorleston. She'd walk arm-in-arm with her two young friends, entertaining them with stories of this 'real world' that she had read all about. Polly and Sadie would listen agog. Polly in particular would be fascinated; Maud's rich imagination and vivid descriptions gave the publican's daughter a place to escape to from the drudgery of the Bowling Green. At fifteen she had probably forgotten more about certain parts of this 'real world' than Maud was ever likely to know, but she no more realised this than Maud did.

On this day in May the three companions happened to pass two men who were both pointing up into the masts of a large ship and discussing some detail of its rig. Maud admired the upright bearing of the taller man in a vague sort of way and wondered what countries *he* might have visited. Then as they passed the two men Sadie leant across her to Polly and whispered:

"Poll, thas Palmer's nephew, int it? I remember him from when I was small. He was a Tabernacle boy, 'cept he left and went to live with his uncle."

Polly shrugged. She had the tact of an innkeeper's daughter and didn't point out that that was years before she was born.

"*Must* be who 'at is, then," said Sadie. "I used to see him with that John Palmer what died. 'Course I was only a littl'un."

"Did you know him well then?" asked Maud, watching the man.

"No," said Sadie, "he was much older'n me. Years older."

They all stole glances back at the two sailors. The other sailor looked briefly in their direction, but Sayer didn't even take his eyes off whatever it was in the mizzen that was so interesting.

That night Maud mentioned this to her mother as they ate bloaters in their parlour. Maggie told her that if the young man were indeed John Palmer's nephew it could only be young John Sayer. She had no idea he still lived in the area. It was his uncle who'd brought him up, she said, and always used to call him 'Tealer', though she had no idea why. Her own memory of John Sayer was as a small child, well-behaved, but always very quiet. She explained that he was one of the Gorleston Sayers, and his mother was a Palmer with Sandcroft connections – all a little reduced in circumstances, but still quite notable local families:

"…so the Howe girl shouldn't be getting ideas! Her people cure fish, do they not?" Maggie chortled at the thought and ate some more of her bloater. Then she put down her knife and sipped thoughtfully at her water.

"But – do you know…?"

And Maud knew what was coming.

"…if young John Sayer does still live here he might be an interesting young man for *you* to become acquainted with. I only say he *might* be. He's not of our church, I'm sure, but that could be overcome. I should make some discreet enquiries."

Maud didn't much rate her mother's talents as a matchmaker. It was Maggie who had trawled the local Anglo Catholic congregations to find a husband for Maud's sister Rebecca. As a result poor Becky was now joined in conjugal felicity with one Pericles Catchpole, an averagely successful, nasal-voiced accountant from Norwich who sought to impress any listener with his reduction of "complex issues" by what he styled the "application of simple principles". He impressed Maud only with his ability to irritate her the moment he opened his mouth. But Maggie had been so emboldened by her success in marrying off the plain daughter that she was convinced she would soon find a match for the pretty one. Only the previous winter she'd made 'discreet enquiries' amongst other young men in Catchpole's circle, causing a succession of stooping, whey-faced bores to beat a path up Cliff Street to present themselves. The most determined suitor had made a valiant attempt to win Maud's heart with an explanation of double-entry book-keeping. To give him his due he'd lasted a full twenty-three minutes before shrivelling in the stony green glare.

Yet, in the case of Tealer Sayer, Maggie had said just enough to set her daughter's fertile mind a-working. There'd been nothing stooping or whey-faced about the seaman Maud had seen on the quay. She now knew that Tealer was a relic of one of the old Gorleston shipping dynasties. That certainly didn't hurt his suit, but the key point for Maud was that Tealer himself was a junior officer serving aboard merchant ships.

He had *travelled*!

The other details her mother subsequently uncovered and passed on to her were meant as mild caveats: that by twenty-six Tealer had not shown the remotest interest in 'settling down'; that his uncle had been an maverick who had let the Palmer business go to pot; that the Sayer business had long since gone to pot; that Tealer himself only seemed interested in chasing wildfowl whenever he was home. But inasmuch as she thought about it at all Maud regarded Tealer's alleged reluctance to put down roots as a point in his favour. The other details she ignored.

She'd made up her mind that she would get to know more of this enigmatic seafarer.

So for the next month Miss Pritchard worked on ways to place herself foursquare in the path of the unsuspecting Sayer. She had no luck at all. She was even reduced to dropping handkerchiefs, but she stopped that when an expensive piece of *pointe d'Irlande* was caught by the wind, blown down the South Denes road and into the river without Tealer even turning round. She started associating with people she normally found immensely tiresome but who she reckoned might know Tealer, or might know someone who knew him, or might know someone who knew someone else who knew him.

She began to frequent the quay rather more than was respectable for a young lady from the Gorleston side of the Yare. On several occasions she spotted Sayer in the distance – what little she could see gave her the impression of a tall, serious-looking man with a direct manner about him that she correctly guessed came from a life of giving instructions. This detail was duly inserted into the tapestry, a tapestry in which strands of truth criss-crossed with others of complete fantasy – such as that the Sayers were scions of East Anglian nobility, an ancient dynasty of which Tealer was the last proud survivor; that Tealer had journeyed the globe; that Tealer had known hardship and privation; that Tealer had witnessed scenes of passion, wonder, cruelty and bloodshed beyond the ken of land-living folk.

And with a girl like Maud it is hard to say whether learning the facts would have curtailed this elaborate fantasy at all.

The facts being, of course, the same facts that Tealer's parents had often reeled off to one another so bitterly many years before, and which related to the fortune poured rashly into a succession of bird-brained schemes for a new Yarmouth harbour (a Palmer); the fortune invested in arms shipments to the losing side in a squalid tribal war in Arabia (a Sayer); the fortune thrown into a plan for a network of Norfolk canals just as the railways were coming of age (another Palmer); the fortune drunk to the lees in the pubs and taverns of Norwich, or frittered away in its gambling dens (various Palmers and Sayers). And, of course, the mighty fleet of scuttled hulks now used as blocks to keep the waters of the estuary from flooding the marshes beyond.

But, as we know, the eccentric uncle with the passion for wildfowling had at least seen to it that his nephew got a position aboard a brig, and, as we know, Tealer was launched on his career as senior mate on other people's ships. And because the money and the status had disappeared before Tealer was born, he felt no disgrace in his profession, and much pride. There was still some equity in a handful of herring smacks, some cash, and some property that included a house in one of the 'smarter' Yarmouth Rows – and Tealer wasn't complaining of his lot.

And Maud was at least right in supposing Tealer had travelled – if only as a mate on passenger packets from East Anglian ports to those on the continent. But the fabulous destinations that Maud took for granted were at that time as unknown to Tealer as they were to her.

After these initial failures to engineer a meeting Maud was more determined than ever to put herself in the way of the young merchant officer. She heard from her spies that Tealer was in the habit of using his Sunday afternoons to look over vessels at the far end of the South Denes, at East Quay, near the harbour mouth. She also knew it'd be very improper for her to be seen alone in such an ungenteel part of the town. But then wasn't that exactly why, if she did go, Tealer couldn't help but notice her? She needed to devise a scheme to get up to that harbour mouth and, as elegantly as possibly, make a spectacle of herself.

The solution was thrown into her lap when Becky and her husband came over from Norwich that Saturday evening for their weekly visit. Within minutes of seating his spare frame at the supper table Catchpole was expounding on the merits of steam versus horsepower, a theme close to his heart.

"It can be shown with fairly simple mathematics that as a means of transport the horse is decidedly uneconomical," he droned. "You see, it can be proved by breaking the work done into units and offsetting that against the expenditure involved at each stage in the operation. By my calculations the sooner society can abandon the horse and move entirely to mechanised travel, the better."

"Perry is always so clever in seeing such things clearly," said Becky. "Though I must say I should not want to see all horses disappear. Such dear creatures! And this afternoon I loved watching Dyer getting our trap through that great throng of people and vehicles at the Vauxhall Station. He managed to bring us through spaces and gaps I should hardly squeeze through on foot. So it would be a pity if *all* such skills were lost to progress. Don't you think, Perry?"

"No, I don't," said Catchpole in a tone that caused Maud's teeth to clamp together. "And I think 'skill' might be an overstatement, dear. Driving those vehicles is no more than an application of simple principles such as any bumpkin is capable of. Pull left to go left, right to go right, and you pull back on the reins to stop. Nothing simpler. And nothing slower, for that matter."

The scheme came to Maud in a trice. "Oh," she said brightly, "then you have tried it yourself, Pericles?"

Catchpole started. Apart from the odd loud sigh, his sister-in-law rarely reacted to anything he had to say. This sudden interest made him uneasy. "Um, yes, I think, once. Several years ago."

"And you found it an easy task?"

"I don't remember it as a challenging one."

"Ah," said Maud, pouring herself some water. "Good."

Catchpole looked at her suspiciously. "Why, has someone told you otherwise?"

"Indeed not," said Maud.

"Why, then," he said and smiled coldly over his spectacles at her.

Maud smiled back. "No, it's good because I have heard that next week there are to be some fine ships moored at East Quay. I should like to have a look at them, and I know Becky would. I can easily procure for us a dog-cart, but we only ever have time for such excursions on a Sunday – so we've always lacked a driver. But now it seems we've had one all the time!"

"Ooh, yes!" said Becky happily, before Catchpole could shoot her a warning frown. "What a nice plan! We can take a cart and you can drive, Perry."

Catchpole licked his lips and adjusted his cravat in a manner that Maud always found uniquely repulsive. "But would it not be simpler to hire that driver we had today, or some other fellow?"

"On the Sabbath? In Gorleston? They are all Non-Conformists from that 'Tabernacle' place at the end of the road. They'd sooner cut their own throats than be seen driving a cart on a Sunday. No, we depend on you, my dear brother-in-law."

So the following Sunday afternoon found Pericles Catchpole, his wife and his dear sister-in-law making their laborious way down the Southtown Road and over the Haven Bridge before heading back south along the quay on the Yarmouth side. The cart and mare, provided as a favour by Sadie Howe's father, had been delivered to them without incident – but from the moment Catchpole had levered himself gingerly into the box and taken the reins from the smirking Howe it was clear that this couldn't continue. However simple the principles of driving a cart, the application of them was soon proving unexpectedly complex. Fortunately the breezy acres of South Denes were almost deserted, and the only obstacles were the acres of nets that the fishermen had pegged out to dry. But it was after many stops and diversions around the dunes that they finally arrived at East Quay.

By the time they got there it was turning into one of those glorious, dangerous days when the sun and the wind combine to make the sea a host of white dragons, seething, writhing and hurtling towards land, throwing angry heads over the harbour wall before crashing down to rejoin the melee below. Clouds of glittering spray were slapping down on to the shingle at the end of the South Denes road, and bundles of foam littered the track like snow. Everywhere along the quay men were hard at work, lashing, battening and belaying; occasionally a canvas would break free and flap madly, or an empty herring swill would catch a gust and bowl noisily across the track. From the heaving ships moored along the quay came an orchestra of creaks and rattles.

As they worked their way along the last few hundred yards of the Denes the three sight-seers were buffeted by the unseasonal gale. Howe's mare was a reliable beast but the conditions made her restive and uncooperative. Catchpole shook the reins and waved his whip about ineffectually. Becky was smiling benignly though gripping the cart grimly with one hand and clutching her bonnet with the other. Maud had taken her bonnet off as soon as they were clear of the more respectable end of the quay, and now her hair was flying about her head in a storm of auburn tresses. She was scanning the quayside for the object of her search, but there was no sign. Perhaps her sources had been wrong. Then she saw the longed-for blond figure right down at the end of the North Pier, much further than she was expecting. Sayer was standing with another seaman glassing the ships that were heading for the harbour to shelter from the rising wind.

"Have you seen what you want to see?" shouted Catchpole hopefully to the two women behind him.

"Go on!" Maud shouted back to him.

"But…"

"Go *on*!" She yelled it with such vehemence that Catchpole turned round. In the place of his bored, sullen sister-in-law he found a Queen Boudicca. Any grizzled Iceni charioteer would have quailed at such a terrible face, and Catchpole was no grizzled Iceni charioteer, nor any kind of charioteer. He licked his lips and somehow persuaded the reluctant mare to take them off the end of the quay and on to the pier.

The wooden structure was vibrating with the force of the water crashing against it. The wind-blown foam was becoming thicker, and the mare kept starting as chunks of it sailed across her path. Then a whole pile of swills crashed over and the horse decided she'd had enough. She reared up in her shafts, neighed, and actually tried to reverse, but her hooves were slipping on the wall and she panicked. A monstrous wave crashed down just ahead of them. Catchpole's reedy-voiced instructions were useless against the wind and the roar of the water. At one point his hat blew off. He tried to catch it and failed, dropping his whip in the effort. Both Maud and Becky were clinging tightly to the cart, which was lurching ever closer to the wall's edge.

The mare's protests were heard by Tealer, who looked round. After a moment's astonishment his features relaxed and he walked towards them shaking his head. He grabbed the mare by the halter and stopped her rearing. He took her upper lip in his left hand, and with his right he stroked her flank, all the time whispering to her to calm down. This she did. Keeping hold of the mare's halter with one hand, he reached down and picked up Catchpole's whip which he flipped over and handed back to Catchpole handle first.

He shouted against the wind into Catchpole's ear "This horse know she shouldn't be on the quay with the sea like this!" He pointed to the mare, "Sometimes they know best!" He grinned good-naturedly at Catchpole, and raised his seaman's cap to Becky. His eyes did not even meet Maud's. Then he guided the mare carefully around and led her gently but firmly off the pier. He watched in courteous silence as Catchpole (after some lip-licking and one-handed cravat-adjusting) managed to urge the mare to start taking them back down the road in the direction of the town. Then Tealer turned and carried on watching the ships making their way into harbour. He said nothing, but the seaman next to him was shaking with laughter:

"Blust, yes, Mas' Sayer! Reckon there's only one o' them lot with a brain, an' she's the one pullin' the cart!" Maud caught every word of this on the wind, and her insides withered in humiliation. From then until the time they finally made it home she said very little, for mixed emotions were washing over her as powerful as the waves over the harbour wall.

But Catchpole was quiet as well. He was of course livid with Maud for having made him look so inept, but he knew that anything he said would only remind them of his original ridiculous boast.

It was left to poor, simple Becky to keep their spirits up by chattering inanely all the way back to Gorleston.

So Maud had achieved nothing, or less than nothing! This mere placing of herself in the way of John Sayer wasn't going to work. She could stagger about the market place with heavy bags till her arms broke; she could carpet Yarmouth with handkerchiefs from the North Beach to the Beccles road; she could loiter on the Denes till she turned into a pillar of salt: passivity, in this business, was going to get her nowhere.

A few days after this recent fiasco, Maud and Polly were walking arm-in-arm along the Gorleston sea-front. Maud was unusually quiet, staring out to sea. By way of cheering her up Polly asked her if she had thought to come to the horkey.

"Horkey?" asked Maud, coming slowly out of her trance. "Oh, do you mean that harvest thing at the Burgh Castle?"

"Yes, the horkey. Thas always on the evening of the water frolic. Week next Sa'day."

Maud smiled indulgently. "No, dear, I don't think so." she said. "Why, might you go?"

"Sadie and me thought 'at might be… quite nice."

"Jigging about with some brawny ploughman in a dusty field? And having to smile at him as he crushes your feet under his hobnails? Polly, really!"

"Oh, they ent just farmworkers go to it," stammered Polly, red with shame. "There's all sorts go – I mean respectable people: f-farmer's sons, officers from the ships, sergeants from the camp, church people, even the parson…"

But Maud had turned back to the sea.

They continued along the front without speaking. Polly decided to say nothing more, since Maud's mind was clearly elsewhere.

Polly was wrong. Maud's mind was centred entirely on what Polly had just said, and ideas were coming to her in a very quick succession:

Officers from the ships – officers from the ships – a week on Saturday – what about Mother? – Mother away that week –London – yearly pilgrimage to cousin Breda – idiot Catchpole also away – pootling auditing job in Ipswich – braying about it for weeks – officers from the ships – leaves only Becky as chaperone – Becky will do as she's told – officers from the ships – must, must make sure he comes – must.

They came to the end of their walk, and Maud turned to her young friend with her sweetest smile.

"Polly, dearest, perhaps you and Sadie can help me in something."

And the more Maud thought, the more she liked her own plan. In fact, she soon made the necessity of attending the horkey something of a virtue. Like the preacher Lovett she'd read Atkins's monogram on the ancient pedigree of the Burgh Castle celebration. Unlike the preacher Lovett she'd been entranced to think it still went on. But she'd never actually imagined going to the dance herself.

Now she couldn't imagine not going.

She started her campaign by setting her two followers various tasks in intelligence-gathering. They were to ask Tealer's friends what might best appeal to him in a horkey.

The answers that came back were not encouraging. It seemed that very little about a horkey would ever appeal to Tealer Sayer; Sadie reported back that she'd been told Tealer was unlikely to go anywhere near the horkey on account of his having 'no time for any kind of loud gatherings'. Maud brushed this setback aside. Was there *anything*, she wanted to know, that would get Sayer coming to that horkey? Duly tasked, Sadie went to see her cousin Charlie Harrison, who she reckoned knew Tealer better than anyone.

Harrison was vastly amused when Sadie told him what she was after.

"What if you mention the pretty girls and the hornpipe tunes?" she asked. "That's what sailing men like, int it?" Harrison shook his head; he knew a childhood friend better than that. Only one enticement would get John Sayer to attend such a party.

"*Ducks?*" said Sadie, when he told her. "What d'you mean, 'ducks'? Are you soft?"

"No, girl, I aren't." said Charlie. "Mark my words. Ducks is the only thing'll get him up that horkey. Leave it to me. I'll go and see someone I know what can help." And trusting to his instincts he paid a call to the Fritton Decoy.

A day or so later Harrison sent word back via his cousin that Maud should be at the horkey. That was all.

Maud had to be satisfied with this, and it was more in hope than expectation that she presented herself at the dance with her sister and friends.

Yet, sure enough, Tealer arrived at the fort just after she did. He scanned the multitude of faces glowing in the setting sun, all laughing, talking and tipping back beakers of ale and cider. His eyes met Maud's – and passed them – and his face only lit up with a smile when he spotted someone right at the back of the throng. Maud was then beside herself – it seemed all her efforts had only gone to putting some other girl in Tealer's purview! Seething, she watched him make his way straight across the stubble. Her fury abated a little when she saw him walk straight past various groups of young women to stop by some nondescript oaf with a dog who was standing well away from the crowd. He appeared to fall into deep conversation with the fellow. She crossed her arms. Jealousy had given way to bewilderment. She had no idea that the presence of this oddity was the only way her friends had managed to get Tealer to come at all.

By contrast, Tealer was rather enjoying himself. He'd not seen old Harry Pole for several years and he'd only half-believed it when Charlie told him that Pole would be at the horkey. So as soon as he'd spotted the old fellow loitering on the edge of the gathering he'd made straight for him, much pleased. There'd been a cursory exchange of nods and gruff monosyllables (the East Anglian version of a greeting with open arms). Then, after five years apart, they fell to discussing what was the most pressing matter to both: whether the duck were feeding better on the stubble north or south of the Waveney.

After a little while Fiddler Goodens started up on his violin and was soon joined by someone else on a squeeze-box, and the dancing got underway. But Sayer and Pole didn't so much as glance up. Instead they carried on their conversation quite oblivious to the jollity around them. From where Maud was standing across the stubble they could have been planning some crime. She began to be nervous. It was all very perplexing.

But the cider started to work its rough magic. Though he was still in deep conference with the mysterious fellow Pole, Tealer began unconsciously to tap his foot to the music. Several pairs of beady eyes noted this, and sly nods were exchanged across the field.

Charlie Harrison moved in to spring the trap. He produced a feather that he'd torn from a stuffed bird in his father's parlour just for the purpose.

"What d'you reckon this here feather come off, Jointy?"

Pole broke off from his conference with Tealer and frowned at it. There was not a single bird in Norfolk or Suffolk whose species, sex and age he couldn't identify just by looking at one such feather – but this one stumped him, because (as Charlie knew full well), no red grouse ever streaked across the skies of the *Gariensis*.

Tealer was craning over Harrison's shoulder to have a look for himself, and it was then that he felt a touch on his own shoulder. He turned around in some annoyance to find himself looking down at a dumpy woman of the kind that always left him utterly uninterested: a straggly covering of lank auburn hair, eyes of an insipid green colour and a ridiculous grin that reached right across her chubby face. He also was vaguely aware of one or two other women behind her.

"Ah, Mr Sayer. Um, good evening," said the woman, "Um… er…I think you might remember me. I mean… us."

"No, ma'am, that I do not."

Tealer was then aware of a noise, a series of grunts and desperate intakes of breath, donkey-like but faster, so odd that for an instant he didn't realise it was the woman laughing. "No, no! You must, I think," she said. "You saved our skins out by the harbour mouth Sunday last. You don't remember it?"

Tealer tried to remember any time when he had had to jump into the Yarmouth harbour to save anybody – or had heard of anyone else having to do so. "No, ma'am, I think you must be mistaken. I've only ever been down the harbour once this last half-month. The only incident I remember was some clueless idiot in a dog cart… or was that? … you mean…?"

The woman made her donkey noises again. "Yeees!" She said, loudly. "Yeees! Er, yeees. That was us! Yes! Um…" but her voice trailed off uncertainly, leaving only the vacuous grin. Then she twitched as if someone had nudged her sharply from behind. "Er…, yes," she said, "you see, I am Mrs Pericles Catchpole."

"Indeed, Mrs Catchpole. I'm right glad to make your acquaintance. And glad to ha' been able to assist last week. But if you'll excuse me…" But when Tealer turned round he found that Charlie had led Harry away into the crowd. He turned back helplessly and Becky continued.

"I… um… I… That is, my mother knew your uncle, Mr John Palmer, through a mutual friend. That's how I knew your name. Ha, ha. Ha, ha, ha."

"Ah, really? Well, there's a thing," said Tealer, desperately scanning the stubble from the corner of his eye for a sign of Harry Pole.

"Yes," said Becky. "She often spoke well of him. Very well of him. Yes, very, very well of him. Um… er…" She experienced another of her strange twitches, and a voice behind her whispered something. "Oh! Heavens! And just look! They're forming up for the next reel. Do you like to dance, Mr Sayer?"

"Dance? Me?" said Tealer, almost in a state of panic. "Hardly! You see, I…"

But Becky suffered a third spasm, the most violent yet, and this caused her grin to become truly imbecilic. She held up one plump hand to her mouth and whispered hoarsely:

"Um… My poor sister Maud is without a partner this evening and is very sad about it. I know this might seem forward. But, after all, my mother was acquainted with your late uncle… Er… now this is my sister, Maud… and these are her two young friends Miss Howe and Miss Bessey.…"

"Well, the thing is, Mrs Catchp…"

But at that point the good Becky Catchpole was firmly moved to one side and her younger sister stepped forward without looking up.

"The thing is …" tried Tealer again.

Maud kept her head down. "I am pleased to meet you, Mr Sayer," she said in a voice that was about an octave lower than her sister's. Then she did look up, loosing two devastating shafts of emerald light straight into Tealer's face.

And… Tealer was duly devastated.

"These are my friends, Miss Sadie Howe and Miss Polly Bessey. We have all heard so much about you."

Tealer didn't even look at Sadie or Polly. He didn't even speak. There was an awkward silence and then an outbreak of tittering from behind Maud that she quelled instantly with a lethal flash of green. But when she turned back to Tealer she was smiling shyly.

"Yes, I should so much like to dance," she said. "Thank you."

Still without saying anything, Tealer stumbled towards the dancers with Miss Pritchard on his arm, and they joined in the reel.

Now Tealer had been about to tell Becky that dancing was an art he had yet to master. As it happened, this was true. But Maud seemed to ignore the several occasions he cannoned her off other revellers, took the skin from her toes, or nearly twisted her little finger from its socket. She concentrated hard on her dancing, and still not a word passed between them.

Then after the first couple of dances Maud suddenly wilted. She leant heavily on her dance partner:

"Please," she said in a small voice, "take me away from here. I am feeling unwell."

"I'll take you back to your sister, she's only over there."

"NO! I mean…, no. Better in the shade of those trees beyond that wall. And fetch me a cider, if you will."

Tealer hurried away to get the drink, thoroughly alarmed at how his none-too-skilful dance steps had done so much damage so quickly. But when he came back he found there'd been an even quicker recovery. Furthermore, Maud's hair, which had been pinned back for the dancing, was now tumbling about her shoulders. She took a sip of the cider, and while she was drinking Tealer tore his eyes away from her to see if her sister had noticed what was going on.

He turned back again and found Maud staring straight at him. For a second or so there was no movement in her face, but then she thanked him and dazzled him with a broad smile.

"Mr Sayer, what country have you just visited?"

The question was unexpected, but Tealer answered it nevertheless. He told her he'd just returned from Bordeaux; this seemed to open a sluice and release a flood of questions that flowed on and on without interval or even a pause for breath. There were questions about the people of Bordeaux, the customs of Bordeaux, the wines of Bordeaux, the seas around Bordeaux, the seas around Norfolk, the Dogger Bank, the Grand Banks, the Cape Horn, the Cape of Good Hope, Cape Wrath, ships that had foundered on Cape Wrath, ships Tealer had served on, ships he hoped to serve on, ships he would not like to serve on, the size of berth he slept in, the Spanish places he'd visited, the Spanish places he'd like to visit, the people of Spain, the customs of Spain, the wines of Spain, Spanish laws, Spanish punishments, Naval punishments, the throwing of men into the brig, the stringing of men from the yard-arm, the forcing of men to walk the plank, Henry Morgan, English pirates, Spanish pirates, Barbary pirates, Barbary pearls, oysters, coral, mermaids' purses, mermaids, giant squid, St Elmo's fire, the worst seas he'd weathered, sea-sickness, homesickness, tropical sickness, death at sea, Davy Jones, John Paul Jones, Captain Kidd, Captain Bligh, Captain Cook, the difference between a Captain and a Master…. And throughout this bombardment the legendary gaze was unremitting, so that in his mesmerised state Tealer found he was providing answers with a candour that he would never normally allow himself.

And in spite of himself he became more and more fascinated. When Charlie sidled over on the pretext of asking him if his mug needed replenishing, he hardly heard him. When he was finally aware of his old friend next to him he tried to pull himself together.

Charlie drew him to one side. "You know thass old Giles Pritchard's mawth' you're talking to there, you crafty old devil. Reckon she ha' got you in her sights. You could do a lot worse!"

"Go you on," muttered Tealer, "you know I never play such sport at the home anchorage."

Charlie nodded derisively. "No, we can see that, boy!"

"No, that's right, I don't. And good reason, 'cause that way there's no…"

But Charlie had already walked away chuckling. Maud cleared her throat, and Tealer walked back to her and she carried on exactly where she had left off: which once again was Spain and the Spanish, and whether Tealer had read Don Quixote…

Recollections of what happened thereafter become lost in a blur of cider, music, earnest questions, fulsome answers, and a hypnotic gaze that was now of an unearthly intensity.

Tealer later recalled there was another small interruption quite early on when Becky had come over and beamed at him with one half of her mouth while whispering to Maud through the other half that Dyer was "ready with the trap to take them home", and Maud had whispered back that Sadie's father had offered to drive her home with Sadie, and Becky had responded with a gentle "But, dearest,…", and Maud had responded with an assurance that Becky should not worry, and Becky had responded with a "But, Maud, *dearest*…", and Maud had responded with one of her Queen Boudicca faces, and Becky had scuttled away.

The next clear memory Tealer has now, as he thinks back, is of standing alone with the late Pritchard's younger daughter in a glade just below the north wall of the fort. She was wearing Tealer's heavy jacket. Several hours had passed and none of the other party-goers was anywhere to be seen. Maud told him later that they'd in fact been talking about some of Tealer's foreign adventures.

The harvest moon was now up in a clear sky and the refreshing chill of a mist coming up from the river below was slowly bringing Tealer back to sobriety, but only to the extent that he could better register what was before him. The moonlight was causing the pale form of Miss Pritchard, now about five inches from him, to glow. Her face, neck and arms were covered with large faint freckles, and these now gave her skin the look of stained marble.

Tealer's fate was finally sealed when he took one of these arms in his hand and told her that you could only find such rare, red-flecked marble in the hills of Tuscany. Very valuable, he told Maud. (He didn't say he'd only ever seen it stacked up on South Quay for the gravestone trade.) Maud immediately pictured Tealer striding through the red-marbled porticos of Tuscany, a land she had only vaguely heard of but which was obviously one of indescribable wealth.

Then, moved to new madness – possibly by the moonlight – possibly by some ancient ghost from the Roman fort whispering in his ear – but most likely by the cider – Tealer asked Maud if it was just her arms that were so marked.

Or... was she... marbled... all over?

Maud came back from Italy and glared at him. She looked quickly round her and back at him again. She slipped off the jacket, thrust it roughly into his hands and for the second time that evening crossed her arms in agitation. For a moment her luminous face lost all expression so that she looked like an effigy, but she never took her unsmiling eyes off Tealer. Finally, with her arms still crossed she took a deep breath, shook her head at him and sighed.

Tealer was surprised, for he was expecting at least a gasp at his effrontery. But much more surprised was he when Maud, still in her cross-armed pose, gave the pure white cotton dress an upward tug and hung it on a nearby willow, and with a few other deft manipulations of laces and cords let her undergarments rustle softly to the grass at her feet. She stepped carefully out of them. She gathered up her hair from her back and shoulders and held it in a great bunch above her. Still holding it she turned one way, and then the other way. Then she let her hair flop down again, but only after she was sure Tealer had seen that every square inch of her flawless, flawed skin from the flame-crowned head to the dainty white toes was the rarest Tuscan marble. Throughout the performance her eyes never left his.

It was an extreme kind of sorcery to have worked on poor Tealer Sayer, but

Maud rightly guessed that this was no time for juvenile attempts at flirtation. Tealer was a sailing man, and she'd read enough to know that with sailing men all business must be done while the ship's in port. And the magic she worked was so potent exactly because this particular sailing man had convinced himself (if not anyone else) that he would never fall into such a trap on his own doorstep.

Two years later the scrape of Tealer Sayer's clogs is echoing against the walls of his street, Row 111, so he takes them off and walks barefoot, not wanting to draw attention, and Yarmouth remains unaware that one of her better-travelled sons has come home.

He carries on his way to his house. It's only ten minutes since he learnt of the change in his life's course from the gap-toothed child on the quay, and he's still dazed. As he has done five hundred times in the last seven weeks, Tealer stops and feels the leather pouch bound tightly at his waist, at first not conscious of the irony of the action. Then he realises what he's done and something between a grin and a grimace appears on his face.

He takes the key from the agreed crack in the mortar, wondering what was going through Maud's head when she put it there.

And what does he feel himself? He finds he's not distraught. He realises that he's been expecting this from the moment he went back to sea. Now that it's happened his biggest surprise is to realise just how little surprised he is.

Still, he thinks, pulls a fellow up short.

Tealer unlocks the small street door and pushes on it. It hasn't been opened for some time and has swelled in the rain. He shoves harder at it so that it suddenly gives. Several spiders and earwigs fall on to the stone doorstep. Tealer watches them thoughtfully as they scuttle frantically away from what they too had thought were safe harbours, and then he steps inside, closing the door with the back of his stockinged heel and shutting out the hum of Yarmouth at evening.

His first impression is of the complete silence, and his second is that everything's smaller. Everything is as he left it, except that there's no sign of his ever having known Maud. She's taken nothing that she didn't put in, and in fact she has left much that is rightfully hers – but nothing remains that could hint at an imminent union.

Tealer goes into the empty kitchen, throws his clogs under the table and sits down so heavily on a windsor chair that it creaks loudly. He notices a letter on the table and looks at it for a long while, though he doesn't pick it up. Instead he reaches in his pocket for a strange piece of shrivelled hide and lays this on the table next to the letter. He takes the leather pouch off his belt and puts it with the other two objects. He contemplates all three – the letter, the scrap of hide and the pouch – for several minutes as if through some unknown alchemy the combination of them will present him with the solution to his predicament. Then he turns to the gap in the window through which he can watch the coming and going in the Row outside the house.

Tealer is a seaman, and seamen are used to having periods of time in which to arrange their thoughts. The mice scratch in the wainscoting and flies bounce against the window-panes. Down the road in the main street there's the muffled clop of a draught horse, and from the far end of town comes the steady thump of the steam hammer. Another hour brings the more immediate clatter of the troll carts being driven back from the market to the various private yards of the stall-holders. Then the sounds of day diminish. Bats begin to flit in the rows. Cats, which have lain curled up on the dividing walls stir, yawn, stretch themselves front and back, lick their lips and survey their hunting ground with widening eyes.

After an hour or so of being almost motionless Tealer reaches out to pick something up from the table. It is not the letter but the scrap of dried flesh. This most resembles a piece of burnt meat with a leather pad on the end. The pad is surrounded with a series of razor-sharp teeth like the mouth of a giant leech. Tealer hefts it in his palm and thinks of the story with which he'd planned to entertain Maud:

Leaning on the rail of a clipper plying the deep ocean off Peru, cold and clear with the waters of the Humboldt current. Becalmed. Tealer and a Philippino crewman are on deck for the first of the night watches. Apart from the helmsman up on the bridge the rest of the ship's company is below deck. It is two hours after nightfall. The moon is shining down on the mighty bulk of the Shadwell Empress, *making her sails glow like clouds in the starry sky. Tealer is chatting to the crewman in the working pidgin of the vessel. They are listening to the echo of the calls of blue whales miles up the coast, but these are now receding. Now there is silence but for the occasional creak as the great vessel moves to the smallest of breezes.*

They notice that a shimmering glow of many colours has filled the waters below them. They both look upward into the sky to see what has caused such a reflection, but the steady gleam of the moon is unchanged. The light in the water is coming from the depths below the ship. It gets brighter and begins to pulsate, and as they watch, a massive glowing shape rises from the deep and waits just below the surface next to their vessel. It is nearly as long as the ship. Tealer at first imagines he must be looking at a whale. But this is no whale, for no whale shimmers in a multitude of vivid colours. And no whale has a huge white-rimmed eye as big as a plate that regards you with the dispassionate scrutiny of the predator.

They watch it, and it watches them. The unblinking eye that holds their gaze takes on an almost holy balefulness as a dreadful limb snakes out of the water and begins to slither towards them, probing the deck as it does so. The Philippino is on his knees and gibbering in Tagalog. The sound of his shrieks in a strange tongue jerks Tealer out of hypnosis and he reaches behind him to where there hangs a bucket of sand and an axe. He takes the axe and swings it as the horrible limb advances towards him. He manages to sever the tip. A great hiss arises from the creature and it slips below the surface. They are able to watch its glow diminish as it makes its way back into the deep. With shaking legs, Tealer goes over to the twitching fragment of tentacle and marvels at its wicked arrangement of bladed suckers.

Of course, none of this happened – not to Tealer at any rate. The *Shadwell Empress* was never anywhere near Peru. Tealer was told this tale himself by a Chilean sailor who'd given him the fragment in return for a half-bottle of whisky. As like as not it didn't happen to the Chilean sailor either, although Tealer knows of plenty of people who have spotted the dreaded kraken, the Colossal Squid. He himself has spent hours on the night watch, peering into the dark waters, hoping to catch sight of the kind of monster that many say can attack whole ships and devour their crews. He has sometimes thought he could see lights way down in the water, but very indistinct. The piece of dried tentacle he is now holding was most likely taken from the stomach of a dead whale. But then only imagine the battle between two such huge creatures, way down in the abyss! Since childhood Tealer has had a fascination for water monsters, and so the kraken story he planned to tell Maud was one that would truly have come from his heart and would have set her peerless eyes shining in wonder. And this withered fragment was to have been the sinister prop.

He slings the dried squid claw into a dark corner. It bounces off the wall and skitters under the stove, utterly forgotten.

After a while Tealer decides to take a drink, and cranks some water from the pump into a cup which he takes back into the kitchen. It seems only minutes since he walked into the house and sat down, but somewhere in the town a clock strikes one. Sitting in the dark he tries to review his position, but still he finds that his thoughts wander back to those events of two years ago...

The Further Witching of Tealer Sayer

It would be hard to say who was more changed by that dalliance among the groves of *Gariannonum*. For all her bold manner, knowing looks and sophisticated ways, Maud had actually arrived at the horkey with her virtue intact. Nor had she planned to compromise herself that evening. But then Maud rarely planned anything in much detail. And like Tealer she had downed a good measure of the innocuous-tasting cider.

The transformation for Tealer was at least as great. No loss of virginity with him, of course. A very much younger Tealer had long since surrendered *his* innocence to a bored whore in Genoa while his shipmates shouted up encouragement, argued over their cards or snored under the tables on the floor below. But it was true that courting was a pasttime he would never have thought to practise in Yarmouth. *That* was what changed in Tealer that evening. The idea of a young woman from Gorleston, the old place itself, having any hold on him! Ridiculous! Yet Maud had employed all her considerable charms – and Tealer had been helpless. All his carefully-nurtured ideas of what was prudent shattered in a few passionate hours. It amused, appalled and fascinated him.

Over the next few days he started acting very strangely. He did not go back to sea but busied himself around his house and his hut by the river. Yet he stopped his river activities: his punting, his shooting, and his fishing. The despairing bachelor friends who'd put him up to the horkey venture now looked at one other grimly, shaking their heads and wondering what they'd done.

Tealer Sayer, of all fellows!

But… too late now. For Tealer had decided that perhaps all his carefree wandering was a lonely business after all. Now the worldly first mate with the roving eye only had eyes for the bookish little witch from Gorleston.

Thus it was that in the weeks of August and September Maud would fob Maggie off with a thin pretence of staying with her friend Sadie in Gorleston. Or she would wait until her mother's hearty snoring was filling the little house in Cliff Street and then she would creep out late into the summer night dressed in a swirling black robe and veil looking as gorgeously witchlike as would settle the case for any doubter; and in this disguise she would fly straight into the arms of her waiting seafarer down on the quay.

Maggie Pritchard was only quite stupid, and even she could guess about half of what was going on – and she decided she knew better than to object. Any scruples she had were more than offset by the prospect of a connection with the Sayers. So considerable had this name been in her youth that she managed to ignore the fact that it had lost much of its weight in recent years. She managed to close her mind to the risk of unwanted consequences – even including the ultimate disgrace.

So Maud and Tealer were almost free to meet in the groves around Burgh Castle to mingle their natural passions with tales and airey reminiscences, all spiced with the breezes blowing off Breydon and the vista of the sun setting over the marshes. They'd listen happily to each other's chatter, though neither had much notion what the other one was describing.

Maud would tell Tealer about the Romans and Saxons and Normans who'd lived here, and their gods and saints, their ghosts and demons. She could move from one topic to the next with incredible rapidity. Ideas seem to assail her all at once, each one demanding expression, so that a conversation with her was a fascinating obstacle course of *non sequitur*s.

She would bring books to read to Tealer, and he would listen open-mouthed. The only books he was familiar with were the Bible and Col. Peter Hawker's *Instructions to Young Sportsmen*. He had been forced to learn the fiercer bits of the first by his parents. The second he had read so many times he knew it by heart anyway. But Maud read to him from Homer, Shakespeare, Milton, Keats, Wordsworth and Byron, Fielding and Defoe. Byron's *Don Juan* was a favourite, as was Defoe's *Crusoe*.

Tealer in turn would tell Maud of wildfowling exploits with his uncle. For example, he was very careful to explain that there were two ways to catch duck: by the net and by the gun. Your netting, he told her, was called 'decoying', where a man used a trained dog to weave in and out of a series of fences in sight of the duck. This would so fascinate the birds that they would follow the dog up an ever-smaller channel and right into his master's net. (There's a fellow I know do it over at Fritton, said Tealer, I'll take you sometime.) Your gunner, he went on, was a different sort of fellow, who roamed the shallows of Breydon in a low boat with an enormous great gun at one end. He would creep up slowly on a flock of duck roosting in the shallows, and, if he could get near enough before they all took off, why, then he could slay twenty at a time. Tealer and his uncle used to use both methods, but they'd kept it quiet, because there was no love lost between the wildfowlers and the net men.

"I'm with the netters," said Maud.

"Ah," says Tealer, "females usually are. They have no love for guns and loud bangs."

There was a glare of cold green at that: "Give me less of your 'females usually are'! I dislike the gun-men because they have no guile or cunning, whereas the netters…"

"*No guile or cunning?*" says Tealer, "Do you know what thas like to creep up on five hundred duck, each one with two eyes and two ears (I know you can't see the ears, but they're there) with no trees or bushes 'twixt you and the skyline, and only the slowest movement of your boat to keep every bird on Breydon from spooking and leaving you with an empty estuary. No guile? Blast, you do talk soft sometimes!"

Maud's eyes flashed bolts of green lightning. She had never been the object of such plain talking, and it thrilled her.

They would explore the groves and copses around the fort, and try to imagine what life had been like for the soldiers who'd once manned it. Tealer would tell Maud the names of some of the plants. Some were utterly unknown to her till that point, though she was delighted by names such as comfrey, sorrel and vipers bugloss. Other names, such as hemlock, elder and valerian she knew from her books, and as they found each plant she would say: "So *that's* what it looks like."

One plant grew as a bold shrub with leaves like potatoes, and it was covered with glossy black cherries so shiny Maud could see her reflection in the skin. She turned to Tealer and asked him what it was.

"Ah, that." he said. "You want to be careful with that. Some folk call it dwale, but most call it deadly nightshade. Thas a good name, an'all. When I was a littl'un they used to give it to me for when I couldn't sleep. But once they gave me too much, and 'at nearly did for me. I won't forget that night too quick."

Maud took a sharp breath and ran a hand over the soft, shiny half-cherries.

"But it's so handsome. How could such lovely fruits be 'deadly'?"

As the cool of the late summer evening turned to straight autumn chill, these meetings in the copse around Burgh Castle had to stop, and so Tealer started to take Maud down to one of two houseboats his uncle had owned on a rond of the Waveney. Here they'd slip into another world. Maud would bring books and read to Tealer on whatever took her fancy. She knew he'd keep quiet and listen. They would pull down the shutters of the houseboat against the damp Breydon mist. Outside the silent flow of the river was an echoing backdrop to the night calls of coot, waterhen, owl and fox. Inside Maud would sit in the glow of the oil lamp, which set her hair glittering around her shoulders like a red aura, and in this position she'd read to Tealer. She would occasionally sweep back a lock when it fell loosely over the page she was holding up to the light, and pluck absent-mindedly at one of the buttons of her jacket as the oil fire began to warm the cabin. She would shoot the odd sly glance to Tealer to see how he was reacting. Otherwise she sat perfectly still as she read.

And Tealer would listen open-mouthed as Maud read to him from *Paradise Lost*, or the exploits of Alexander the Great, or the stories of Rob Roy MacGregor, the Scottish outlaw.

Oh, I've met a few outlaws myself, says Tealer. Where, Maud asks, where? In Marseilles, he says, the docks are full of them. Tell me about them, she demands. Nothing much to tell, he says. I reckon the best outlaw I met was here in Norfolk: Shortie Thomas. He once killed a swan on Breydon and hid it under… Oh, swans, Breydon – pish! she says, I want to know about Marseilles. So he would tell her whatever nonsense came into his head about the pirates of Marseilles, and her eyes would shine.

On one occasion Maud brought a book of poems by someone called Ovid. The poem she liked best was Pygmalion. Listen to this, she said, and she read of how Pygmalion, a Greek sculptor, carved a statue of a woman so perfect in the shape of her neck, breasts, waist, thighs and slender legs that he fell in love with his own work. So he prayed to the goddess Venus for the statue to come alive. Suddenly it pulsed with life, and beckoned to Pygmalion.

And Maud shut the book and stared into space as though thinking.

What, asks Tealer in a voice so husky he has to clear his throat and say it again, what was the statue made of?

"Oh, marble, of course," said Maud, "all the ancient sculptors worked in marble in those days. Do you want to hear...?

"You're a witch," said Tealer, as he stifled the lamp.

And these liaisons by the river continued for months. In the reedbeds around their lonely houseboat the whisper of summer had turned to the rattle of winter. Tealer would return from a voyage with tales of places he had visited in Europe. None of these was remarkable to him – but to Maud, for whom fact was so easily augmented with imagination, they were riveting.

But Tealer knew the day was fast approaching when he'd have to tell Maud of something much closer to home. He knew he'd been putting off the evil day for months. He knew that Maud was soon going to have to learn of the White Lady of Breydonside. Maud wasn't the type to play second string. The White Lady was the only other partnership in his life, and the longer he hid her existence from Maud the harder it would be for Maud to believe the hold that White Jenny had on him. He had to think carefully how to explain that he had inherited Jenny from his uncle. It wasn't right to call her his mistress, he decided to tell Maud, but she was the centre of his world – well, until Maud appeared, of course – and he still felt a strong duty of care. Yes, that was how he'd phrase it: 'a duty of care.' Maud was sure to understand. He had abandoned Jenny over these last few months, but now the winter was approaching and the flocks of whistling wigeon could be heard gathering on Breydon, and the urgings of the White Lady could no longer be ignored. He resolved to explain this to Maud one evening just before Christmas, the day after he returned from Copenhagen.

Immediately he arrived in Yarmouth Tealer sent a message to Gorleston. That evening Maud appeared on South Quay with a bottle of dark wine and an arch smile. They went straight down to the houseboat at Burgh Castle where they lit the stove in the tiny galley. Once Maud had warmed the wine she poured out a measure into one of the pewter tankards hanging on the galley wall. She took a long draught and gave the cup to Tealer. She made him drink it all. It was a blackberry wine suffused with cinnamon, and Tealer knew that she had fermented it from the brambles that grew along the base of the ruined fort. The initial effect was no worse than that of any other strong liquor – but then he was seized by some more potent force and had to sit down, taking deep breaths. That's the wormwood, she told him. And with a gleam in her eye she added that there was a third ingredient he would soon feel, an ingredient so wicked and wonderful that she 'could not possibly divulge it', but its effects would not become apparent till much later.

So began a strange, fateful night.

As Tealer started to feel the glow from the potion he relaxed and felt ready to begin to explain to Maud the strange pressing business of his white mistress of Breydonside.

He explained that he felt that White Jenny could not simply be abandoned. He assured Maud that since their coming together he'd realised that things would never be the same – nevertheless his late uncle had many years ago made him solemnly swear that Jenny would always be well provided for and never be neglected, cast out or forgotten. He said that in recent months he realised that he had not been fulfilling this undertaking. He hoped Maud would understand that he would have to devote at least a little time to making good on this recent failing. He promised that while his uncle might have devoted almost the whole of his life to this strange diva Tealer himself had never been under such a spell. Maud could be sure of it. But from now on there would have to be days when Tealer attended to Jenny...

Maud listened unblinking as Tealer explained all this, and he noticed how her eyes seemed to glow with a black light. If he'd thought that this was the prelude to the storm he was to be proved wrong. Maud only looked at him closely, with eyes wilder and blacker, and the smile ever archer, and said:

"La Belle Dame sans Merci hath thee in thrall."

"Who?"

"La Belle Dame sans Merci. You visit all those places in France and still don't know what I mean? The fair damsel without pity."

In that supposedly creative state that precedes befuddlement, Tealer suddenly saw what a perfect way this was of Maud's to describe his uncle's white lady. He was more than a little relieved at Maud's equanimity!

"Yes, I… see what you mean, girl. Where's that from?"

Maud took a book from her portmanteau and read him a strange little poem.

"*La Belle Dame sans Merci*. Do you not think it very apt a poem to read in this little winter bower of ours, now that 'the sedge has withered from the lake'. It is by Johnny Keats. What thinks Johnny Sayer to it?"

Tealer recalls now how Maud looked up at him as she spoke.

"Do you know, girl, your eyes are as wild as the mawther's in the poem."

She gave a squeal of laughter and said "Then it's working!" and she took a mirror and held it up to him and showed him that he too had developed an uncanny look in the eye.

That night was one of unnatural intensity. Maud's high-pitched gasps turned to a rhythmic screaming of a kind that couldn't have been heard on the Burgh Castle rond in many a year; a yelling so elemental that it threatened to stir the Romans and Anglo Saxons and Vikings from deep within their plots around the old fort and bring them marching down to the staithe to hammer on the roof of the houseboat with the pommels of their swords for some quiet.

Tealer likewise felt some unearthly energy – though through it all a part of him felt detached from the frenzy. He felt a great dryness in the mouth, but any discomfort this caused was stifled by mounting waves of passion. How long they continued he never knew, but by the time the fires of this heroic congress had lessened to a smoulder the weak light of a winter dawn was leaking in through the portholes. Maud, still panting, with auburn curls dark red with perspiration where they touched her face, eased Tealer off her, propped herself up on one elbow and whispered deep into his ear:

"La Belle Dame Sans Merci! Was I not right?" And she flopped back down on to the cushion. Tealer wondered why she'd chosen to bring up White Jenny at this of all times and looked at her for explanation, but with eyes closed in exhaustion she could only smile weakly and nod in affirmation of her own statement before going to sleep.

And then Tealer himself fell into a long dozing reverie full of vivid images. He was flying over Yarmouth, he was flying over the whole of Norfolk, alongside the great black-backs and the swifts. The sleek cold form of the White Lady seemed to mingle with the quickening marble form of Maud lying next to him. Then the images were more sinister, and he had nightmares of the kind he'd not known since childhood. These increased in intensity until he sat up in the bunk with a shout. Next to him Maud didn't even stir. Then he slept a deep sleep in which he must have dreamt calmer dreams or no dreams at all, because he didn't wake up till midday. Apart from the raging thirst (which he was only able to quench with two ewerfuls of water), and a curious bulging ache in his eyes, he felt wonderfully rested – and the following morning as he made his way down to his ship he thought about this last, strange postscript to his night's exertions.

"Must have been the drink," he said to himself.

It was a couple of years and very much trouble before he knew how right that was.

Tealer proposed to Maud in the middle of the field surrounded by the fort walls one misty evening in February. Maud found this impossibly romantic, and accepted. Maggie Pritchard was also pleased. By now she knew very well that as well as the official Sunday afternoon visits that Maud was making, chaperoned by her dim, amiable sister, she was also seeing the young shipman unaccompanied. But still Maggie did not remonstrate. She knew better than to try. Even when Maud was seven poor Giles had once remarked that putting a check on his younger daughter when she had a passion for something was 'like trying to stop the Light Brigade with an upraised hand'. And the intervening decade had hardly made her more tractable. So Maggie shrugged and soothed herself with the prospect of a link with the houses of both Palmer and Sayer in one 'I will'. After all, she reasoned, if her daughter was so utterly oblivious to the wittering and twittering of the Gorleston trading classes, perhaps she could be too.

It was on either one of the chaperoned or the unchaperoned visits that Maud started to rearrange things in the house she might soon be mistress of. It was several years since a female hand had sought to enhance the faded elegance of the house behind the town hall, and Tealer could only watch as essentials – an etching of the famous gunner Colonel Hawker, a stuffed spoonbill, and a seven-bore muzzleloader with a burst near the fore-end that had taken four of Tealer's great-grandfather's fingers with it – were whisked away into a cupboard, and some fetching copies of paintings by a Mr Millais and a Mr Hunt were put up in their place.

The plans that Tealer and Maud made together were vague. Tealer would re-establish his family's failed shipping concern and Maud meantime would take over her mother's failing milliner's business. Theirs would be a life of genteel Yarmouth trade, interspersed with regular trips together to foreign parts.

Winds would be favourable, people would flock to buy hats, and everything in the garden would be lovely (notwithstanding the house in Row 111 didn't have one).

Tealer breaks from his reminiscing and decides he could do with some liquid fortification. He gets up, puts his clogs back on, and begins to search the house. He shines his lamp around the kitchen. It's devoid of any food or drink. He goes through to the parlour and searches there. Along the mantelpiece where he'd often leave a bottle of rum or gin there is nothing. He shines the lamp in the cupboards. They are bare. Then he swings the light around the parlour at random. Its beam catches the large chip in the lintel where his uncle's drunken father once tried to shoot a spider with a duelling pistol; then he makes out the scratches on the door left by his uncle's dog Buck, who never accepted the parlour was out of bounds. A dark brown stain on the wall marks where Maud once threw an oil can that Tealer had put down on a letter from her cousin Niamh. A dark red stain marks where Maud once threw a glass of punch because Tealer had dropped off during a love scene from *Don Juan*.

But the room itself seems empty of any refreshment.

Then he has an idea. He goes to a small recess near the fireplace and reaches in. With a curt nod of satisfaction he pulls out a bottle. It has no label. He uncorks it and pours some of its contents into a glass. He is immediately transported by the strange aroma of fermented blackberries, wormwood and whatever else. A little of this, he decides – with plenty of water to take with it – will eventually calm him and let him think clearly about what he will do next. He looks around for water. Where's the water? He hasn't pumped any from the yard since he arrived. Damn the water. He goes back to the kitchen for a tumbler, pours out a healthy measure and downs it. He sits back and lets his mind wander as the fumes take effect.

After another half-an-hour Tealer suddenly sits up, aware that someone is moving about in the house. Someone is moving from room to room swinging a ship's belaying pin, and hissing "Damn this thieving Scot." He listens again with the hairs on his back all a-tingle. It takes him a few moments to realise that it is he himself, no longer sitting but pounding agitatedly from the kitchen to the parlour and back, repeating this mantra. Another waking dream, he decides, of just the kind he has had of late, but sharper and clearer than before.

I am overwrought, he decides. He pours another measure of Maud's wine.

It's now the dead of night. Tealer takes a tinder from his pocket and lights an oil lamp on the table. He goes into the small front room of the little Row dwelling and casts his eye about.

The Millais and the Hunt have gone again.

The mice are now more active, and their scuttlings mix with the groans of the oak panelling as it contracts in the cool of night.

Tealer remembers how Maud was delighted with this room when she first saw it. She gasped at the thick patterns in the plasterwork of the ceiling, neatly cut in half by the wall at the end of the parlour. She loved the doorways that opened up not to reveal rooms but cupboards, and the cupboards that turned out to be staircases that spiralled up for a few feet before hitting a dead end. The tiny bedchamber with a window nearly as large as the wall that framed it. The kitchen with the window so small that the scullery door had to be left open to give light to cook by. She correctly imagined the house must once have been much bigger, and she thought it must once have been divided into two. Tealer told her the truth – the modest dwelling in Row 111 had been a Palmer dwelling since the seventeenth century, but by the time of his uncle the Palmer share of the building was about one fifth its original size.

"And every partition a stage in the Descent of the House of Palmer," said Maud as she gazed sadly at the oaken panels. "Or a Paradise Gradually Lost. But… I'm sure Paradise can be Regained." She smiled and Tealer smiled with her, though he didn't much care for the images. He'd been very happy here as a boy.

Now Tealer finds himself staring at that same truncated plasterwork, the only reminder of one-time Palmer grandeur in that strange house of half-rooms and doors to nowhere.

He finds himself looking at one door he has never noticed before, even though he's lived here off and on since the age of eight.

Curious, he thinks.

He wanders over to it and opens it and very nearly steps down off the ship's side into the deep black waters of the Atlantic. He slams the door with a bang, trying to haul himself out of another of his damned waking dreams. He rubs his eyes, and when he opens them again he finds they have settled on the letter

The Further Witching of Tealer Sayer

which is still lying alongside his leather pouch on the table. He resolves not to be discomfited. He picks the envelope up without ceremony and holds it to the light. Just a 'T' with a full stop. He opens it as though it were nothing more than a bill of lading and sits down to read it.

It consists of three pages explaining things – and it is vintage Maud: tearstained, luxuriantly tragic, and written with complete disregard for the fact that Tealer can barely read. He squints at the script from different angles, muttering each word aloud. Only after two or three attempts does he get the gist.

Broadly, Maud is sorry, Maud is very sorry, but she's realised that there is no future for her as Mrs Sayer. Tealer shouldn't try to contact her. By the time he reads this she'll be married anyway. She wishes Tealer well. There would always be a corner of her heart… etc. etc.

Again Tealer tells himself: you knew to expect this. You've been getting ready to hear this for months. You've been like a crewman on a leaky vessel: always one eye on the lifeboat.

Still, pulls a fellow up short.

He takes a grip on his belaying pin and again resolves to give the unknown Scotsman a thrashing. Then he uses the pin to brush the letter off the table. He eyes the unmarked bottle, wondering if a little more liquor might not be in order. A little more is drunk, and soon Tealer is relaxing from his mixed emotions, his dreams and nightmares and fevered visions of damaged Scotsmen. He begins to lose sensation in his limbs. All his energies seem to concentrate in his head, and he comes very thoughtful. He wants to decide, as a man of action, what exactly his next action should be.

But he finds questions about the future are being crowded by questions about the past.

Chief among these: "How am I here alone?"

Paradise Postponed

How? Because impending marriage brings with it impending domesticity - and with domesticity comes reality. Reality for the future Mrs Sayer was the realisation that one may not, after all, have an automatic right to see one's dreams come true. It began to dawn on Maud that her betrothed really wasn't all that wealthy. Wealth was not what had attracted her to Tealer, but she was beginning to find that a measure of prosperity did a match no harm. She also realised that although Tealer had ambitions, these were little connected with the sea but with his passion for the hunting of local wildfowl. His goal seemed little more than to become the Colonel Hawker of Norfolk. Why, he'd once actually said as much, and at the time Maud had laughed her head off at the quaintness of the notion. At the time she'd thought she could afford to. Only later did she begin to see that one of them was going to have to return to earth, and that one was going to be her.

And sitting alone in his house and thinking back Tealer now admits to himself that Maud did make valiant attempts to learn the arts of cooking and housekeeping. She started watching her mother's housekeeper. She found none of it easy.

Occasionally she would rage at Tealer, calling him feckless and shiftless. She had thrown her lot in with a dreamer, she'd say.

Yes, she had. And always a risky venture for another dreamer.

Then one day the following March, Maud and Becky arrived at Tealer's house boasting about how they were going to give it a cleaning with 'their own hands'. Neither was much used to manual work, and both rather enjoyed the sensation for the first two or three minutes. Becky started to give the carpet a beating out in the yard, and by standing downwind of it nearly asphyxiated herself with dust. Maud got on her hands and knees and gave the floor in the scullery a scrub. (She'd known this would be hard on her shapely knees, but had not been not ready for the ache in the wrists and shoulders!) It then occurred to her that this kind of work might be more than an occasional novelty.

This might be her lot.

As she held her hands over the grate to draw some life back into them, she turned to Tealer, who was cleaning a gun. Not any gun, but a single damascene-barrelled four-bore flint-lock by Joseph Manton. A very rare piece, a classic piece even. Not many such guns...

"Tealer," says Maud, "Tealer, we'll need money."

Whatever Tealer thought, Maggie agreed with her daughter. The marriage would have to be delayed, and Tealer would have to go back to sea. Not coastal trade, but something lucrative.

Now, Tealer had heard of the good living to be had from the tea clippers and windjammers that plied the routes to the Far East and the New World. It would mean long periods at sea. But with such an income he and Maud would be able to start a household, to employ servants and to avoid having to beat carpets or scrub scullery floors.

After some searching around Tealer learnt of a clipper company sailing out of London. He secured a post on a tea-route that took him away for four months. A second took five months; but when he came back he reckoned he had amassed sufficient to see them both well. He reckoned Maud would agree, but when they talked about it she surprised him by saying that she wanted to be sure they had enough to develop her mother's business. She wanted none of the tiresome borrowing and scrimping that seemed to make life so tawdry for so many of her friends.

Of course, to any mariner truly experienced in navigating the seas of life the signs were clear as a lighthouse beam. A wistful smile which was ever more wistful. A faraway look which was ever further away. The sea-tales Tealer told that no longer seemed to thrill.

And Maud had stopped raging at Tealer if he began to nod as she read to him. Now she'd only shake her head and take up her needlework.

Even Tealer began to realise that they were moving into stormy waters, and that resolute decisions were needed if he were to save the day. So he agreed he should seek more such positions before they married – long ones like the first, and, with luck, lucrative ones, to put the issue beyond doubt. At first he had no idea whom to approach – there were no vacancies on any tea-clippers he was aware of. Then through a chance conversation with a fellow in Felixstowe he learnt of the rich rewards to be had on the coffee-clippers plying the Brazilian routes. He made a few more enquiries. These ended with him winning the post of first mate on an ageing bark berthed down at Rotherhithe but owned by a Yarmouth man who'd known his uncle. The pay was excellent. He came back to Yarmouth triumphant with the news of his appointment.

Brazil!

Maud's spirits revived. The storm was ridden! Calm returned.

A loud cat fight below the window causes Tealer to jump. He realises that he must have been staring at the empty wall of his kitchen for hours. His stomach rumbles. He last ate when the *Empress* was still fifty miles down the coast. Yet he's got no appetite. Instead he sinks another slug of blackberry spirit, stretches, slips his clogs on, and walks around the house to get the feeling back into his limbs.

In the silence it seems to him that the groan of the floorboards under his weight must wake the street. He clomps up the stairs and makes his way to the window, which he opens. He leans out and looks up and down the Row, listening. Daybreak is still several hours away. The windows of the building opposite are wide open against the summer heat, and the thick air carries a mingling of sounds: the squalling of a restless infant, the rhythmic gasps of procreation, the terminal cough of a consumptive. Beyond these are stranger noises of the kind only familiar to night-walkers – the distant, vague screams and moanings that might be human, or animal, or supernatural.

And out to sea is the tolling of the bell that warns sailors of shoals around the very entrance to the haven.

Tealer's position for the last nine months has been as first mate of the *Shadwell Empress,* and at the moment he feels he would sooner be back on the *Empress* than in this the house he grew up in. He has – or till a few hours ago, had – reason to be happy: he's back from his last voyage with a very decent wage, but also with something of much greater significance. He feels for the pouch by his side and unties it. He takes out the contents and scatters them on the table with the same mirthless smile as in the street a few hours ago. He takes them in his fist and squeezes so hard that they leave indentations in the palm of his hand.

What use now? Might they not just as well be shells, or pebbles?

Oh, he will give that Scotsman a thrashing! A *thrashing*! Yes.

But there's no force behind the resolution now. He sits back and stares and stares at the contents of the bag.

And as he stares a jumble of sound and light begins to fill his head. He hears the wailing of gulls, the banging of guns, snatches of familiar songs, the roaring of a crowd, the voices of many people from down the years – Maud, Palmer, Charlie Harrison, Harry Pole, Daisy Bales – all calling his name. The room is rocking back and forth. Tealer grasps the table ends to brace himself against the familiar roll and pitch of the *Empress*. But he finds he's not on board ship but sitting in a tree that is swaying in a stiff sea breeze. Laid out below him is the Bure. The sultry August night has turned into a chilly May evening. The banks of the river are thronged with chattering crowds eager to see what's going to happen next…

The mice in the kitchen start to reappear as the solitary seated figure in the kitchen droops and becomes silent. Outside the house the moaning, whispering summer night rolls on.

For several hours more the sleeping form of Tealer Sayer is part of the restored silence in the kitchen of the house in Row 111. Once more the mice can only hear one anothers' scratchings. The thinnest of lights starts to seep in through the crack in the shutters, and the faint sounds of early morning are just beginning to mix with the vaguer noises of the dark.

John 'Tealer' Sayer could be dead but for the smallest movement of his chest. His breathing is inaudible.

Then of a sudden his lips quiver and his eyes open wide.

"The Shuck," he says.

The mice scuttle for cover at the croak of his voice.

After a few moments he succumbs again to the effects of Maud's strange wine and sinks back into the world of his distant past. In time the mice recover their nerve, and again their faint scratchings are the only sounds that break the silence.

An hour on. From the cataleptic form in the kitchen there is no sign that, deep within, some small part of John Sayer is travelling the vivid routes of his early life. The rest of him is near death.

Two hours on. Morning light has filled the room.

Without any warning there's a sudden urgent banging on the door to the street, followed by someone or something heavy pushing against the woodwork. Again the mice vanish. But Tealer doesn't stir. He doesn't react at all to the shadow that falls across his window or the face that peers through the crack in the shutters into the gloom of his kitchen.

The cause of both the noise at the door and the shadow in the window is a bearded man of his own age. A man with a serious expression and piercing blue eyes that seem to take everything in at once: the strange objects strewn about the table below the window; the wary gull on the opposite roof; the children playing at the far end of the Row; the light falling on the top of the house wall above his head; the steely blue sky beyond.

This man is Charlie Harrison, who has come down to the house in Row 111 because he's heard that the *Empress* has docked on South Quay. But having just knocked on the door without an answer, and having leant against it to no avail – and not realizing that the door has simply warped into its jamb from lack of use – he has wrongly decided that it must be shut and locked from the outside. Now, as he peers in at the window and can make out only the table, he decides that Sayer can't be at home after all. (Tealer is in fact not four feet away from him, but slumped over the end of the table, just out of view behind the wall.)

Harrison looks up and down the Row for any other clue that might suggest that Tealer has come home. Then his eye catches something that makes him forget all about why he is standing here in the Row at all. It's a sight that makes him gasp and stare. It is nothing more or less than the August sun playing on the masts of the ships moored on South Quay at the end of the narrow alley.

"Now *here's* good stuff," he says, and he fumbles for a piece of paper and a stick of charcoal from the inside pocket of his jacket. He then walks briskly down the Row towards the light.

In the darkness of the house Tealer sleeps on. His breathing is very shallow and his limbs are motionless. Mice run straight past his head and round his feet, unheeding. Silence has returned to the kitchen in the little house half-way down Row 111.

But just as a stone dropped into the deepest part of the sea will eventually reach the bottom, so Harrison's banging on the door finally plumbs the depths of his friend's unconscious – though it is a good fifteen minutes after the painter has wandered away that Tealer fully resurfaces. And immediately he feels outrageously thirsty.

The *Empress* must have foundered, he thinks.

It must have hit a reef. Yes! He heard the banging!

Yet he still feels a swaying.

So he must be sitting on a raft in the Atlantic, he thinks, shipwrecked and dying from lack of water.

Then the rocking ceases, and he can feel no elements on his skin, only the raging lust for water which must be quenched before it kills him. He's puzzled as to where he is – but the priority is to drink. He gets to his feet, reaching out to steady himself on rigging that isn't there. As soon as he's upright his legs buckle and send him crashing to the floor. He drags himself to his feet again and staggers to the door, which swings open to let him into the back yard where the daylight hits him like a volley of spears. The urge to vomit forces him to bend over with his hands on his knees for support, but when the spasm comes it merely wrenches at his empty stomach. Another agonising heave has the same effect. With eyes screwed shut he falls against the pump and works the handle with his whole body for several strokes before realising the water is simply draining away. Somehow he manages to kick a nearby pail partly under the spout so that it slowly fills. He picks up the pail and pours the water over his face, some of which by luck gets into the leathery cavity that was once his mouth. Having quenched this epic thirst he then becomes aware of an infernal ache in his eyes. He keeps them firmly shut except where they are needed to see him back out of the yard. He hears himself muttering that there's a Scotsman he must kill, but now he neither knows nor cares what he's talking about. Now that he has drunk the water he only wants to get out of this appalling light.

He makes it back into the kitchen where he closes the shutters on the little window harder than he means to, and he cringes as they crash into place. He sits back down in his chair. Through the half-light he makes out the bottle of blackberry spirit which he reaches for and empties.

John Sayer doesn't know that his condition is no simple hangover.

He soon feels that someone in the room is nauseous and he thinks this might be him. Soon he ceases to worry about it. He is soon slumped back into his chair with his arms on the table and his head on his arms.

Unbeknownst to Tealer; Yarmouth awoke hours ago and the daily rhythm of men, women and horses in the rows and streets has already begun to slow to the speed of a warm afternoon. The steady thump of the steam hammer has been shaking the quay-side every few seconds since early morning.

The last two or three weeks have been hard for Tealer Sayer. Heavy seas kept the crew of the *Empress* awake for days on end before they hit high pressure and calm waters approaching the British Isles.

And in any case Tealer hasn't slept well since leaving South America.

And then, of course, there was the truth to confront about Maud.

Mix these ingredients with those of the singular green bottle on the table in front of Tealer's hunched form and you begin to realise why the cycles of day and night have become meaningless to this shattered man in the darkness of his darkened kitchen.

A further bout of thirst forces Tealer back on to his feet. He stumbles out to fetch more water. When he returns it is with something approaching amusement that he watches himself in the windsor chair, rocking with the waves as he sinks back and back, back down the pathways into his past.

As he watches he thinks: "That fellow sitting there had better have no more fruit spirit."

Then he feels weak and goes back to sit down – and is again one with the fellow who had better have no more fruit spirit. And with body and soul thus reunited he floats back three months and five thousand miles to where great waves crash down on to the dazzling shores of Rio de Janeiro.

Rio

When not occupied with the business of first mate on board the *Shadwell Empress*, Tealer would spend hours watching the frigate birds. He'd first noticed them when the *Empress* was many miles off the Brazilian coast and he had assumed that they must be birds of the open water. Then when the Empress was docked at Salvador he saw that they also patrolled the skies up and down the shore. He asked one of the Empress's paying passengers, a man called Alvares Williams travelling from Salvador along the coast to Rio, what they were.

"Devil birds, *senhor*", said Williams, "and when the time come for honest men like me to die, those bastards they fly above the house. They come to steal our spirits for to take them down to Hell. They steal everything. They will steal the food from the lifeboat with a crew who is dying, and then when they can they will steal the eyes from the crew. They chase the other birds, and catch them, and if they can they eat them, and if they can't they shake them about till the other bird he vomit up everything he ate, and the frigate he swallow that. They are sea birds, *senhor*, but they never swim. They never even touch the water. You see, they are devil birds." And he laughed and spat over the rail and went back to his canvas, which he was preparing 'for to paint our coming into Rio'.

Tealer had never crewed a South American route before, and this fellow Alvares Williams seemed heaven-sent. From the time Williams had wangled and wheedled his way on to theq *Shadwell Empress* for passage from Salvador down to Santos by way of Rio he'd been a constant fund of anecdotes, explanations and advice about Brazil. In addition to the practical knowledge needed for his duties, Tealer was especially interested in the bird-life, and Williams had stories and legends about every kind of bird they saw following the ship. The man could paint, though not very well, and he claimed to supplement his income as a coffee-broker by selling Brazilian landscapes to the rich of the coastal towns. No-one believed him, and he probably didn't expect to be believed. He claimed he was half-Welsh and admitted he was half-Portuguese. As soon as Tealer got to know him he realised that Williams in fact had a chameleon talent for mixing in with any of the many races in Brazil, because he had antecedents from all of them. Captain Press, the *Empress*'s master, had taken one look at Williams waiting on the quay in Salvador – the long, greasy black hair that sprouted out from under a floppy, wide-brimmed hat, the oversized, stained white cotton suit, the grubby orange neckerchief – and had muttered to Tealer he wouldn't be trusting 'that half-blood cove any further than he could spit him'. But then Williams had offered to pay half his fare up-front, which had surprised even Press.

The only other passenger on that leg of the route was a bespectacled, Fagin-like caricature of a Jewish merchant by the name of Jacob Levison, and whose card, which he gave to everyone from Press to the ship's cook, alleged that he was an exporter of Brazilian goods. He said his specialities were sugar, nuts and garnets, though there seemed nothing related to business that didn't interest him, and nothing not related to it that did. From the minute he climbed aboard he was pestering anyone who spoke English or Portuguese with questions about the *Empress*: its owners, its customers, its cargoes and its routes. He even secured a private interview in the master's cabin to discuss a 'nice little chance' that he felt Press might like to consider. Tealer was in his own cabin and he heard Press's angry laugh through the wall.

Rio itself was a fantastical dream to Tealer. It would not have been possible to imagine a land more unlike his own. Huge lumps of rock stuck straight up out of the water, and between were verdant forests and deep lagoons. What would Maudy say of the beetling heights, with their tops lost in threatening thunderous clouds that were regularly lit with brilliant flashes? The nights, too! Not the evenings – those were paltry affairs that simply marked the border between light and dark – and Tealer missed the magnificent sunsets which stain the Broadland sky for hours before nightfall. But with the chirruping and whirring of armies of frogs and insects the nights themselves were as alive as the days, and they were another shock to a man for whom the sound of darkness was the wind whistling under a shut door, or a total silence broken by the occasional call of a fox, duck or peewit.

Above all, though, it was the birdlife which most impressed Tealer. After the gentle duns and browns of the waterfowl of Breydon, he found the bronzes, azures and vermilions of the Brazilian birds outrageous. (He thought of those tweedy collector-fellows who pester the gunners at the Bowling Green for the broken corpses of avocets and greenshanks. What would they make of the toucans, the macaws, the hummingbirds!) And where Tealer was used to plaintive cries echoing over the marsh, here the forests resounded to strident screams and whistles. As a man who had spent much of his life watching and listening to the birds of the sparse wastes of Norfolk, even a walk through the scrub at Rio's margins could force his eyes to dart around until he was tired with fascination. The richer life of the forest itself, higher into the mountains, left him feeling literally giddy.

Soon after the *Empress* dropped anchor it was clear she wouldn't be leaving in a hurry. There was no sign, nor even any news, of the shipments that Press had been told he could expect. This had him fuming. He wandered around on the bridge muttering about missed trade winds and sharp merchants. But Tealer and the crew found the sun genial, the rum cheap and the smiles of the Carioca girls dazzling. The missing coffee was no great concern to them.

Williams was happy, too, when he heard the news.

"But it is good, Senhor Tealer! I thought I will have a day, maybe two, to show to you this town of Rio. Now we have a week, I think, at least. For example, I think you like the birds, *senhor*? I will show you many! The hills above Rio is good for birds. I go to paint the views. You will come. But first I show you what a good town is Rio. Then we go together to the mountains."

Williams was as good as his word. He took Tealer along the beaches and around the markets. He took him to the horse-races and the cock-fights and the taverns with glistening African dancers. He took him to sinful dens where they were able to drink rum with limes, and drain the milk from fresh coconuts. Everywhere there was noise, rhythm and music. Above all, there were girls of every conceivable race, chattering, gossiping and whispering, but always – it seemed to Tealer – always smiling.

"What do you most like in this town, Senhor Tealer?" asked Williams as they quaffed rums under an awning in a leafy side-street overlooking Guanabara.

"The women," said Tealer.

"Ah, the girls. And you like these *Carioquinhas*? Why do you like them?"

"They seem honest mawthers," said Tealer. "They walk around as though they want you to look at'm, and smile at you if you do. You don't get much o' that where I come from. Where I come from you could stand on a street corner a-watching for weeks and not see one woman that would compare with these. Must be all this nice weather, I reckon."

"Yes they are very beautiful women, Mr Tealer. But you know…," he leant across the frail table causing it to creak, and he fixed Tealer with a gleam in his eyes, "they are nothing to Indian girls."

"Indian girls? Blast, I never knew you'd been to India an'all. You get about, Mr Williams!"

"India, *senhor*? I do not mean India, I mean Rondonia – the jungle. To the north."

"Ah," said Tealer. "Well, what about them?"

"Ah, well," said Williams back in his throaty whisper, still staring at Tealer and ignoring a large fly that was buzzing around his face like a familiar, "do you know what the men here they say? The men here they say: you take a candle of the hardest wax – the *hardest* wax – and put it in a Brazilian girl, and she will melt it. *Piff!*"

Tealer chuckled and drained his glass, which Williams immediately filled. "But not the Indian girl," he said, leaning back and waggling his finger. "She will *not* melt the wax."

"No?"

"No." He leant forward again, and brought his face even closer to Tealer's. "The Indian girl, she will light the candle."

They looked at each other in silence for a few seconds and then roared with laughter. Tealer in particular was enjoying himself. This voyage was turning out easier than he'd expected, and this fellow Williams was good, sporting sort of fellow. The sun was pleasant, the rum went down easily and the girls….

"You want try for yourself?" Williams asked.

"Well, as you see, I ha'nt got a candle to hand," said Tealer, still laughing.

"No, *senhor*, I am serious," said Williams. "You cannot leave Rio without you try all it has to offer! These girls are not to describe. They know things no Christian woman should know." He ran his finger round the inside of the orange neckerchief where it was sticking to his neck. He had stopped laughing but was still grinning conspiratorially.

Tealer was caught off guard. He returned the conspiratorial grin, but was pulling himself up.

Now, let there be no mistake: our John 'Tealer' is no saint. Before this voyage to Brazil he had visited brothels in every port from Copenhagen to the Gibralter Rock, but such lusts had melted away like a summer frost since the red-haired Maud had captured his heart. (He didn't mention this to Williams.)

"Well, Mr Williams, I don't know. You see, five year ago, I did a passage to Malaga, and someone rather like you got me to try some of *their* local goods. And when I got back to Blighty I realised I'd caught more than a bit of the sun. Took me a fair few weeks to get back on an even keel."

This mixture of the nautical and the medical foxed Williams for a moment, then he smiled and waved his hand dismissively,

"But *these* girls are virgins, *senhor*."

"Oh, are they, though! Well, then, how…?"

"It's… how to say? It's in their blood. They are like animals, born with knowledge of such things."

"But… *virgins*!"

"Well, virgins maybe not, but they are very high class girls, *senhor*. They do not sleep with every dirty mule driver with a few coins in his pocket. They are good girls. Yes. Now let me think – there is one address in Catete that I have once visited – yes, yes, I confess it – very, very good. I remember it well: Rua Cristoforo. No. 15. Very secret, very private, very good. I have not been for a year or two, and if I speak the truth I even do not know if it is still open. I remember one girl, no more than fifteen, who… well…I cannot tell it! Her name was Lucia, and she spoke English and Spanish I remember. I think you speak Spanish too."

"Some," said Tealer. "But: a native mawther fresh from Rondonia, speaking Portuguese and Spanish – and English to boot! She sound quite a rare one to me, master Williams."

"Trust me, *senhor* Tealer. If you grow to be an old man, and you sit in your chair remembering your life, and you remember that you missed such an experience, what will you say to yourself? You will say to yourself: "I was a fool." You will be a very angry old man, I think. But if that place in Cristoforo is still there, I do not know. The girl Lucia would be maybe eighteen, and perhaps has moved to other work, or is married. To some lucky man, if yes. But..! But…! There are other such places in that district, it is for certain. I can find out for you. What have you to lose? And, please, don't say me you can lose your own *verginita* or I laugh very much!"

Indeed, what had Tealer to lose? The midday sun was devilish hot and Tealer was a long way from home, and it was Maudy who had wanted him back at sea, and what she could never know could never hurt her, and the image of a lighted candle did made his heart race a little, and that afternoon he found himself knocking on the door of a quiet bougainvillia-strewn house set discreetly back from a side street called Cristoforo in the *Catete* district.

He was met by a smiling lady of middle age as elegant as a piano teacher, quite in keeping with such a respectable brothel. He was taken through a tastefully decorated house and into a quiet shaded garden where small colourful birds flitted between enormous purple and orange blooms. The madam showed him to a mahogany seat and clapped her hands softly, at which point a native girl of about twelve came out with a jug of coffee which she poured for Tealer. The madam supervised the operation with a benign smile. As the girl finished pouring and walked back into the house Tealer took the opportunity to ask the woman if she knew of a 'Lucia'. Knowing no Portuguese, he tried in Spanish. The madam showed no sign of understanding: she simply bowed her head, smiled politely and walked out. A minute or so later she returned with a tray and a bill that she placed before Tealer with the utmost discretion. Yet for all this finesse Tealer felt that he would rather have liked to see the goods before parting with any money. Then he noticed that the madam had been joined by another girl. The madam beamed at Tealer and gestured to the girl.

This was certainly a comely lass with jungle-thick hair that was plaited and adorned with various flowers. The girl shook Tealer by the hand and curtseyed in a modest fashion before gesturing delicately to the stairs. The madam bowed as he paid his due and spirited herself away into some other part of the establishment.

The girl was neither called Lucia, nor was she Indian, nor was she a teenager, nor did she speak English, nor was she a virgin, nor did she do any exotic tricks with candles. But Tealer couldn't claim that Williams had led him on a wild goose chase by slipping him the name of this leafy bordello. The girl showed all the discreet efficiency of her mistress. She took Tealer's greasy cap from his head and hung it carefully on a hook behind the door and then helped him out of his jacket as though she were about to measure him for a new one. And in everything from then to the time she had her tawny thighs locked round his midriff she showed a sophistication that he found admirable. There was none of the tiresome moaning and squirming that so insulted the intelligence of a man of taste. In fact, Tealer was very impressed. A top-drawer harlot, he reckoned. Yes, definitely one for the connoisseurs. Williams was not entirely guilty of exaggeration. Williams was a sterling fellow.

And after the first transaction was completed "Lucia" got up, tidied her hair and gestured Tealer towards a divan by the window. Once he'd lain down she rubbed some sweet smelling local oil into his back (and again didn't try his patience by cooing a lot of bilge about what fine muscles he had). When she'd finished she offered him a silk gown and a passable glass of wine and asked him in Portuguese what his name was. He answered in Spanish, a language he'd picked up in the Mediterranean. She gave a dignified squeak of surprise and said in Spanish.

"Ah! But you speak my language."

"A little," said Tealer. "Are you Spanish?"

"No. I am from Montevideo. My name is Maite. Tell me, I want to know. Are all the English who come to Brazil the younger sons of aristocrats? This is what I've heard. Are you? Are you rich?"

Normally the secretive Tealer would have told anyone, female or otherwise, asking this sort of question to mind their own affairs. But such ingenuousness in woman so experienced in other ways amused him, and he saw no harm in humouring her.

"No, *señorita*, I am not rich. Not very rich. But I have enough. I have about a couple of hundred pounds collected, but the girl I want to marry says I need more."

"What's your work?"

"I am the mate. I am the captain's second-in-command. On a ship. I am also in charge of finding provisions for the cook and for paying the crew."

'Lucia' took all this in with wide brown eyes, and nodded to show a level of interest that was polite and not inquisitive. "And you have all that money for yourself?"

"It isn't mine. And it is locked deep inside the ship. But yes, it is my job to look after it."

She nodded thoughtfully again. "If I had any money at all I'd surely have a lot." Tealer looked puzzled, so she added "I mean that if I had a little money I could invest it and become very rich. This town is growing very quickly. Those who buy part of it are soon rich. But first you must have a little money to begin." Tealer nodded. She went on: "But if I were like you, I'd borrow or even steal – only for a short time – the money on your ship to invest in the railways or the coffee planations or the mines. It's so sure."

Then they talked of other matters. Tealer asked the girl if she had heard of Alvares Williams. She frowned and said she hadn't. They talked of the voyage of the *Empress*, of her captain, and her crew. It turned out that the Levison family were quite well-known for their business in semi-precious stones, of which there were many fine examples in Brazil. They talked of Tealer's itinerary, and of his adventures, including the fictional one with the kraken. Downstairs one of Maite's colleagues was plucking idly at some stringed instrument. The wind billowed the muslin screen over the windows and sent large dead leaves scraping around on the balcony outside. The coarse, hard-won pleasures of Yarmouth seemed a long way away.

The sky was in fact becoming very black. The *Empress* had sailed into Rio at the end of the Carnival, and the thunder clouds were now piling with rain to throw down on the ravaged town and cleanse it, washing the detritus of celebration away.

The girl got up from the divan and wiped the oil off her hands. She went to the window and looked out cautiously, keeping her naked body in the shadow of the curtain until she could see there was no-one in the garden below.

"There's going to be a storm," she said. "Rio changes her face in a storm. Just you see."

Then she leant boldly on the balcony with her hair flowing behind her. The smell of her body mingling with the unguents was wafted round the room on the breeze.

Tealer lay back. A second voyage into Uruguay was imminent.

This was the first of several visits to the brothel, and after each one Tealer emerged on to the street feeling sated, relaxed and guilty.

On what was to be the final visit the feelings of satisfaction and relaxation evaporated leaving only the guilt when he heard a woman's voice calling him and he looked up to see Maud staring straight at him from across the street. She was shouting something indistinct, drowned out by the racket of human voices, barking dogs, whistles and the relentless undertone of the cicadas. But it was surely Maud, and Tealer was rooted to the spot with stones in his throat. Jostled by the stream of people and donkeys streaming up and down the street, he could only stare at the girl in the sultry, thundery dusk, too surprised to question how or why she could be calling him frantically on a street in Rio de Janeiro when he had left her quiet and thoughtful half a world away on the quayside in Yarmouth. Finally she turned and walked away into the crowd with the splay-footed gait of an Hispanic girl, quite unlike the long, straight stride of Maud. It was just another daughter of the great Brazilian crucible; perhaps some Irish antecedent had left a trace of auburn hair and pointed chin to make him think it was Maud. Then even that was shown to be a deception: as the girl passed under the glow of a street trader's lamps her hair was as black as any other Brazilian's. The rest was too hard to make out in the fast gathering gloom.

At times like this the indistinct tormentors of Tealer's early life, those phantasma too distant to identify, still had the power to re-emerge, albeit for an instant. And so a long-suppressed part of Tealer caused him to gaze foolishly at the unknown girl in the concourse.

But simultaneously, another, more recently-crafted part of Tealer Sayer was already reacting to something else.

This second Tealer, hardened from experiences in fifty different docks and waterside ghettoes, was swinging round on a shadow behind him and at the same time slipping a length of wood from its home in a long narrow pocket inside his jacket. But the weapon, an oaken belaying-pin hollowed at one end and filled with lead, swished uselessly in the air as the thief melted away into the gloom. Tealer felt at his pocket with his elbow, but on finding it empty he didn't waste time berating his own stupidity in falling for such an ancient trick. He simply gave chase, relying on a body honed by years of sea-voyaging to give him the stamina to keep the pickpocket in view.

The chase went on for several minutes. They tore up alleys with dark, stepped passages, and then across streets, through yards and into more passages. People and dogs in the way were simply pushed aside or bowled over. Onlookers regarded with casual interest the small drama of another street robbery. Eventually the thief found himself in an alley blocked by a handcart and he turned to face his pursuer. A knife appeared in his hand as a magician produces a bouquet of flowers. Tealer slid to a halt thirty yards away from him, slipped his jacket off and bound it round his left wrist with a deft series of swings. He had broken up too many crewmen's brawls to feel overawed by this situation, though he knew no knife-fight is ever a casual business. He saw the thief stiffen, and he realised that the man had thought the display with the knife would have been enough to persuade Tealer to let him go. The thief surveyed Tealer with the cold anger of the street robber – who might die if he thieves, but will die if he doesn't.

And so began the age-old, oft-repeated drama of a fight between two armed assailants in a side street in the poor quarter of a poor city. Such were the weapons, a knife and a cudgel, that at least one life would likely end in the conflict, but the town didn't gather round with bated breath to see if their local boy could disembowel the pale-skinned stranger. A city like Rio has ten thousand other life-struggles to concern it. Yet, here was a contest far more real, more immediate, more honest, and played for a much higher stake, than the most eagerly-awaited prize fight. It was a contest utterly free of bombast or match-rigging and there would be no plaintive excuses for defeat at its conclusion. As the bodies of the two men ducked and wove, wary of the side-swipe, the downward strike, the forward thrust, the deliberate miss that carries on into a full circle and a second unexpected slash, their concentration was so total that their spirits might easily have left their taut forms and looked down at the combat with relaxed curiosity. That was certainly a sensation Tealer later remembered.

Yet in the first few moments after it was over and Tealer was nursing a cut eye, the shock of combat left him indifferent to what had just passed. Then as he caught his breath the desperate seconds of the fight came back to him bit by bit. He remembered how, as he'd readied himself, he'd realised that robber had only really wanted to escape, but also that it'd been too late for that. Tealer would have had to step back to let the man pass, and in such a narrow alley he couldn't have risked it – the more so because a thief from a town like Rio would only have expected to be bludgeoned to death even if he had offered the wallet back. Then of the fight itself Tealer's main memory was the desperate scuffling of his boots on the cobbles as he'd danced his deadly pax-de-deux with the pickpocket. The alley was greasy with the scum of rotting vegetables and urine and he'd remembered slipping and landing on his back. He must have instinctively brought his legs over his body to lash out at the bare legs of his assailant, because he somehow managed to regain his feet – and he later remembered how, in the midst of the crisis a fleeting image flashed before him of a childhood fight when he'd done the same thing. He remembered noting that the knife was not long, meaning that the robber would not try to stab but to slash. He remembered how he had waited for the slashing movement and had jerked back so that his midriff was six inches beyond the arc of the blade. He remembered how he had then swung his own weapon angled slightly downward and had caught the thief's forearm as the knife commenced its back swing. He remembered the crack as the belaying pin made contact with the lithe brown forearm. He remembered very clearly the screech of pain from his assailant as Tealer himself again over-balanced and fell on the treacherous surface. And it came back to him how he had again brought his knees up to protect his body and again kicked out, this time catching the thief on the back of the leg and bringing him down. He remembered how the thief had bounced back up and jumped right over him, throwing the knife down at him as he went, catching Tealer a glancing blow that had caused blood to flow immediately.

And it took Tealer several hours of reliving the event to realise that the reason the thief had thrown the knife at him – something no true knife-fighter would ever normally do – was that his belaying-pin had shattered the man's right arm.

He stood up after the fight and brushed as much of the slime off his clothes as he could with a handkerchief. He threw the handkerchief into the gutter and made his way out of the alley. In the background the city was coming alive for the evening, while in the quiet of the alley the only noises were Tealer's boots and his heavy panting. He realised the injury to his temple was still bleeding copiously. He made his way to the quay and hired a boat back to his ship. Once in his cabin he cleaned his head-wound with wet cotton and treated it with witch-hazel. He looked in the mirror at himself and tried to decide if this had been a good night's work or a bad one. He had won more respect from Williams, a fellow whose style he liked. He'd had another turn with Lucia, a gold-standard courtesan he could describe to friends for years to come. He'd lost a monogrammed wallet that had belonged to his uncle. He was saddened to have lost it, as it was a memento of the halcyon days of his later childhood, but there was little in it save a few fishhooks and a pipecleaner. He imagined the hoodlum shaking it with his good hand and then throwing it away in disgust on to one of the rubbish tips that sprawled down the steep rock faces below the shanties of Rio. Tealer looked at himself in the mirror and grinned encouragingly.

He had arranged to meet Williams on the quay the following day. At the appointed time Williams arrived wreathed in smiles, which abated slightly when he saw Tealer's face.

"You have had an accident on that ship, *senhor*?"

"No," said Tealer, "this was ashore."

Williams laughed and said " I hope it was not in that bordello on rua Cristoforo. If it was then Senhora da Silva has girls with a different… what to say?… *style*… from the girls that I remember."

"No, that weren't the whorehouse. *That* part has been good, I grant you."

Then Tealer told Williams the story and Williams stopped smiling. He tutted and shook his head.

"You should have let him escape, *senhor*. This is too dangerous."

"I couldn't, my man. We were too far up a blind alley. I had to try to disable him. I dussn't let him pass."

"And he took your portmonnaie?"

"My wallet? Yes."

"You have lost much money?"

"Not after my visits to your Senhora da Silva."

Williams ignored the irony. "Was it valuable?"

"Not really. That was my uncle's. 'At was embossed with his monogram. Mind you, 'at never had much money in it in his day, either. Don't worry on it. 'At weren't really that important."

"But you like you have it again?"

"Well, yes, but…"

"Perhaps we can do something."

Tealer looked at Williams, and then at the bustling town shimmering in the liquid heat of midday.

"Thas like a jungle!" he said. "You'll never find anything."

"A jungle," said Williams with a laugh. "Yes it is kind of jungle. But I know some roads through it." He paused and took a deep breath to indicate he was changing the subject. "Will you come with me tomorrow? I go to paint the town from the Corcovado. There you will see many birds and animals."

That suddenly seemed to Tealer a more wholesome use of this enforced delay than a session with the finest prostitute in South America. He agreed willingly.

The Mortuary

It was at the swift Rio dawn that Tealer arrived on the quayside again. He looked back at the *Empress* waiting patiently out in the harbour for her turn to come into berth. As he sat down Williams handed him his wallet.

"Lord," said Tealer. "How the hell did you ever…?"

Williams waved his hand. "I had no idea who the thief was. But I know men in this town who know everyone. This is not my town – I am from Santos – but it is my country, and I do not want good men such as you to return to Europe to tell your friends that we are all savages."

"Well, thank you, *senhor*."

"Nothing," said Williams. "Now we must enjoy the forest on this fine morning. There are some rain clouds in the sky but not too many. The views will be good. When we arrive at our destination there is something I want to show you and something I want to talk to you about."

The cockerels in the back yards of the houses were vying with the shrieks of the wild birds. Not much of a dawn chorus, thought Tealer, but then not much of a dawn. Nevertheless, he was looking forward to experiencing another facet of this sublime town.

His fascination turned almost trance-like when they reached the outskirts of the town and began to climb. At first the vegetation was unremarkable; Williams said that the trees had long been cleared for rows of coffee , but now it was realised that these were depriving Rio of its water, and so a team of workers was at work re-planting the forest. But as they climbed away from the town the surroundings became wilder and more rugged. The trap driver brought them to a small hut in a clearing above the town where three donkeys were waiting, one each for Williams and Tealer and one for Williams's easel and paints. They mounted and set off further up the path which became little more than a trail once they had passed the last habitation.

Away from the sea the heat was fierce, and at certain points the track was so steep they had to dismount and climb on foot. As they climbed, they entered an area where the re-planted trees were oldest and had already become tall, with long, snaking creepers that dropped to the forest floor. The extravagance of life that festooned and cascaded around, along and over the path defied the senses. The donkeys' hooves crunched on huge brown leaves. At almost every step butterflies flew up and away on slow wing beats quite unlike those of the peacocks and swallowtails Tealer knew from the reedbeds of Norfolk. Several particularly gaudy specimens were sipping delicately at the eyesockets of a dog which must have climbed up here to die only the night before. Massive jewelled spiders sat ominously in the centre of colossal webs so strong that they had caught even the heavy stalks of dead vegetation that had fallen into them.

The upward path was unrelenting, and Tealer, who had never really encountered such terrain before, quickly found that his muscles were trained for the sea and not the saddle, especially a saddle that was mostly in the vertical from the steepness of the hill.

At about midday their climb ended. They reached a clearing that from the distance seemed only to open to the sky. Then Tealer realised the enormity of what he was seeing. He was looking over the town from the summit of one of the rocks that dominated it, and to him the view bordered on the impossible. He gawped helplessly at the sight of the mighty *Shadwell Empress* as a toy boat among other toy boats far down in Guanabara Bay. In another direction the beaches of Copacabana, Ipanema and Leblon seemed to stretch for an eternity of sand on which breakers crashed without a sound. In the foreground, seemingly almost directly below them, glowered the dark, quiet waters of the Rio Lagoon.

"It is very beautiful," said Williams, as he put up his easel and shook himself into a painter's smock. "I am lucky I have a talent to capture some small part of this beauty." He pulled a box of water colours from his bag, and began to prepare them, "Do you know," he said, "I think about the day soon when I can do this and not have to worry about anything else."

Tealer was still mezmerised by the view and wasn't listening.

"One day I will be rich," Williams went on. "One day I will be rich and this will be just one of many pleasures."

"We all dream like that, Mr Williams," said Tealer without turning around.

"But for me it is not a dream, but reality. Soon I will have made enough money from this stupid painting to buy one of the mines. Then – yes – I am rich."

He began to daub colours on to his canvas.

"Do you wish to be rich, Mr Tealer?"

Tealer was still too taken with the vastness of the place to answer at first. Then he asked:

"What's the name of this here rock we're on?"

"Corcovado."

"And that there plantation we now rode through?"

"Tijuca. But I have asked you a question, Mr Tealer. Do you wish to be rich?"

"Of course." said Tealer, thinking of Maud for a moment, "But that won't be for a while yet."

Williams painted a little more while Tealer watched a hummingbird through his spyglass.

"You could be very rich very soon if you want, *Senhor* Tealer."

"How?" said Tealer, still watching the hummingbird.

'With these, *senhor*,' and he pulled a bag from somewhere and held it out. Tealer dragged himself away from the hummingbird and took the bag, which he opened. He shook the contents into his palm. A few rough-looking pebbles with streaks of bottle-green lay in his hand.

"What are these, then?" he asked.

"They are emeralds, *Senhor* Tealer," said Williams.

"Emeralds?" said Tealer, "I don't think they are! I've seen emeralds. They sparkle, like green diamonds."

Williams clicked his tongue with impatience. "Only if they have been refined. Do you think they are found in the ground like that – or perhaps you think they grow like that on trees? In the jungle? Really, *senhor*, I thought you were a wiser man! To men who know such things, these, *senhor*, are worth a small fortune – and with others like them, a big fortune. And this will soon be my fortune. And it could be yours."

Tealer laughed. But already he was listening, as ideas unbidden began to spring to mind. Emeralds – emerald eyes – Maud – riches – money – the leisure to hunt and shoot and fish and never worry about tomorrow. "Go on, then,' he said, 'How? Dig a mine?"

Again Williams tutted reproachfully.

"No, no. Leave the digging to fools with strong spades and weak brains. This country is young, Mr Tealer, and everyone who has the courage can be rich. I? I invest in the mine that produced these gems that you see here. But I need a merchant in Europe. Here such stones are only little valuable, but in Europe they are in great demand. I have been watching you, *Senhor* Tealer. You are a man of taste and a man of good sense. Such men are rare in these colonies."

"Why haven't you gone into business before, Mr Williams? If these gems are as valuable as you say you should rich already, to my way of reckoning."

"The mine which I have bought part of is only beginning – and remember these stones are not as valuable here as they are in Europe. And I have been determined not to start my business until I found a man I could trust. Thieves are always easy to find, *Senhor* Tealer, and especially in this son-of-a-bitch country."

Tealer looked back at the view, perhaps hoping not to appear that concerned. He suddenly put his glass up to a frigate bird banking on the updraft from warming rocks far below, but Williams continued:

"Recife, Santos, Porto Alegre, Rio – everywhere you go along the coast you find the streets are full only of liars or idiots. Especially idiots. Men who sit in the sun drinking rum and scratching their bellies and telling each other of the days when they will be rich. I do not need dreamers. I decided long ago that I would not develop my plan until I found a man I could trust. If I am honest, I have to say that I think you are such a man."

And Williams explained his idea: Tealer should buy ten stones at ten pounds each, and take them to London or Amsterdam or some town 'where people know of such things'. And when he sold the stones at a profit, he would know that this was no dream but a quick and easy way to make money.

Tealer liked to be told that he was wise, and he liked to be told that he was trusted, and that he wasn't a dreamer, and he liked to think that he'd found a scheme to get rich that did not depend on anything that he'd been taught but that was entirely a discovery of his own. And he liked the idea that at last he could show Maud that he could provide her with the lifestyle she craved.

But Tealer was a Norfolkman. For a Norfolkman it is never done to show too much enthusiasm for anything, ever.

" 'At sound as though 'at could be a good idea, Mr Williams. Let me think about it."

"Of course, Mr Tealer. Only a clown accepts such a contract without he think about it, in spite it promises much. I think your ship will sail the day after tomorrow. We have time. Here, keep a stone – no, keep it! – pay me later, only after you have shown it to one good jeweller. Only I ask that you tell no-one else. As you have seen, it is not safe in this town to carry things of value with you!" Then he poured the rest of the emeralds back into the canvas bag which Tealer now saw fitted neatly into a concealed drawer in the paint-box.

They went back down to the town, where they parted company. Williams said he was going straight back to the Empress to leave his painting equipment before returning ashore one last time to visit an acquaintance he wished to see before the ship set sail again. Tealer couldn't join him because he firstly had to make his way to the market to procure provisions for the voyage to Santos – but as he negotiated with the dealers his mind was on Williams's proposition. He remembered Williams's advice to find a discreet expert opinion of the uncut emerald, but he knew of no jewellers in Rio and was loath to ask where he might find one. He began to think he would chance his arm. Williams after all had turned out to be a good friend.

He arrived at the quay late that afternoon to take a boat over to the *Empress*. He was surprised to see the trim, bespectacled, straw-hatted figure of Levison waiting at the quayside. It turned out that the merchant's business had been concluded more quickly that he had anticipated in Rio, and that he was now looking to go on to Sao Paulo by way of Santos – but only if he could negotiate the right fare with Press.

As they were rowed over, Levison asked a few questions about the missing coffee shipment. Tealer answered only in curt generalities. He never had much wish to engage with Levison, whom he found over-inquisitive and tedious. And at this particular moment Tealer wanted space to think. Not getting much mileage out of Tealer, Levison talked a little of the coffee trade himself:

"Of course I don't claim any special knowledge of it. As you know it's sugar and stones are my business. And nuts of course. Mainly sugar, though. Did you know, Mr Sayer, that since that hurricane in the Carribean last year the price of sugar …"

But on a reflex Tealer interrupted him. "I'd forgotten you work with precious stones, Mr Levison."

"More my brother than me, Mr Sayer – and semi-precious, not precious. It's garnets are what we know most about. And, do you know, it's a good trade to be in, too. You see, it's easier to ship your assets about when you can carry them in your pocket or sew them into your clothes. Very useful when my people had to get out of Russia in a hurry. Now me personally, I never went into the trade like my brother Mordecai. It's me eyes, you see. I can feel the quality of a sack of sugar and smell it in a barrel of brazils, you see. But for stones a man has to have good eyes, which any fool can see I ain't got. Of course I don't say I couldn't tell the genuine article from a bit of paste, precious or semi. That much my father did teach me, rest him! Even with my eyes. Did you know…?"

"What about emeralds, Mr Levison?"

"Er… what *about* emeralds, Mr Sayer?"

"Would you know a real emerald if you saw it."

"Of course. As I said, I know that much about any stone you want to name. Not that I would touch the emerald trade with a very long stick, mind. Nor brother Mordecai, neither."

"Why not?"

"Too much trouble, Mr Sayer. Far too much trouble. You see, they're precious, like your diamonds. And your rubies and sapphires. There are men not half a mile from this boat as would slit your throat for a single diamond. Less likely to for a single garnet, though. You see, there isn't *that* sort of value in garnets. Value enough, mind you. Did you know…?"

Tealer let Levison ramble on for a while in order to give himself time to decide what to do. He decided to cast his die. He checked the oarsman wasn't looking, leant over to the merchant and passed him Williams's emerald. He asked very quietly "What d'you think about this, then?"

Levison, who by this time had got on to a drop in the value of amethysts, stopped mid-sentence. He took the stone and turned it over in his palm. He took off his spectacles and produced a magnifying glass from his top pocket through which he squinted for half a minute without saying a word. He dripped some seawater on to the stone and rubbed it and viewed it again through his glass. Finally, he muttered:

"Where did you get this?"

"I won it in a card game."

Levison nodded without looking up. Then he said:

"Well then, win some more. This is certainly emerald. It needs some work, but it is very nice. Very nice."

"Are you sure?"

"Am I sure? Of course I'm sure. Why would I say it was if it wasn't? As I said, precious stones are not my family's business, but I could easily have it cut for you if you wanted. For a very reasonable fee. Did you know…?"

But Tealer was not about to let anyone else muscle in on his new venture so soon after it had started. He took the stone back and said he might think about it.

Once aboard, Tealer retired to his berth to escape the sun, but was almost immediately summoned to the master's cabin. The master was waiting with the second mate and was looking very angry. There was still no sign of the coffee train, and there were rumours ashore that it had been either been waylaid by republican bandits or Paraguayan guerillas. He was wondering how long they were going to have to sit at anchor in Guanabara Bay. As there was no imminent sailing Tealer was to stand the men down.

As Tealer came out of the cabin to execute his orders he met Levison who was going in to see Press to negotiate a further passage to Santos. As they passed, Levison raised his eyebrows and smirked knowingly.

Levinson was unable to agree a fare with Press. In fact, the discussion lasted about thirty seconds. The merchant didn't seem too perturbed, though. With a shrug he resigned himself to the next bumboat back to the quay. Before he climbed down to it, he slipped Tealer his card.

"I think your ship might be in port for a day or two yet. Trouble up country, so I've heard. So… while you're waiting, if you decide you need advice on cutting that stone…" he nodded the rest.

Tealer nodded back and watched him disappear across the water. He congratulated himself on his shrewdness in not having let Levinson in on the act. And as if to confirm this, Press told him later that Levinson's idea of a reasonable fare to Santos had been what most people would reckon to pay for a ride across the bay in a rowing boat.

"Damned cheapskate," said Press, and Tealer agreed readily.

Of Williams there was no sign. Nor was he back by the next morning, even though he couldn't have known the ship was to be further delayed. Tealer began to be concerned.

Perhaps Williams had found a more willing customer for his venture.

jThen that afternoon Tealer was summoned to a second meeting with Press; again the master looked out of spirits. "It gets ever better, Mr Sayer. While you were ashore the local militia came over with the British consul. It seems that fellow Williams has managed to get himself run through in some kind of tavern brawl. Damnable thing is, the authorities were somehow able to trace him back to us. I wish the devil would take this confounded city!" He took a breath. "In any case, I want you to go directly to his berth, collect his chest and anything else he had and take 'em over to the Prefect's palace. The consul's told them to expect you this evening. They want someone to identify the body, and they won't let us sail till it's done. Not that we had any reason to sail anyway. Blast the man to hell, he still owed me half his fare. I don't suppose we'll be seeing much o' that!"

Tealer returned to his cabin, shut the door, and thought.

He pounded the cabin wall once, very hard, and thought some more.

This was cruel! Damn it all, this was cruel! To have a sure route to riches placed before you and then plucked away. It was with the feeling of a man cheated that Tealer went down to Williams's berth to pick up the man's effects. He pulled the sea-chest out from under Williams's bunk, opened it and surveyed the contents. These were surprisingly few: a light jacket, a pair of trousers and the dirty white smock for painting. A not-so-clean shirt and some shaving utensils. His easel, folded up.

And his box of water-colours.

Now Tealer was a Christian man at heart and certainly an honest man. He hadn't been a chapel-goer from the time he was orphaned – but even the agnostic Palmer had brought him up to have a regard for his fellow human being. It was with reluctant hands that he fumbled for the catch that sprung open the secret drawer on the box of paints.

He found the catch and released the drawer which revealed the bag to be still in place. He loosened the knot and spilled the contents out on to the bunk and looked at them. He was struck by their nondescriptness. A pile of pebbles. Nothing suggested a potential to change lives.

Certainly nothing that eight months hence would leave a man deranged and near death on a frozen waste thousands of miles from this humid port.

A pile of dull, greenish pebbles.

Yes, dull they may have been to most, but Tealer knew what they were.

And what they were *not*.

And what they were *not*, was Tealer's.

Time was very short. He must decide what to do.

He reasoned: Williams was dead; he couldn't take the gems with him; he had told Tealer he had no family. Who else had any right to them? Williams had said that Tealer should have them.

– Yes, but to buy, not to steal. They might be the only wealth Williams had, the only money for a decent burial.

– No, come on, now. Williams wasn't so poor. Anyway the town authorities would find enough for a burial. And Williams himself would want the rocks to find a good home. Stop worrying.

Yet Tealer did worry. An early childhood amongst evangelical tabernaclers had trained him well in the art of worrying. The battle went on within him for five minutes or more, during which he clenched his teeth and picked up a handful of the stones and ground them together in his palm.

Then he heard someone coming quickly down the steps to the passenger quarters. The trunk was wide open and the stones still scattered about. Tealer snapped into action, and in less than three seconds he had scraped the stones up, slipped them into the bag, put the bag back in its niche, and shoved the paint box under the bunk. Even though he was expecting the brisk knock on the door it still made him jump when it came. A seaman put his head into the room to tell Tealer the boat was ready to take him ashore. The man's eyes may have strayed briefly down to the bunk, they may not – Tealer could not be sure. He nodded his reply, put the lid down on the sea chest, shut the door and locked it. He handed the chest to the seaman and followed him back on deck.

They climbed down on to the boat and made their way across the darkening waters of the bay.

There were flocks of frigate birds in the sky, and though deep in thought Tealer couldn't help registering that they were gathering over the town. The crewman rowing him over was Portuguese and also spoke reasonable Spanish, and Tealer was able to ask the man what he'd heard about the incident. The man said he'd spoken to some fellows on the quay who'd told him there'd been an argument between the 'trader' Williams and two men in one of the dockside bars. Some people were saying it was revenge for an arrest Williams had brought about. Others were saying it was for lack of payment for a deal. Others that it was over cards. The oarsman shrugged. It made no difference. There'd been a brawl in which Williams had been fatally stabbed and his body thrown into the lagoon. Hardly a talking point in Rio.

The man fell silent and rowed on.

Tealer studied his own hands, the hands whose scrabbling of a few minutes ago had turned him from an honest seaman into a thief. He looked at the glowering sky, the deep waters of the bay, the spikey silhouette of the *Empress*. He looked again at the oarsman, who seemed to be glancing at him curiously between oar-strokes. He looked again at his hands. He looked towards the Rio shoreline.

Then the dead figure of Williams rose up out of the sea some three hundred yards off from the boat's starboard side. It slipped across the waves of the bay and sat on the prow behind the oarsman. It looked over his shoulder and stared at Tealer.

"I trusted you," it said, and disappeared over the side back into the waters of the bay.

The *Empress* became smaller and smaller. Tealer opened his mouth to speak to the crewman, but no words came. The crewman shot him another curious glance, but kept rowing.

Then all at once Tealer was resolved: "Turn around immediately, I reckon I ha' left some items on the ship!" But the words only echoed in his head, and his dry mouth uttered no sound.

The *Empress* was smaller still.

The journey out of Guanabara and round the headland to the Ilha Fiscal was against the breeze, and by the time they tied up on the island the short Brazilian evening was underway. The rock-faces above the city were now featureless and brooding. Above them flashes of light in the western sky marked the progress of a jungle thunderstorm far inland. Rio had quickly become dark and oppressive. The frigate birds wheeled ceaselessly in the sky, now joined by turkey vultures.

Tealer presented his documents at the main gate of the prefecture. A message was sent and in due course an officer of the military police in bright blue uniform complete with tall cap, shiny boots and steel heels came out to the entrance. He regarded Tealer coldly for a moment and beckoned him to follow. He led him down a causeway to the next island leeward, the Ilha das Cobras, on which stood the city gaol. They went down a long, poorly-lit corridor, their echoing footsteps sending all manner of small creatures darting for cover in the dark corners.

They went down a dank staircase and entered a basement cell with a low ceiling and one tiny window high up that gave out on to the base of a slimy wall. A sentry in the cell drew himself up to attention. The atmosphere down here was particularly stifling and smelled of whale-oil, alcohol, damp soil and excrement. It took a little while for Tealer to realise that the cell was serving as a morgue. Any light the room might have enjoyed had long since waned and the place was illuminated by one poorly-trimmed lamp. The militiaman took this lamp and held it up to show a long bed-board suspended from the far wall by chains.

On this board lay Williams. He was staring straight up at the ceiling as though dreaming of the day he would be rich. At the point where the stiletto had slid in between his ribs a slight red stain discoloured the sodden white linen of his over-large suit. He was dressed exactly as Tealer had last seen him, even down to the garish orange neckerchief. Only his hat was missing, revealing a bald crown that Tealer had never suspected in all the days he'd known the man. It was this baldness that did most to make the corpse of the cocksure Williams seem pitiable.

But at this moment it was guilt that was wracking Tealer, not pity.

He strained his eyes in the dark to take in the details before him. A cockroach ran across the table. In fact the repulsive little room seethed with cockroaches. For a moment Tealer yearned for the cold, clean air of a Breydon night.

He nodded to the militiaman as a confirmation that the body was indeed that of Williams. The militiaman scowled at him and fired a question in Portuguese. Tealer could understand enough to know he was being asked how well he knew the dead man.

"Quite well... er... *muy bien*... er... *muito bem*." The unsmiling man gave him another long look and then turned back to the damp corpse. He pointed to the sea chest and said something else which Tealer took to be "And these are his only belongings?"

Williams stared on at the ceiling.

Without looking at the militiaman Tealer nodded to indicate that, yes, the contents of the box were the sum of Williams's possessions on the *Empress*.

The militiaman looked straight at Tealer, this time for what seemed an age, and said nothing.

Williams stared on.

Tealer regarded the corpse slowly from head to toe with an expression that alternated between casual interest and boredom. It was a look he had cultivated from years of dealing with foreign port officials who were trying to be intimidating – but on this occasion the look belied real nervousness. He could feel sweat dripping off his temples and running down the inside of his chemise. Fortunately the room was so dank that sweat was unremarkable: the militiaman and the sentry were both perspiring profusely.

The militiaman remained silent. A gigantic brown centipede surged out of the gloom beyond. It coursed up Williams's arm, on to his shoulder and over his unblinking eyes before vanishing into the black beyond the lamplight. No-one spoke.

Flies buzzed.

In some distant, ignored part of the palace a door slammed and feet marched. Somewhere out in the town a church bell was ringing.

Then the militiaman, still looking at Tealer, snapped his fingers and held his hand open.

A flush of panic surged though Tealer. *How could this man know? How could he possibly....?*

The militia man snapped his fingers again – but this time he turned to the sentry and grimaced impatiently. The sentry drew a sabre and handed it over. After a moment's puzzlement Tealer felt a flood of relief. This relief changed to apprehension when the militiaman held the sabre up and regarded it thoughtfully so that for more than an instant it was on a level with Tealer's eyes. Then lowering it, he used the tip to loose the catch of the chest, threw up the lid and rummaged around for a bit before kicking the lid back down with one polished boot. Again he fixed Tealer with his sullen stare, and without taking his eyes from him he threw the weapon back to the sentry, who just managed to catch it.

"*Tudo?*" he said. "Everything?"

Tealer slowly looked away from the corpse and met the smouldering gaze of the militiaman. He shrugged, and looked back at the corpse. Another long interval passed in which he didn't know if the militiaman was looking at the corpse or watching him. He shook his head gently a few times. He wanted the militiaman to think that the reason he was looking at Williams so fixedly was that he was thinking sad thoughts about him.

Finally the militiaman said: "*Obrigado senhor. Boa tarde.*" He walked over to the mortuary door and held it open.

Tealer walked out, taking care neither to be too quick nor too slow.

Williams stared on.

Even the damp evening air of Guanabara Bay seemed a liberation after that gruesome basement, and Tealer looked up into the dusk with relief. As he did so he noticed that the only frigate birds left in the darkening sky seemed to have collected immediately above the prison.

As the oarsman took him back on the now familiar route out of the inner harbour towards the anchorage Tealer thought over his predicament.

What predicament? The stones were hidden under Williams's bunk, not his. If anyone found these and tried to connect him with them he could simply claim he had missed them when he searched the cabin. And even that was if the authorities knew of their existence, which they most likely did not.

Yet Tealer knew his nerves would be like torn shrouds in a gale until the great basalt pillars of Rio were distant and receding forms. Sometimes this fear was

The Mortuary

simply that he was sure he was going to lose the stones. At other times it was a fear that he would be hauled back to the prefecture where the humourless militiaman would once more snap his fingers and hold open his hand.

At other times his unease stemmed from the memory of a face that watched sadly as cockroaches and centipedes scuttled across the slimy ceiling above it.

The waiting was to go on all night. And so with the next day. And the next night. And the next, and the next.

Finally Press lost his patience and decided to set sail. Tealer didn't relax even when the *Empress* weighed anchor. It was only several days later, when they had negotiated a cargo of coffee at Santos and left Brazilian waters altogether, that he began to sleep a little easier.

It was to be a while before Williams came a-visiting. There weren't yet any ghostly scratchings on Tealer's door – even after he had quietly entered Williams's former berth, taken the stones from the box and put it back under the bed.

There were other, more immediate dramas. The *Empress* was a clipper. Tealer's senses were forcibly filled with mountainous Atlantic waves, the shrieks and screams of the winds in the sheets, and the groans of the old ship's tortured timbers. One crewman had half his leg torn off by a piece of flailing rigging. The sunny climes of Rio were soon a distant memory.

Only once, during one of the lulls between several storms, did Tealer lock the door of his berth and take out the stones. With the immediate dread of retribution receded he felt for the first time a flash of sympathy for the white-suited man dismissed by most as a rogue, but a fellow who'd been a real companion to him.

"Poor old Williams," he thought.

Then almost at once a message came to report back to the bridge. He was needed in the stern business of manoeuvering six hundred tons of wood, canvas and coffee through trillions of tons of heaving brine.

WHITE JENNY

And I awoke and found me here
On the cold hill's side.

John Keats – La Belle Dame Sans Merci

Jenny's Lair

Tealer is woken with a jolt by the racket of a troll cart being pulled past his window at speed.

He blinks in the half-light of the shuttered room and looks around him blankly. For hours – or years – he has been re-treading the paths of the past from his earliest childhood to the Rio of a few weeks ago. Now he must fight to remember who he is, where he is and why he's there. As with the last time he woke he finds he has a choking thirst, and again he goes into the yard to pump himself some water. He feels automatically for his pouch again, and again relaxes to find it still there, though at the moment he couldn't say for certain why the pouch is important.

Very slowly he fumbles for a sense of the present; he knows he is John Sayer, first mate on the *Shadwell Empress*. But he isn't *on* the *Shadwell Empress*, of that he's also sure. No, of course he isn't – he's in his own house. He has awoken from a long sleep.

He can just remember that it was very early morning when he was last conscious.

And he can feel that he has been sitting here for hours and hours since then.

Yes.

So… why isn't it darker than this?

He tries to tell the time by looking through the window at the sun, but is confounded by the high walls of Row 111. He goes to the street door, opens it and looks out.

Now he is badly confused. Rather than dipping below the walls, the evening sun seems far higher in the sky than it should be. Then he notices something strange in the shadows on the chimney stacks. They're back to front. As he gazes at the daylight with swollen, smarting eyes he grapples in vain with the evidence. But he can't deny what he sees.

Time has gone backwards.

He goes back into his house, sits in the windsor chair and tries to work out as calmly as he can where he's gone wrong. And after several minutes still being unable to make head or tail of things, he begins to feel a sense of panic. Is he back in Brazil…? Did he ever leave? But even there the sun doesn't move backwards, nor does it set in the east! What topsy-turvy land has he woken up in? If the laws of nature have been so mischievously subverted, what hope for a man trained for years to tell the time and log a position by the certainties of sun, moon and stars?

Tealer feels the sweat at his temples. He looks at the cobbles, at the yard wall opposite, at a cat at one end of wall that is watching him, at a gull at the other end of the wall that is swearing at the cat, at a moth that has found itself blinded in the daylight and is crawling round and round in circles at his feet – and this is when he notices that every object he lays his eyes on – the wall, the tools leaning against the wall, the cat on the wall, the gull, the moth – even his own shakey hand – everything – is sanctified with an unearthly halo.

Has he died and gone to Heaven? If so, he doesn't think much of the place. Or is that just it? Is he in Hell? Has he been marooned in some strange mariner's hell?

Still grasping for some island of sense in this sea of confusion he wanders back out for a second look at the Row. Another troll cart filled with empty crans comes crashing down the alley towards him. It's one of scores that work the Yarmouth Rows, yet it's suffused with the same cloak of light as everything else in Tealer's view, making it more like a fiery chariot than a small grubby wagon. Tealer steps back and watches open-mouthed as it passes. The driver salutes him with a wave of the hand without even taking his eyes off the horse as it negotiates the tight walls of the row. Tealer tries to shout after it but dissolves into a fit of coughing, and he has to lean against the wall to steady himself. He closes his eyes and opens them again, but the sun is still obstinately in the wrong quadrant, and every object in the world is still shimmering.

Presently another cart appears in the row and comes thundering down. Tealer finds himself stepping into the path of the cart, raising his hand and calling to it to stop. This time he finds his voice, something nearer the calm, penetrating tone he might use on the deck of a clipper during a blow.

The driver leans back on his reins and the troll cart stops. "Whassup, bor?" he asks.

"What seal o' day is it?"

"*What?*" asks the driver, scowling with irritation. Then he catches a certain look in Tealer's eye. He fumbles inside his smock and brings out a simple time-piece.

"A five-and-tweh' past six."

Tealer gives a slight nod, and the carter whips his horse back into motion, glad to be moving on. Tealer watches the cart clatter down the row and disappear out on to South Quay. Then he leans against his door with his eyes shut. How – oh, how – can it be five-and-twenty past six with the sun where it is?

Realisation swamps him like a tidal surge. The sun hasn't moved backwards, and Tealer hasn't awoken in some malign parallel world. He has simply been asleep for many more hours than he first imagined. What he thought was the light of early evening is the light of early morning. He walks down the Row and out on to the South Quay. The clamour of ships, hoists, men, horses, wheels, dogs and gulls is painful to him, and every object is still unnaturally bright, but old chaos is welcome, and so is the savour of the salt air. The orange-blue sky and the silver sea in the distance promise another warm August day. And as Tealer climbs out of the coma he's been in for the last day-and-a-half he begins to feel refreshed, though the halos of light persist around everything he sees. He walks back up the Row to his house and shuts the door.

And as he walks round his kitchen he finds himself watched by a stranger. He starts before realising the stranger is his own reflection in the mirror. He goes close up to the glass and studies himself. There's a blackness about his eyes that's curious and yet in a way familiar. It gives him such a wild and intense look that he can see why at first he didn't recognise himself – and why the troll-carter was so quick to be on his way. He throws open the shutters and goes back to the mirror to look more closely. He sees that this strange look is caused by his pupils being open to their widest – in spite of the light in the room. And he realises that this is what's giving the world its strange sheen. He's not unduly alarmed because he now remembers having experienced this sensation before, if not so markedly.

Tealer then feels a dampness in his undershirt and finds that in the early morning cool of an English August he is sweating, and probably has been for hours.

But now that he's becoming clearer-headed the memories of the last few days, rather than his more distant past, begin to come back. He realises he must now confront a sombre present. Yet he also finds himself seized by a great listlessness. He has hardtack in his bag which he takes out and chews on, but his mouth is too dry and he throws the morsel away. He goes up to the yard to pump himself some water, and with his thirst quenched he takes another bottle from the alcove in the parlour and pours a measure of the fruit spirit, though smaller than before.

Then he wanders around the house. He puts firewood in his stove but doesn't light it. After an hour or so of aimless moving about he then remembers the fire and does light it, but he forgets to put the kettle on. Then he remembers the kettle and boils water to make tea which he forgets to drink. He paces around the floor swinging his belaying pin back and forth, swearing mechanically to bludgeon to death the first Scotsman he lays eyes on. He throws himself down on a chair and starts totting up his recent pay. He adds this pile to some savings he takes from under a loose floorboard in the parlour. He loses count repeatedly and has to restart. In a sudden loss of temper he hurls a handful of coins down on the table where they bounce and scatter to the four corners of the kitchen.

"Triflin' stuff in any case," he says, and strokes the leather pouch containing the Williams jewels.

But what's he to do? His uncle, with whom he shared so many adventures, is gone, and now he finds his wife-to-be has left him. The only others he was ever close to now live elsewhere or have passed away. Five years ago Daisy Bales dropped down dead on these very kitchen flags a moment or two after she'd finished scrubbing them. Poor Susan Durrant left for Swindon three years later, away from sad memories of her 'dear John' and the scandals that together they had quietly engendered. Charlie has married and is now surrounded by a bevy of young'uns, and the other men of Tealer's youth are likewise preoccupied. Who is there that means anything anymore? Why does he stay in this town? Shouldn't he leave and continue the life of a true sailor-nomad, the life he'd decided on after his uncle had died, and before he met Maud?

Then for a third time the strange concoction begins to affect him, and again he feels weak, and the weakness is this time compounded by lack of food. He takes out more hardtack and begins to suck on it; but he feels a greater need to fill the void in his head than the one in his stomach. So he goes into his parlour, takes the nearest book from the shelf, brings it back into the kitchen and begins reading in a half-hearted way. As it is almost the only book in the place, it's no surprise that it is Col. Hawker's *"Instructions to Young Sportsmen"*.

Tealer is calmed by the familiar illustrations of waterfowl flying, swimming, and roosting, all stalked by men armed with every kind of weaponry. It cuts through his feeling of isolation. For a moment Hawker's pencil etchings of waterbirds in anonymous creeks seem better known to him even than his own house. He regards the illustrations more avidly.

It is then, finally, that he remembers White Jenny.

The idea that comes is almost painful in its stark brilliance. A solution so obvious, so blindingly clear that he shouts out loud:

"*Jenny*! Blast, there's still Jenny. Lord forgive me, I *aren't* left alone in the world. Blast! There's still the White Lady." And he sits back in his windsor chair with his heart beating and his mind racing. Jenny: beloved of his uncle above all others. Jenny: whom he himself had faithfully promised to look after, and instead had allowed to be neglected as his affair with Maggie Pritchard's daughter ran its course. Jenny: so sacred that Tealer was not allowed to see her till he was fifteen, or even know of her existence till he was twelve.

Jenny: as changeless and reliable as a gemstone in this decrepit world of failure, false hopes and shattered dreams.

Of a sudden Tealer sees a plan. He starts up from the windsor chair so violently that it flies back with a crash on to the flags, and he resumes his furious pacing up and down the floor. But this time he isn't thinking of Scotsmen. He's seen a way to take the helm once more. No more angry recriminations or wild resolutions! Here's a higher calling!

He rights the chair and sits for a few more minutes, though his knee bounces up and down in a restless fidget as he thinks.

Then a broad grin breaks out over his haunted face.

And at precisely three minutes and twenty-two seconds past one on the sixth afternoon of August in the year Eighteen hundred and sixty-nine, John 'Tealer' Sayer bangs the table in the kitchen of the much-partitioned house in Row 111.

"*That* is what I shall do. What a dullard I am that I ha'nt seen it before! Yes, *that* is what I shall do!"

He goes to a cupboard under the staircase and drags out a large chest. This he flings open, and is satisfied at the smell of oil and moth-repelling herbs which waft around the room. He takes out clothes of a very singular kind. It's two years since he's laid eyes on them, and he inspects them almost as though they were sacred vestments. They're all there! They have kept their shape, and more importantly they have kept their colour, which is a kind of grey-white. Grey-white hat, grey-white smock, white trousers and over-trousers and grey-white boots. He lays them back in the chest, shuts down the lid and shoves it back under the stairs. Then he reaches behind the stair well and takes a well-greased key from a concealed hook.

The evening of that same sixth day of August in 1869 finds Tealer Sayer on Oulton Dyke in a rowing boat.

He's making his way to the dyke mouth where he will then push on up the Waveney towards Breydon. Flocks of mallard pass him on the river, following the line of the bank before veering off to some quiet dyke in the marshes of north Suffolk. Each flock of duck he looks at hard, as he does the party of coot that are squabbling in sprays of water. A single grebe is oblivious to him as it dives into the murky depths to reappear with a roach or perch fry. As he rows he is not gazing idly at these birds. He's watching them intently.

Suddenly he himself veers off toward the bank and disappears through the reeds into a concealed inlet. He rows and then walks along the bottom of this small inlet to a low-slung boathouse with an unusually stout oaken door. As he wades through the mud the welcome stench of rotting plants rises up around him and reminds him that he's home. He unlocks the door with impatient twists of the wrist and swings it open.

He's shaking.

There's a sigh of some relief from Tealer Sayer at what he sees inside. A long flat-boat is lying perched on the cross beams of the low hut well above the water. It's about twelve feet long, and sports a fading nameplate, 'Sturgeon'. He takes a short ladder lying along the wall, climbs up and looks in.

The boat is in good condition – in fact just as good as he left it. It is well-varnished, and inside it lie a variety of paddles and a quanting pole. A greased canvas bag contains a short mast with a small sail bound tightly round it. Everything – the boat, the paddles, the canvas bag and various smaller pieces

Jenny's Lair

of equipment – is in the same grey-white as the clothes Tealer was looking at earlier. But to Tealer, the boat and its issue of paddles and canvas are of only passing interest. It is the sleek form resting along half the length of the boat and out over its prow that takes his attention.

For this is the object of his childhood dreams, and the reason for his resolute thumping of his kitchen table.

She was abandoned two years ago, and is now regarded almost apologetically by her prodigal lover. It is with shining eyes that he gazes at her noble lines. Perfectly balanced in the boat which forms her cradle, and decked out in the same off-white, and with hardly a blemish to mar the effect, White Jenny lies silent.

Tealer gazes for a minute or two and then runs his hand along her barrel and slips his fingers into the dark mystery of her interior. He actually mutters aloud to himself:

"Look out, Jenny! Look who's back."

Alone in this lonely boathouse in the outer reaches of the Beccles marshes, Tealer might appear to have lost his wits. But many others, confronted with the same sight, have reacted in the same way.

She has a muzzle more than two inches across. She takes nearly two pounds of shot, and with a measure of powder rammed into her mighty breech she can fling the load 150 yards to cut a path through the largest flock of duck or geese. Breydon has other great punt-guns, each with her own history, but none comes anywhere near in size to White Jenny. Other Breydon gunners, even when they're a full four miles away at the opposite end of the estuary, always know the titanic thunder of her discharge, and they'll say to themselves, 'Hell! There go ol' Jenny agin. Hope she 'a left some fer the rest on us!'

Indeed she's so big that the act of lifting her in and out of this craft is a job for three strong men. And she was nearly one hundred and fifty years old when Tealer was born. In the first century of her existence she never knew the inside of a punt; she was a pigeon-slayer. She'd been commissioned to a gunsmith in Norwich by an officer who had fought at Malplaquet. This man had watched in horrified fascination as French gunners had withered his own lines with grapeshot before Marlborough had driven them from the field, and he'd later had the idea of a heavy gun on wheels, hidden behind a large hurdle screen, which he would use to lay waste not to Frenchmen but to the swarms of woodpigeon that ravaged the crops on his Norfolk estates. Years later it was Palmer's grandfather who'd realised that what Jenny could do to pigeons on plough she could also do to duck on water. He bought her from the officer's grandson and had the *Sturgeon* built to bear her great weight across the flats of Breydon. He replaced her old flint-lock with the more weather-proof percussion mechanism – no longer would perfect stalks across the mud be ruined by the dreaded 'flash in the pan', when a damp primer failed to ignite the main charge.

White Jenny became mistress to Tealer from that special evening when he and his uncle had abandoned the mullet at Breydon's mouth to pay homage to her. From then on Palmer took Tealer with him on all his gunning expeditions. At first Tealer had been left on the bank to watch through a spyglass as Palmer took the *Sturgeon* to stalk across estuaries from Blakeney in north Norfolk to the Blackwater of Essex. Tealer's job had simply been to watch and learn.

Then one day, without a word, Palmer gestured to him to get into the front of the *Sturgeon* itself. Tealer obeyed, also without a word, though he knew full well what, for the first time, was being asked of him. He was being given the dread task of pulling the cord which would ignite the charge deep in Jenny's breech and send a curtain of lead hurtling across the mud toward the unsuspecting rafts of wigeon or mallard. How that moment comes back to him now! With his head jammed in the well between the magazine and the low gunwales of the *Sturgeon* so as to be out of the sight of any birds, the blood pumped a furious rhythm in his ears. He could see nothing except the boat timbers in front of his nose. He could hear the occasional whistles of wigeon on the water ahead of them, and the suppressed grunts of effort as his uncle, also lying flat, paddled the *Sturgeon* slowly forward to within range. There was a crisis when it seemed the front birds in the flock stopped feeding, and his uncle very quietly cursed. They then had to remain perfectly still for twenty minutes, and although Palmer had chosen a time when the tide was on the turn, there was a fair breeze coming off the marshes which meant that they were blown quite badly off-course. That put another half-hour on the stalk, and that meant that they were now trying to approach across an outgoing tide. But the flock settled again, allowing the craft to slip gradually into range.

Jenny's Lair

Without a sound, Palmer brought the two short paddles out of the water and laid them on Tealer's inert form, and then Tealer felt two sharp prods which he knew would be his uncle's elbows resting on his back as the older man glassed the flock with a small telescope.

"Mixed wigeon and teal." said his uncle in a tiny whisper. 'More than I thought, an'all."

Tealer had now been staring rigidly at the same knot of wood in the boat's timbers just below his nose for forty minutes, and his heart had been pumping so loudly he reckoned the flocks of birds must surely hear.

When…? When…? When would he be given the word to pull?

Agonisingly, his uncle slipped the short paddles back into the water and began to push the *Sturgeon* even further forward. He wanted to be nearer still! Now, more surely than ever, even the tiniest scrape of a paddle against the side of the boat might alert the flock and send it off in a *whosh* of wings.

But his uncle eased them forward for another five minutes, and yet another five.

With his head still forced down tight below the gunwale Tealer could only imagine from the sounds what was happening.

Then, with no warning: *"Pull away!"*

Tealer jerked on the cord so hard that he hit the magazine with his hands and took the skin off his knuckles. From his position deep in the prow he was spared much of the colossal blast, and when he tried to come up to see the result he found he was wedged between the magazine and the side of the boat, and he had to push hard to free himself. Finally, through the acrid billowing smoke, he was able to survey the mudbank in front of him, and he saw a sight which amazed him. About twenty duck lay floating on the shallows, bobbing about among a mat of feathers and bits of Norfolk News that Tealer's uncle had used to wad Jenny's breech. Most had died instantly. A few were bidding farewell to this cruel life with a waving of their paddles or slow flapping of their wings. But one or two were only pinioned and were making their way urgently from the killing ground, and Palmer was looking all around, marking their positions.

"'Stoppers, quickly, boy! *Quickly*!" he yelled, "both sides."

Tealer had to snap out of his dazed state; he swiftly dragged the four primed sixteen-bores, the 'cripple-stoppers', from the prow of the *Sturgeon* so that he and his uncle could dispatch the wounded birds before they were able to run off on to the soft mud and out of reach.

A little later Palmer and Tealer had accounted for every bird. They were sitting in the punt with Tealer at the prow, speechless with pride, examining every single duck in the bag. His uncle was at the stern, wiping the sweat off his face and smoking a clay in a glaze of deep relaxation. When the clay was empty he took it out of his mouth and picked up one of the teal, running his hand over the glossy green and chestnut plumage of its head.

"Well, boy," he said with a chuckle, "I never seen so many teal in one bag. That look as though we're go' have to call you a 'tealer' from here on. 'Tealer' Sayer. Ha! I don't suppose that's a name we'll find in the Bible. What ever'd your poor mother ha' said? Still."

Eleven years have passed since that first loosing of Jenny's stays. But never once has Tealer primed Jenny, climbed into the *Sturgeon*, lain down behind the great gun, and slipped his hand forward to set her at half-cock, without feeling an echo of that first thumping in his ears. He's been on a hundred stalks with her, and marvelled again and again at the devastating swathe she can create in a flock of birds – or whatever else lies in the path of her fury. *The fair maid without pity*. That's what Maud had called her. And Maud never realised how right that was...! Because Tealer knows dreadful tales of gunners, who – sometimes through their own misadventure, sometimes from the foolishness of others – have been damaged or destroyed by a mishandled punt-gun. He remembers for an instant the one most terrible case involving White Jenny herself, but he puts it to the back of his mind, as though this goddess in brass and gunmetal might somehow read his thoughts and think him disrespectful.

The fair maid without pity! Oh, yes!

Tealer reaches in his pocket for a full clay and lights it to keep away gnats. He looks back at the boathouse. The memories that flooded his head back in the kitchen of his home are still washing around...

No more than a decade ago, and he and his uncle were standing on the rond not ten yards from this very boatyard. They were packing the great gun away for the summer, having scalded her barrel and oiled and greased her so that her parts moved without the smallest friction. When they finished Palmer cracked open his flask of gin, darkened with sloes from the Wickhampton side of the estuary. They talked about the various winter stalks they'd gone on in that first magical season with 'old Jenny'. As the gin took effect, Palmer waxed a little more lyrical.

"Boy, listen," he said. "The wilderness here is becoming a smaller place, and all kinds of know-alls and upland simpletons are venturing out on to our precious estuaries. They're folk who know as much about the marshes as you or I might about the breeding o' unicorns. And many of them will tell you that a punt gun is a weapon of easy use and casual destruction. Well, I hope you ha' now learnt how far that is from the truth.

"But you should also know that this here gun and her kind are more than the means to a special kind of fowling sport. This here White Lady, our Jenny, has been the saviour of many a poor estuary family in her long history. Yes, she certainly have the power to take life away, but also a power to save it. The man who wield her here on the open mud have the means to keep himself alive through the bitter winter months, but not just himself – also his family, his fellows and his neighbours. I aren't o'erstating the case if I tell you that in harder times than we live in today, Jenny fed many a desperate household on both the Norfolk and Suffolk side of the Yare. So, that's her right to be treated with respect. I don't mean simply that she's dangerous. Blast, she certainly is. What I mean, though, is that she's *good*, and to be the man who pull her cord is an honour never, *never* to be taken lightly. Take you a look at her barrel, her fittings. Look how much care generations of marsh-hunters ha' lavished on her! Men who were dead a hundred year afore my father were even thought of. She's nigh on two centuries old, and yet she's as good as she'd been forged last week. Jenny ent some pitted drainpipe braced up with bits o' wire. No-one ha' ever fired bent nails and smithy cast-offs down *that* flue, I can tell you! Only the finest grade lead. She ha' never been left out in the snow to end up all cratered up with rust. She," he said, pointing at the great machine with a passion, "is White Jenny. The mightiest gun in the marshes. And men who ha' been stalkin' in the lashiest sort o'weather, and ha' got home bent double with the cold, wi' freezin' salt-water a-seepin' through their clothes – half-dead, some on 'em – and *still* they ha' dried and cleaned and oiled Jenny before ever they e'en thought about lookin' to themselves."

He took another slug from his flask. "One day, boy, I'll be dead and gone, and you'll be Jenny's guardian. Well, I ha' told you that I don't hold much with fables of ghosts and demons a-haunting the Breydon marshes. And that I don't. Well, not much. But," he waved the flask fiercely at Tealer, "if ever Jenny is left in the open, or if she be abused , or in some way neglected, I promise – I swear – I will rise up out of the mud, and I'll take her away. Even if she proved to be the death of me herself, I'd do it! That I would. If old Jenny end up untended and uncared for, beached up on the mud like one of them there worm-eaten wherries acrost the water, I will surely come back and spirit her away far out to sea. Far out to sea, if necessary. So do you watch over her, Johnny. 'Cause *I* surely will!"

Tealer sighs as he puts back the sacking that covered the great length of steel, and turns to leave. As he does he says out loud:

"Just a couple of months more – give the wigeon a chance to come in – then you and I are goin' home, girl."

He locks the boathouse and makes his way back down the dyke and out on to the open, deserted river.

A rustle in the reeds from the far bank makes him start out of his reverie, and with keen fowler's eyes he scans the reedbed. Not the angry spirit of uncle John, he thinks in jest to himself, for surely I have come to pay homage to the very White Lady herself. Surely uncle John would love that. He smiles to prove to himself how comforting he finds that thought.

He continues to look through the dense sedge, and as he does so he sees an indistinct white-coloured shape disappearing through the stems, a figure of the kind that only men with a guilty conscience are haunted by. And that does not include Tealer, of course. For what has Tealer to be guilty about? He's always looked after Jenny as his uncle required, and he has never done any real wrong to any man.

Well, not here in Norfolk, at any rate.

Yet he scans the reed bed again, for a long-dormant spirit has just whispered in his ear. But the ghost in the reeds seems to have gone, and so the whisper, never very distinct anyway, is silenced.

Besides, what matter? Tealer has renewed his bond with the mightiest gun in the marshes, and he's unassailable.

Tealer makes his way quietly back to Yarmouth, and spends the rest of the day packing what he'll need. That evening, under the cover of darkness, he loads the belongings on to a hand-cart and slips quietly away to the same houseboat which was once his winter courting-place. He unloads the contents of the cart into the houseboat, and his last act before leaving Yarmouth for his next voyage is to take the key of the house in Row 111 and throw it high into the air over the river. He waits for the splash of the key hitting the water, and he nods savagely when he hears it. Then he turns and disappears into the darkness.

The 'Green

With John 'Tealer' Sayer back abroad this is perhaps a good time to drop in at the Bowling Green Inn.

The 'Green.

The 'Green is loved by punt-gunners, shoulder-gunners, eelers, out-of-work sailors, wherry men and loafers.

The 'Green is disliked by most wives of the above, avoided by townsmen and loathed by excisemen and preachers.

The 'Green is, depending on your point of view, a refuge against the fierce elements of the East Coast, a den of thievery, a place to exchange cautious notes on the movements of birds, a sink of idleness, a source of delight for any man with a love of nature and the old ways, a source of despair for any man with a love of godliness and progress.

The Bowling Green is ideally located for rapid flight. Whether the danger is from constables, excisemen or angry wives, just as long as a crony with a seat near the window raises the alarm in time, you can disappear along the banks of two different rivers or dart into the maze of the Yarmouth Rows. Or you can jump into a boat and slip upstream to Stokesby, or downstream towards the harbour, or out across Breydon itself. Once away from Yarmouth you have all around you the anonymous creeks and marshes of the *Gariensis*. These unwelcoming places have always been a refuge. It was here that your fathers and grandfathers used to hide the contraband from off the various Dutch ships that slunk about in the Roads waiting for the flash of their lights. Even these days when – let's face it – the stuffing has been knocked out of the smuggling profession, there are still times when you need to park the odd bag of something in the deep marsh.

The Bowling Green in summer has a fragrance of mugwort and sea lavender, and its interiors are dark and cool. Fellows in shirt sleeves sit mumbling in the gloom with their panting dogs spread out on the clay floor at their feet. They stare at the harsh yellow light in the yard outside and wait for the orange of evening to bring some respite.

The Bowling Green in winter exudes a thick odour of burning coal and driftwood. This thickens through the day as the wind hammers down the chimney in gusts that send flame and sparks blowing out from the great black stove in the centre of the room. There's the occasional banging about and swearing when someone realises either his jacket or his dog or his beard is smouldering; otherwise the fowlers and mullet-fishers sit and gaze silently into the embers as the feeling comes back into hands crooked from rowing in the freezing channels and drains.

In any season a man entering the 'Green can depend on the calming musk of oaken table-tops seasoned with a century's worth of spilled nog and the smoke from many clay pipes. There's also a permanent reek of the blue-black Breydon mud drying on hobnails and waders, and this mingles with the warm scent of the sawdust thrown down to mop it up.

The Bowling Green's a temple to the simple ambitions and triumphs of the Breydonsiders whom it serves. It is adorned with the tools and mementoes of the marsh. Each of these decorations has a special significance for the man who brought it in.

There's the scythe with the engraved blade used by the winner in a reed-cutting contest of some thirty years ago. There's a whole Roman belt buckle from up by the fort. There are umpteen mounted birds in varying states of decay, all shot at one time or another on the estuary outside. Pride of place amongst these goes to Wellington, a sea eagle whose great outstretched wings take up one quarter of the west wall. She was bagged as she hunted for flatfish along the Ship Drain, and the man who shot her decided to prepare her himself. Alas, his gift for mounting specimens didn't quite match his skill at shooting them, and the misshapen, mildewed, bossed-eyed result has never attracted a buyer. For the last quarter-century Wellington has been about to take off, impervious to the icy blasts, the sweltering heat or the drenching storms just a few inches on the other side of the tavern walls. She's long been a talisman of the 'Green, in spite of no-one ever even realising her gender.

Very few of the regulars of the 'Green are known by the names they were baptised with. In good Norfolk fashion every man has his second identity, to be used at all times except the most serious trouble with 'the Authorities'. They are names redolent of the estuary, recalling occupations, characteristics or even memorable incidents associated with it. This has the useful effect of ensuring they are rarely bothered by strangers… Whoever's going to address a man he doesn't know from Adam with a name like 'Cadger', 'Fiddler', 'Wiggy', 'Salt-fish', 'Deaf', 'Old Stork', 'Generous', 'Horse', 'Joyful' or 'Poker'?

At any time when two or more regulars are gathered here the Bowling Green becomes a hotbed of debate, though you could walk in and sit for twenty minutes and never realise it. Raucous, riotous behaviour is almost unknown at the 'Green. Even when Bessey the landlord decides to shut up shop and turn his clients stumbling out into the night, any dissent is confined to scowls and whispers. These are men who've spent a lifetime on the mud, creeping up on nervous flocks of birds and avoiding excisemen. Loudness is anathema. An argument may be raging about the weather, or which was the best year for brent, or who crossed whose line in a stalk out on the mud, but the arguing will never be more than a series of ferocious mutterings.

At the particular time that Tealer Sayer is making his way back out to sea as a newly- confirmed bachelor, the topic of this muttering isn't the weather or the bird-life, but that Breydon might have a ghost.

Breydon, of course, has thousands of ghosts.

But this particular spirit has been making its presence felt more than most. A key piece of evidence seems to be the recent strange behaviour of the birds. Flocks of dunlin, knot and lapwing have been behaving oddly around Duffels Drain and all along the north side of the estuary up to the meeting of the rivers. A casual birdwatcher would find nothing unusual in the clouds of birds sweeping up, down and across the muds from one feeding station to another, thrilled though he might be by the spectacle. Yet to men whose livelihoods depend on understanding these birds, any variations or abnormalities in the flight patterns of the huge flocks are of great significance.

There have been many such abnormalities of late, and the consensus in the 'Green is, therefore, that all is not well.

But there's more. A shadowy figure has been seen lurking in unusual corners of the marsh at dusk. Again, nothing untoward in that – ask Tealer Sayer for one – and in any case, these men themselves sometimes lurk in strange places, usually carrying armfuls of things from vessels up the coast, straining the dusk for a sign of any excisemen out to stop them from earning an honest smuggler's wage.

But this apparition hasn't been seen holding anything at all. And when fowlers have taken refuge on the water it hasn't pursued them in some other craft as a law-man or gamekeeper might – it has simply stared after them. Sometimes it's seen in the reeds, sometimes away on the far bank of the estuary, and, just recently, in and around the windpumps – but always watching.

So it is the agreed opinion of everyone there (except Joyful Norris – there's always some obstinate old devil who won't believe the evidence of his own eyes) that there is an unquiet spirit abroad on the mudflats.

Some of the men have much to say on this subject, others are quiet.

One of the quiet ones is Wiggy Thacker, one of the younger of the fowling men. But then Wiggy's got more cause to fear the unquiet dead of the marsh than most. One winter's evening two years ago another shadowy figure crept down to the waters edge with a strange little bundle and rowed out on the high tide to the main channel. It's not this second shadowy figure that's the cause of Wiggy's nightmares, because the figure was Wiggy himself; rather it's the bundle that he weighed down with stones and threw into the channel. A kindly wherry-skipper who'd learnt of his plight had taken pity and lent him the boat. And the same old fellow had even taken the girl off Wiggy's hands by finding her a place on the wherry.

So: all's well that ends well.

It's just that Wiggy has never since been able to row his punt in that stretch of the channel without casting furtive glances at the silty, swirling water. For in the many bad dreams he's had since that sad night, the bundle has slipped anchor and a tiny, black, bloated hand has appeared on the surface to point at him. This is why Wiggy is one of those not to be found joining in the talk about ghosts on the water.

You might remark, though, that it's an ill wind that blows nobody good: things at least turned out well for the kindly wherry skipper – our good friend Joyful Norris, no less – for he acquired the services – all the services – of the young woman, and at no cost to him at all.

Yes, but even there you'd be wrong. Joyful himself is *also* one of the quieter ones – at least till the drink takes hold. Is that because he too fears an accusing Fury, this time not with a tiny hand but with a huge one, pointing firstly at him and secondly at the gaping hole in its head where its brains have been dashed out by a flying winch handle? It might be, but you'll never know, because Norris is a miserable old devil any way, and whenever he's had anything to say, it's only ever been a sneer. On the subject of the unquiet dead, as on any other subject, "What a loaderol' squit," is the most you're likely to get out of Joyful.

So Wiggy and Joyful are a couple of the quieter ones. There are other Bowling Green regulars who have much to say on this subject of the phantom out on the mud, and for several weeks the talk amongst these has followed a rough pattern:

"I sin it with me own eyes. 'At don't come arter you or nothin'. 'At just stare."

"Thas worse when they stare. That mean you' a' had it 'fore the year's out."

"I sin it up by Duffel's."

"I wonder who 'at is."

"Could be anyone. Arter all, how many men ha' died on the mud since Noah's time?"

"Thas right. 'At could be a Roman from the fort."

"Don't talk s'much squit! 'Course 'at int a Roman from the fort."

" 'At could be."

"Not wearin' a gent's top-hat, that int! They didn't have 'em in them days."

"Sandcroft used to wear a top hat."

Ah! Sandcroft! Now at the mention of Sandcroft there's always a moment's quiet. Sandcroft! Yes, there's a name to tighten the grip on a few of the 'Green's pewters.

For what the gunners of Breydon fear above all else is the return of the vengeful spirit of Jack Sandcroft.

Sandcroft was one of those oddities who gunned not for the money but for the sheer joy of the sport. He was well-known amongst the fowlers of the 'Green, and quite well-liked, though never really 'one of them'. How could he be? He had *his* living from sources other than wildfowling. He knew the chagrin and disappointment of a missed shot, but not the sinking feeling that he and his family might be going hungry for the rest of that week because of it.

It's several years now since that dark September evening when Sandcroft came floating down with the ebb tide. All the men on the grass stopped their bowls playing and peered over the river wall as he passed by – and realised that Jack was not stalking a roost, but lying very still in his punt for some other reason – and they feared the worst.

It had only been meant as a prank. The night before, as he was drinking in the 'Green, a couple of fellows had hauled his punt up and taken off the gun which they knew he'd left primed ready for the dawn stalk. They had hooked out the wadding, tipped the shot out of the muzzle, and rammed in an extra charge of powder followed by half a barrel of wood chips. This would have been harmless enough. It was when they heaved the gun back on to the punt and re-engaged its trunnions into their mortises that they made the terrible mistake. Working quickly in the darkness they didn't check that they had properly re-secured the breeching lines. These are the lengths of rope that save a gunner's life every time he fires, for they take the full force of recoil as the great weapon of the marshes erupts.

The pranksters went back to the 'Green and made sure Sandcroft was filled with ale. Then at the end of the night someone bet him he couldn't take out ten redshank with one shot. "Oh, can't I, though?" says Sandcroft, too far gone to see the winking around him. "We'll see about that first thing in th' mornin'."

The rest played at their bowls expecting Sandcroft to arrive back furious after stalking a flock of redshank for half a day and with nothing more than a shower of sparks to show for his efforts. They heard the great crack of the gun from an area of the estuary where a drainage channel known as Duffel's joins the main river channel. They didn't even bother to glass the scene but merely looked at one another and grinned and carried on with their game.

Then afternoon turned to evening, and they assumed that Sandcroft had hauled up elsewhere to go home in a sulk. Only at dusk when the flood tide had turned to ebb did the current bring his punt down the channel sideways on. When they saw that something was amiss they grappled the craft, hauled it in and surveyed wordlessly the horror on display.

The giant gun had shot back to smash Sandcroft's forehead as easily as any of the men standing there had smashed the skulls of a thousand winged duck. The great white cape he used for wildfowling was covered with his gore.

The authorities called it 'accidental death'; they concluded that Sandcroft must have set off without properly checking his equipment. Of course, the truth was that he'd checked it meticulously, but before his evening drink. He'd have seen no reason to check it again in the half-light of the morning.

Except amongst themselves, the brotherhood of Breydon have since remained silent on the subject. These are hard men, these men of the mud. Accidents are common – accidents with powder, set off in its magazine by the stray spark from a hobnail, or accidents with guns which go off when they're 'empty', or when an ancient damascened barrel pitted with salt-rust finally bursts and takes most of a man's hand with it. And none of these men swims so strongly that he could survive a tumble into the freezing brown streams of the *Gariensis* on a high flood tide. And sometimes the sheer cold of the winter estuary can deprive a man of his senses – and very soon after, his life – as he lies stranded on the soft mud in the middle of a blizzard, waiting for the rescuing waters to creep back in, inch by agonising inch. Yes, these men surely felt bad for having been the death of Jack Sandcroft, who in his time had stood many a round in the 'Green. But life is life, and the tides and the light and the duck wait for no man, and there's little use in fretting over what can't be changed…

Well, true enough, but wildfowlers are just as much at the mercy of the elements as sailors and fishermen are, and so they're just as superstitious. So when the estuary darkens they are always glad to haul up and get back to the snug haven of their houseboats or the fiery cheer of the 'Green. Once night has fallen all kinds of strange sounds begin to be heard on the mud, and then it is never too hard to believe, as their forefathers did, that the plaintive wails of the peewits in the dusk are the cries of lost souls calling from Perdition. And since the mishap with Sandcroft there has always been a briskness about the way in which the fowlers of Breydon have packed up their gear and headed home after the last stalk of the day – especially those who've been stalking in the area of Duffel's Drain. None spends much time peering into the gloom that he's leaving behind him, for none especially wishes to catch sight of a spectral punt bearing down on him with the ghastly, smashed face of Jack glaring at him from over its gunwale.

The Demon at the Casement

Five months have passed and Tealer Sayer is back.

And it so happens that, like the chaps in the Bowling Green, Tealer seems to be the target of troublesome visitors from the Other Side. In his case this is particularly strange, for we know his life with John Palmer taught him to dismiss notions of ghosts and hauntings as so much claptrap. The ghosts of his early life have been laid long since, haven't they?

Tealer's plan four months ago was to sell his emeralds and use the money to live a life not unlike that of his uncle: one of occasional work and regular leisure. So on leaving Yarmouth he had firstly taken a boat to Amsterdam.

Yet Tealer never did sell his stones in the Netherlands. Once in Amsterdam, he'd wandered around the Jewish quarter like a man lost. He'd watched the stone merchants scurrying in and out of jewel houses intent on their business, oblivious to him, and he found himself lacking resolve.

He reckoned later that it was Holland itself that had unsettled him and led him to hesitate.

Holland was undoubtedly a curious land. The curving gable ends of the Amsterdam houses could not but remind him of Yarmouth; likewise the city's flat hinterland of marshes and dykes. The clothes and the tools of the marsh-workers were the same as men used in the Broads eighty miles across the grey North Sea. Even the men themselves – fair-haired, broad-shouldered, wide-mouthed, with slightly overshot upper lips – could be the cousins of many of those who walked the lanes around Breydon.

And yet it was as a well-known place seen in a mirror. It was Norfolk – but with familiar objects in the wrong locations, or familiar sounds in the wrong order. The sea was the same grey, uninviting waste, but it lay to the west, so that there was no glorious silver sunrise. The traffic trundled up and down the canal-sides keeping to the right, as in the more foreign lands of southern Europe. At a distance, the stresses and intonations of the local language could have been English, and to a Norfolkman some of the words were clearly recognizable, but, when Tealer came close enough to catch the foreign raspings of the Dutchies, the illusion faded. The effect was of people talking in the next room, or across a busy street, or against the roar of the sea. Or in a dream.

Yes, Tealer decided, and that was it! This town of Amsterdam was all too much like a dream. It was cockeyed, back-to-front, unreal, and this was what had unsettled him. There was, he told himself later, something about this town he hadn't liked. This was why, he told himself later, he was never in the right frame of mind to get the best price for his gems. And this, he told himself later, was what caused him to find a path by a quiet canal, take the emeralds from his leather pouch, heft them in his palm a few times and then put them back, resolving not to sell them here after all.

And perhaps all to the good, too, he told himself – later.

But, in telling himself all this later, he chose to forget that he had never been adversely affected by any of his previous trips to Amsterdam – and that his disquiet had not started the moment he'd set foot on Dutch soil but had been growing for weeks beforehand. So he managed to avoid the notion that the true reason for his edginess might not lie in the vistas of this chilly *alter*-Norfolk, but thousands of miles away in the thick dark of a foetid Brazilian crypt.

When Tealer returned to England from this latest trip to Holland it was Felixstowe rather than Yarmouth he arrived at. He then made his way straight to London – not to seek out one of the many jewel merchants of the City – he decided he was too busy – but to secure a short contract with a company sailing packets to the south of France. This has been his work until now – he has just made his way back to Yarmouth having returned from one of several sailings to Bordeaux. The work has been monotonous and the cargoes uninteresting, but Tealer has been relatively occupied.

Of course, he's had some time to reflect on his plans. On his lighter days he's been looking forward to midwinter and the return of the wigeon to the marshes. And, he's decided, as the wigeon return, so perhaps might Maudy return – and then he'll be able to show her the rough green rocks that could be the key to the life they both yearn for.

That's the way he's been thinking on his lighter days at sea.

On his darker days at sea he has found himself pouring the gems from one hand to the other, thinking of Maudy's eyes bewitching some other man. And of how some other man would now be running his damned hands over that peerless marbled skin, no doubt whispering all manner of insincerities as he helps himself to what, by right, belongs to Tealer, and…

It was on one such darker day, just after he'd finished his watch on the bridge and was lying on his bunk, dozing with the roll of the packet, that a most unwelcome thought came to Tealer Sayer. He'd been turning the facts of his jilting back and forth in his mind.

Suddenly he sat up.

"I'm being punished," he thought. "I'm being punished for taking what wasn't mine to take. And what *was* rightfully mine has been taken from me because of it."

He put this idea to the back of his mind.

It came to the front again.

No, Tealer said to himself, Williams was dead, and couldn't have taken the emeralds with him.

He went into a fitful sleep. He didn't feel rested when he woke to take up his watch with Bordeaux only half-an-hour away. The sun was shining, but it was a hard, scorching light, and the air was filled with the harsh sounds of the gulls.

Then a few nights later, on a return journey, again he came off watch and went to lie in his cabin. This time he drank a little of Maud's fruit spirit which he carried in his sea-chest in the hope of avoiding another sleepless night. And indeed he did sleep, but dreamt one of his vivid dreams: firstly of black-backed gulls and then of frigate birds. He dreamt again of the hot stuffy basement room, and of Williams in his white suit with the bloodstain in the chest, hands by his side, staring straight up. He dreamt there was a buzzing of flies in the room, loud and discordant. He dreamt that Williams turned his dead, glassy eyes to Tealer and smiled a ghastly smile that showed all his yellow teeth, and that one of his hands flopped down open-palmed on to the slab. That was when Tealer woke up with a start, for an instant utterly lost in the coffin-smallness of his berth. This was not the first time he'd dreamt this dream, but he found it no less disturbing for that. He decided to take the air on deck, and opened his locker to take out his jacket.

Williams was there, hanging on a peg, swaying with the roll and pitch of the ship, still smiling. Tealer shut the locker with a bang.

On another night, during another voyage from Bordeaux, Tealer was woken with a 'Johnny! Johnny!'. It was Maud, standing at the end of his bed. She was radiant in a white night dress that contrasted with the sublime discolorations of her skin. But behind her a dark figure stood with its hand on her shoulder. And Tealer started to fumble under his pillow for the emeralds, shouting all the time, 'Look, Maudy, what I have! We're rich, girl!'. But he couldn't find them, and as he scrabbled, Maud faded away. He shouted: 'Wait, Maudy… wait! Wait!' But she'd gone, taking her dark accomplice with her, and the crewman on watch had put his head round the door wanting to know if anything was amiss.

On another night Maud woke him again. This time she was holding out her hand, and was gazing down at uncut emeralds lying in her palm. But when she looked up, Tealer saw that her own peerless emeralds had gone, leaving eyeless sockets where the crows or the frigate birds or the butterflies had feasted.

Dreams, Tealer said to himself that following morning. Dreams. And this bag of emeralds is reality, he thought, squeezing the hard, sharp lumps in the pouch at his belt.

But these visitations, these reminders of a distant past, are now troubling him almost every night. They've been like the unexpected return of a loathed relation long thought dead.

Yet Tealer is made of stern stuff; throughout this growing torment his consolation has been the thought that once he's back in Yarmouth such sombre visions will be blotted out by the enormous light of the *Gariensis*, and the small, accusing voice that has started to sound in his ear will be drowned in the familiar ringing cries of wildfowl.

So: the upshot is that Tealer has now returned to Yarmouth with the emeralds in his pouch unsold and even unexamined. He has resolved to hide them up under the floorboards of his houseboat, or under the gearing of a windpump, or up the chimney of the now-empty house in Row 111 (if he can find the spare key). There they can wait until Maud returns. And, if she doesn't… well, there they can stay till the crack of doom, when the sea rises up in a vengeful brown froth, breaches the walls and roars back into the *Gariensis* to claim its own.

Tealer makes sure once more to slip back into Yarmouth unnoticed. A few acquaintances of his uncle's might still recognise that 'quiet young chap what the Pritchard girl ran out on'. And Tealer, as we've seen, is an especially private fellow with no desire to be the subject of finger-pointing. Having paid a carter to deliver his chest to the houseboat on the Burgh Castle rond he waits around at the Vauxhall station till the leaden sky finally starts to dump the rain it has been threatening. Then he makes his way into the emptying market-place to buy provisions. At this ungentle time of year, when the damp wind scours the market-place leaving the stall-holders pinched and huddled with hands blue from handling cold fish and wet, soily roots, Tealer doesn't look out of place with the cape around his head and the rim of his sou-wester over his eyes. Few shoppers or traders even glance at him, so busy are they in their own struggle with the elements.

However, invariably there's someone – and usually it's a young girl – with sharper eyes than the rest. The young girl today is Polly Bessey, the publican's daughter. She's buying fish, and happens to look up at the next stall just as the heavily-caped form of Tealer is striding past it. His face is concealed but Polly sees something familiar in the loping walk. Automatically she grabs her fish and starts to follow him, trying to place him. He stops at a bread stall and curtly asks for a loaf – and she knows him. She's fly enough not to call out because she remembers the kind of man he is – and what has passed. Instead she waits until he's clear of the stall and then she comes up behind him and gives his cuff a gentle tug. He turns round sharply, and there's such a hunted, haunted look in his eye that poor Polly starts back.

"Lord!" says she, "Tealer Sayer, I thought 'at was you. But you're enough to make a girl's hair curl with that angry face."

Tealer's eyes blaze for a moment longer, but then Polly sees just a hint of that shy grin that used to have even the sophisticated Maud shakey about the knee joints.

"You're Polly Bessey. I remember you. You're... you were... are... one of Maudy's friends, ain't you?"

"Yes," she says. They both look around them, but the market is too busy trying to keep warm to pay them much attention.

"Have you heard from her?" asks Tealer, sooner than he means to.

Polly shakes her head. "Not much since she went off with that Fraser. Just one letter."

"Was that his name?"

"Didn't you even know that? But,'course, you ha' been away so long." Polly looks up at the tall rough-shaven seaman with the haunted eyes and feels sorry for him. "Come you with me up the 'Green, Tealer. Thas cold here. I'll make you a cup of tea."

Tealer looks doubtful.

"Don't you worry, there ent no-one know you there. They all knew Maud, of course. Who didn't? But you were just a name to them. Besides, they'll all be out at this seal o' day."

She takes his arm, and they set off against the wind and the rain, out of the market place and into the maze of the Rows which are glistening darkly in the poor light of winter. Sleety water is gushing off rooftops and down pipes and splattering loudly on to the cobbles. Vicious blasts of air are blowing up each alley driving the freezing spray into their faces. They squeeze past other walkers in the Rows causing Tealer to sink lower into his cape, but no-one even glances at him – everybody in Yarmouth is far too intent only on getting indoors and out of the vile January weather.

The 'Green is, as Polly has promised, deserted. Tealer relaxes, and in spite of his eagerness to hear what Polly has to say he can't help dallying to look at Wellington and the other delights laid out around the walls. Polly shakes her head and smiles and says that now she remembers him better, and she hurries him into the small kitchen at the back.

Over tea she tells him how the man Fraser came to Yarmouth to sell cattle, and caught sight of Maud when buying a hat for his sister in the shop. He impressed Maggie Pritchard with his obvious wealth and it wasn't long before he'd been invited around to the house on Cliff Street for afternoon tea. At first he pretended to be cultivating the mother's company, so Polly reckoned. He was invited back, several times. He'd go and regale them with songs and ballads of his native land (he had a fine voice, Polly admits, having heard him on one occasion herself). Maud told Polly that Fraser had told Maud that with such red colouring she must be of Celtic blood, perhaps even descended from one of the 'High Kings'. Maud described word-for-word how he'd then entertained her with some of the old tales of the Celts of Scotland.

Tealer nods, for it all makes sad sense to him. He knows how lonely, dreaming Maud would love some of the old tales of the Celts of Scotland.

The Demon at the Casement

Polly tells Tealer she wouldn't have trusted Fraser an inch, though perhaps she says this only out of kindness to Tealer, because she adds: "but he was always right polite with me, which is more than Mrs Pritchard ever was." Maggie Pritchard, Polly reckons, never much liked Maud associating with a mere publican's daughter, and she cuts Polly whenever she sees her – which means that Polly has heard no news of Maud. And apart from one letter stamped Glasgow, full of all kinds of rambling nonsense about the Catholic Church, neither has Polly heard from Maud herself.

Polly wants to know Tealer's plans, and Tealer sees no harm in telling her.

"I've had it with the sea, girl, so I'm go' take up fowling, part for profit, part for sport. I won't be living in that place of my uncle's in the Rows – not now, I won't. I'm going to set up in my houseboat on the rond by Burgh Castle. I ha' got some money and one or two valuables," and as he says this he feels for the leather bag in an instinctive movement not missed by Polly. "And," he adds, "I ha' got Jenny, of course."

Polly looks up: "Jenny?"

"Yes," says Tealer, "My boat gun. White Jenny. My old Jenny. She'll never let me down."

Polly suddenly has the memory of a tearful Maud sitting just where Tealer is sitting now.

Outside the slanting rain is rattling harder against the window panes.

It's turning to sleet.

And the sleet soon turns to snow as another spasm of the fearsome winter of 1870 rocks across the open waters of Breydon. The raw, wet day when Tealer met Polly marked the end of one of the milder phases in this winter. Now the cold is returning to the land. Before long the mud of the estuary has turned back to being glittering black sheets, and the grasslands around it are once more sparkling with frost. This is a delight for those who only have to look at it from a distance – for those who live and work in it, the soft, sticky world of the marsh has once again become an unyielding, diabolical landscape of razor-sharp peaks. The icy dykes ring to one other at the dead of night as they are bound more and more tightly in the deepening freeze.

Then for a while the crystal night skies, into which all of the small heat of the landscape has been slipping, cloud over, and snow falls on the the jewelled, tortured world, muffling it into an utter silence. There might be a slight thaw, but even if there is, the wind will once again swing into the east to freeze the land, and the harsh beauty of the hoar frost will be replaced by the dour grip of the wind frost, which has no beauty but is no less harsh. The heads of the reedmace and the branches of trees will clank with their burden of ice as the snow which covered them is frozen mid-thaw.

It is, above all, this cycle of cold followed by thaw followed by more cold which is battering the resolve of even the hardiest men and beasts of the *Gariensis*.

But through it all the fast-flowing main channel of the estuary and one or two of the tributary drains remain open. It is around these streams that Tealer hopes to dust off the exacting fowling skills taught him by Palmer.

His first step is to take a dinghy on the flood tide down the Waveney to the hidden boathouse, to launch the *Sturgeon* and secure her during the slack. He can then tow White Jenny home on the ebb to her rightful place at Burgh Castle. The bitter evening has made the large boathouse key into a brand, and Tealer has to concentrate on turning it with two numb hands clamped together. When he gets in he again approaches the covered form of White Jenny with reverence, and when he uncovers her he stands once more transfixed by her wondrous form.

This time, though, he has come to take possession, and using the geared pulleys bolted to the central timber of the hut roof he slowly eases the punt and its great gun from its dunnage above the mud and manoeuvres it on to the ice. He pushes the craft to the edge of the ice and into the water where he tethers it to the back of his dinghy. Finally he goes back to lock the door.

As he turns the lock he hears a hiss behind him, and he recognises it as sound of a heron flying up from within the reedbed. He wonders what has disturbed the bird, and scans the bank opposite. At first he can't see anything, but then makes out something white through the reeds that seems to be human in form. Yes, at more than forty yards the face is indistinct, but someone seems to be watching him from the rond. He calls out: "Whatever you doing out on a night like this?" But the breeze is against him and his voice doesn't carry. There's no reply and the figure makes no movement. Eventually it sinks down below the tops of the reeds.

Tealer stares at the swaying reeds, and begins to doubt that he's seen the figure. He's no longer given to the fancies of his youth – well, no more than any other man when out on the marshes alone on a winter's evening. That's why he finds the first thought that comes to him – that the light-coloured apparition seemed to be wearing the dirty smock of Alvares Williams – ridiculous.

Ridiculous. Williams was in Rio, and Williams is dead.

No, Tealer's lived too long in the marshes to fall victim to such fantasies. It's too easy for foolish notions to fill the head when darkness falls on the *Gariensis* – the stark silhouettes made by dead alders on the rivers edge, the keening wind blowing through the freezing mace, the despairing cries of the plovers and curlews, the loneliness. Why, nowadays he has even taken to teasing his own senses for sport. He'll be sitting on a duck flight, waiting for the first bird to appear, and he'll *deliberately* listen for the distant *churr churr* of partridges in the upland corn on a summer's evening! And part of him can *still* imagine it is the panting of a demon dog coming ever closer! How easy, too, to see the shapes in the autumn mists – which he knows to be rotting gate posts – as skinny things from coffins and crypts creeping slowly towards him! Or to hear the busy scurrying of some tiny mouse or vole in the dead winter sedge and picture some much larger creature readying itself to pounce. He can play such games with himself till the hair rises on the back of his neck and the grip tightens on his gun! And all imagination!

So Tealer begins to row down the river, watching the space where he saw the apparition.

But nothing more appears.

Williams? *Williams?* Here? In the cold of the Breydon marshes? What an absurd idea! Williams was a sweating creature of the tropics. Lord knows what would happen to him in this corner of the earth. He'd freeze to the spot, just like some jungle spider brought home with a crate of fruit. In the darkness Tealer smiles at the very thought.

It doesn't work. His sense of unease only grows.

He lets the oars hang in the rowlocks as he waits for the slack to turn to ebb, and through the gloom he tries to spot any flotsam of the river that might give him a sign of change in the current. As he does so he finds the doleful grey-brown winter dusk lit up by thoughts and memories of Brazil. Dazzling days, gaudy cicada nights, dark green forests full of bright screaming macaws, the blistering blue skies where the turkey buzzards and frigate birds wheel in the thermals, the grog dens, the markets and the beaches with half-caste girls with light cotton dresses, honey skin and shining smiles. The glitter of the spray as the great Atlantic rollers crash on to the sands of Ipanema. And the heat, and the sweat and the dogs with eyeless sockets lying in dusty roads, still grimacing in the agony of death, and the airless cellar of the Islas das Cobras with flies buzzing terminally and huge centipedes scuttling between dark corners, and Williams lying on a board staring straight into the soul of Tealer Sayer.

That was Williams back there by the boat house. You know it was.

A thought is inescapable – for all that it is just the spawn of a dark night alone on the Waveney. The thought in question is as follows: *the putrefying corpse of Williams has climbed out of a flowery, fetid crypt in the Jardim cemetery and has staggered blindly down to the sea and has swum – so slowly but irresistibly – across the Atlantic and round the coast to Yarmouth, and will now slop around in the estuary with its unblinking eyes always fastened in the direction of Tealer And one night, moaning the moan of the unquiet tomb, it will appear from the Waveney mud and reach out to drag Tealer down with it into the freezing black depths for having taken what was not Tealer's to take…*

Enough, Tealer Sayer!

Tealer finds himself rowing more quickly, and looking into the darkness behind him.

Enough!

He rows on, with the punt creaking slightly on the rope behind his dinghy.

The figure must only have been a marshman come to check that none of his stock has not walked across a frozen dyke and escaped. Tealer can relax. He rows with the ebb tide back up north towards Burgh Castle.

He's looked forward to this time for a long time, hasn't he?

So he'll enjoy it, won't he?

But he's dismayed to feel the now familiar unease colouring his elation at being back on his oldest hunting ground. Even the magic of the *Gariensis* night hasn't succeded in warding off the Brazilian incubus…

A marshman checking his beasts? There are no beasts left on the marsh in this winter weather. They've all been taken upland.

A fowler, then.

But the figure had no gun.

What business is that of Tealer's? Stockman or fowler, it makes no difference, it's not his concern. He determines to put the strange watching form out of his mind – though not before he's felt the reassuring hardness of the leather pouch on his belt.

In this mixture of spirits he rows home.

The following morning the snow changes back to sleet again and this goes on for the rest of the day and into the evening, rattling against the sides of Tealer's small dwelling. He decides to batten down his hatches against the weather. The sheer pleasure of having the *Sturgeon* tied up alongside his houseboat, with White Jenny stowed under a protective canvas – so long dreamt of, and now a fact – means that he has been able to push many of the unwelcome fantasies out of his head, and he prepares for the night in a happier frame of mind. He lights the same oil lamp by which Maud used to read to him of lives and loves and myths and monsters of ancient times, and after his supper he sits down to a tot of Maud's fruit spirit and one of a collection of books he has bought in Yarmouth since his return.

Book-reading is a habit Tealer got from Maud, though he has never found the same pleasure in reading to himself as being read to by her. He still labours over each page, sometimes mouthing syllables to interpret them – but at least he can now read of people and places that before were only names.

He has already worked his way through Tennyson's *Idylls of the King*, and Byron's *Don Juan*. He has started on Shelley's *Frankenstein*, and also has Defoe's *Crusoe* to read. Tonight, though, he's weary, and feels only like the re-reading of a little well-known poetry. He takes a copy of the *Lyrical Ballads*, and thumbs from the back till he finds the *Ancient Mariner*. It's a poem he read with Maud, and he laughed merrily at Coleridge's ghoulish descriptions. Now he is less inclined to laughter, though he still tries to smile at lines that were once his favourite:

> *Like one that on a lonesome road*
>
> *Doth walk in fear and dread*

And having once turned round walks on

And no more turns his head

Because he knows a frightful fiend

Doth close behind him tread.

He flicks further back through the poem for something more cheerful, but in doing so he comes across four lines which he never really paid much attention to with Maud:

An orphan's curse would drag to hell

A spirit from on high.

But oh! More horrible than that

Is the curse in a dead man's eye.

He slams the book shut and straightaway picks up *Frankenstein* as being the nearest to hand.

It offers no relief:

'I trembled and my heart failed within me, when, on looking up, I saw by the light of the moon the demon at the casement. Yes, he had followed me in my travels: he had loitered in the forests, hid himself in caves...'

Tealer throws the book down, angry at himself, and he reaches for the copy of *Robinson Crusoe*. Here at least he finds more congenial scenes. The brilliant shores of the tropics he knows and can easily transport himself to.

Although he doesn't realise it, Tealer is again very tired. He has travelled constantly since his last brief return to Yarmouth. The heady brew caused him to sleep, but only in a restless and very dreamful way. More recently he's laboured feverishly to get the great gun Jenny and her punt back into his domain. Now, as he retires in his den, he relaxes and soon begins to doze over his book. In this state of mind he becomes Robinson, striding the desert beaches of some unknown South Sea island. But soon the scene in his head is the dazzling shoreline of Rio. Then, against the roar of the surf, clear as a bell, he hears Maud call out, *'Tealer'*. He looks up expecting to see her, and he gets up, but the lamp has burnt low. He strains through the darkness to find her, and eventually she appears behind him, carved in marble, sitting in the chair he's just risen from. She's smiling and beckoning with a languid hand. But of course she's a wraith, just as Williams, who then appears in her place, regarding Tealer with the glassy gaze of the corpse and stretching out a dead white palm, is also a wraith. Even in his half-waking state Tealer knows to stare this second apparition down, and indeed it slowly fades until it is just the two cold eyes gleaming at him through the darkness. And then nothing. And then Tealer wakes up, and he finds himself still sitting in the same chair. He takes a deep breath and yearns for the bright hard light of the estuary, the reality of the cold wind and the familiar calls of the wildfowl. They'll drive these phantasma out from his world, he thinks. He puts out his lantern and listens to the *hoop*-ing of the foxes in the ruined fort above him till he goes back to sleep.

Then once more he wakes up, this time with a start. There is movement outside his houseboat. He can hear laboured breathing and a fumbling at the hasp of his door. Something is trying to get in. He hears shuffling as the same creature then works its way around the stern, testing with a light touch the battened portholes – he can trace the slight scratch of an object, perhaps a hand, around the outside of the houseboat, sometimes just the thickness of the cabin wall from his own ear. This time he waits, but this time the disturbance continues – and he knows that that is because it is real. He can feel his ears twitching to every scrape. Finally he hears the movement of a body passing through the reeds near the houseboat door. Of a sudden he throws himself at the door, but he trips over his own boots and falls with a crash. He's immediately up again, and he flings the door open.

There is no rotting horror from a tropical grave waiting to greet him, but he can hear the sound of a heavy form moving through the reeds away into the darkness. He reaches for the nearest object to hand – his wooden belaying-pin propped up by the jamb. He hurls it after the retreating sound. With the hiss of the wind in the reeds he doesn't hear the pin land, but something disturbs a waterhen roosting in the ronds much further along the bank. 'A fox, then,' he says to himself, 'no more than that.' He shuts the door, feels the pouch at his side, lies down on his couch and goes to sleep.

In the morning, in spite of the continuing bad weather, Tealer starts to prepare White Jenny for her first outing. He drags the *Sturgeon* out of the water to the lee side of his hut. Here he loosens the breeching lines and levers Jenny off her mounting. He pours boiling water down her muzzle and rams it hard so that it flies out of the port at the other end in a black jet. This he continues to do until the jet is clear. Then he sets to work scraping points on the barrel of the great gun where two years of inactivity have left bare patches in the blue-white paint. The resulting scoured areas he then carefully touches up with more paint. As he works he becomes more and more absorbed in his job and he begins to forget his experiences of the night before. When he finishes he gets up to admire his work, and without even giving the paint time to dry he sets about the task he has looked forward to most – the priming of White Jenny. Having swabbed her great flue with a dry mop he pours a hornful of powder deep into her and rams it home, grinning the while. On finishing he walks over to his rain butt to wash his hands.

This is when he notices a footprint in the mud on the bank by his door. He assumes it's his until he remembers the events of last night. Just like Crusoe in the book yesterday evening, Tealer puts his own foot against the print.

Like Crusoe, he finds that there's no match.

He looks around for further signs, and now realises something that he missed earlier when he was preparing White Jenny for priming – that the magazine on the *Sturgeon* has been forced open. He quickly checks the contents – powder, powder horns, shot – nothing missing. For a moment he's much relieved. Then it comes to him that whoever was searching the magazine might have been after something quite different – something altogether unconnected with the sport of wildfowling. With that thought there comes once more to Tealer Sayer the old flush of anxiety that is followed by a sustained, all-absorbing melancholy.

And Tealer decides that this is enough!

Of course, he's decided the same thing many times before, but he decides it again this morning.

Instead of moving to his next job, that of pouring the twenty-four ounces of shot into Jenny's barrel and ramming it home, Tealer decides first to sit down, pour himself a goodly portion of Maud's blackberry spirit and work out just what it is he is so unsettled by.

Right, now… Firstly: is he afraid?

He's sure that he's not unduly afraid of physical danger.

After all, hasn't he already known plenty of that…? Only think of the time on the *Empress*, voyaging south of the Azores, when Tealer was on the port rail close to the bow on a heavy swell, and supervising the trimming of sails. He suddenly saw the faces of every crew member on the deck look up to stare in open-mouthed disbelief at something behind him. And he turned to see what had had this effect, and saw a mountain advancing fast on the ship. A mountain, far out in the middle of the ocean. A mountain of water, a wave so unlike its fellows, big as they were, that it was as one large wave on a flat calm sea. Its towering crest seemed to be level with the top of the mainmast. It picked the *Empress* up and lifted her higher, higher and higher still above the rest of the blue-black ocean. The great vessel rose with the water and came down the other side, for the gigantic wave didn't break. They were saved, yet the episode turned every man's bowels to liquid. There was no mistaking that feeling. No-one aboard tried to deny it, though they all joked furiously when the squall had passed.

And what about Cape Verde, when Tealer had woken one morning inland and pulled on his cotton chemise without thinking? Simultaneously he felt the scuttling on his arm and saw the black shape through the cloth make its way up to his shoulder. He grabbed at it and held it tightly in a fold, and rivulets of sweat flowed instantly down his back. He yelled to the second mate in the next room, kicking hard at the timbers with his bare feet. The man came running, pulled out a clasp knife and cut the fold out of the shirt with the creature still in it. They went outside on to the verandah and threw the bundle down, and a large and terrified cockroach shot away out of the light. Again the laughs were loud, especially from Tealer who had been tensed for several minutes against the hot stab and the searing pain that lead to a gasping death.

He takes a long draught of his spirit.

And what about his race across the marsh with Irstead Supreme all those years ago? *That* was fear, though! Yes, now *that* was a jolt to turn any man to jelly, and Tealer was then still a lad.

Yet on all of these occasions he was able to think and then act. Snatching the wheel from the terrified helmsman and bringing the *Empress* about; grasping the imagined scorpion so as to secure its tail; making straight for the deep dyke instead of running blindly for the marsh gate.

Yet now he finds himself wilting in the stern gaze of… Of what?

So Tealer decides that it isn't a fear he feels, but a more insidious dread, and with this dread comes a melancholy. It also brings an anger, like the frustration of a animal that has fought its way to freedom and now finds itself back in its cage. He feels a surge of agitation and storms back out of the hut. He goes to the footprint in the snow and stamps on it.

'Right, then!" he shouts aloud, "That ent a fox! Thas a snooper. Well, he's a-getting nothing off me, whoever he is. *Whoever* he is.' And he shouts it into the reedbeds. 'He's gettin' nothin' off *me*!' In a growing rage he grasps the bag of emeralds set aside for the days of bliss ahead. And he shouts once more into the reeds. 'He's gettin' nothin' off *me*!' He takes a horn of powder – for the second time – and pours it down the barrel and rams it.

As said, Tealer is a tired, confused man.

Oblivious to the huge powder charge Jenny is now carrying, Tealer pours down a twenty-four ounce load of shot.

He starts wadding this shot, but he's soon consumed by another fit of fury. He stops his work and glares around the Breydon skyline, daring his monster to show itself. Then he turns back to the gun and hesitates for an instant, unable to remember what stage in the priming he's reached. This should cause him to start again, but it doesn't.

He's again scanning the Breydon shore. "He'll get nothin' off me, whoever he is!"

And with shaking hands he pours in a second twenty-four ounce load, now hardly aware of what he's about.

"Nothin'!" he mutters as he rams it home. "He'll get nothin'! Nothin'!"

With a last defiant look around the shore he turns to Jenny and pats her, as though he's noticed her for the first time.

"You and me, girl! Eh?" He covers her with a canvas and strides away.

Quiet descends once more on the rond.

White Jenny remains motionless under her canvas. There is nothing in her cold lines to suggest that her distracted master has primed her dark womb with a truly awesome seed; a charge far greater, perhaps, than her ancient, pitted breech can withstand.

The Demon at the Casement

Jenny is, after all, just a lump of gun-metal.

Tealer needs to make further furtive forays into town to obtain the essentials of his new life as a wildfowler.

There's still a numbing sleet in the air, and while this has caused others to stay indoors the heart of Tealer exults at it. It also gives him the excuse to put on the heavy white smock and sou' wester from his chest. The smock is of good quality and wonderfully warm, and its oiled material keeps out the vindictive damp of the east coast. And he reckons that disguised like this he can pass through Yarmouth market unnoticed.

He's nearly right.

Having bought his provisions he sets off across the market square to make his way home by boat back to Burgh Castle. Once again the market-goers are bent against the remorseless wind, little interested in Tealer or anyone else. Indeed, the population of Yarmouth is today a faceless order of monks clad in cowls, hoods and capes, bowed down and forced into introspective silence by the elements. All do their transactions and shuffle on to their next station with none of the usual chat or banter.

All the more surprising to Tealer, then, to realise that he's being watched very closely. At first he thinks he's imagining it. But he looks more steadily across the market at the mass of cloaks, capes, hoods and umbrellas, and there can be no doubt that one featureless form in this sea of oil-skinned anonymity is both perfectly still, and staring straight back at Tealer.

At this point he forgets every shopper in the market. He forgets that he's in the market. He can only stand rigid as this apparition fixes him in its hooded gaze. The details of its eyes are lost in the depths of hood, but he catches their smouldering light. And then, slowly, and with awful certainty, the figure raises a trembling finger of accusation. It disappears for a moment as other figures block Tealer's line of sight, but when they have passed it is still there, pointing.

Finally the figure slips off down one of the Rows, but all the time keeping Tealer in its thrall. He can only look helplessly after it and then at the dark Row into which it disappears.

The other market-goers continue to shuffle past quite unaware.

Tealer's mind races, firstly to grasp whether or not he's actually just seen what he thinks he's seen; secondly – having decided that indeed he has – to explain it away.

It was Williams's height.

Williams? What the hell has Williams to do with it? Why ever think of Williams?

It was Williams's height.

Yes, it was roughly Williams's height, but too far away to be sure.

The figure was pointing at him.

Or someone behind him.

The figure was pointing at him.

Well then, the figure was some half-witted creature of a kind you often get wandering the streets of any town.

The figure was pointing at him.

Or simply the figure, whoever it was, mistook Tealer for someone else.

At any other time Tealer would have been amazed at his own imagination in explaining the event away; now he's acutely conscious that he doesn't believe any of these explanations. He again feels the familiar flush of heat from the back of his head which suffuses his whole body and which he knows will leave him in a mass of melancholic nerves. And he will be assailed by the thought that even here, in the familiar, beloved stamping grounds of the *Gariensis*, he hasn't escaped his demon. Worse still, the sensations that come with it are those from much earlier in his life, and which he thought long extinguished.

Whether or not this strange haunting is real or comes from inside him, Tealer is becoming tired of it. He's becoming angry at it. He will *not* allow himself to believe it is the ghost of Williams that he's just seen in the market, or on the rond, or heard scratching around outside his houseboat. He is determined to believe that in each case there is some other explanation.

There is some other explanation. There is some other explanation.

There is – some other – explanation!

Sandcroft's Ghost

Given this unhappy state of mind that Tealer is in, we can doubt that he would be much reassured to hear that there are others who also think dark forces are stalking the streets of Yarmouth.

No, indeed, if he's seeking to show to himself that he's simply the victim of nerves and coincidence it certainly would not help Tealer Sayer to learn of events in the Bowling Green this same morning. For if he'd been in the Bowling Green he might be forced to conclude that there must *really* be special places or times when malignant spirits and hooded demons swarm up from the Vasty Deep, or back from the Hereafter, or over from the Other Side, to harry all manner of the guilty, both young and old. And whether such a conclusion would comfort him in his misery or confirm him in it, he further would have to conclude that his dead-eyed Mr Williams was just one of many such tormentors, and he one of the many tormented.

But fortunately for Tealer he has no idea of events in the Bowling Green this morning.

This is what happened there:

At about midday the door of the 'Green is flung open and Deaf Watson staggers in. He asks for gin, a spirit he rarely drinks. The other regulars of the Green don't miss this, and watch with great interest.

"Whatever's up wi' you, bor?" they ask.

"I reckon I just now seen him, thas what!" says Deaf, after a gulp of gin.

"Who?"

"Sandcroft!"

There are sceptical snorts and various mumbled versions of "Don't talk squit" from the other drinkers, but these all sound a little hollow – everyone knows that Deaf is not normally the sort to take on like this.

They ask him where he saw Sandcroft.

In the market, he tells them.

What did he look like? they ask.

And Deaf then gives a description of a grim, hooded apparition unhappily similar to that which has just upset Tealer so much. And Deaf's voice comes as close to a shout as the voice of a fowler will ever get:

"That was the eyes. Cor, blust, that was the eyes. They went right through me! They were wild, cold eyes. I couldn't see nothin' else on account a' his hood. But I can tell you that was Sandcroft! Thas who that was! An' his eyes, blust! They bunt right through me!"

"You just now said they were *cold* eyes," says Joyful Norris, all sneering disbelief.

"What?"

"I said: you now said they were *cold* eyes."

"That they were!"

"Then how could they 'burn right through'? Stoopid old goat!"

But Deaf is in no mood for quibbling over the mixing of metaphors. He's had a turn, and the drinkers of the 'Green, and even Norris, can see it.

"An' how d'you know 'at was Sandcroft?" asked one of the others.

"Well, 'at looked like him. An' if 'at weren't Sandcroft, all I can say is someone else round here must ha' done suffin' right wicked to bring a creature like that a-walkin' round the market a-starin' at people. Thas all I can say!"

At that last outburst, all traces of smiling, fixed or otherwise, disappear from the faces of Deaf's audience. A few glance sharply at Polly, the rest just look out of the window or down at their drinks. Polly pours Deaf another gin and listens with mild interest, but no more – in the three years she's been serving the fowlers and fishermen of the 'Green she's heard it all.

Come the evening Polly is busying herself in the scullery, and allowing herself the odd smile as she thinks back to the scene earlier in the day.

There's a knock on the door. She unbolts it to reveal the unsmiling form of Tealer Sayer wrapped up against the elements. Polly promised to cook him a pie last time they met, and he's come round to collect it. She stands back and in he walks. Before he says anything he helps her force the door shut against the wind. She brushes the sleet off her hands and dress and turns round to find

Tealer looking no better than when she left him.

"How are you keepin', Tealer?" she asks anxiously when he sits down.

"Oh, life go on," he says, with a wry laugh.

"You don't look to me as though you ha' been sleepin'."

"Well, no," he admits, and again with the unconvincing laugh, he adds "If you want to know, girl, I sometimes reckon I'm being a-chased about."

"Chased about? Who by?"

Another half-laugh. "A ghost…I suppose.."

Polly nearly says 'Oh, don't *you* start', but something from her barmaid's intuition tells her not to.

"What kind of ghost?" she asks.

"I don't know. I suppose 'at could be the ghost of a man in Brazil I borrowed from and never gave back to."

"You mean you stole somethin' from him?"

"Not exactly. I kept something of his back from the authorities after he died. I 'a still got it."

With Tealer's eyes straight on her, Polly resists the temptation to look down at the bag he now invariably wears at his side.

"Did he have family?" she asks.

"No."

"Well, if he didn't have no family, and himself gone where he can't take nothin' with him, I can't see as he ha' got any reason to go a-hauntin' you."

"I don't know," Tealer says sadly, as he sits and drips melted sleet on to Polly's newly-swept scullery floor.

"What is he? A ghost, or an evil spirit, or what?"

"A ghost, I suppose. At first I only dreamt about it, but since I been back I seen it on the rond down at Burgh Castle, and outside my hut at night, and last time was this afternoon. In the marketplace."

Now even sensible, practical young Polly jumps at that last one, and she turns to get Tealer's pie and cover it with a cloth as an excuse for hiding her face while she thinks. She doesn't really believe in such things as ghosts – she's far too busy – but …

She decides to keep her counsel.

"I reckon you're just tired, and imaginin' things. Thas probably some poor soul from the madhouse. There's no end on' em get out and cause frights."

"Thas what I thought."

"There you are then. You don't even believe you seen a ghost yourself. Go you home and eat this pie, and have a good rest."

He thanks her and walks back out into the sleet with his pie.

Polly meanwhile sits down and thinks for a while. Was she right not to have told him about what Deaf saw in the market place? Yes, she was. It couldn't be the same ghost, because Deaf can't have upset anyone in Brazil – Deaf has never been to Brazil. Deaf has never even been to Gorleston. And yet two different ghosts haunting two different people in the same place on the same day? Well… granted… she's no expert in such things… but that seems a bit coincidental.

Anyway, Polly has mugs to wash, fires to lay and floors to sweep, and ghosts or no ghosts, those are jobs that won't wait.

Tealer shouldn't be living down there alone in that little houseboat, Polly thinks.

Tealer, of course, tells no-one else of *his* experiences, and Polly would be the last to betray such a confidence. But Deaf Watson's story soon spills out beyond the storm-weathered bricks of the Bowling Green and across the whole of the *Gariensis*, which has already been murmuring about spectres sighted in the marshes for some months.

People are now agog. Suddenly it is as if all the evil spirits of East Norfolk have entered the streams and watercourses, slithered down the riverbeds, and are now bursting out through the muds of Breydon to terrify mortals all along its fringes. Accounts of chilling events spread from the estuary up into the marketplace, through the Rows, and out to all the villages and hamlets of the area. And the villages and the hamlets soon reciprocate with their own ghastly tales. There's the railwayman whose job it is to trim the oil lamp on the deserted

Berney Arms Halt; he tells of being half-aware of someone at the other end of the platform – yet when he looks up after finishing the job the platform is empty, and no sign of humanity for miles in the wide-open, whistling flats. Then a marshman from north of the Bure recounts how the hackles of his placid old dog have started to go up every time they pass the great, gaunt mass of Runham church. A maid in one of the big houses in Halvergate describes the evening she was preparing supper for her mistress when she glanced up through the pantry window and caught sight of a 'something' in the kitchen garden – though the garden is walled and always locked on the inside. In the shops, at the pumps and down by the staithes, village folk vie to broadcast the latest news of a spectral this or an uncanny that. Black Shuck the hound seems particularly busy: if the sombre prophecy concerning the fate of those who spot *him* is fulfilled, why then, a year from now Norfolk will be an empty old county. And as for the eelers and fowlers themselves, who spend their time in the loneliest places in the area, short days bring long shadows. The cries of marsh birds seem to be more plaintive. Even experienced marshmen are happy to be off the water and round the stove of the 'Green. Of course there are others who dismiss the tales as 'codswallop', just like Joyful Norris – but even they cast the odd look back on their way home through the dark hawthorn lanes. Just like Joyful Norris.

But far from being anything new, this is merely the latest act in an old drama. In the past, wars, floods and plagues have often threatened the *Gariensis* and the inhabitants have always looked for portents and explanations. And the wilderness of the marshes has invariably obliged, with panoplies of ghosts, lights, devil dogs, glowing horsemen and other horrors. These apparitions have served both to remind folk of their mortality, but also to reassure them of their immortality. This time it is probably the vicious emptiness of winter itself which has summoned up the demons. The arctic weather is killing the old and the weak – nothing imaginary about that – and it is reminding the survivors of the cold quiet of the grave that awaits them too.

And when such bouts of superstitious wonderment are so widespread even the sober and level-headed can find themselves drawn in.

Take Charlie Harrison. Here's a solitary sort of chap, a sign-writer by trade and a catcher of vistas on canvas by calling. Evening after evening you can find him out on one of the riverbanks studying the elongating shadow of a windpump, or the steady course of a wherry as it slices a way through a marshland scene. Sometimes the very beauty of that scene will make his heart ache, and he'll be torn between a desire to gaze and an urge to record it all on canvas, and he'll curse the slowness of oils. He's a stickler for detail, but only the detail that is of use in telling the epic of landscape. Trees, clouds, lilies and water he reproduces with loving care. Amid this celebration of space, even birds and animals are of but passing interest. People he reduces to a few occasional brown shapes, perhaps manning a staithe or chatting over a gate at the far end of a marsh, but always indistinct, formless and faceless, like the peripheral figures in a play. What Charlie Harrison really sees is earth and sky, and what he sees he sketches, furiously, as though it is his mission to record every angle of every scene in every light.

Just recently, before the weather turned wet, Harrison was making regular visits to sketch the deserted acres of the Roman fort at Burgh Castle. On the last clear evening he watched as the mist rolled in from the coast and covered the frosty grasslands to create the phantom inland sea that so many before him had wondered at. Harrison in turn gasped at it. "Damned if I aren't seein' what one of them Roman guards would ha' seen standin' here two thousand year ago," he thought to himself. "The old estuary before the Dutchies come and drained it." Then as he stood marvelling, the last rays of the horizon lit up a drainage mill poking up above the mist in the middle ground between the two forks of the river. He paced up and down, desperately seeking the best angle. He sketched and sketched until he worked out a way to catch the glowing red brick without losing it in the vast orange bath of the sunset-sky behind it.

Then it occurred to him that the very spot he stood on, with its singular ruins, would also make a perfect picture, but from down below. He wanted to catch the light before it disappeared. He threw his materials into his haversack and sped away down to the river where he had a small pinnace moored.

So intent was he in his task that he didn't notice a figure appear at the other end of the fort, moving slowly towards where he'd been standing.

Once on the other side he sketched at lightning speed; soon the sun was gone and the fort was now only a long, dark shape against the night sky. Then he spotted the figure watching him. He tingled slightly at the sight, because like everyone he'd heard strange stories of the Fort. Did not the figure at a distance look like a Roman legionary?

By Heaven, yes, a legionary, spear in hand, standing guard, and staring straight down at him.

"Now I'd have to say that was a ghost – if I knew no better," he thought. 'But ghost or no ghost, he int botherin' me, so I'll ignore him. No, wait, I'll stick him in the picture.'

And so he did.

But later on that evening, as he surveyed his work at home, he looked at the figure he had included on the wall of the fort and tingled once more, and on an impulse painted it out. Then the following day he surveyed his tableau of the fort perched on the Lothingland bluff above the river and the marshes – great, gaunt and very empty. Great, gaunt and very empty. Very, very empty. He shivered a third time, and he painted the figure back in again.

Even a level-headed fellow like Harrison!

There is one, however, for whom it can safely be said all the sprites of the misty marsh hold no dread at all. This is Titus Gooch, now a junior officer with the Excise, still a servant of the Cliff Street Tabernacle and a man as devoid of imagination as he is of humour. Any belief in the supernatural on Gooch's part is entirely confined to a mystical reverence for Authority, whether Authority takes the form of God or of the Excise.

He is also terrified of his wife, of deep water, and of dogs.

But idle chatter about ghosts and spirits? Fairy tales, reckons Titus. Yarns and fables put about by wrong-doers to keep honest folk away from the scenes of their nefarious activities.

Well, they won't be keeping Titus Gooch away! For is not ruthless – quite ruthless – in his persecution of the poachers and wrong-doers who think to use the lonely wastes of the *Gariensis* as cover for their illegal trade? He's proud to think of himself a driven man, and of his work as a sacred vocation. He has inherited the Tabernacler's hearty loathing of 'wilderness': and what more lawless, godless wilderness is to be found than the estuary and marshes of the *Gariensis*? A useless, dangerous swamp, providing escape routes and refuges for those who would seek to put themselves beyond the law. The men who live and work in it are all suspect to Gooch simply for having chosen to earn their keep in a place so far removed from the watchful gaze of Authority – fiscal or celestial. It matters not a jot that some of these men have no more to their name than their flimsy huts, leaking boats and rusting guns. Any talk of the pitifully tiny profits they can make on an occasional box of un-taxed cigars leaves Titus Gooch unmoved. And don't go bothering him with sad tales of winter fuel hard to find, wives with consumption or children with rickets. No concern of his. The difference between right and wrong, lawful and unlawful, is the difference between black and white, and between him and them.

It is therefore along the banks of Breydon Water that Gooch spends most of his time prying and spying for Her Majesty; and he'll go to extraordinary lengths to ensure said monarch is not defrauded of her dues. He will lie drenched, roasted or half-frozen – the more uncomfortable, the more virtuous he feels – ready to give chase to fowlers and marshmen whom he imagines he's taking by surprise. Usually he fails, for when challenged the scoundrels invariably take to water; then, like Burns's Cutty Sark or Mr Stoker's vampire, Gooch has to back away, for since a certain famous incident by the Bure he's had a mortal dread of the swirling currents. Well, we can forgive him that, at least.

Sometimes he succeeds in detaining a suspect before the villain reaches the sanctuary of the river, yet only rarely does he find him in possession of incriminating evidence. However, Gooch represents this very lack of success as a cause to celebrate: if the wretches are never caught with smuggled goods, he reasons, why then, his eternal vigilance must be preventing them from transgressing in the first place. Of course, only Gooch himself is taken in by such egregious delusion – his immediate superior in the Excise, old Matthew Jermy, knows otherwise, but is happy to let sleeping dogs lie. Unlike Gooch, Jermy has much regard for the resilience of the impoverished Breydonsiders, and he would prefer to concentrate on more serious offences; this is just why he lets Gooch fool around on the banks of Breydon. He knows Gooch is no countryman, and that the fowlers will have usually worked out where Gooch will be hiding long before Gooch has himself. The shrewd old exciseman reckons that the best favour he can do them is to let Gooch rush uselessly up and down the mudflats in the belief that he serving Her Majesty some purpose.

But a recent repeated failure to bring about convictions has forced even Gooch to come to terms with a lesson familiar to any estuary man: the great importance of patience. Of waiting silently in one place and noting everything. Now, even Gooch realises the value of lying for hours and hours with a telescope, watching the tiny movements of distant figures on the horizon. Even Gooch has discovered that the bland vacant landscape of winter marshland, far from being lifeless, actually teems with activity.

Thus it is that one night, at about the time of our story, Gooch is busy scanning Breydon's shores for signs of wrong-doing. And he sees something through his trusty telescope which would petrify many other Breydonsiders but simply puzzles him: he reckons he sees Jack Sandcroft, whom he knows to have been blown apart by one of his own infernal guns several years ago. Mouth agape, he looks up from his 'scope to get a different perspective. This doesn't much help, so he peers through the scope again, straining in the wan light of winter to make out the features better. Then a mirthless smile creeps over his pallid visage: "I know what them devils are up to… they ent go' scare me that easy!"

Now what Exciseman Gooch lacks in imagination he makes up for in zeal. The belief that the fowlers are trying to ward him off the estuary only drives him to more extremes of dedication.

Which is what leads to an ugly little incident in the backyard of the Bowling Green.

It's the following morning, and here's Polly Bessey, going to empty some waste on to the compost heap at the end of the yard at the back of the 'Green. As she steps out of the scullery she gasps involuntarily at the sharpness of the cold, and her eyes begin to water. The handle of the heavy copper pail makes her knuckles blue as she grips it, and with her other hand waving about for balance she concentrates hard on trying not to slip on the freezing flags. She gets to the low hedge, steadies herself and throws the contents in the direction of the heap. A particularly treacherous eddy of wind, however, catches the mixture of vegetable peel, stale beer and spittoon water and takes it right over the hedge. There's a noise rather like 'Gaaah!' from the other side, and a grotesque face appears over the cropped spikes of hawthorn. Polly lets out a scream and drops the bucket, so that it clatters loudly over the icy ground. Then she recognises the gargoyle visage of our friend Gooch the Exciseman, pinched into an even more hideous state than normal as he tries to shake the heady mixture out of the brim of his hat.

"*Dagh*! *Yagh*!" says Gooch.

"Whatever are you doin' there?" asks Polly, still very shocked.

"Never you mind!" growls Gooch, "Look at my clothes. *Yagh*! You're lucky I don't get the constable."

"*You're* lucky *I* don't get the constable," says Polly. 'Whatever you doin' there?"

"I said, never you mind,' said Gooch, picking a piece of rotting orange peel from the collar of his greatcoat. Then he fixes her with his sour stare. "You work here, don't you?"

"No, I walk round the yard with a slops pail for the fun of it."

"Don't you get saucy with me, girl, do I shall have the Law round here in a flash. I have the Authority, you know. And I reckon there's a few of you here wouldn't want that very much. Ha! No! That they wouldn't!"

But Polly is a girl from the world of men and not to be intimidated by the likes of Gooch:

"You hint got no right to be hidin' round behind people's hedges, whoever you are," and then, remembering something she's heard about Gooch, she adds: "I've a good mind to let the dog out."

Gooch whitens as he catches sight of a huge old shin-bone lying in the yard and instinctively puts a protective hand to his rear. He has no idea the bone belongs to Tiger the Norwich terrier, the ancient guardian of the 'Green, who has been gnawing away at it to no effect for years.

"This is a public highway, and I certainly have the right," he says with an indignant, high-pitched voice. Then he collects himself and tries a more profound tone: "I want to know which one of that lot in there's been messin' about in the fort recently. And who's been dressin' up to make himself look like Jack Sandcroft?"

"How should I know? Jack Sandcroft, I shouldn't wonder."

"Don't get saucy with me – Jack Sandcroft died years ago."

"Jack Sandcroft's ghost then," says Polly, and with a toss of her head she takes her bucket back to the scullery door. She wants to be well away from the cold sea wind, and away from the cold, sour Gooch and his witless questions.

"I'll have the Law up here! You'll see!" shouts Gooch. This gets no response from Polly, so he adds "And you can tell them inside I know suffin' strange is goin' on down there, and I'm go' find out what." Then he thinks for a moment, and shouts louder still: "No! On second thoughts, don't you go tellin' them nothin'!"

But Polly closes the door behind her with a bang. And the tiny grizzled face of Tiger the Norwich terrier appears in the scullery window, and gives a single, hoarse, toothless yap. Gooch looks at the dog, and then at the gigantic bone.

'*Dagh*!' he says.

Tealer's Last Shot

Meanwhile tealer is on the water at last! He's blissfully unaware of the various brouhahas both within and without the 'Green. And though he might be tormented by unwanted companions when he is deep amongst the reeds, out here on the open water he feels wholly in command.

He dons the white coat and hat of the wildfowler, and climbs into the cream-coloured boat and adjusts the blue-white gun Jenny. Like all gunners, it's as though he is obsessed with painting the world in these light blues, creams and whites. He checks his clothes for any blemish. He checks the sides of the punt for any discolouring chips and his paddles for any muddy stains. And the reason for this obsession with whites and off-whites becomes clear as he lowers himself into the craft – for both he and his boat immediately become part of the low skyline of the *Gariensis*. Open estuaries provide neither bushes nor hills to creep behind. A waterborne gunner must disappear into thin air, and he can only do this if he merges perfectly with the grey-white glare above the surface of the mud. As he approaches within two hundred, one hundred, or even seventy yards of a target flock, he must convince every single pair of eyes and ears in that flock that he's non-existent. Just one bird need see an unfamiliar shape on the surface and all is lost. Likewise if any bird hears the slightest wash of a body moving through water, or the creak of a rowlock, or the faintest rattle of poorly-stored equipment in the magazine, or the slap of a paddle as the fowler pushes it furtively behind his prone form, or the wash or drip of water as he pulls it back out again – then that wary bird will hurl itself into the air, alerting the others, and the skyline will change in a storm of beating wings.

The gunner needs to be slow, but not so slow that the rising tide pushes the roosting quarry off the mud and away to some point four miles down the estuary; or so slow that one or more useless shelduck takes up position between the gunner and the wigeon or mallard he is stalking. (Every fowler at some time in his life will try to disprove the collected wisdom of the marshes by showing that there is some use for shelduck flesh - and as a result his hut will be uninhabitable for days from the stench of boiled duck oil, rotting seaweed and mud.)

The gunner must also watch the ripples on the water for the direction of the wind – because he doesn't want to be pushed off course, nor does he want noisy wavelets slapping too hard against the sides of his craft. Nor for that matter does he want to be swamped by the freezing waters of the *Gariensis*. Above all he must watch that the ever-changing tide doesn't leave him aground on the mud, or wash him away into the channel and out to a lonely death at sea.

This is why the fowler is a man for whom concentration must be total, with no distracting attention to anything other than the job in hand. Tealer's uncle drummed it into him from a very early age.

"*Just react, boy. Once you get near, don't even think. Keep your mind clear and react – react to the wind, to the tide, to the water, to the light, to the birds. Do it automatic. Apart from anything, the birds will hear you if you think. I mean it. They'll hear you. Keep your mind clear and trust your own senses.*"

Already Tealer feels something he hasn't felt for some time. It's the feeling of being in two places at once – of being outside the boat and watching himself as he sets about his stalk, utterly absorbed.

To Tealer, it's also the very welcome feeling of being back.

But the conditions aren't ideal. The art of wildfowling is no pursuit for the fairweather hunter, as it takes its students on to the most exposed landscapes in Britain at the dead of winter. But even by these harsh standards the conditions on Breydon are bad, and getting worse. The sheets of ice, which only decreased slightly in size during the recent 'mild' spell, are again getting bigger with the return of the bitter cold, and some are coalescing to form big, dangerous floes which could crush a boat like paper. No other wildfowler is on the water – most have retreated to seal themselves into their huts, or have repaired to the Bowling Green Inn to contemplate the glowing coals of the lounge-stove.

Tealer, however, doesn't notice the freeze, because the smell of the mud and the whistles of the wigeon and the weak orange light of the intermittent winter sun are arousing such instincts as he hasn't known for several years. Jenny is primed, and backed up with two loaded 'stoppers! No matter that the navigable water between the ice sheets is getting ever sparser, Tealer is back on the estuary!

His first stalk serves to remind him just how much edge he has lost.

As he brings the *Sturgeon* out of the shelter of the river channels and starts to scan the mudflats for roosting birds there's a sudden change in the colour of the horizon. He immediately recognises this as a flock of two hundred mixed fowl which has been disturbed, and disturbed by him.

Chastened, he scans around more cautiously for a second target as he drifts on the gently ebbing tide toward the broader reaches. Eventually he spots a mixed flock of dunlin and redshank, all probing for scraps in the paltry line of open mud between the fixed ice of the banks and the frozen sheets. The stalk begins some half a mile away... but ends not long after, because Tealer has forgotten to mark the bitter east wind which blows him off his line, thus requiring heavy paddling, which in turn leads to a careless scrape of a paddle on the side of the hull. The tiny noise carries towards ears sharp enough to hear the scratch of a lugworm in the silk-soft ooze. The dunlin and redshank spring into the air in a mesmerising cloud.

Another flock of redshank lands in the middle distance, but is off again as the dark shape of a peregrine darts down and scatters them before making off to some remote tree with its kill.

And the great gun White Jenny, with her cataclysmic overload of powder and shot, remains unfired. Untested.

Tealer glasses the mud further - and his heart stops. He mouths a happy curse. He stares again down the telescope and gives a laugh of disbelief. Where there is still open water amongst the frozen mud and ice, Breydon is wearing a brown mat. Tealer looks again – a mat not of scum or seaweed, but, yes, of living birds. And now that he strains the wind he can also hear a noise which he realises was there all the time; only just audible from being downwind, but, unmistakably, the incessant piping of a wigeon flock.

He marks the one piece of estuary currently holding enough open water to allow him an approach. With more stealth and more control he eases the craft forward. He keeps his port paddle working harder to make up for the easterly wind, which in any case is now dropping. Lying flat on his stomach, trying almost to become one with the timbers of his punt, he works the paddles behind him with a rhythmic pumping that creates no wash and sends him steadily down the channel in the direction of the piping, whistling mass of birds. Two hundred, one hundred and fifty, one hundred yards – and then with quivering slowness he ships the paddles. The wind has now dropped off almost entirely.

This is a blessing, as it would otherwise be blowing every sound from him to his prey. He can hear the whistle and clatter of a train miles away, carrying people cocooned in gaslit carriages, utterly unaware of the existence of Tealer and his quarry deep in the freezing gloom beyond their windows.

Tealer watches his own hand move as he might watch a creature in no way connected to him. The index and middle fingers edge forward toward the hammer and pull it steadily back, allowing not so much as a fingernail to appear over the gunwale. Then he reaches forward another two inches to allow his hand to pass from the hammer to the trigger cord. It is at this point that a small but terrible rattle comes up from the boards, and he thinks that he must have struck a streak of shingle, but almost as soon realises that the leather pouch at his waist has come undone and several of the stones have fallen out on to the deck. Only the nearest birds hear it, but it's enough. They peel off the ice and gradually take the rest of the flock with them. Tealer could fire, but he knows he would only get a few tail-end birds. He was taught well enough to know not to engage in futile displays of irritation, but simply to stay still and watch. Sure enough, most of the circling fowl have no idea where the disturbance came from and they are not leaving the estuary. Instead they're making their way down-stream to the bank on the south side of Duffel's Drain.

Jenny, grossly overcharged, still inert, still untested.

Tealer watches the departing flock with resignation, and then down at the dull green stones lying on the floor of the punt. He tries to pick them up but the freezing cold has taken all feeling from his fingers, so he has to brush them on to the corner of his smock and funnel them back into their pouch. As he looks at them, thinking how they have ruined his stalk, a sudden black thought takes him, a sliver of doubt from the past few weeks which tries to pierce his heart.

But it's deflected. Here in his element Tealer can be more resolute, and here the magic that dominates is the white magic of the marsh. He merely shrugs off a portent which days ago would have left him in an agony of doubt.

He sits up and glasses the north west corner of Breydon. He knows that this is where he must now head for. This corner is the area of Duffel's Drain and is not at all well-known to Tealer. He and his uncle usually left it to the Yarmouth fowlers. But today there are no other fowlers the length and breadth of the estuary, and with a sudden rush of adrenalin he realises why. It is now very,

very cold – perhaps colder than any man here has ever known. He's on Breydon at a forbidden time.

The thought exhilarates him.

He prepares his stalk.

The tide is now moving out quite fast, and Tealer begins to feel himself buffeted by lumps of ice in the flow. He knows this will be his last stalk before sunset, and, through his excitement to be underway, a moment's reason tells him that he must make sure he finishes near firm ground or risk spending the last night of his life in the freezing open, stranded out on the mud in his punt.

He considers the position. He decides he needn't fear the wind as this has dropped and he therefore won't be blown off course. However, the tide in the channel is now getting stronger, and if he uses it to get down to the mouth of the drain there's a danger he will be swept straight past the mouth without being able to swing into it. Therefore, for as long as he can, he'll want to use the shallow water over the mud at the edge of the channel to make his way down, rather than the fast, deep waters in the middle – until, that is, the outgoing tide makes the mud too shallow to be navigable.

Yet all that means that he will be much slower getting to his quarry. This is not a problem with regard to the birds themselves – with the tide going out they will be in no hurry to set off inland from this sanctuary. No, his problem is that being too slow might mean that he's simply not able to beat the fading light. He begins to realise this is getting hopeless.

Then he hears something in the air which electrifies him.

Among the cacophony of whistles from the wigeon flock is the *wink-wink! w-w-wink-wink!* of some other creature.

Geese!

Geese!

There are geese around Duffels Drain! The wildfowler's prize, the king of all waterbirds. Tealer now becomes utterly single-minded. No matter that his face and hands have no feeling or that the muscles of his back are aching from being hunched constantly against the cold. This is a stalk he will not forego, come what may.

Failing light, quickening tides and arctic temperatures. This is a wild, foolhardy business, and if Tealer were in any other frame of mind he would see that. But old Tealer hasn't been thinking straight for some time.

He sets off.

As he travels downstream to the mouth of the drain, Tealer is aware of a strange hush falling around the estuary. At the back of his mind he recognises this as the prelude to snow. The calls of the wigeon have fallen to occasional whistles and the geese are silent. He wonders if they will flight at all tonight given that they'll know their usual feeding grounds are frozen solid. Perhaps not, which suits Tealer.

With one elbow on the magazine and his spyglass lined up along Jenny's broad barrel, Tealer scans the middle ground. Slowly the great flock changes from being a dark stain amongst the ice and water to being recognisable as a mass of birds. He can see individual duck fly up and move on to more comfortable positions, and he can also now see the larger shapes of the geese in the background.

Then he sees a sight to make his heart sink. From somewhere in the great grey void above his head drops a flock of eight or ten shelduck. They land some one hundred yards up the main channel from the drain mouth, and thus between him and his quarry. He curses again, this time not lightly. He will have no choice but to drift toward the shelduck, drift past them, then drift away from them toward the wigeon without their even seeing him as a moving shape. He watches them carefully – they're jumpy, for in such conditions their enemies are as hungry as they are, and they well know that on ice that is even remotely strong enough a hungry fox will risk all to feel his teeth meet in the oily neck of one of them.

Tealer forces his eye from the wigeon to the shelduck flock and keeps it there. As he approaches the shelduck they move about restlessly, but he knows this is a good sign - their attention is not fixed on the river. He watches their brightly-coloured heads bobbing up and down and tries to follow his uncle's injunction not even to think about them. Then they seem to become immobile, which is what Tealer dreads – it is such bland woodenness in a flock of duck which he knows is the forerunner to a noisy escape, and this one will take the wigeon and geese with it. He expects at any second the clap of many wings against the ice.

But he doesn't hear it. He begins to hope against hope that he isn't spotted after all. He slips further down the side of the main channel past the motionless shelduck. He turns slowly to the wigeon in the distance to his right front – his very eyeballs moving slowly from fear of being detected. The wigeon are also very still, and it's then that he begins to wonder if there's something else disturbing them.

But who else would be stalking Duffel's Drain in such weather?

Or is it a fox, or another late-hunting peregrine?

He can see nothing, so he starts to line up for the final approach across the main channel into the drain. He's concerned to see the main flock is further up the drain than he'd like, but he's not abandoning his plan now. He takes a deep breath and pushes diagonally over the fast waters of the main channel, and succeeds in bringing the *Sturgeon* into shallow water on the south side of the drain mouth. A drop of sweat pours out from under his woollen hat and immediately chills on his temple. He begins to be more confident that he isn't seen, and this confidence grows as he finds himself now able to target a mixed flock which will allow Jenny's spread of shot to take both duck in the foreground and geese in the background. He pushes the *Sturgeon* forward and tucks her into a position in the mouth of Duffel's Drain that helps him avoid being pushed back into the main channel by the growing current coming down the drain.

The birds are settled, and within range.

A shot will carry off the water up onto the mud and claim several layers of fowl; wigeon in front, brent geese behind them, and even the possibility of a few pink-footed geese behind the brents. It's a tableau of gunning straight from the pages of Hawker!

But did Hawker ever venture forth with as gigantic a charge in his gun as Tealer has unwittingly stuffed into Jenny's vitals?

And now this same White Jenny – disastrously overprimed, coldly obedient – is pointing straight up Duffel's.

Silence.

Silence.

Then – mayhem.

A maelstrom of flapping wings and calling birds transforms the very shape of Duffel's Drain. Where some two thousand fowl were sitting in the shallows there is suddenly not one. Yet Tealer hasn't fired, or even thought about firing! Instead, he's staring straight ahead of him at something on the far bank, silhouetted against the last vestiges of western light.

It is a figure, and it is facing him, and beckoning with long, slow sweeps of its arm.

At this, a great conflict rages in the soul of Tealer Sayer. The faceless figure has jerked him back into the world of guilt, doubt and fear which he'd been confident the magic of Breydon would exorcise.

But then he *is* stronger here, for before he would have crumpled and shrunk from such an apparition! Now, though, he's in his element, and no longer so vulnerable. Yet still he's twisted and tormented by this thing that has pursued him. Is it Williams? Is it Williams's ghost? Is it the frightful cadaver from Williams's stifling tomb, impervious even to the arctic chill of the worst winter East Norfolk has known for years?

Or is it something far worse, even, than that? Is this an older, even less welcome friend, long thought to have been vanquished, now returned, simply using the punctured corpse of Williams as its latest incarnation?

Whatever it is, it is definitely here, and desecrating even this holiest of sanctuaries, the very waters of Breydon herself. Tealer blinks and blinks, but the figure remains. It is impassive against the skyline.

Now desperation replaces uncertainty. Tealer *cannot* be vulnerable *here*! Rio – Yarmouth even – but not here! This is his… *home*!

And yet the silhouette continues to beckon, now no longer with the whole arm but with a mocking crook of the finger – and all Tealer can do is lie in his boat and stare in disbelief. Months of this chase, and all the lonely, persecuted years that it has resurrected, crowd in on him, and he wonders if he can endure any more. Then he feels himself take a huge breath, and for the first time in his haunting – for the very first time in his life – Tealer actually shouts out aloud to his tormentor.

"Why me?" he cries. "Why me? Why can't you leave me alone? You're not

Williams! You have followed me all my life. For once, leave me alone! Leave me alone or I'll blast you to hell!"

The figure is silent and now very still.

The rage in Tealer grows, and he yells even louder. "LEAVE – ME – AL…..!"

But the last syllable is lost, because as he utters it, Tealer's hand jerks convulsively on the cord that holds in check the dread forces stored in the chamber of the huge weapon beside him. The hammer snaps forward from full cock and crushes the little copper cap of detonating charge, which in turn ignites the lethal double measure of black powder which has lain dully in the dry depths since Tealer rammed it into place outside his houseboat three days ago.

In the first instant, in the first one thousandth of a second that follows, there is only an intense, noiseless white light on the face of the estuary. But then the whistlings of the wigeon, the calls of the geese and the piping of the lapwings are obliterated, as are the failing light and the dark sounds of the marshes – as is the relentless thud of the steam hammer and the whistle of another passing train and the rhythm of a working Yarmouth on a winter afternoon – as is, along with all these, the beckoning apparition in the distance… But also, as is the image of the lifeless Williams in a dungeon in Rio de Janeiro; and the visions of Maud with the dancing eyes; and the visions of Maud with the gouged-out eyes; and the devil dog with the glowing eyes; and the shrivelled red goblin with the one evil eye, and the many-armed kraken with the saucer-sized eye, and the great pike with the pitiless Norris glare; and the malicious grin of the young Gooch, and the mirthless wraith of Georgie Stolworthy; and the expressionless face at the garret window – and as are the happy memories of days on the Roads, days on the Broads, days on the mud – and as are all the dreams; all the visions, all the illusions, all the nightmares...

Everything.

Everything is blotted out.

Everything is swept into oblivion when, after three long years of silence, White Jenny, the mightiest gun in the marshes, Belle Dame without Mercy, roars out her challenge in a shattering clap of sound that shocks and numbs the air across the *Gariensis*.

As the initial, apocalyptic blast dies away there is a lull in which the whole landscape remains stunned. All movement ceases, and even Time itself seems to have been suspended. Then the monstrous echo sets off on its long journey, waves of thunder that roll and cascade across Breydon, crashing against its shores and rousing the whole four miles of the estuary as it goes; every one of the ten thousand roosting fowl jumps reflexively off the mud into the iron-dark sky to begin a desperate search for some new sanctuary. The echo rolls on over the marshes and sets dogs barking in remote dwellings. It continues to the villages on the edge of the uplands. It stops townsfolk in their tracks as they shuffle through the lanes of Cobholm. Weak yellow lights appear in the portholes of the few houseboats on Breydon's fringes as the occupants break away from the huddled comfort of their stoves and push back drapes to peer out, trying in vain to place the source of the din in the waning afternoon light. The same lone railwayman, again trimming the lamp on the Berney Arms station, loses his pipe as it drops from his mouth.

The whole of the estuary is made to stop and acknowledge that, after a long absence, White Jenny is back to re-claim her crown.

When he loaded the great gun Jenny, Tealer must have secured her breeching lines well – because he is still alive. His inadvertent feeding of her with twice her normal charge has stretched the hempen fibres to the utmost, and the sharp recoil has brought Jenny so far back that she has actually split Tealer's lower lip. He's been part-blinded by the huge orange flash of her detonation, and he is coughing on the acrid fumes of spent powder. Through the clouds of this choking smoke he can only just make out points of flickering light on the water ahead of him where brands of burning wadding have landed on the ice. The shot has carved a great trough in the mud and has sent plumes of icy spray flying far into the air. These are still drifting back down on to the surface. At the estuary edge, just visible against the tiny remnants of daylight, fragments of dried vegetation are fluttering in the air where the top of the pattern has ripped through the reeds, causing their sere heads to disintegrate.

Beyond the reeds there is nothing at all to see.

The figure is gone.

Whoever or whatever it is that has sought to pursue Tealer Sayer in this most sacred land is surely annihilated. The winter horizon is once again one of deathly emptiness.

For several minutes Tealer is too dazed to move. Gradually the calls of the frightened birds subside, as does the barking of the dogs in backyards from Cobholm to Belton. Freezing silence reigns once more. Slowly he lifts his head up from where he instinctively thrust it at the shock of Jenny's report, and he strains the darkness. He can see nothing.

Then he comes suddenly to life. He grabs a cripple-stopper with shaking hands and thrusts it out into the gathering darkness, swinging it wildly in a complete circle around him.

But where the figure was standing on the Wall beyond Duffel's there is only the last light of the day turning to night. For a few more seconds Tealer swings the cripple-stopper. Then he uncocks it, and lays it gently down, and a grin appears on his face. He takes his flask filled with the last of Maud's fruit spirit and drains it to the lees. He drops the empty vessel into the bottom of the boat.

"That was Jenny, that was!" he shouts into the dusk, "That was old Jenny! What did you think o' her, then? Hey? *Hey*?" He looks down at the huge punt gun, smoke still pouring out from her muzzle – and still intact in spite of the awesome pressures she has had to sustain. Then his grin becomes manic, and he tears the pouch from his side and holds it high above his head. "I tell you what!" he yells "If there's still aught left of you, come you here and get them!" he yells. "They're all here. Only we'll be waitin' for you, Jenny an' me! We'll be a-waitin'!"

He throws the precious pouch back into the punt and takes the powder horn from the *Sturgeon*'s magazine. But he doesn't put to shore. Instead he unhitches Jenny's lines and with a short staff he levers her trunnions out of their mortises and then, with desperate, shaking tugs, he drags her great weight backwards into the *Sturgeon*. He picks up the ramrod and begins the inadvisable business of re-charging the mightiest gun in the marshes while still afloat.

Back at the 'Green

Now, earlier this evening, just before the start of all this excitement out on Breydon, Charlie Harrison came in through the door of the Bowling Green holding something in a hessian sack.

The savage cold outside had left him so stiff that he could barely nod to Bessey and his niece; he slowly scanned the lounge for a particular face but couldn't find it. He was looking for one of the finely-dressed 'gents' who occasionally brave the deafening silences of the Bowling Green to enquire after rare birds or other curios to take back to London. He'd heard that such a fellow was interested in a landscape of the area and that this fellow would be in tonight; but this was not the case. Not everyone's ready to make the journey down to a Breydonside tavern in cold like this.

Harrison put the hessian sack down and massaged some feeling back into the fingers of his left hand which were crooked from carrying his bundle. He took a pint of Lacon's and sat down in an easy-chair a little away from the main body. As a painter of quiet and lonely places Charlie is no more loquacious than the fowlers. They know him as an occasional visitor but have little interest in his trade. So after a few curious glances the regulars returned to their muttered conversation.

Then there was a lull in even this level of communication, and, as in all good English inns, a spell arose when no-one talked because no-one felt the need to. Everyone stared at his boots, or the amber depths of his Lacon's, or the discoloured eagle, or the ageing Tiger sleeping on the rug by the stove, or the smart lines of Polly Bessey quietly cleaning a mug. Finally, one of fowlers, Generous Hunt, turned to Harrison, nodded to the sack and asked casually:

"What, yer brought us a present, Charlie?"

The painter fixed Generous with a piercing blue gaze, but went with the flow. "No present, but I reckon you can have it if you ha' got the money."

There was a slight chuckle around the lounge at that, for Generous was said to be so tight his eyelids squeaked when he blinked.

"I reckon I oughta see the goods, fust."

Harrison looked at him for a moment longer, and then shrugged. He pulled off the canvas and showed them a picture in oils. No-one complimented it, but then Harrison wasn't expecting them to. The only response was Cadger Brown who asked him: "Where is it?"

"Yarmouth, from Breydon."

Cadger tilted back and forth to look at it from different angles. "Yarmouth from Breydon?" he said. "Can't say I can see it."

Poker Lamb gave an irritated laugh. "Blast, just look at him a-twistin' his head about like an ol' starlin' on a gate! Cadger, you hint got eyes, thas your problem!" And he then turned to Harrison. "Don't you take no notice o' him Charlie, he wouldn't recognise hisself in a mirror – that's why he allus look so rum of a mornin'. *I* can recognise it; any fule can see that there's St Nicholas in the distance, and that there's that wherry palk by the north shore."

Harrison nodded.

"So where were you when you painted that, then?"

"South side of the Drain."

"What, the Ship Drain?"

"No, Duffel's."

At the mention of Duffel's Drain there was suddenly a surge of real interest – which meant that eyes previously half-opened were now at full extent and people were even darting the odd look at one other. No-one spoke at first, and the quiet was broken only by the sound of Polly's cloth on her mug and the rhythm of Tiger's back leg on the floor as he scratched himself.

Then Fiddler Goodens cleared his throat. "Tell me now," he said in a nonchalant manner, but all the same looking at Harrison straight in the eye, "Hev you... seen... anything up there on the Drain? When you been a-paintin', I mean."

"What like?"

"Anyone. Standin' around."

"No, only me."

"Oh."

Polly looked up at the group thoughtfully for a second and carried on cleaning.

"Should I ha' done?" asked Harrison.

"No, no. Er… no," said Goodens, as though that were an end to his interest in the matter.

"What the ole fule mean is," said Joyful Norris, who was slowly coming to life as his ale took hold, "hev you seen Sandcroft's ghost?"

Harrison looked up sharply at the group, who were all glaring at the smirking wherryman. "What, Sandcroft what was killed?"

A few of them nodded. The others just watched him.

"No" said Harrison simply, "not up at Duffel's. Can't say I seen anything."

"What d'he say?" asked Deaf Watson, who had become aware that something had caught the real interest of his fellows.

"He said he hint sin *Sandcroft's ghost*," said Cadger loudly.

"Where?" asked Deaf, the colour draining from his face.

"*Duffel's*," shouted Cadger into his ear.

Deaf turned to Harrison and said "I sin him, too. In the market."

"No, no," said Harrison, "I said I *haven't* seen him."

Norris shook his head, and said: "There you are, then. Thas what I said. Thas all a heap o' squit."

"But," said Harrison, "I have to say that I have seen *some* rum things down on the marsh just of late."

"What sort o' 'rum things'?" asked Goodens.

Harrison took a deep breath and sighed. "Oh people, figures. Figures in the landscape. In the mist. In the distance."

"Ghosts, you mean?"

"Well, perhaps they were ghosts," said Harrison, and almost muttering to himself, he added "and then perhaps that don't make a shred of difference."

"What d'y'mean?"

Harrison looked at Hunt and the others, all of whom were now watching him even more intently.

He swilled his beer around in its glass and watched it settle, and said "Well, the likes of you and me make our livings down here on the marshes and the mud away from other people. The way I see it, we have to face things here that other men can avoid. Your folk that work in the towns or villages, or even upland in the woods or the hills – they always have streets or valleys – hidden places, at any rate – they can hide up in. But for us," and here he gazed through the window at the light of the dying day over the estuary, "for us down here in the flat land, there int nothin' 'twixt the top of our heads and the wrath of Heaven. Nowhere to run and shelter. Nowhere to hide. Now, normally, I love this area – well, and so I should, seein' as I paint it! – but I have to say that there have been times when there's been a certain light in the sky, or a piling-up of thunderclouds, or a hush on the water, and I've suddenly realised I'm all alone out there. I don't know if any of you boys ha' ever felt it, but myself, I feel… watched, I suppose… at times like that. Singled out, you could say. Too easy to spot. Almost like the last mortal on earth. And when a man's in a nervous state like that I don't wonder that he see odd things now and again. I know *I* have. Figures where I weren't expectin' them. Ghosts, perhaps…"

"What ghosts are they then, Charlie?"

"Ghosts from my past, I suppose. They may not be the same as the ghosts you see, or anyone else see. And whether they're real or not – perhaps that int the point. They're real enough to the people what see 'em."

The comity of the 'Green looked at one other and back at Harrison. If some didn't quite follow the drift, it wasn't from lack of attention. And a number of them were studying their own boots fixedly, suggesting *they* followed the drift only too well.

Harrison then put his glass down, leant back on his chair and crossed his arms. "But then, maybe even *that* int *exactly* what I think." And here he took another deep breath, and let out another sigh. "You see, I reckon that we all see ghosts down at marsh from time to time… *because we want to*. Because, if we didn't see 'em, we'd look into that there gret ol' open space and we'd see nothin'. That just the word I mean: 'nothin''. Nothin' at all. Or, put it another way, we'd see into eternity. Or infinity. With just ourselves, and nothin' else, in the whole universe. Then we'd *truly* feel alone. And that'd scare us worse than any ghost."

The men around him stared, and Polly frowned from among the mugs, and there was more silence, because the Bowling Green Inn is not used to such philosophy. Homespun theories on the behaviour of ducks or wives, yes – but not this kind of talk.

It was Deaf Watson who first spoke up, mainly because he hadn't even heard most of what Harrison was saying:

"But, but… did you see ol' Sandcroft? Thas what we want t'know."

Harrison was still looking out of the window, but he turned to Watson and said: "No, I can't say I seen Sandcroft." He gave his beer another swilling and smiled at it. Then he seemed to remember something: "I did see a strange sight up at the old fort, though. Ha! Would you believe! I reckoned I could see one of the old Roman soldiers looking down at me. He was hunched on his spear and starin' straight at me. Now, was he real? You tell me! Did I see him 'cause I was alone on Breydon of a winter's evening, cold as death, with the tide a-comin' in around me? Or did I see him 'cause out by that there fort I wanted to think there was something living and breathing under the stars apart from just me? Do you see what I mean?"

He took another draft of his Lacon's, and half-closed his eyes as the fumes of the beer combined with his tiredness and the warmth of the lounge to relax him further.

Then he opened them again and continued: "But then perhaps I *have* seen Sandcroft, now I come to think on it. I did see some strange-looking figure walking about near Sandcroft's rond, and I weren't expecting that, seeing as Sandcroft ha' been dead all this time. So perhaps I ha' seen Sandcroft after all."

"Wh-what was he wearin'?" asked Hunt.

"White. All in white."

"What w-wildfowler don't dressh in white? That don't mean nothin'!" said Norris with an inebriated snort.

"Thas true," said Harrison, "but this was much whiter than normal, and 'at seemed very clean."

This riveted the drinkers yet more. They remembered Sandcroft's habit of dressing in camouflage so spotless that it dazzled the eye. They looked at each other darkly, and silence reigned again.

"Lorro' shhhquit," said Norris after a while, and he downed his pint.

He couldn't have chosen a worse time. As the beer disappeared down his throat in a great gulp, a deep boom seemed to reverberate around the tavern, causing him to choke violently. It was a noise from outside, from the middle of the dark, empty estuary. It was not so much loud as profound, elemental. In another Yarmouth hostelry, perhaps one located nearer the sites of quay-side industry, or simply a place more prone to outbursts of rowdy laughter, such a sound might even have gone unnoticed. In the Bowling Green, filled with some of the quietest men in Norfolk, and lying at the point where the only movement is the silent mingling of the waters of the Yare and the Bure, it was heard by everyone. Even old Tiger picked up some vibration and started to yap furiously. And lest there were any who could persuade themselves that that first rumble was imagination, it was followed by a distinct rolling echo that left thousands of seabirds and wildfowl in uproar.

There was a murmur of alarm, and then a rictus seemed to descend on the fowling men – and Harrison looked from them to the window and back to them again.

"Well, what the devil was that?" he asked. But he got no answer, for the men were all looking at one other grimly, all except Joyful who was still coughing. So he turned to Polly "What was that? Do you know, girl?"

But Polly shook her head. "That I don't." And she called over to Fiddler. "Surely there ent no-one out on the water tonight?"

Fiddler said stiffly, "You're right, girl. There ent."

"So what was that noise just then? That sounded like a big-bore gun. Mr Norris, do you know?"

But Norris who had just stopped coughing, simply shrugged and shook his head.

"He know," said Deaf, in a bitter voice, "he know, but he won't say. Well, I'll say, and anyone who don't reckon I seen Jack Sandcroft in the market place had better listen right well! All of us men here know that worn't no normal gun could ha' made a row like that. And wi' my ears I wouldn't navver a' heard no other gun – not from in here, I wouldn't. That was ol' Jenny, that was."

The others all looked at him and then at the floor and walls.

Deaf got more excited: "We hint heard her for many a long year, but thas what we ha' just now heard. There int no point in sayin' that weren't. That was ol' Jenny, that was." He looked fearfully out of the window.

"Who's Jenny, and what's she got to do with Sandcroft?" Harrison asked.

Poker said quickly: "Jenny was Sandcroft's gun. She was the biggest what's ever been used on Breydon. There ent no mistakin' her racket. That's what we just now heard, alright. I reckon Deaf's right."

They all nodded, and several of them started to get up and peer through the window into the gloom. But the lamps of the lounge had solen their night vision, and they could make nothing out. And they began muttering to each other nervously, 'This is gettin' worse – I aren't goin' out there n'more – that couldn't be nothing else – even that ol' dog heard it, and he's deafer'n what Deaf is – we oughta had the parson down here – cor t'hell, I wish that'd leave us alone.'

And so it went on.

Polly was watching this hubbub open-mouthed. Then of a sudden, she called over to them, "Listen! Wait a moment!" But they took no notice, so with a voice beyond her years she shouted again. "Wait...! Cadger! Generous! Fiddler! Listen! You stupid donkeys, will you listen!" And she brought a tankard smartly down on the table. "*Listen!*"

And they all jumped, and stared at her in astonishment.

And they all did listen to Polly – even Ben Bessey himself, who'd come down to find out what the commotion was about. She glared round at them all, hands on hips, and looking, at a slender seventeen, every part the mistress of the 'Green.

"This 'Jenny' you're on about – was 'at ever called '*White* Jenny'?"

"Yes, yes, she was," said Poker "How ever did you know? That was years afore your time."

Polly took no notice, but went on: "And this man Sandcroft you're all goin' on about, did he know... or did he have anything to do with... a John Palmer?"

As the men had become grimly unforthcoming, Polly was answered quietly by her father from the stairs behind her: "He *was* John Palmer, mawther. John Palmer-Sandcroft. He preferred men to use his mother's name down here, so's not to attract attention. But never mind him, though, there's still glasses need cleaning."

But Polly turned back to the men and pressed on: "And thas the same John Palmer that had a nephew, John Sayer? Who everyone call Tealer?"

" 'Course he did," said one of the men. "The boy Sayer. He was the one that was go' marry the Pritchard girl from Gorleston – 'cept she ran off to Scotland with a cattle-man. What's he got to do with it? And what are you a-lookin' at us like that for?"

For Polly was looking from one to the other, mouth still open, with a mixture of amusement and pity, and given their recent upset, they didn't much care for it.

"What are you boys like?" she said. "What *are* you like? That int Sandcroft's ghost out there, you daft crew, thas his *nephew*!"

After they'd thought about this, Saltfish Jex, who liked to think things through at his own pace, spoke up in his quiet voice:

"Now you're wrong there, mawther. You can't explain it as easy as that. Everyone know the boy Sayer went off to sea. He was go' come back to marry the Pritchard mawther, but she then went and ran off with a Scotch cattle…"

"He's been back several days. He's living out there on Sandcroft's rond."

The fowlers, mulleters and eel-men of the Bowling Green took all this in true Norfolk manner – not one muscle in one face moved – but inside they were digesting the news. In the meantime, Harrison broke out in a broad grin.

"And I don't know what you're laughing at, Charles Harrison," said Polly, trying not to laugh herself, "you're half the cause of this foo-fer-rah!"

"Oh, yes? And how's that, my girl?" said the painter.

"Where did you paint that there picture under that sack? Duffel's Drain. How long has it taken? Three weeks. What's it called? 'When Night Creep On'? So, when have *you* been hanging around there painting it? No! Let's guess! How about… when night creep on? No wonder these boys ha' spent the last three weeks mardlin' on about a strange figure in the twilight – I don't reckon they come much stranger than Mr Charles Harrison in his painter's smock. And no wonder the duck have been flighty around the Drain the last few weeks. And no wonder poor old Tealer Sayer reckon he's been haunted. Because when you hint been puttin' the wind up the wildfowl round at Duffel's, you ha' been hidin' about in the reeds opposite Sandcroft's rond trying to catch Tealer's back on canvas. You're lucky he didn't take a gun to you!"

Harrison was enjoying all this, and his grin was getting broader. "I suppose that could have been old Tealer, now you come to say. Difficult to tell in the half-light. But you haven't told me about the ghosts *I* seen. I haven't been hauntin' myself, you know."

"I ha' thought about that, an'all. I reckon thas that toad from the Excise – Gooch, I think his name is. He told me he saw you up at the fort, and – if you want to know – he reckon you're up to no good. He's started usin' a telescope on a stick. I seen him creepin' up Bowling Green Walk with it. I should imagine that was your 'soldier's spear'. Oh, and you other boys what ha' been saying the Berney Mill's got a ghost – Gooch ha' been hiding up there, an'all. And – *and* – I reckon Gooch was another one what's been makin' the birds nervous in the reedbeds. Cha! You lot, you're better'n a fairground turn – the lot o' you!"

The men looked sullen and unconvinced, and Deaf, who'd been straining to listen with his hands cupped at his ears, suddenly shouted:

"Thas all very clever, but don't forget I saw Sandcroft in the market."

"Oh, yes, you did, didn't you?" said Polly. "And did you see his face?"

"No, 'at was hid, but…"

"Then how do you know 'at was Sandcroft?"

"I could tell from his clothes – they were the same gunner's clothes what he always wore. Good quality oilskins, they were. I'd know 'em anywhere."

"And do you imagine that his nephew wouldn't take 'em over after he died? You soft ol' fule. That was his nephew you saw."

"But why should the boy Sayer want to stare at me in such a horrible sort o' way?"

"Probably 'cause you were a-starin' at him in such a horrible sort o' way."

"That I worn't! I… "

"That you were. You put the wind up him, an'all. He told me! He thought *you* were a ghost. I didn't work out myself what's been goin' on till just a few moments ago. Now I can see you boys ha' all been runnin' around the marsh scarin' the daylights out of one another. And out of half the rest of Norfolk, for that matter. What a rum team you are!"

That was half-an-hour or so ago, and the fowlers have been muttering and mumbling amongst themselves at the back of the lounge ever since. Muttering, and aiming the odd scowl at Polly behind the bar, who has been cleaning her mugs and at intervals looking back at them and shaking her head.

The sense of unease is intensified as two sets of footsteps are heard marching crisply up the frosty gravel path towards the door.

It is briskly opened, and in walks the stately, caped form of Constable Chapman, closely – very closely – followed by Exciseman Gooch, who is looking drawn, shaken and unhappy. PC Chapman nods to Polly and her uncle. Gooch darts quick looks at the multitude as though meeting anyone's eyes will cause him to turn to stone.

The assembled company regards these latest additions with slack-jawed astonishment. Only Polly is collected enough to slide a box of unlabelled bottles under the counter with her toe and then say in a bold voice:

"Good evening, gentlemen. Could one of you shut the door, please?"

PC Chapman gestures to Gooch, who complies – but only after he has tried a haughty scowl at the girl who made him look such a buffoon earlier today. But his attempt at menace isn't convincing – he's never actually set foot in the Bowling Green before, and he resembles a cat that has walked around a corner on to a pack of dozing terriers.

PC Chapman, however, is not overawed in the least. He strides over to a chair near the main body, takes his cape and helmet off, brushes the snow from them into the grate, sits down and comes straight to the point:

"Now, you men, I want t'know who's been shootin' at Mr Gooch here."

No-one answers, partly because they're all too stunned to speak – events are moving rather faster than is normal for the 'Green.

He goes on: "I aren't sayin' 'at was deliberate, but 'at *is* serious. Someone hollered at him about blastin' him to hell and then let fly with a heavy-bore gun, and Mr Gooch tell me if he hadn't ha' ducked at the hollerin' that could ha' took his head off. Look at his telescope."

They all look at Gooch's telescope. A sorry sight. The glass is cracked and etched with dots like the surface of the moon and the brass frame has unsightly dents in it. The stand, which Gooch is still clutching as a Roman sentry might his spear, is pitted with shot holes all the way up its varnished length.

Harrison is the first to speak, and Gooch has the feeling that he's trying not to laugh.

"When was this?"

"You must know when 'at was. You must a' heard the noise if you were sittin' in here," says Constable Chapman.

"We did hear something 'bout thirty minute ago, Mr Chapman, but we couldn't make up our minds as to just what 'at could ha' been. For my part, I can't imagine what any man with half a brain would be doin' anywhere near the estuary on a night like this. Er, savin' Exciseman Gooch here, of course."

Gooch glares at him, and whispers something to Chapman.

The constable asks "Were you down by the red mill the other evening, Mr Harrison?"

"Yes, that I was."

"Now what you were doin' down there?"

"My job. I'm a painter."

Gooch looks at him with a true Tabernacler's disgust for such an occupation, and then whispers something else to Chapman (who's looking a little bored at being whispered to), and he gives him a large wooden belaying pin.

"Do any of you recognise this? Few nights ago 'at was thrown at Mr Gooch down at Sandcroft's rond, and 'at… er… hit him on the head." Chapman's voice goes hoarse toward the end of this statement, and he has to cough a little.

Poker asks "And what was Mr Gooch doing down there, then?"

"He was… he was… carrying out an investigation," says Chapman, as he regains control.

"Serve him right, then," is muttered from somewhere at the back of the group.

This brings Gooch to life. "Don't you get saucy, do I shall call a constab…, do we shall…, do you'll all be in trouble."

"Mr Bessey," says Chapman, ignoring that last exchange, "have these men been here all evening?"

"That they have," says Bessey, relaxing now that he has realised the unlabelled bottles near his daughter's right foot aren't the reason for the visit. "All on 'em. All evening."
"In that case the man who fired the shot might well still be down there," says Chapman, and he gathers up his helmet and cape.

"Yes, but you int go' find him tonight, Mr Chapman. The tide'll be comin' in by now, and if he ha' got any sense, he'll a' used it to go up river. And look at the weather."

They all do. In the darkness immediately beyond the panes they can see snow falling, and they know it will be settling readily on the frozen ground.

"Well, I can't let it drop – if you men hear anything, I shall expect to be told,' says Chapman in a voice which suggests he expects no such thing. He walks out, followed like a shadow by the exciseman.

For a few moments there is a bewildered calm in the Bowling Green as men take in the events.

There then starts to be heard a sound not often associated with that establishment – more a sound you would likely hear coming out of those rowdier hostelries further into town, like the Crown or the Ship. It starts off innocently enough as a gentle wheezing which spreads across the gathering. Then men begin to shake in unison. And this is followed by intakes of breath, and then, like a great wave breaking on a shore there are bellows of laughter which engulf the room and make the glasses vibrate. Men are helpless, and slap and thump each other and hit the tables. It subsides slightly, giving room for certain spluttered observations which in turn cause more shouts of mirth. Tiger is again disturbed from his slumbers by the uproar, and even Wellington seems to rock gently on her perch as the noise courses around the 'Green and past the glowing embers of the stove and up the chimney and out to meet the falling snow in the chilly darkness of the Breydon night.

Bessey, who is relieved at the departure of the officials is also laughing – and even Polly can't help a smile or two at poor Gooch's discomfiture.

"But where will Tealer be now?" she asks Poker when the rumpus finally subsides.

"Long gone, I should reckon," is his reply. "Blust, I heard o' men peppering keepers and bailiffs at a distance, but – lettin' ol' Jenny loose on an exciseman – well, that do take some beatin'! No, he'll be long gone. 'Sides, he won't want t'be hangin' about on the water on a night like this. Blust, he must'a had a basinful of that fool a-pokin' about at his uncle's cabin to want to go and do a thing like that. Blust me!"

Eventually the drinkers of the 'Green come to the end of one of their more memorable evenings and make their way, still chuckling and chortling, out of the door and into the muffled black and white world beyond. Some disperse to houses in Cobholm while others start the long slippery trudge round the estuary wall to their huts.

Bessey retires for the night and the 'Green becomes quiet. The heavy odours of ale and tobacco begin to mingle with the lighter musks of the oak and ash furniture, and soon the only sounds are the occasional sputter of the coals in the stove and the sighing of Tiger dreaming of his younger days, when neither cats nor excisemen ever dared come within a furlong of his yard.

Just Polly is left. Her job as always is to clear the debris of a winter's evening from the settles, benches and tables. Then she sits down in one of the empty armchairs and thinks about what has happened. She realises that through all the jollity she hasn't been entirely happy. She gazes beyond the window into the snow-heavy night and wonders where Tealer is.

Finally she takes her lamp and makes her way to her tiny room overlooking the yard. The flakes are now coming so fast that she can't even make out the shape of the rain-butt just below her window. The familiar lights of Yarmouth are invisible. She undresses and climbs into bed, where she dozes fitfully for much of the night.

She's awake again long before light. She dozes, and thinks, and dozes.

Then of a sudden she sits up, wide awake, and says aloud:

"He doesn't know! He didn't know 'at was Gooch! He must ha' thought…"

All kinds of implications race through her like flames of a spreading fire. She throws her clothes on, wraps a shawl around her and without thinking goes downstairs into the scullery and opens the door. A numbing blast sends a cloud of flakes into the room. The snow is feet thick around the door. She comes to her senses. To venture out would be suicide.

Thus begins for Polly a miserable wait until the grey light of morning begins to bring the featureless snowfields slowly into view. When dawn finally breaks she's already sitting in the empty guestroom with an ancient spyglass pushed up against the smoothest pane. At first she can't see a thing, and it takes several breaths and much rubbing with the hem of her dress before she can make out more than shapes through the dusty lenses. Gradually the north shore of Breydon becomes visible. At one point she finds movement on the horizon, but it is a fox, foraging up and down the shore for casualties of the night. Then she makes out the two posts which mark either side of Duffel's Drain where it enters the estuary. She concentrates on the estuary around this point until she thinks her head will split.

And then she catches sight of a rise in the snow, a discoloration in the uniformity of the estuary immediately below the horizon, and this makes her catch her breath. She stares at it and stares, until her heart beats harder for want of air and causes the image in the telescope to jump up and down. She stops and takes another breath and looks again, and then realises what she's looking at.

"Oh, no," she gasps, "Oh, no," and she throws the telescope down on the bed and runs out of the room, down the steep stairs of the inn and out into the white, wrapping her shawl around her as she goes.

Back on the Ice

The breaking of a winter's day on an English estuary...

Long before any real light is visible in the sky the dawn is anticipated by the grunting of the brents as they reassure one another that they're all still together and that all's well. They are huddled in the middle of the estuary, well away from land and beyond the reach of foxes and men. As you listen to them you are lulled by their distance, so that the sudden, strident *te-te-teup* of a redshank only a few feet away, but still invisible in the half-light, makes you start. The grunting of the brents continues, and then you jump again as a wailing peewit shoots just over your head with a violent soughing of wings. Then there are the telling whistles of the wigeon flocks – they also sound close but are really hundreds of feet up. A buzzing, a swishing and a series of tiny splashes are the only clue that teal are dropping into the gloom all around you. Next, the piping of oystercatchers, the squeaks of dunlin and the mournful monotones of golden plover combine in a chorus of primordial melancholy. The rasping croak of a passing heron seems at odds with the languid, graceful form which appears out of the dusk to make its way down to its first stand of the day. The approach of the curlew is more tuneful – the call of no other bird speaks so completely of the marsh.

The stage is set for the main players. Against the faint light of the coming dawn, lines appear, twisting, coiling and writhing like snakes. At first they are silent through sheer distance, but as they approach the air slowly fills with a ceaseless cacophony of cries that demand the total attention of the watcher. In waves of energy, and a seamless barrage of sound, the lines descend and show themselves to be skein after skein of geese – whitefronts, greylags and 'pinkfeet' – which have now left some secret roost and are heading over the estuary wall to the grazing marshes beyond. And in periods when the Scandinavian lands are truly arctic, these geese may be joined by wild swans, whose ringing calls led the Old English to give them the name 'hwoper'.

Neither on Breydon, nor along any other stretch of Norfolk mud, nor indeed on any British estuary from the Solway Firth to Pevensey Levels can there be a fowling man so devoid of soul that he has not at least once in his life allowed the ghost of a smile to crack his windburnt face in pure wonderment at the morning flight of wildfowl.

Yet these birds are driven by the simple imperative to eat. The massed ranks are a necessary defence in a landscape where to be single is to be singled out. And so, on most winter evenings and most winter mornings, the great movement of birds back and forth between roost and feeding ground is repeated – the theme never varies, yet no two flights are ever quite the same.

But there are the times when there is no flight at all. The reason is usually severe cold.

It is such a cold this morning that has crushed the *Gariensis* into silence.

Yes, there have been some grim winters in recent years, but no-one remembers anything like this. The land is bound in iron, the waters of the dykes are thick, black glass, and the great, bountiful estuary of Breydon has become a barren place of ice-floes and whistling north winds…

The snow that last night forced Polly back indoors was heavy but it wasn't prolonged, and later the clouds dispersed. Any vestiges of warmth have since drifted up toward the black spangled sky, leaving the earth below colder than ever. So now, come the morning, there are neither flocks of waders nor flights of wigeon to usher in the dawn. Only the tireless great black-back and one or two hopeful crows circle and spin above the motionless craft, waiting for Tealer Sayer to die. Their occasional calls are all that break the silence of the muffled world they scan.

Then they spot movement, not from the boat but away on the 'Wall', the earthen rampart which hems the estuary in and separates it from the marshes beyond. They swing away. The figures which have driven them off are moving urgently through the snow, sometimes slipping, sometimes tripping on the frozen lumps of mud hidden below the white powder. Duffel's Drain is now covered with ice, and one brave soul, the lightest of the group, dares to step out on it. There's not the slightest creak, because the freeze is already three inches thick. And so the other figures, four in all, run after him as he makes his way to where the *Sturgeon* lies jammed in the ice with the barrel of White Jenny still pointing blankly into the reeds. And behind her, and staring down her line, is the deathly form of Tealer Sayer.

With little ado the five men load the stiff body of Sayer on to a stretcher and begin the stumbling journey back round the estuary to the 'Green.

They bring him into the lounge and lay him down next to the stove which Polly has already prepared. Like so many creatures of the estuary at this time, he's barely living.

Medical help is sent for, and in the meantime Tealer is left in the care of Polly and a couple of the fowlers.

If there's any growing to womanhood left for Bessey's young daughter, it's now. It's two years since her mother died, and she's become her father's mainstay. She has ministered well to the good-hearted but cantankerous, unbending group of men who frequent the 'Green, and she's learnt much about the world. But her ceaseless round of chores has left little time to enjoy any of the adventures that seem to be filling the lives of more affluent friends like Maud Pritchard. Most fellows would say she was a 'fair-lookin' mawther', distinctly comely in her woollen frock, with crisp apron tied tight round a slim waist, and regular, smiling face framed in a spotless starched bonnet. Yet at seventeen she hasn't known so much as a beardless delivery boy scratching at the scullery door for a furtive squeeze. What pleasures of womanhood she has so far enjoyed she's had to enjoy second-hand. She can still only guess at the sensations of courtship that her friend Maud used to describe in such detail, let alone the more secret matters that even Maud only ever hinted at. Nowadays it is just the odd dance or fair that allows her to escape the cycle of service and drudgery that is her working day. Mostly she cheerfully accepts her lot; but there have been times recently when she has found herself gazing into the suds of the laundry sink or leaning on her shovel after banking the tinkling embers of the stove. And she has wondered just what might be passing her by.

Now, at a stroke, this same girl finds herself not only having to watch, but to direct, the concerned marshmen as they hasten to peel every stitch of Tealer's clothing from his ashen frame and dunk him into the tin bath to thaw out. She also has to supervise the unceremonious funnelling of brandy down his throat. The pallor in his face, the wordless muttering from his bleeding lips, and his half-lidded, unseeing stare soon drive out any bashfulness on Polly's part. Concern is her only feeling as she surveys the helpless form of the man whom her all-knowing friend Maud used to talk about in such hushed tones. This man may once have been at the centre of her girlish fantasies. This man may once have been able to cause her to blush and look down simply by catching her eye. But now this same man is very ill, and depends on her for life itself, and instinctively she responds. In an urgent, clear voice she directs the men to pour another copper of warmish water gently into the bath. She sets to work rubbing, kneading and pummelling Tealer's knotted muscles into recovery. (The older of the two men, Fiddler Goodens, helps her in this frantic massaging. Years before Polly was born he once had to do the same, and many times over, at a place not two hundred yards from this spot.) And when Tealer moans in agony as even the tepid water brings a return of blood to his frozen limbs, it is Polly who is ready with reassuring words.

Finally she feels confident enough to send the attendant fowlers on their way, and she covers with heavy towelling the areas of Tealer's body not immersed in the tub.

But it is only very much later when Tealer's cries have ceased and his cold, taut body has warmed and relaxed to her touch that she feels more at ease. He seems to be out of immediate danger. Only then does Polly find the slightest curiosity vying with her worries for his well-being.

Polly is a practical girl. Trust her soon to have the matter well in hand!

And where has Tealer Sayer himself been while all this has been going on around him?

Earlier this morning, close to death, he could only watch dully as a small line of people approached. This wasn't the team of hardy marshmen sent to rescue him, all buttoned and caped against the elements. This was a motley crew of men and women dressed in summer clothes, or their Sunday best, or their winding sheets, making their way in procession across the icy flats. Jointy Pole was in front with Charlie Harrison, and between them they were holding something like one of Charlie's pictures covered with a cloth. Behind them came Maud Pritchard and Polly Bessey, both supporting the battered form of Sarah Stolworthy with blood pouring out of her, leaving a trail of crimson on the ice. Alvares Williams brought up the rear arm-in-arm with Tealer's parents – he very smart in his red-stained cotton suit, they equally smart in the shrouds they'd been buried in. The little company gathered solemnly round the frozen form of Tealer. Pole and Harrison placed the object in front of Tealer's face while the others looked on.

No-one smiled.

Then from behind them a kraken burst up out of the ice and loomed right over the top of the little group, dropping one great tentacle to pull back the drape that covered Charlie's picture. Tealer peered through the cold; in the frame he thought he saw a face.

"You don't paint faces, Charlie. You never have," said Tealer.

But Charlie said nothing.

The kraken rapped the picture with its tentacle and Tealer looked harder. He saw that the one face had become several and that they were the faces of hideous, un-human creatures. They became clearer. Now they were the glassy-eyed victims of the Cory Bridge. They all glared straight at Tealer. Then they were one face again, a deathly cherub carved in the image of little Georgie, surveying Tealer with its bland marble eyes and reading every nuance of guilt in his soul. But in the time Tealer took to blink, pimples and pustules appeared all over its bloodless flesh and the all-seeing gaze had become a reptile stare. A Gooch stare. Dead and cold as a fish. A pike, perhaps. But now a pike with furious eyes that promised vengeance. A pike with the face of Norris! Then the eyes glowed redder still, like the eyes of a mad dog. A rabid dog, dripping venomous froth from its maw. Or a rabid preacher, with froth oozing down his beard as he denounced Tealer to the world. And then the beard was frothless, and the eyes weren't mad but merely sad, and Tealer's father James was quietly shaking his head at the pass his son had come to. And finally, there was Georgie again, shaking what was left of his head at the pass his friend had come to.

Tealer dropped back down on to the burning cold of White Jenny.

"No, I know these now," he whispered into the depths of the *Sturgeon*. "These are all fantasies. Tricks and illusions. I ha' faced 'em all my life, and they can do me no more mischief! They're only masks. And I... ha' got Jenny. Jenny's real."

But when he brought his head back up and his faltering eyes slowly focussed he found the little delegation still there, and in the middle the kraken still had its own, great, dish-sized eye fixed on him. And it tapped hard on the painting again. And again. And again. And each time harder.

Tealer knew in his heart what it wanted. He knew what they all wanted. They were here to tell him that the running, hiding, pretending, turning away, laughing off, playing down and ignoring of the last twenty years must end.

They were telling him that all the different masks he'd stuck on his pursuer must now be pulled off. That it was time for the Spectre behind the spectres – the Tormentor behind the tormentors – the Face behind the Faces of the Fiend of Breydon – the one true Demon in the life of John 'Tealer' Sayer – to make itself known.

Yet Tealer Sayer was not ready to be turned to stone by any old Gorgon that happened upon him in the snow. There was still some fight in him! He looked down again, shaking his head at the timbers of the punt in defiance. He refused to face the loathsome thing that had hovered in the shadowy areas of his life since his boyhood. He refused to be so much in thrall to it!

Instead he reached for the cord that would once more unleash the dreadful force of White Jenny. Yes, then let this malignancy know what vengeance Tealer's Queen of the Marshes can wreak! She wiped away all the other visions! Now watch as she blows this one into oblivion!

Tealer made to reach forward. But his arm was a lifeless block of wood that dangled from his shoulder. The lethal length of cord lay not three inches from his dead fingers, but it could have been at the other end of the world.

So there was to be no saving blast.

And the mighty mistress of Breydonside was to stay silent.

And the Nemesis would be faced. No longer disguised as Nobody, or Stolworthy, or Norris, or the bad dog Shuck, or the screamer of a far-off scream in the small hours, or the gleam in a herring gull's eye.

Not even as the undead corpse of a wronged friend.

Not this time, Tealer.

Tealer knew that the Truth was there, waiting for him to meet its gaze.

And finally, defeated, he had no choice but to to do so.

And when, at last, their eyes met, and he knew his torturer, he could offer no more than a weary groan.

"Yes…," he said. "Yes. I reckon I knew all along 'at was you."

And then Charlie stepped forward and covered the frame, tucked it under his arm and led the little procession away. The kraken slithered back under the ice, and Tealer was left behind.

Then all memory of this strange little meeting faded, because Tealer's very brain was beginning to fail in the cold. He placed his head on Jenny's icy breech, oblivious to the burn of her freezing surface, and he prepared to die.

# Jenny's Last Victim

But AS WE know, Tealer wasn't destined to die out on the ice. Foolish fellow! – it was the thickness of his uncle's greatcoat that saved him, though it was a close-run thing.

After two hours or so in Polly's care, his eyes, which have remained half-closed from the effects of brandy, warm water and exhaustion, are beginning to flicker. He's still delirious, and from time to time he mutters unintelligibly. The only words Polly thinks she can recognise are 'stones' and 'frigates' and the name 'William'. At one point he lifts an arm out of the water, and looks at it in a mildly distracted manner. If anything, he seems to have been enjoying a rather pleasant dream. His hand drops back and with his eyes shut and he slowly feels for something in the area of his waist.

Then of a sudden his eyes snap open wide and he shoots upright, clutching the sides of the tub and sending water flying over the floor of the saloon. "Where's my pouch? Where am I? Where's Jenny?"

Polly tries to ease him back into the water, and he turns round and looks at her. "Maudy, what are you doing here? Where's my pouch? Where's Jenny?"

Polly says "Your pouch is here by the bath. Stay still."

"Where's Jenny? My God, where's Jenny? He'll come for her!"

"Tealer, get you back in the water and lay still."

"No! He said he'd come for her if I ever left her out! He…"

"The men are lookin' after your gun," Polly lies. "Now get you back in the water and lay still."

For a moment Tealer stares uncertainly at the little barmaid. Then the spurt of strength deserts him and he sinks back into the tub. He tries to think things through but his mind is still dulled from the cold and he returns to a state of semi-consciousness.

Much later a physician is called who pronounces him over the worst. He'll lose two finger tips, and for months he'll also carry a mark on his forehead where it rested on the cold metal of Jenny's barrel.

But within hours he begins to think and speak more lucidly, though he still rambles.

It's a couple of days later, as he is lying in the bed of the spare room at the 'Green, that his eyes focus unsteadily on Polly.

"Polly. Polly Bessey."

"Yes. Are you feelin' better?"

"Polly, give me my pouch."

Polly does so, though not without some anxiety, as she knows the pouch is empty. Yet when Tealer takes it and feels nothing inside it, he almost smiles, and murmurs "Good. I weren't dreamin'." Then he stops smiling and a shadow crosses his face. "Unless…" he says to himself. Then he says in a louder voice to Polly. "Polly Bessey, there's a bag with some things in it lay under the bunk of my house boat. I need it. Can you bring it, girl?"

Polly nods, and Tealer goes back to sleep. That evening when he wakes, there is Polly watching him with a large canvas bag by her side.

"What's in it?" he asks.

She feels around and brings out a box.

"That's the only thing there?"

"Yes."

"See, there's a secret drawer at the bottom. You push it from underneath."

She does so and gives a little start when the compartment springs open.

"Now, what can you see in it?"

"Tealer, there ent nothin' in it at all. What are you…?"

"No, girl, thas good." says Tealer, "Thas what I wanted. Good. They're all gone." Polly puts the box at the end of the bed and sits down to watch him. He has lain down again and seems to have gone back to sleep. But without opening his eyes he says, slowly and drowsily:

"That box… that box of paints you can give to any painting fellow that want it. What about Charlie Harrison? Do he still come up here to drink? If he do, give them paints to him."

Polly nods again. "We see him in here from time to time. He come up to see you when you were very poorly. You wouldn't remember, though."

"Yes, well give 'em to him. He can have 'em. I don't want to see 'em any more.'

And with that, and with his eyes still closed, Tealer smiles unreservedly for the first time Polly can remember. He nods, and still with eyes closed he murmurs, "You're a good 'ol mawther, Polly Bessey."

If Tealer Sayer had been listening to the literature on one of those book-reading nights with Maud, he'd know that, according to Shakespeare's Hamlet, "conscience makes cowards of us all". But he hadn't really been concentrating on the famous soliloquy... not after the point where Maud had read of 'when we shuffle off this mortal coil'. The lamp wasn't properly trimmed on that far-off evening and it was throwing a flickering light on the higher contours of her form, leaving her eyes as dark green pools that darted alternately between the Shakespeare and the intent face of Tealer. He forgot everything in the soliloquy because Maud read on into the scene, right up to the bit about the 'nymph' in her 'orisons'. 'Nymph' was a word that seemed tailored to Maud's shapely mouth, and so *that* was the quotation Tealer took with him from that evening's reading, and the line about 'conscience' passed him by.

Perhaps this was a pity – if he'd understood it, he might even have saved himself much self-torment.

But then... perhaps not. Had he not decided to settle his account with his demon out there in the snow, might he still be just another solitary duck-gunner, at once seeking welcome refuge in the anonymity of the twilight, and yet fearful of the images it brings?

More of that later. The point here is that 'conscience' is now also making a very nervous young fellow of Ted Wood, who was the light-footed boy first across the ice to the trapped *Sturgeon* when the men set out to bring the frozen Tealer back to the 'Green. As they loaded Tealer on to the stretcher Ted's gaze was torn between the terrible look in the dying man's eyes and the legendary white gun of Jack Sandcroft. The apprentice rope-maker has always listened opened-mouthed to tales of White Jenny; on that silent snowy morning with the rescue party he found it difficult to believe that the great gun was lying not six feet from him. And then he noticed that the others seemed ready just to leave her there. Young Ted found that hard to believe!

Jenny's Last Victim

Well, it's now three days after Tealer's rescue. There's still no change in the weather. Snow flurries alternate with bouts of freezing calm. No-one has been able to get even to the shore of Breydon because the snow has collected in treacherous drifts which cover the deep channels and dykes that surround the estuary.

Young Wood has been looking for the first sign of a let-up, and when it comes in the form of a whole day without snow he waits for a time when he won't be missed at the rope-works and stumbles his way along the icy streets out of the town. He plunges on through the deep snow round the Breydon wall to Duffel's where the *Sturgeon* is still lying fast in the grip of the ice.

The youth approaches the punt as if it contained a body lying in state. Gingerly, he clambers into the vessel and eases his way up to the breech of the gun. Instinctively he runs a finger along her lines just as every man has done who has ever come anywhere near her. Ted has never managed to get his hands on anything more lethal than a rusting thirty-two bore, and the sheer size of this creature enthralls him. He takes in every fraction of every inch of her, from the gaping muzzle right down to the hammer.

That's when he notices that Jenny is on half-cock.

And his young heart beats very fast. Cocked! And being only on half-cock none of the men noticed! Ted thinks about this – Tealer must have managed to prime the weapon without going back ashore. Ted marvels, knowing how difficult this is with any large gun, let alone a leviathan like White Jenny. But he doesn't yet know the strength of a desperate man. Now a dreadful temptation comes over Ted to pull Jenny's cord. No-one's about, and by the time anyone gets over here to find out what's going on he'll be able to vanish into the gathering darkness undetected. On an impulse he pulls Jenny's hammer to full-cock.

But then the truth of the observation of Shakespeare's Danish prince is demonstrated. As he reaches for the cord to fire the weapon Ted suddenly finds himself wondering if he is fit to lay hands on this most hallowed of Breydon guns. If he were precipitate, he might just pull the cord and... Yes, but no-one has ever been precipitate with White Jenny – not in the cold light of day at any rate. Her very size and her formidable reputation have always ensured that. Everyone knows what happened to Sandcroft. Ted's no exception, and his eyes are drawn to the breeching lines. They look secure enough, but he doesn't know enough about punt guns to be sure. This wave of doubt develops: the thought comes to Ted that it is impossible that he can be in such a forbidden place and not be watched, even though the flat landscape around him is utterly deserted.

So he decides not to fire.

How can he not at least lie with her, though? Will he not kick himself later that he did not at least lie down in the punt and feel what it must be like to aim the great gun? He casts around for a reason to justify this and decides that – yes – he should be responsible and leave Jenny in a safer condition than she's in at the moment. With this excuse to 'conscience', he reaches forward to take the cap from Jenny's pan and ease the hammer down. But the spring on the hammer is looser than he expects it to be, and in brushing past it to get at the cap, Ted knocks it forward.

So shocked is he that he does not so much hear as feel the famous report, a 'Whumpf!', that seems to blow his spirit from his body.

Jenny has once again given voice.

Once again the roar circles the *Gariensis*, and once again the cold, tired birds of Breydon Water hurl themselves up into the air before wearily dropping down again a few minutes later. Ted Wood is vaguely aware of a myriad of tiny green lights sparkling for a split second in the clear evening sunlight – but nothing else, because for fully five minutes he buries his head behind the magazine, hardly daring to move.

Finally, and still very shocked, he puts his head up over the gunwale and looks around him. There are no people about, and from far away on the other side of Yarmouth, over the still ice, comes the steady thump of the steam-hammer and the whistle of a train coming into the station. Beyond the Wall the marshes are silent but for the wheezing of two short-eared owls whose quarterings have brought them into angry contact.

Then he sees a single duck flapping on the ice, which he realises must have been in Jenny's line of fire. Without further ceremony he races across the frozen mud, despatches the bird and puts it in his knapsack.

Then he steals guiltily away along the Wall, glad that the gathering darkness will have lessened his chances of being spotted.

Oh, but Ted *has* been spotted! No less an exciseman than Titus Gooch has been watching him from his vantage at the top of a windpump upstream from Duffel's Drain.

Gooch has been using this pump as an observation tower for some months. It is one of the tallest windpumps on the marshes, and gives a commanding view of the estuary. He always tries to creep up to it unannounced – that's so that the sly, insolent fellow in charge of it has no chance to warn people that Gooch is there. He was delighted when he first discovered this lookout. However, for some reason, there's never been much in the way of unlawful activity on the nights he has chosen to wait up there, which he's found a bit irritating. (We can reckon he'd find it a bit more irritating if he ever noticed that the huge sails of the windpump always seem to be left as an upright cross rather than at their usual diagonal position whenever, and only whenever, he's hiding inside.)

Tonight, though, it seems his wisdom in selecting his new vantage is at last being rewarded. He has just heard Jenny's great report and after a (perhaps understandable) dive for shelter, he has recovered quick enough to see Wood stealing away up the Wall.

At last, after the frights and humiliations, revenge beckons to Titus Gooch. He's stirred to action! Grunting with excitement and determination, he almost falls down the ladders that separate the two floors of the mill in his race to get out on to the marsh. Once out he hides up against the large channel known as the 'soke dyke' on the marsh side of the Wall. Eventually the crunch of Ted Wood's feet tell of the lad's approach. And out jumps Gooch:

"Stop!" he shouts, and Wood stops, not yet being old enough to find Gooch merely ridiculous.

"Give me that there bag," he says, and Wood, wanting no trouble, hands it over. "I know who sent you here, boy! And why! Don't think you fooled me by the firin' of that there infernal gun. Now off with you!"

Ted Wood slinks away into the failing light.

"I have you now, Mr Sayer," mutters Gooch to himself. He can't see into the bag in the gloom and he dares not tip things out into the snow-covered sedge of the footpath for fear of losing evidence, so he hurries home to Gorleston.

Once in his front room Gooch turns the bag over, and the mallard falls out together with a few breadcrumbs and an empty clay bottle, the remnants of

Wood's lunch. Disappointed, he then takes the bag and shakes it up and down several times.

Nothing.

He feels along the lining of the bag.

Nothing.

He feels along the strap.

Nothing.

Then his wife comes into the kitchen and demands to know why he's late. He's lost for an answer, so he shows her the duck.

"A free dinner, my dear! Just fancy!" The argument is indeed a powerful one to Mrs Gooch, and she grunts and says nothing.

The following evening she roasts the duck and they sit down to eat it. After a few mouthfuls Mrs Gooch lets out an angry squawk and spits what appears to be a green pebble out on to the table. At the same time Gooch feels something hard take a chip from one of his molars.

He takes the object out of his mouth and looks at it. Then he looks at that of his wife. Then he frowns for a few moments. Then he has an insight so brilliant it dazzles even him, and he makes the rare gesture of ignoring the rantings of his spouse and begins to tear excitedly at the carcass of the duck.

Nine o'clock the next morning finds Gooch striding briskly through the yellow-grey snow of the market-place toward Bramley's, opposite the church of St Nicholas. Bramley the jeweller has just unlocked his door for the day, and Gooch bustles in immediately. He puts about ten greenish stones on Bramley's counter, stands back and looks at him triumphantly.

Bramley is a very precise little man with the air of one who often has things put on his counter by people who then stand back and look at him triumphantly. He studies the stones with an indulgent smile.

"Ah," he says, "Ah. Well, now. Goodness. Un-cut emeralds. Yes. Might I ask you where you got them, Mr Gooch?"

"Ha!" says Gooch, "I was *right*." And for once a genuine grin appears on his vinegar face. He tells Bramley how he's been tracking the movements of a suspicious character since the fellow first arrived in town last summer on a merchantman from South America. Then two nights ago he nearly cornered the same man on the estuary as said man was (obviously) trying to smuggle *something* from a small cabin near the old fort to some hideaway across the estuary. It could well have been contraband, but even if it were merely stolen goods and no direct business of the Excise, Gooch still felt it was his duty to intervene and apprehend the suspect. He explains how the fellow threatened to 'blast him to hell' and he ducked before making his escape, which was lucky, because then the fellow fired a punt-gun at him and nearly hit him – and then in trying to sit it out overnight on the water the same fellow got caught in the ice and had to be rescued in the morning.

The constable is still waiting to question the suspect, Gooch adds.

Bramley nods, totally absorbed. "Yes, I think I heard that there was recently some kind of... *to-do*... on the estuary."

"Oh, yes," says Gooch, "but Constable Chapman won't have much to get from him now. I've worked it all out m'self. Chapman would ha' told me if any goods had been found on the man when they rescued him, but nothin' was. So I *knew* there must be suffin' hidden in that there boat."

"And you searched it and found these?"

"Just one or two – layin' loose in the timbers – and at first I didn't know what they were – 'course, if I seen 'em with a lot of others, well, I would ha' guessed right away they were suffin' important. Right away. But, yer see, the cunnin' devil had hid the rest up the barrel of the gun. *Very* clever. But I *did know* there had to be suffin else in or near that boat *somewhere*, so I kept watch from one of my Observation Posts. Sure enough, not a day later, a lad come along – clear to me that the suspect had sent him to fetch 'em. Thing is, this fool of a boy went and set the gun off. Well now, at the time I thought that was just to trick anyone around into thinking he was doin' some fowlin', instead of collectin' the goods. But I now realise he dint mean to fire it off at all. Anyway, I catch the lad but - well - I let *him* go. Yer see, Mr Bramley, I was arter the mackerel, not the sprat. And now I got the evidence! And once you ha' valued it I have a notion the Authorities will be very satisfied with the outcome! *Very* satisfied!"

Bramley frowns: "But what led you to believe that there were more of these stones hidden in the... gun-barrel?"

"Ah! Well, would you believe, there was a duck on the ice nearby that was hit when the gun went off. Lucky for me I caught the lad when he was trying to make off with it. He was only too happy to get rid on it and escape so lightly, I can tell you. I, um, dissected the duck, and sure enough, there they were."

Bramley is still nonplussed. "But… if at the time you knew nothing of what was in the barrel, what prompted you to search the corpse of the duck?"

"Er, yes,' says Gooch, clearing his throat. "Well, as 'at happen, I was… that is to say… Mrs Gooch and me, we bit on to them when we were… *eatin'* the duck. That seemed a pity…um…"

"Oh, quite right" says Bramley. "Waste not, want not." Then he thinks for a moment or two. "But… *another* puzzling aspect to me is that of why the gun was primed again."

"Primed?" says Gooch.

"Yes," says Bramley. "If this miscreant, having first tried to shoot you, had then hidden the gems in the barrel of the gun – as you say he did – it is hard to know why he would prime the gun first. Where would be the point? Especially if he then risked losing them in the estuary should the weapon for any reason go off."

Gooch thinks for a moment. "Well… well… perhaps he thought that that way he could destroy the evidence if 'at looked as though he was go' be caught on the water. Or perhaps… yes…! perhaps he din't realise I'd made off, and instead he thought I was still about, and so he wanted to have another go at me, and…and… loaded the weapon with the only thing he had to hand! Yes, yes, of course," he says, as he warms to his own theory, "thas obvious when you think about it!"

Bramley nodded slowly. "Ye-es, I suppose either scenario is… plausible. But whatever the case, I have to say he went to a great deal of trouble for no good reason."

"No good reason? What d'yer mean?" says Gooch through his triumphant smirk.

"Simply that the specimens you have here," says Bramley as he picks up one more of the stones in his tweezers and inspects it through his eyeglass, "are worthless."

The smirk dissolves. "*Worthless*! But…but you now said they were emeralds!"

"Indeed they are - but full of flaws, Mr Gooch. I've never seen such rubbish. Left over from the cutting process, if you want to know. I have no idea where this fellow who took such a dislike to you out on the estuary obtained them, but I do know that more than once I have had merchant officers in here trying to sell me stones of similar… er… quality. Almost always it transpires that they have bought them from some sharp dealer in Brazil or Chile at what they have been persuaded is an advantageous rate. The suggestion made to them by these rascals is that they sell them on in Europe for a small fortune. Of course it is all very believable. Indeed, I understand they will go to some lengths in their deceptions. For instance, one commonly-reported ruse is one in which a local accomplice, supposedly unknown to the first villain, masquerades as an expert from one of the big Jewish gem-houses. This second scoundrel appears fortuitously from nowhere to corroborate the value. And… um…. " Bramley's voice drops to a discreet whisper. "…um, I am even told that the most sedulous of these criminals are not above firstly encouraging their victims to consort with ladies of… um… er… um… *loose*… um… virtue, whose commission of course is to establish that the victim has access to enough funds to make the operation worthwhile. Men deemed to be pursers or paymasters are regular targets. So you can easily imagine that these fellows who come into my shop expecting to realise a fortune in precious stones can become quite… *upset*… when I tell them the truth. In fact, on one occasion, I had to send my assistant for a constable." Bramley shakes his head sadly. "Mr Gooch, you wouldn't believe how much wickedness I am witness to in my business. Or how much *foolishness*!"

The freeze continues for weeks more. Men and women become used to the unforgiving hardness beneath their feet, and after several painful falls they learn the winter shuffle of middle Europeans. There are no more releasing thaws, and layer after layer of frost settles on the snow. The weather is by turns dull and bell-clear. Sometimes a cruel east wind blows, sometimes the landscape has the quietness of a tomb. But there's no thaw.

The whole of Breydon is now locked. Duck and geese are gaunt statues on the ice. They are too cold and weak to resist the attack of the starving foxes that tip-toe across the forbidding mud to break their necks and chew on their shrivelled flesh. The drains are covered with ice, and even the brackish main channel is now sluggish. In Duffel's Drain, White Jenny remains pointing in the same direction as she has since Tealer Sayer was dragged unconscious from the hull of the *Sturgeon*. She doesn't move. No-one approaches her – no-one approaches the estuary at all. Even the most vital sounds of the town are subdued. Everyone and everything – from the richest burger hunched over the fire-place in the too-large parlour of his splendid townhouse, through the pinched coster in the market trying to keep both his customers and himself interested in the paltry roots laid out on his stall, to the shivering sparrows huddled amongst the chimney pots above the heads of both – everyone and everything is now concerned with the single struggle to survive the destroying cold. Hordes of famished rats, bold and dangerous, have been surging out of the frozen sewers and into the streets, firstly at night and now by day. No other creature ventures abroad in Yarmouth, and out on the estuary only the cold-eyed black-backs and the bright-eyed crows scour the landscape to tear at the latest corpse in the short time before it freezes solid.

Thaw

Then one morning in mid-March, just before sunrise, the breeze moves into the south. From the darkness beyond the shuttered windows of the dwellings around Breydon comes the half-forgotten sound of dripping and trickling. Birds that have long been numbed into silence begin to call again as the weak winter dawn breaks across the marshes. Plants and objects which have been gripped in glass for weeks are freed. The loosening landscape seems to sigh.

The thaw continues on into the evening and through into the next morning. At first light of that second blessed day there comes from one corner of the estuary the hollow groan of timber chafing on ice. A little later a sleek blue-white punt carrying an enormous fowling-piece slips slowly down Duffel's. Moving alongside the punt are lumps of driftwood, slabs of melting ice, and the corpses of many birds.

The craft is drawn into the choppy waters of the estuary.

Up on the Wall above Duffel's Drain a heavily-cloaked figure watches her progress until her pale colours make her invisible from the shore.

When the boat reaches the meeting point of the Bure and the Yare rivers she is spun round by the joining currents. Then on through Yarmouth she floats, gaining speed with the gathering ebb. The streets are still choked with snow even after a day and night of thaw, and there are no early-morning loiterers on Yarmouth quay to witness her passage between the hulks of the ocean-going vessels.

This is to be the last voyage of the punt and the great white gun, because the relentless ice has taken its toll. The sturdy timbers of the *Sturgeon* are cracked, and she's shipping water. She enters and passes through the harbour, and exits out into the open sea, where the warm southerly begins to push her up the coast. Two or three wigeon, which last night were inland gorging themselves in their first proper feed in weeks, climb aboard to preen on the slowly sinking punt. Eventually they are forced off, for White Jenny's huge weight causes her loyal bearer to founder and slip forever beneath the waves of the Yarmouth Roads.

Back on the mud of Breydon the strong southerly muffles the sounds of the re-awakening town. It's a town that can now count its cost. And it's a town that can now, finally, bury its dead. Till now, mattocks, picks and spades have rung as sweetly as bells whenever they've struck the soil; but they've made no impression in it. The bodies of those who've had the misfortune to succumb in the last few weeks have had to be stored in sheds and mortuaries, some packed in ice, others pickled in brine, against the day that the earth of Lothingland is ready to admit them.

Two of these corpses have been a cause for more than the usual discussion.

In the case of one of them there seems to have been a resurrection...

It was the Devereaux's headkeeper who found Jointy Pole. It was a few days before the thaw, and he was seated comfortably on a wicker chair outside his hut on Decoy Lake. In fact, he was frozen to the chair. He was staring serenely across the glassy broad from which in life he'd harvested so many birds, pulled so many pike and pailed so much water. "Fust time I ever seen the ol boy with a smile," said the keeper when he described it later to the Devereaux's steward up at the big house. "You can see it for yourself. But you want to get down there 'fore the wind move into the south, do he'll start a-thawin' out and you'll miss it. Blust, he look so happy you'd think he'd just seen Jesus Chroist Almoighty a-walking 'crorst Decoy t'wards him."

The gamekeeper had also found Jointy's dog, one of Mart's successors. It was still alive, standing guard, but in a confused and pitiful state. The keeper wished to do right by his old friend the decoyman. He found a morsel in his pocket with one hand and aimed his short single-barrelled gun with the other. The grateful creature was still gulping down its treat as it was sent to join its master on the summery banks of some celestial decoy. The keeper roused some fellows and together they took the corpse, still seated in its wicker chair, and set it up inside the hut. The keeper laid the dog next to it. After the party had doffed their caps, bowed their heads and shuffled out, the keeper shut the door of the hut and locked it. Their idea was to take Jointy for interment – as and when Tibbenham the sexton could do anything more than jar his wrists on the iron clay of the churchyard.

But by the time the frost and ice had finally disappeared, so had Jointy. The undertaker's party could only look around the hut in blank incomprehension. Both man and dog had come to life with the thaw. Jointy had managed to unlock the door from the inside, and had been careful (as he always was) to lock it again from the outside.

If this turn of events was bizarre, what was yet more remarkable was the lack of any reaction amongst the locals when word of it got round. By way of comparison, just think of the Bowling Green. Think of the stir there was *there* at the merest suggestion that the spectre of Jack Sandcroft was haunting the Drains! Yet the reported resurrection of Harry Pole caused nary a twitter in the Decoy Inn, whispered or otherwise. Some of the youngsters were mildly curious. From the older drinkers there were a few grunts and a few knowing nods. Nothing more.

Only Tibbenham the sexton had anything much to say on the subject. Tibbenham was not a practised drinker, but whenever his wife made one of her periodic visits to her aged mother in the next village, Ben would make one of *his* periodic visits to the Decoy Inn, where he'd always end up having a tankard more than was good for him. On this occasion he started blaring to all and sundry how he knew 'every blessed inch' of that churchyard: yes, every headstone, footstone, pebble, and blade of grass. For instance, he bawled, a week back he'd noticed where lichens had just recently been dislodged from round the edges of the Deveraux vault. Just a few lichens and bits of moss, but you 'couldn't fool Ben Tibbenham'. Ben knew "what was up", did old Ben.

That was when the landlord decided that Ben had had enough. He was duly helped out of the house, his hat was shoved on his head, he was pointed in the direction of his cottage, and he was helped along his way with a hobnail planted firmly in his rear.

If poor Ben had been allowed to continue he could even have said that the day after he'd noticed the vault had been tampered with, he found someone had lain a foreign-looking plant lying across its top. One of those fancy foreign flowers. Such as grow in the conservatory up at the big house.

But since Ben was shown the way home the subject hasn't been raised in the Decoy Inn. After all, the honest souls who drink there are not free agents like those across the estuary in the Bowling Green. The fellows you find in the Bowling Green may be grindingly poor, but they all have only the weather and themselves to answer to. Very different in the Decoy Inn. Take any night in the Decoy Inn and there's hardly a soul there who doesn't make his living from the Devereaux estate.

The only reason so few mourned the passing of Jointy Pole was that so few knew him.

No-one at all was much put out by the passing of Joyful Norris, though many knew him very well.

He is our other notable corpse.

This was found out on Corton beach a day or two after the thaw. Men who know the way the *Gariensis* waters flow round the Lothingland peninsula reckon that Norris must have fallen in when a part of one of the rivers was still open. His body would have been invisible under the ice, especially when the ice itself was covered with snow. Then on the melt the body would have been taken downriver through the harbour and out into the Yarmouth Roads before finally being flung back on to the shore by an incoming tide.

There was an inquest and some excitement, because the coroner found evidence of death from causes other than exposure or drowning. Rumours spread up and down the Yarmouth quay and out through the rivers and broads. Norris had had his head 'bashed in', they said. With a heavy object, they said.

- What, like a winch helve? Like the one what brained poor Tom Pye?

- That's what they're a-sayin...'

- Cor, blust! That make yer dudder, don't it!

In fact, the inquest found that the old wherryman had died from the severing of his carotid artery. He *had* suffered a head injury, perhaps from falling on to hard ice, but this wasn't what had killed him. The coroner was informed by the surgeon who had performed the post mortem that death was most likely due to a sharp object with a serrated edge being thrust with considerable force into the throat. The surgeon suggested a rusty carving knife, or perhaps a bread-knife, and this the coroner duly recorded in his report.

What neither knew was that the wielder of this knife had disappeared out of the county weeks before what was left of Norris popped up to bob about in the Roads. The attempt to locate the culprit, whose identity is not much in doubt, has been going on since that inquest, though it can hardly be said the investigation is being expedited with much vigour. The inspector in charge knows that even an arrest would achieve little. With Norris's reputation a defence of lawful killing for reasons of self-preservation would be both inevitable and unassailable. In any case such an arrest is very unlikely to come about. London nowadays is a few hours by train, and its burgeoning, smokey suburbs are filling with the newly-genteel. Ever more grates to be blacked, ever more flags to be scrubbed and ever more buckets of night-soil to be poured away. Few references are being sought from the many Annies who daily arrive in the capital from all over the country, ready for the work. Few awkward questions are asked.

Elsewhere, on the waterways, on the streets and in the villages those who have survived the great freeze of 1870 are now picking up the threads as though they've just returned from a long journey. The fowler who emerges from his hideaway is heartened at last to hear the piping and trilling of gorging waders – though groans from the sheets of melting ice warn him that it still isn't safe to go into the Drains with his gun. As he walks through the slush towards the Yarmouth end of Breydon, noting the patches where the birds are most densely packed, he might also catch other sounds that, perversely, are in their way just as welcome: the concert of bangs, clanks and whistles from the quays and workshops have now rejoined the remorseless thump of the steam hammer to signal that Yarmouth has come back to life. In a day or two this cacophony will go back to being the joyless music of industrial grind. But for a short while it is enjoyed like a popular new tune.

Whether the thaw brings great joy, simple relief, sadness or sorrow, it is forcing folk to look at their world anew. Some have lost family, and others their own health. Others have been changed in subtler ways.

Charlie Harrison, for example, is introduced entirely by accident to a whole new branch of his craft...

We return to that first evening of the thaw...

Tealer is still being nursed back to health in the guest room of the Bowling Green, listening by day to the calls of the feeding waders through the window. By night he's been entertaining himself by straining to hear what people are saying from amongst the murmur of drinkers' voices in the lounge directly below.

On one particular night he hears a gruff laugh that he thinks he recognizes as his old friend Charlie Harrison. He's right – it *is* Charlie, being impolite to Polly. She has just handed him the paints as Tealer asked.

Abovementioned gruff laugh, and then he says "Damn watercolours! No use to me, girl. I'm an oils man."

"But Tealer want you to have them," says Polly crossly, "So do you take 'em."

So the artist shoves them into the poacher's flap of the greatcoat slung over the back of his chair and thinks no more of them. Then later, when the 'Green has tipped its contents into the raw night and Charlie is splashing his unsteady way through the melting slush towards Yarmouth, he's suddenly aware of the unfamiliar weight in the hem of his coat. He pulls out the paints and grunts again. "Lot o' rubbish," he says as he walks along the Bure, and is about to throw them into the river when he remembers through the haze of ale fumes what Polly has said, and the way that she has said it: *Tealer want you to have them.* So when Harrison blunders into the house he takes the box of paints out of his pocket before hurling the greatcoat in the general direction of a coat hook. He leaves the paints on the kitchen table to look at tomorrow.

This is where one of his children finds them early in the morning, and by the time he comes back down, complete with thumping headache, they have broken into the paints and are trying to make the dry tablets produce colour. In spite of his head, Harrison laughs:

"You little devils, that ent the way. You need a drop of water," and he wets the paints with the dregs from the ewer he is carrying and gives the children an old piece of paper to play with. He watches them with amusement for a few moments as they splosh colours about, and goes out to the pump to wash the sleep from his face and re-fill the ewer. He grins again as he passes them on the way back upstairs – then he stops, and with the ewer still in his hand, he comes back for another look. He puts the ewer down and runs a finger over the surface of the children's picture.

"Blust me!" he says, "Thas already dry."

His children look at each other and back at him in bewilderment. He takes a brush from one of them and dabs some paint on and paints a few tree-like shapes among their childish blotches.

"And so easy, too!" he murmurs. "A man could work fast with these." He takes the paints back from his protesting children and packs them in his pocket. "You can have'm later," he says, "I need'm now." Without further ado he takes his easel and sets out for the shore of Breydon as fast as his crashing headache will allow.

It's about eight in the morning when he gets there. He assesses the dawn scene and wastes no time in starting, with brush leaping from water to watercolour to canvas. He marvels at the speed of his own work. At first his brush strokes are crude and ineffective, but he quickly learns how little effort is required to achieve a desired effect. And then it's as if some spirit in this box of colours has seized control of his hand and is taking over the direction of his work.

In his excitement it takes Harrison a while to register that the thaw is now truly underway. New shades of light, mud and water await capture. He gazes across the moving, melting world, and the bitter wind blowing off the flats causes his eyes to stream.

Then he notices someone moving briskly along the other side of the estuary. He's not especially curious, any more than he was about the figure on the fort three months ago. As we know, he knows full well that there are always distant, anonymous figures on the *Gariensis*; and Charlie, at least, is little bothered by them.

A little later he also sees a small boat in the middle of the main channel. He decides to include it in the sweep of his canvas. It is just a long, dark shadow mid-estuary, and he logs it into the picture with a few impatient sidestrokes of his brush. As always, manmade objects are incidental to his work. He is concentrating on the watery dawn itself.

"Yes," he thinks as he paints, "yes, this is it. Watercolours, though! Whoever'd a' thought it? Now I'll catch all that strangeness afore the sun get any higher and burn it all away. It can be never so quick but I'll catch the devil!"

And when he finishes, he stands back and gazes at his work. Then he notices for the first time the boat he has so casually included in his scene, and he looks up to see where it is now. It has gone, and he grunts in surprise at how quickly, but then thinks nothing more of it. He has other matters on his mind. His life has just turned a corner, and he knows it. He blows on his blue fingers and continues.

Two and a half years later, Charles Harrison is standing in much the same place, though this time in very different conditions. Now he's in shirt sleeves and painting the same scene with beads of sweat forming on his brow and matting his beard. It is another of those late harvest days, and the Yarmouth shore of Breydon is again dotted with strollers young and old, all enjoying the priceless calm of a Broadland summer evening. In the distance, three figures approach, a man, a woman and a small child. The woman is walking awkwardly.

"Hey ho, Charlie Harrison!" shouts the man from twenty yards off.

"Mr John Sayer! Are y'alright?"

"While since we seen you."

"I ha' been in London this last year. I aren't goin'back there though – ent the place for me! And how old is your littl'un now? Eighteen month I guess he must be, and already faster on his pins than what I am. And soon to have company, I reckon!"

Polly Sayer blushes down at the cracked clay of the Wall.

"And how goes it with our Charlie H?" asks Tealer.

Harrison throws a paintbrush on to his palate and stretches his back. "Fair to middlin'. Did I ever thank you for them paints?"

"Paints?"

"What you gave me when you were took poorly up the 'Green."

His sharp blue eyes catch a slight lessening in the grin on Tealer's face. "What, them?" says Tealer, "Glad to get shot of 'em. No use to me. You aren't still using them, are you?"

"Don't talk so soft – 'course I aren't! I'd finished them a few days after Polly give 'em to me. These are their great-great-grandchildren, I should reckon. Still, that was you put me on to water-colours, you old toper. Only trouble with watercolours is that you don't get no fly legs on the paint as you do with oils."

"Fly legs?" says Polly.

"Yes, my dear," says Harrison, "your client like fly's legs stuck to the paint – then he know – or he think he know – he's lookin' at authentic field-painted work and not some fancy studio job. But water-colours, they're fast – they're just what you need for painting a sunset like that there."

They all look at the setting sun turning the Breydon mud a fierce pink. After a few moments Harrison turns to Tealer.

"What ha' you bin doin'? Don't you take that old gun out n'more?"

"I go down to marsh with my twelve-bore now and then. When business allow. But I haven't been out on the estuary for two year or more. Not since I was nearly done for out on the ice that time. I took that as a sign. Besides Jenny… she… would you believe… she disappeared with the thaw. Best thing for her, I reckon. I don't reckon anyone could ha' stole her. Hell, no! She'd be a noisy sort o' secret to keep! No, I reckon she loosened in the thaw and floated away on the ebb."

Harrison says nothing. He just looks at Tealer and nods.

" 'Sides," says Tealer, "she's better off wherever she is. The days of the big guns are finished here on Breydon. Too many new rules and regulations from up-country. Whole place is being run by bird-fanciers and ministry men and any number of other folk that wouldn't know a hawk from a harnser. Jenny was from a different time. She's well out of it."

"Whatever would your uncle John Palmer ha' said, though?"

Tealer looked across to the far shore of Breydon where someone, a fellow stroller perhaps, was glassing their little group as they talked. "I really haven't a clue what he'd say, Charlie."

Polly looks at where Tealer is looking, and then at Tealer, and then says in a bright voice:

"Probably he'd say there were too many excisemen about."

"Yes, girl, I reckon he would," says Tealer. "Too many o' *them*!"

They all have a chuckle.

Then suddenly Harrison has an idea. "You never saw that first picture I did with the water colours, did you? No. Come you over this next Sunday afternoon, both o' you. Bring the littl'un. Edith can make you tea, and I'll fetch it out."

The Demon Drink

Tealer is now looking forward to this tea-party; an opportunity to catch up with one of his oldest friends.

In the meantime, he has business in Norwich.

The battlements of Norwich Castle are a fine place from which to consider Norfolk's woody capital. Below you are the streets and alleys that this great block of Norman stone was put here to cower. To your northeast are the dark heights of Mousehold, whose scrubs and briars seeth with the ghosts of honest rebellion. To the southeast are views of the wide valley where the waters of the steady Wensum and the secretive Yare mingle and begin their slow course through the county's eastern fringe. To the north, the spire of Losinga's cathedral soars above the affairs of men. To the west, beyond the reassuring bulk of St Peter Mancroft, the vital, unassuming farmlands of central Norfolk stretch away.

For more than a century the gentry and senior yeomanry of the area have used the meadow below the castle to buy and sell livestock. But for nearer a millennium it has been a place to meet and discuss the business of the day. Ventures planned and agreements reached on this hill have moulded the landscape and fixed the destiny of the county arrayed around it. Even now there's an authority, an inimitable assuredness, in the manner of those who gather on its lofty vantage to watch the buying and selling of beasts.

And it's no surprise that nowadays we should find John Sayer Esq., Shipowner, in such company. He has just taken lunch with a merchant in a hostelry by the Guildhall to discuss a shipment of crockery to the continent. The business is soon concluded to his satisfaction and his train doesn't leave for Yarmouth for some time, so it being market day he's naturally drawn to make the short journey from the Guildhall, down White Lion Street and on to Castle Hill to see who's at the sales.

Tealer Sayer, you see, has come up in the world.

Not long after he married Bessey's daughter he sold the unused properties that passed to him from his uncle and used the proceeds to buy into a small concern sailing cargos to and from The Hook. It has turned out to be a sound idea (as Polly's ideas generally do). The junketing of a few years ago is well behind Tealer, and the only marks of his travails are a scar over one temple from a 'tumble with a scoundrel in a street in Brazil', and two missing fingertips on his right hand lost to frostbite during 'that hard ol' winter of two year ago'. Now in a modest way this resurrected branch of the Palmer-Sayer dynasty is prospering, and in the summer sun Tealer's brushed hat shines as resplendently as any on Castle Hill.

The pleasant breeze on the hill mirrors Tealer's good humour. He's enjoying the easy fit of his newly-tailored trousers. He's enjoying the fluttering flags and bright billboards and the rows of bleating, grunting and lowing animals. He's enjoying being able to nod and smile at acquaintances, some of whom are hard at their negotiations, but most of whom, like Tealer, are here simply to relax in the shade of the elms and to watch the enduring rituals of commerce.

This is all a far cry from a few years ago.

Nowadays there would seem to be little that could discompose John Sayer.

Nevertheless, as he watches the sale of a pen of Angus steers, John Sayer suddenly finds that he is discomposed. He feels as though something hot or sharp is boring into his back. It causes him to turn around to a young woman standing behind him, and this in turn gives rise to the even stranger sensation that he is staring straight into the fiery, laughing, scornful eyes of Maud Pritchard. It is a sensation due entirely to the fact that he *is* staring into the eyes of Maud Pritchard – or more precisely, Maud Fraser – but definitely Maud.

There've been some changes. The wanton ringlets of auburn have been marshalled with nets and pins into a set of loops and twists, and topped with a fetching summer bonnet. The face is slightly less youthful, but only in that motherhood has defined some of its edges and given it more character. And, of course, the eyes are utterly unchanged – the same Celtic green set in a broad Anglo-Saxon forehead; part vulnerable, part indomitable, wholly unpredictable.

"I thought it was you," she says, "even in those remarkable clothes."

Tealer splutters in a search for coherence.

"M-m-m...," he says, "Er... Mer-mer-mer...,"

The eyebrows arch mockingly. "Mer-Mer-Mer-Mrs Fraser," says Maud. "Mer-Mer-Mer-Maud Pritchard as was."

"H-how…? Wh-where…? I mean, how…?"

"Ian is come down to sell livestock – these are his beasts you are looking at here. I have taken the opportunity to visit my poor old mother in Gorleston and my sister Catchpole here in Norwich. We stayed in Yarmouth last night and I met Polly in Yarmouth this morning and heard all your good news. We're now just arrived in Norwich for this sale. Will you take tea with us? This…

"Well, now…"

"…evening we start to make our way back to Scotland. Look, there is Ian, over there talking to the auctioneer. Can you not see him? No? He isn't the tallest. He's behind that gross yokel of a man leaning on the stick. And there is Marjory, my sister-in-law, and there's Callum…"

"Yes, but…"

"…our son. He's two. He has hay-fever, which is a trial for us all, but mostly for him, I suppose. A good Highland name, you'll agree, but a little foolish, for Ian is from outside Kilmarnock, which is no higher than a tall lamp-post. He should be finished with the auction very shortly. Ian, I mean, not Callum. I shall call him over. You shall meet him. I shall tell him that your father and my mother were once acquainted. Why do farmers always have to talk in such loud voices? Ian has no knowledge of our former connection. Is that cravat from Norwich? It's a fine style, but not the colour for you. Ah, I'd forgotten how hot Norfolk can be in August. Still, it is very pleasant here by the castle. Ian! *Ian!* No – he hasn't heard me."

The barrage continues, switching effortlessly from recollection, to criticism, to confidence, to observation and back to recollection. Tealer knows from the past that this isn't flirtation but simply a product of the speed at which ideas come into Maud's head. He's given no chance to dwell on any of it, and only has time to note that Maud's speech still carries an unmistakable Norfolk cadence (an accent she would never admit to), though some of the vowels have acquired a distinct Caledonian curve.

Eventually she breaks off to wave her parasol in an attempt to catch the attention of someone in the crowd that surrounds the auctioneer's dais. Tealer can't make out whom she is waving at, but it gives him the chance to note that the figure in the matron is as sleek and firm as it was in the maiden.

At that point there's a lull in the auction and the watchers disperse. A timid-looking young woman with a small child comes over. Tealer takes her for the child's nurse, but he's told that this is Maud's sister-in-law Marjorie, and the child, Callum. Marjorie curtseys briefly to Tealer and mumbles something unintelligible. The child looks at him with critical green eyes that leave no doubt as to at least one half of its lineage. Presently a fellow walks over who Tealer again imagines must be a servant of some sort until Maud turns and says "Ian, I should like to present Mr John Sayer, whose wife we met in Yarmouth only this morning. What a coincidence that we should meet the husband here!"

Tealer finds he's looking down at a man no taller than Maud herself. In the days and weeks after he'd discovered Maud had gone Tealer had imagined that he would one day have to come to grips with some sturdy, black-bearded young highlander like those in the illustrations of Maud's Walter Scott novels. Yet this man is, if anything, older than Tealer himself, certainly seven inches shorter, with a shock of fair hair not unlike his own, and a lopsided, disarming grin.

"Pleased t'make yer acquaintance, Mr Sayer."

"And I yours, Mr Fraser. Um... how... um... how... er... how do you find our county of Norfolk?"

"Aye, tis braw farming land, nae doubt about that. But awful flat round by Great Yarmouth."

"Yes, well, er... I suppose that is a bit rum if you aren't used to it."

Fraser is about to say something else but is interrupted by the auctioneer's assistant announcing the next lot, so that this four-line conversation marks the entire exchange Tealer has with the man he used to dream of beating into a pulp with his belaying-pin. Maud says to her husband:

"We won't detain you, Ian. Mr Sayer can accompany us into Tombland to take tea. I believe Becky and Perry are already there. We shall meet you down at the station at five o'clock."

"Aye, dear. Don't be late. The train'll no wait. A good afternoon to you, sir."

"And to you, sir."

Hats are put back on heads. Fraser turns to the auction ring, hands behind back, totally absorbed in the sale of his cattle. Tealer turns to Maud, who raises her eyebrows at him expectantly. It appears from this that they are to take tea, and he must arrange the transport. He leads the way to find a carriage, into which he hands the two women and lifts the child. He climbs in and sits down. So far he's had the chance to speak about twenty words.

They are driven off Castle Hill, through Bank Plain, down Tombland and into the forecourt of the ancient establishment where tea will be served. Maud is talking incessantly, and Tealer is still only able to nod and grunt in agreement. The sister-in-law Marjorie is gazing silently at the spire of the cathedral, whose pinnacle is gleaming in the blue sky more than three hundred feet above their heads.

Maud tells Tealer mainly of her life in Scotland, and the business of her husband which often takes him to Galloway and sometimes across to Ireland for long periods. This gives her more opportunities to read, she says, which she very much enjoys. Her favourite author was always Scott, and now that she has seen the hills and glens described in his works she can enjoy him all the more.

They enter the hostelry's venerable interior and creak their way towards a table by the window. After the dazzling brightness outside, the tearoom seems almost in pitch darkness, and it takes their eyes some time to adjust.

Sitting in the gloom are a fat woman and a thin man. Tealer realizes with a shock that the fat woman is Maud's sister. Becky was never a slim girl, but now she has put on weight massively, which with her shapeless red hair and freckled face has turned her even more into a burlesque of Maud. The thin man is Catchpole, with the same look of strained civility that Tealer remembers from a few years ago. (Amid a torrent of other asides Maud has already whispered to Tealer that 'Ian pulls poor Perry's leg mercilessly'.)

The waitress brings them tea which Maud pours out without the smallest pause in her descriptions of her adopted land. Her sister simpers at the more acerbic observations, while her sister-in-law contributes nothing beyond the odd shy smile. Catchpole occasionally grimaces in agreement and spends the rest of the time shooting nervous looks at the child Callum from the safety of the other side of the tea-table. Callum is restless, and in a rare lull Tealer takes out a miniature spy-glass and hands it to the child to look through. Marjorie helps him try to find the cockerel at the top of the cathedral spire. Then the child tires of the telescope, and Tealer reaches across the table to take it back, which is when Maud's green gaze falls upon the mangled stubs of his index and middle fingers. Without taking a breath, or even blinking, she turns to ask her sister if she and Catchpole would mind taking Marjorie and Callum and showing them the cathedral. A raised eyebrow from Catchpole shows he thinks there could be some impropriety in this arrangement, but he is skewered by a glance from Maud that sends him into a small frenzy of cravat-adjustment. He nods to Tealer and hurries out after the others. As soon as they are gone Maud reaches out, takes hold of Tealer's wrist in one elegantly gloved hand and turns it to inspect the damage. (Tealer valiantly tries to block the memory of that very same hand, minus the lace glove, raking lines up and down the skin of his thigh.)

Maud asks him how he lost his fingertips. Tealer tries his usual dismissive reference to a winter gunning trip that went wrong, but it has never sounded as unconvincing as it does now. He is very thankful that a thick lock of his hair is covering the knife scar across his temple.

"My poor Johnny," she says. "I remember dear Polly said that you were very nearly lost on the ice a year or two ago, but she didn't tell me you were maimed in this way. Why in the world were you shooting in such weather? Why didn't you just return to shelter when it became so cold?"

"I was out with my punt-gun, and 'at got stuck on the mud."

"You mean that frightful cannon thing that so obsessed you?"

Tealer admits that he means White Jenny, and he adds that it would have been inconceivable for him to desert her on the estuary, even if he'd been able to. He tells Maud briefly about that fateful expedition, if not of the visions that went with it. He finishes by adding: "I suppose you were right when you called old Jenny the 'Belle Dame without Mercy'. She either saved me or nearly did for me, I'm not sure which. She certainly taught me not to rest my hand on her barrel when there's a freeze on."

But as Tealer utters the words 'Belle Dame', Maud stiffens. For once it is she who is lost for words. He regrets having made the reference, thinking that he must inadvertently have reminded her of their nightly liaisons in the Breydon houseboat. He hunts frantically for another topic of conversation.

"Callum, your young'un…"

But she interrupts him: "La Belle Dame? What do *you* know of that?" she asks. Instead of blushing she has gone pale.

"Oh, you must remember. 'The Belle Dame sands mercy' was what you once called old Jenny – 'at was when I told you about my uncle John, and how he'd said I was to look after her. But, look, never mind Jenny… tell me about your young lad. He look a strong young…"

But Maud isn't listening. She drops her fabulous gaze down on to the table and frowns in deep puzzlement. Then she looks back up at Tealer, puts her hand to her mouth and gasps in a kind of horrified amusement.

"Oh, Johnny! You surely never imagined that that was what I meant by "La Belle Dame Sans Merci"? That beastly gun of yours?" She even allows herself a mild peal of laughter. "Good God! Oh, good Lord! Yes, I see. Yes, she *did* have you 'in thrall', that White Jenny. And 'without mercy'! Well, if you lost some fingers, I suppose… Oh dear! Dearest John, please don't imagine I'm laughing at your expense, it's just that… Oh yes, I see why you were confused! But… no, no. No, no, no. I should explain. I am laughing, but God forgive me, it is not a matter for laughing."

So she does explain, and she does stop laughing. She explains that it was her cousin Niamh Walsh from Dublin who sent her a pamphlet about the cult of La Belle Dame. This pamphlet was written by a scholar of the poet John Keats.

"You'll remember – but no, you won't remember, because you never listened to anyone who spoke of anything other than slaying duck on Breydon Water – so let's say you *would* remember if you *had* been listening – that I told you that Keats was a consumptive. He used to take laudanum as a palliative." And Maud goes on to explain the theory that on one occasion the poet Keats realised he'd taken too much laudanum and had tried to restore his equilibrium with an antidote, and that being an apothecary's assistant he would have known that the best of these was belladonna.

"It is the very same juice that some foolish girls place in their eyes to make the pupils wide and lustrous like a *bella donna* – beautiful woman – which is why it is so called." The theory of Miss Walsh and her fellow-thinkers, she went on, held it that this belladonna must be what Keats meant by his *belle dame*. For belladonna has its own effects, which are recurring nightmares and strange trances, and Miss Walsh convinced her cousin that Keats wrote his lay *La Belle*

Dame sans Merci after he had recovered from an application of it. She also told her that it was a herb much in use by necromancers and sorcerers.

"...And I must say that at the time this fascinated me. I had read so much of such matters, and now I saw a chance – may God forgive me! – to enter that world myself. After all, I reasoned, most of the people in Gorleston thought me a witch in any case, and so I reckoned I might as well be hanged for a sheep as for a lamb."

So she describes how she prepared and took the juice of the deadly nightshade, firstly in very small doses that merely made her very drowsy, and then in larger amounts.

"And then I had the most extraordinary experiences. I went to such places, Johnny!" There's a crack in her speech, and she swallows hard. "Extraordinary, terrible places!"

She gazes into the distance for a while, and then shakes her head. "Oh, but what folly! I have since learnt how little mercy this drug belladonna really has. And I have since learnt how small is the difference between fever followed by a deep sleep and fever... followed... well... by death. One of Niamh's friends experimented as I did, and, alas, succumbed. I mean, succumbed. And horribly, by all accounts. And therefore how close was I was to perishing by my own foolish hand. Or at least to losing my mind. *That* is why, forgive me, I started so when you talked just now of *La Belle Dame*."

"And... er... what exactly did you see? When you took this drug?"

Now a Polly would hear the foreboding that there is in poor Tealer's voice as he asks this, just as she would notice the colour draining from his own face as he learns the answer. But Maud, as ever, is too much caught up in recounting her experiences to notice.

"Ah, Johnny, I can hardly tell it," she says.

"I'd be right interested. You see, I was once given too much nightshade myself. 'At when I was a littl'un, and I often wonder..."

But Maud launches off again before he can finish. "Well, the strangest part is that many of the visions you cannot remember, though you know you have had them. One I *can* clearly recall is that of flying. The most bizarre feeling of flying. But that was only the seduction. Then when you went away and I was left alone, I tried the drug again. That's when my… my torments began. Dreadful sensations. Doors appearing in bare walls. Faces… but ghastly, *ghastly* faces… everywhere. In the dark, in windows, in mirrors. And at dusk, everyday objects took on frightful forms! And, worst of all, the watching figures in the distance. Those were the worst! That strange, flat landscape around Breydon seemed full of them. People in the distance, standing and watching, staring. Quite, quite horrible. And the worst of it, Tealer, was that the dreams didn't finish with sleep. They went on, and on. Sometimes for the following night and the night after it; sometimes for weeks. Sometimes waking dreams, in the middle of the day. Yes, I used to see shapes and figures in broad daylight. It was only when I left Norfolk that the infernal visions ceased. And… it's one reason I left so precipitately. So perhaps I am glad really that you mentioned *La Belle Dame*, albeit so accidentally. It has perhaps given me a chance to explain myself. I only hope you can understand it."

Tealer notices that in spite of the heat Maud is shivering.

"Yes," he says, "I probably understand better'n what you might think. Where did you get the belladonna preparation from?"

"Nightshade bushes somewhere near my home. I can't remember. Anyway…"

"Could it have been them nightshade bushes we once found below the Roman fort at Burgh Castle?"

"Yes, perhaps." (Now Maud *does* redden slightly at the associations, and there is the hint of irritation in her eyes at Tealer's indelicacy). But this time it's Tealer who disregards the niceties. He takes a deep breath and looks straight into the two green lights. "Maudy," he says, "I want you to think, now. Did you ever give any of this nightshade to me?"

Maud blinks in surprise at his directness, just as others have done when the soft-voiced, diffident John Sayer has suddenly spoken from the heart. She says "I think perhaps I might once have let you taste some in the wine I made. Well, yes! Yes, I must have. Only a small measure, though, I am sure. Why, yes, of course, for that is what I must have meant when I said you were in the thrall of the *Belle Dame* – though I confess I don't recall saying it."

"And did you put it into them bottles of blackberry spirit you used to make?"

"Yes, I think so - possibly. It was a long time ago. But why do you stare at me so,

Johnny? You look quite fierce."

"Did you leave any of the bottles in my house when you went off?"

Maud looks at him uncertainly. "Yes, I believe I may…" And then the hand goes up to her mouth again, this time in pure, unmixed horror. "Oh, Johnny, who drank them?"

Tealer takes a deep, deep breath and looks to where the afternoon sun is streaming into the open window of the tea-room. Outside, a succession of carriages is rumbling down Tombland, through the Erpingham Gate and into the cathedral close, each to deliver its cargo of the richer faithful dressed for vespers.

"Johnny. Johnny. *Tealer*! I asked you who drank them!"

"No-one," he says, finally. "I took 'em down my house-boat. And when I thought one of 'em didn't taste quite right I hulled 'em all in the Yare."

Maud sighs. "Holy God. That is a relief." For a moment or two she is quiet.

Tealer uses this pause to think things through, and notions are racing through his head faster than ever. Meeting and listening to Maud has brought back to him those haunted months of a couple of years back with an unnerving clarity. Three quarters of an hour ago they were just a part of his life that he had managed to shelve. Now, in a flash they are on him again. Now all at once it is the following two years of contentment that seem remote.

Were all those bad dreams and dark visions, feelings of being watched and followed, were they all caused by the juice of the nightshade bush? Is that possible? He looks round the peaceful tearoom as though the answer might be engraved on the walls or written on the faces of the other customers. But the strongest potion in this quiet place is finest Ceylonnese tea, and the atmosphere is refined, sedate and distinctly un-otherworldly. He catches sight of a bloated image of himself in a polished copper cauldron hanging from a bar in the inglenook – prosperous in his new jacket, Nankeen ducks, chemise and cravat whose colour might or might not be his. How could a successful, confident fellow like him ever have been brought to such a pass by a dose of nightshade juice?

Then he thinks of his poisoning as a child, and (if he allows for the effects of childish imagination) how similar the trances and visions of those far-off times were to what he suffered more recently. All those years of collected torment? All those years and years? Caused by nightshade juice? A lump comes to Tealer's throat, and he actually feels tears beginning to well up in his eyes. He coughs and fidgets to avoid making a spectacle of himself.

He looks again at the reflection.

And he regains control. Yes, perhaps that *was* all it was. Perhaps like Maud he should be grateful for this strange little meeting. Perhaps it has explained a lot.

Well, now. Well, now. Who would have thought?

Yet… isn't there something else? Something he's missed?

And it is just then that – just for the smallest instant – the distorted image of himself in the cauldron changes to a face which rivets him. In a flash he is back in the *Sturgeon* out on the ice, staring into a face that stares back at him, penetrating him to the core of his being. Then the image disappears again, a fragment of a forgotten dream, whose significance is lost with the memory. Yet it leaves him with the distinct impression that, however potent the nightshade spirit, the belladonna has only ever been the key to the entrance of a deeper, darker…

"Johnny…, Johnny… *John Tealer!*" says Maud, bringing him back to the gentle interior of the hotel. "I beg your pardon, Johnny, but you were dreaming, and I must go. I must find Becky and the others and make haste. But before I do there's one more thing I should like to tell you. Let us finish our reunion on a happier note." She takes his hand again, but this time with both hers, and tightly.

"I used to see a figure on the marsh watching me," she says.

"I know. You said before."

"No. This one was different. It always looked the same."

Tealer grits his teeth, wondering what exactly will be 'happier' about the promised 'happier note'. "You aren't the only one, girl. I… I mean… we… most of us who spend any time down at marsh have had that experience at some point or other."

"So who is it? Who do people say it is? A ghost? A departed spirit?"

But Tealer is not going down that road now. He is just *not*. Look at that reflection in the polished cauldron; it is back to being what it should be: a successful businessman in Norwich on a pleasant weekday afternoon in late August. Such things as Maud is talking of are in the past now – and will remain so if Tealer can help it.

He adopts a dismissive tone: "Could be anyone, I reckon. Marshman, gamekeeper, trick of the light."

"Well, it was't a gamekeeper watching *me*, Johnny."

"No?"

"No, it was not. This was a figure that kept beckoning. And I thought that by escaping from Norfolk I might leave it behind, as I left behind the horrors of my self-inflicted poisoning. But *this* vision followed me to Scotland. I used to sight it at the other end of a street in Kilmarnock. Or at the other side of a loch. Or in a clearing half-way up a wooded mountain. Always a little beyond the distance at which I could identify it. And this is what I want to tell you, John. It was not menacing in any way. I felt instead it pitied me. I felt a wonderful warmth from it. It took me so long to realise who it was."

"Very good," says Tealer carefully. "Who was it, then?"

"It was our Redeemer. Oh, how slow I was to realise it! He followed me to Scotland."

"I see," says Tealer.

"You do not see. But I very much want you to see. I have put away all the foolish notions I had, John, and now I follow His precious teaching. I… I feel as the Magdalene must have felt when she spied Him through the bushes of Gethsemane and first recognised Him. Ian's church is Catholic. I have joined it. Not a great step, of course, for my mother is Anglo-Catholic anyway. Ian is a good, dear husband."

Maud carries on in this vein for some time, talking of her conversion from the Anglo Catholic faith to the Roman. Most of it is a little over Tealer's head – no difference from the Maud of old there. But after his initial relief that she's not going to dredge up more unwanted phantasma from the murky past, Tealer finds himself intrigued. The green eyes that formerly sparked with youthful romanticism now flash with evangelistic zeal. The passion itself, for all that it is differently directed, is undiminished.

"I ha' got a feeling," he says, "that our meeting up on Castle Hill was a touch more than chance."

Maud doesn't answer, but Tealer is amused to see that even Salvation has not extinguished the arch Pritchard smile.

They sip the last of their tea and regard each other curiously over their cups.

"And do you have a church, Tealer?"

"The Besseys are Anglican people. We go to St Nicholas each Sunday. That was where we got wed. You know my own people were Tabernaclers. And you may remember me telling you my uncle Palmer had no patience with any of it – high church, low church, any church. For my part I've always agreed with an old boy I knew called Harry Pole. 'Jointy' we used to call him, God rest him. He was a churchgoer as regular as they came. But he always said the best church of all, the best place to 'look for the Lord' as he'd say, was the woods and fields. I reckon I agree, an'all."

"Why, there you are! This Mr Pole clearly thought much as I do. Was he a very learned man?"

"In his way."

Maud seems satisfied with this evidence of spiritual development in Tealer. As she gathers herself to get up she grins at him again "So, to finish where we started; you no longer hunt poor birds with that great machine?"

"White Jenny? No. She came to grief."

"Of course, yes. I heard she was pushed into the sea."

"Who told you that?"

"Polly, I believe."

"No-one pushed her," says Tealer slowly and carefully. "She was stuck in the ice, and then there was a thaw that took her down the river and into the Roads. No-one pushed her."

"I understand," says Maud, clearly deciding that enough sensitive issues have been broached for one afternoon. "Anyway, I must leave now. Ian will be finished in his transactions, and we have the evening train to take. My fondest greetings again to dear Polly."

A few minutes later Tealer is outside in the sunshine watching the cab containing Maud, Becky, Pericles, Marjorie and the child Callum disappear up Tombland. When it's out of sight he blows through his cheeks. He's recovering from the maelstrom of sensations that is a cup of tea with Maud Deirdrie Fraser (née Pritchard).

Day's End

The following Sunday brings us back down the road to Yarmouth, and to the promised tea-party in the small front room of Harrison's terrace in Middlegate Street. Outside there are yells as the Sayer toddler plays in the sun-warm dust with Harrison's children. Beyond are the subdued noises of Yarmouth on a Sunday evening. The inexorable thump of the pile-driver is absent. Indoors there is a Sabbath quiet broken only by the ticking of a small clock on the mantelpiece. The scene might almost be that of the Sayer living room in Cliff Street of twenty years ago. The happy yells of children on the doorstep give the lie.

Tealer is in another world. He entered it when he first walked into Harrison's front room and his eyes got used to the gloom. Pictures cover the walls, they lie about on the floor, they stand on easels and are propped up against piles of books. In this dark room are not just all the nooks and crannies of East Norfolk. Here are windows into the very soul of the Broadlander. Here are the places Tealer has always tried to drift to while lying on his berth sweating out a fever in some stifling tropical port.

One canvas, for instance, has been painted from a boat sitting on a small broad, and captures a distant church through the gap in the oaks that line the broad's edge. In the middle ground lies a corn field. The eye is made to flit back and forth between green-brown waters in the foreground, with its lilies and hint of great pike, across the dessicated wheat and on to the church itself, with its promise of a cool, dark nave as a refuge from the searing afternoon.

Another canvas provides a glimpse of a bright summer's morning with a small craft moored outside a marshman's cottage, and the river sliding by. In another, a working wherry is moving gently to its mooring at sunset. It is at the end of the staithe, it is at the end of its day.

There are other scenes of fields, woods, ponds and broads. A silent loke, where beeches break the autumn sunlight into shafts that dapple the carpet of newly-fallen leaves. A summer marsh, whose shimmering air is a symphony of skylarks, bees and crickets. Two swans on a choppy river, curling their folded wings like sails to catch the breeze.

There is one huge canvas that shows Breydon in winter. A smouldering sunset imparts no warmth to the scene of frozen punts, stakes and eel traps strewn about in the gloom. This last one Tealer looks at with great interest.

Harrison sees him studying the picture. "I call that *When Night Creeps On*. Blast, 'at caused a bit of a kerfuffle when I was painting it," he says with a grin at Polly. "They all mistook me for a ghost. I don't suppose I shall ever sell it."

"Which is why we live here in this little Row-house," says his wife Edith, who has just come in with the tea-tray. "Charlie's no businessman. Look at that one lay in the corner there." She points to a canvas propped against the wall behind the door. It depicts a large country house and is near-perfect but for a great ugly streak from top to bottom. "Daft ole' fool. He did that in a fury. He went shanny all 'cause the lady that commissioned it wanted him to paint in a path that weren't there. Would he paint the path and take the money? 'Course not. That would ha' been *dishonest*, wouldn't it? Daft ol' fool!"

"I'll only paint what I see – I don't have to make nothin' up," says Harrison. "Not living here in the Broads with all Creation to paint, I don't. I don't need to. Now what was I then lookin' for? Oo-ar! That first watercolour." He goes over to a chest and pulls out a watercolour in a simple frame. "'Course, 'at was only an experiment, but…"

Tealer who has been dazed by one fine tableau after another, looks away from *When Night Creeps On* to where Harrison is holding a rough watercolour. The wondering smile disappears from his lips, and he goes rigid and points to an object in the middleground.

"That's ol' Jenny!" he says. "That's White Jenny!"

Harrison is quiet for a while, and then says, "What your old punt-gun? Are you sure, boy?"

"Only Jenny stuck out that proud of a punt, and the *Sturgeon* was the only clinker-built punt on Breydon with a double set of rowlocks." says Tealer, almost in a whisper, "Blast, I never thought I'd see her again. When did you paint this, then, Charlie?"

"But you know. When you first give me them paints. I believe you were laid up at the 'Green – and I painted this just when the thaw started. Damned paints would ha' froze any earlier!"

Tealer thinks about this for a moment. "But I never took her out after that time I was caught on the ice."

They all survey the painting with new interest.

"The *Sturgeon* loosened in the thaw and went out with the tide. I've always reckoned she got swamped in the Roads and took Jenny with her. D'you know, Charlie, you must ha' caught her just after she'd come loose?"

Outside the sun is still quite high in the sky, and the red bricks of Middlegate Street are still warm to the touch, but in this little room Harrison, Tealer and Polly are trying to penetrate the raw gloom of a March dawn long gone. Edith Harrison pours tea into four cups, but no-one even turns round.

"Well, then," says Harrison with a laugh, pointing at a vague human shape in the picture, "Perhaps that there figure on the Wall's you. To be honest, I'd forgotten I'd put that in."

"No," says Tealer firmly, "no, I never actually saw it all happen. I only it worked out later – what happened, I mean. Fact is, I never saw Jenny again after they pulled me out the *Sturgeon*. So that couldn't be me there."

"You did go wandering about the morning of the thaw, dear," says Polly. "I never knew where you went, but I remember giving you what for when you came back! You still weren't quite right in the head, you know. Perhaps Charlie's right – perhaps thas you on the Wall."

"Poll, I never saw Jenny again! That can't be me!" There's an echo in Tealer's voice of a tension that Polly recognizes from a few years ago, and doesn't care for.

"Maybe Charlie put the other figure in later, then" she says, and with Tealer still peering at the boat in the picture she looks at Harrison hard.

Harrison catches the look and says: 'Well, yes, trees and lilies are what I do best, and I like to be truthful with *them*. People, I aren't so worried about. I must ha' put it in later. In fact, I reckon I did, now I come to think on it. 'Sides, you know yourself, boy: Breydon's a rum old place in the evening, and you get hell-an'-all tricks o' the light!"

Tealer looks at Harrison and back at the painting for several minutes. Eventually he nods and smiles. Harrison goes out to fetch the children in, leaving Tealer

Day's End

to stroll round the room looking at other canvasses. Polly sits down to chat with Edith but is watching her husband carefully out of the corner of her eye. She notices one frame in particular seems to take his fancy, and he seems even more engrossed by this than he was just now by the first Breydon watercolour. She fancies he's muttering to himself.

He finally comes back to have another look at the Breydon painting. Polly holds her breath, completely oblivious to whatever it is Edith is saying to her. But she gets some relief when she sees Tealer shake his head at the painting and smile again, this time broadly. He sits down as his old self – which is to say his new self of the last couple of years – jocular and relaxed.

Polly herself then relaxes by several degrees, though she still feels a little uneasy.

What Polly does not know is what has just happened in that minute or two in the far corner of the room. What's more, from the angle she's sitting at she can't see that it was not actually a painting but a small looking-glass that caught her husband's eye.

She has no inkling that a great deal of much significance to John 'Tealer' Sayer has just taken place in that small period of time.

For in that modest looking-glass on Charlie Harrison's parlour wall Tealer has just caught sight once more of the apparition that had so transfixed him as his life was ebbing away on the ice, and the same that appeared again, fleetingly, in the polished cauldron when he was sitting with Maud, and indeed the same that has been coming to him in various visions and dreams since early childhood, though only ever leaving a vague outline in the morning. But in this last appearance of a few minutes ago it was quite distinct, and Tealer was able to take in every detail. And at that point the laughter of the children was blanked out, as were the conversation of the other adults and the rattles of the crockery. Even the ticking of the clock stopped.

Tealer was alone in the house, and alone on earth, but for the Being opposite.

Yes, indeed it was his long-time Persecutor – the Spectre of all the spectres, the Demon of all the demons of the marshes, the Face behind all the faces of the Fiend of Breydon. And it was staring out of the mirror into his soul, just as it had out on the ice on that desperate night of two and a half years ago.

Ah, well… That it might have, though. That it might have.

But, you see, the Tealer that was standing in front of that mirror a few minutes ago was a different Tealer from the one out on the ice two and a half years ago. The Tealer in front of the mirror was not a Tealer at his wit's end, nor a Tealer on the verge of death. Nor was he a Tealer with a brain addled by days of imbibing an essence of poisonous berries. Nor a Tabernacle child with a head full of fundamentalist superstition. No, the Tealer in front of that mirror was a confident fellow, a married fellow, a father and a businessman, humorous-looking, well-barbered, with a silk shirt and colourful cravat, and a characterful scar on the forehead – in fact, really no different from the humorous-looking, well-barbered, silk-shirted, cravat-wearing Demon with a characterful scar on the forehead, staring back at him from the same mirror. The Demon may have been grinning triumphantly at Tealer in that strange, suspended minute, but that was only because Tealer was grinning equally triumphantly at the Demon.

And for the third time in his life Tealer realised this.

But for the first time in his life he did not forget it again moments later.

Which is why he was able to put his face close to the glass and whisper "Things ha' changed, sir. Let's have no more nonsense. I now know who you are – after all these years. And I know you for *what* you are, an'all. You're a wretch and an impostor. And nowadays *I'm* a-runnin' the affairs of John Sayer. So – good day!"

And this is why, having thus made perfectly clear to the Demon how things now stood between him and It, he was able to turn quite calmly on his heel to join the others at the table for tea – forcing the Demon to do likewise, presumably for some illusory refreshment in a parallel world beyond the wall of Charlie Harrison's parlour.

And this is why, when Tealer came to the table at which he's now sitting, he was smiling so serenely.

Of course, Polly, not knowing any of this, remains uneasy, and so when Harrison comes in with the youngsters and they all noisily take their places around the table, she uses the cover of the hubbub to lean over and murmur to her husband, "Are you alright, dear?"

"Never better, mawther."

"You know you ha' been talking to yourself, don't you?"

"Yes, girl," Tealer whispers back, and after a deep breath, "Yes, you're quite right. You're quite right. I reckon I have."

There's some more shouting from outside, and the oldest Harrison child rushes in clutching a wooden model of Brunel's *Great Eastern* that Harrison has fashioned, and the child wants to show Tealer. The other children gather round excitedly. They ask Tealer if he's ever been in an iron ship, and if such a ship can really float. Yes, he tells them, it can float, and it is driven as much by boilers like those in steam-trains as it is by the wind. And it has no paddles, but great shafts of steel with twisted blades called screws which spin round and drive it through the water. It can carry as much cargo as a hundred of the biggest wherries, and it has laid a cable from Newfoundland to Ireland which means that men will be able talk to one another under the Atlantic sea. How? they ask. By electricity, says Tealer. That's the same energy which makes lightning, and one day will power the world.

The conversation continues on into the evening. The children ply Tealer with a stream of questions. Has he ever eaten a pomegranate? Has he ever seen a giraffe? Or a polar bear? Or a sea-monster? They are desperate to know more about the guns and nets and spears and stuffed creatures that Harrison has told them fill the Sayer house in Row 111. But also they want to know more about the wonderful new inventions and discoveries that are transforming Tealer's work. They want to know more of steam-boats, gas-lights, and machines run by electricity.

So he goes on talking happily to his young circle, long after his own boy and the youngest Harrison child have nodded off. Eventually, Edith hands her child to her husband and puts a lamp on the table, where its pool of light is reflected in the shining eyes of the older children. Tealer takes out some photographs that he's brought to show them. These are not as colourful as Charlie's paintings, he grants, but they show trains and ships and bridges as strange and new as Harrison's scenes are old and familiar. The little company around the lamp is taken to times and places far removed from the parlour of a small Row-house in Yarmouth.

Quite unnoticed, day has steadily turned to night. The last rays of the autumn sunset have gone from the walls, and the old scenes and images of the *Gariensis* have faded, merged and disappeared into the darkness.

About this Book

THE CHRISTMAS APPEAL JAMES ALLETT

All the main figures in *The Faces of the Fiend of Breydon* are fictitious with the exception of Charlie Harrison, whose character is based very loosely on the 19th century Yarmouth water-colourist Charles Harmony Harrison (1842-1902). Tradition has it that this Harrison was converted from oils to watercolours, the medium most associated with him, after having been handed a set of paints accidentally left on an Indiaman that put into Yarmouth. (I should say that I have no evidence that the father of the real Harrison was a drunkard.)

Both the collapse of the Bure Suspension Bridge and the Seamen's Riot are historical events; the bridge collapse (which occurred a few years earlier than is suggested by the narrative) remains Great Yarmouth's worst peace-time disaster.

Most of the rural locations mentioned in the story can still be visited, though much of old Yarmouth itself, especially its unique network of 'Rows', was destroyed in World War II when the town was heavily bombed.

The Bowling Green Inn was well known as a meeting place for the fishermen and fowlers of Breydon and the surrounding marshes. It was demolished in the 1930s, and the site, perched on the confluence of the Bure and Yare rivers, is (at the time of writing) a derelict grain store.

Descriptions of Breydon Water in the 19th century, and of the hardy community that depended on it, are based on details I found in Harrison's own paintings as well as in the work of the early photographer P H Emerson. I also built on scenes described by such Victorian travel-writers as Nicholas Everitt, Ernest Suffling and C G Davies. The biography of the Yarmouth essayist Arthur H Patterson (1857-1935) by his great-granddaughter, the late Beryl Tooley, was also an invaluable fund of anecdotes and illustrations.

But the most vivid descriptions are those by Patterson himself, who was a meticulous recorder of the Breydon and the Norfolk Broads of his day, and a naturalist of the first rank – and it's to him that I will leave with the last word:

The question has often been put to me 'What can we do with Breydon?' My invariable answer has been, 'Let it alone.'

Acknowledgements

The Faces of the Fiend of Breydon would never have happened at all without the help of Garth Coupland, who always managed to combine honest critical appraisal with enough enthusiasm to make me feel like continuing. Mike Pearson, Fiona Thompson, Alison Barber, Anna Sadler and my partner Agnes Debacker also provided valuable manuscript-reading services. Dr Trina Ruth provided an incisive critique from a North American perspective. Lt Cmdr John Pressagh (RNVR) gave me some useful pointers on vintage maritime issues. A few minutes' chat on nineteenth-century Yarmouth with the late Percy Trett was always worth days of research. (And next door to where Percy lived was, and still is, the wonderful Time and Tide Museum, full of excellent things.) In Rio de Janeiro it was various members of the Faulhaber family who patiently answered all manner of very strange questions on the history of their extraordinary city. The sections on punt-gunning followed an unforgettable day with G D out on the glittering mud of the Blackwater back in 1998. Tom Barber was a source of much good, practical advice on book-production, based on his expertise as the creator of the extensive *Sam Archer* series. And of course, huge thanks are also due to my publisher Paul Dickson, together with graphic designer Brendan Rallison, for bringing the *'Breydon'* project to fruition. Finally, I will always be grateful to the organisers of the WH Smith *Raw Talent* competition for the impetus provided by their short-listing back in 2002 – even though I took my time to pick the ball up and run with it!

Cover photograph: Ian West, Alamy stock photograph. Berney Arms Drainage Mill, seen from near Burgh Castle on the River Waveney. Sunset. June.

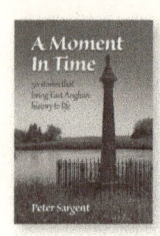

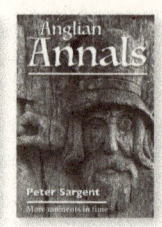

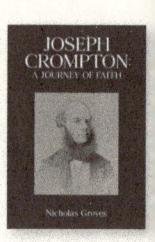

PAUL DICKSON BOOKS
Books by Norfolk writers published in Norwich

Paul Dickson has lived and worked in Norfolk for the past 33 years, initially for the National Trust, then as an independent PR practitioner and latterly as an independent publisher and tour guide.

A meeting with Illuminée Nganemariya in 2006 saw Paul assisting with Miracle in Kigali, Illuminée's story of survival during the Genocide against the Tutsis in Rwanda and subsequent life in Norwich.

After a spell as a director of Norfolk's Tagman Press, Paul decided to branch out on his own in 2016. Since then he has embarked on collaborations with Norfolk writers, Tony Ashman, Janet Collingsworth, Sandra Derry, Steven Foyster, Neil Haverson and Peter Sargent.

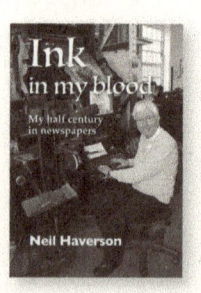

www.pauldicksonbooks.co.uk